Sweet Haven

Sweet Haven

Lakambini Sitoy

ANVIL
Publishing Inc.

Sweet Haven
by Lakambini Sitoy

This Philippine Edition is published and exclusively distributed by
ANVIL PUBLISHING, INC.
7th Floor Quad Alpha Centrum
125 Pioneer Street, Mandaluyong City
1550 Philippines
Trunk Lines: (+632) 477-4752, 477-4755 to 57
Sales & Marketing: marketing@anvilpublishing.com
Fax: (+632) 747-1622
www.anvilpublishing.com

Cover design by R. Jordan Santos
Photography by Yummie Dingding

The National Library of the Philippines CIP Data

Recommended entry:

    Sitoy, Lakambini.
      Sweet haven / Lakambini Sitoy. – Mandaluyong
    City : Anvil Publishing Inc., [c2015].
      pages ; cm

      ISBN 978-971-27-3195-2

    1. Philippine fiction (English) I. Title.

    899.2103 PR9550.9S5 2015 P520150289

Printed in the Philippines

10 9 8 7 6 5 4 3 2 1

YOU SEE I DIDN'T LOVE YOU. If only there'd been a way to send you back, keep you from pushing your insistent way into the world. What were you in such a hurry for? Go away, Naia. Shrivel. Shrink back into a wet, pulsing mass, into what you were in the first unknowing hours after I made you; go back to the beginning, membrane by membrane, protein by protein, until you are one with my tissues again, until you are no more.

I think of you often, of the night you were born. I cannot understand how these memories come in such clarity — as far as I know I was completely out of it: flat on my back, drugged, praying for liberation from the creature in my body. One hundred and sixty pounds, the center of me risen like a yeast bubble, my legs in the stirrups, sex shaven. The violated follicles emerging as pale bumps — a chicken-skin cunt, like something on a meat counter.

I rise, out of myself, registering the rubber-gloved hands of the doctor, the sick-green walls tiled against surprise fountains of blood. Deep, lowing sounds reverberate through the delivery room and the halls beyond, with their worn wooden benches — empty, for it is long after midnight in this hospital built by the American missionaries back in the 1930s, wing after wing slung upon the wooden structure after the Second World War, the whole place rattling with ghosts. Spectral myself, I listen, detached, levitating, to my cries of birthing distress.

Between my spread legs, your skull emerges. You rip through the curtains of my sex, sliding your fine body out — at birth already an athlete — and in your tiny face a glimpse of the beauty you are to wear to adolescence, though you are compressed, unsunned, knowing air for the first time. Red all over — a good sign; it means your skin, wiped free of blood and mucus, will be pale, unlike mine. The doctor hoists you up by the ankles. You swing. Your eyes, black and beady, seem to take in the entire world at a glance. Oh, I see the life in their depths.

Nothing else follows. I must have rushed, appalled, back into my own body at that point, unable to face this creature, this hungry new organism — a fetus with a will.

I wake up, and you are in the nursery down the hall. You are powdery white and pink, a complexion that is perfection itself, while all the other infants in the ward are a proletarian terra cotta. Although you are only a day old, it is obvious you are blessed. Naia. My Naia. I descend into feigned sleep, arms over my chest as though to ward you off, dreading the moment I must hold you in my arms.

One

IN THE VIDEO, the girls lie supine on the same narrow bed. They appear to have been filmed unawares, through an aperture in the ceiling: we are looking through a blurred circular frame, a light fixture perhaps. We who watch them do not know exactly, and in those opening moments of anticipation and dread, we don't really care.

Though the footage was probably taken months apart, the girls seem to lie twisting on the same filthy sheet — helpless, served up for our gaze, on the same hot afternoon. Three girls. Through the magic of computer editing, the camera proceeds from one naked woman to the next without explanation, as though an infinite number of succulent females queues beyond the round black frame. From time to time the camera startles us by wandering over a body, venturing so close that identification is irrelevant.

It is hard to tell whether the same man services all three — how can one be certain from the mere look of a nape or the muscles of a young back?

Sweat slicks their chests and glistens off their foreheads. Their features twist as though in alarm, as though in the final stages of strangulation. On the grainy screen, their complexions are the flat, bruised gray of death.

All the crucial details — of face and breast and dark, split sex — are visible, and that is what counts.

NARITA was the first of the Pastors to see them. She knew instinctively where to look, slipping out of the office an hour before usual and catching a ride to the Quiapo quarter of Manila, where a web of vendors' stalls sprawled about the Church of the Black Nazarene.

It was March, the month of spontaneous fire, when timbers and thatch flared up from tossed cigarettes and small children died screaming, forgotten by families as they fled. The trees were shedding their leaves, their branches stark against the blazing sky. The heat pulsed, out of asphalt and sidewalks, from tons of concrete and sheet glass, from roof tiles and hollow-block garden walls, from fetid mattresses, from pounding scalps.

Earlier that afternoon there'd been a freak shower that turned the streets into ankle-deep sewers. On the wet road, a passenger jeepney rammed the taillights of the car in front of it, and both drivers stomped out into the road to argue and wave iron bars at each other, slowing traffic for a kilometer on either side.

Jammed into a Tamaraw FX with nine other passengers, Narita waited. She was a sharp-eyed, nervous woman, dieted down to a passable thinness, in a black T-shirt and jeans. She had happened to sit behind the driver, where she could see nothing of the road up ahead. She had no idea how long the traffic jam was, if there was any movement at all in the gridlock in front of them. The air outside the vehicle was thick with fumes, as foul as the interior air she breathed. She had rolled down her window an inch, and needles of rain speckled the brown skin of her arm. Pulp of a more ominous shade slicked the asphalt: mud and rags and human excrement and scraps from the cardboard boxes beggars slept on, all pressed into an indeterminate muck under thousands of grinding wheels.

The others in the car dozed, sent text messages, stared resignedly into space. Try as she might, Narita could not shut out the collective odor of their skin and clothes. They were all glued together by perspiration and a full hour's inertia. The road was a giant alimentary canal. The commuters advanced, boluses of humanity, in pulses, a car length at a time.

Desperate for movement, she unlocked the door and eased herself into the steaming air. The FX had gotten as far as the Church of the Black Nazarene. The streets around the building teemed with frenzied transactions.

She slipped past stalls selling roots and drying greens: abortifacients, cures for impotence. Vendors crouched beside displays of movie star magazines, chrysanthemums for the dead, brass fertility amulets, mobile phone cases, cigarette lighters with naked women on them, lucky red seeds to adorn the wrists of newborn babies, playing cards, timepieces being fenced, prawn chips, fish curls. Wads of new spit glistened on the asphalt, like medals.

She came to a street that sold only pirated videos and music CDs. They lay upon sheets of woven plastic, fanned out atop low display tables of wood. A riot of color and possibility. The traffic cops just one block away seemed impervious to them.

At random, she chose a hawker.

"*Sweethaven Girls?*"

The vendor shook her head once, not looking up, and continued to bag a purchase.

Narita repeated the question to the woman's neighbor.

This man had a narrow display case of wood, like a card table, open to reveal a row of animated films. A clear file held sample liners for what must have been a hundred other movies. You pointed to the title you wanted, and he'd disappear for a few minutes, to some secret stall or the back of a van, to fetch the disc and an empty case and a liner. A neat, portable operation — police-proof.

The vendor examined Narita, her stylish close-cropped hair, the logo on her studiedly casual T-shirt, the way she clutched her genuine-leather purse close to her body to deter snatchers. He did not blink. He looked about forty, a few years older than she, with flat black eyes and a goatee like armpit hair.

"I don't sell movies like that," he said in disdain. "Try those people over there." He pointed with his lips. "They do the dirty stuff. If you're lucky, there'll be one or two copies left."

But the men who minded identical stalls a few meters down the stretch were of no help. The video she sought was sold out, they said, old news.

"We have the *State University Girls*," one of them volunteered, calling after her as she resumed her quest among the other stalls. "The *Loyola U Girls*. The *Southern Nursing College Girls*. Hey, miss! Miss-ss-ss!"

At last a young woman reached without fuss beneath her foldup table of plywood and drew out a DVD in its case. She was eighteen, maybe, her skin egg-smooth and fair.

"Don't say I didn't warn you," she smirked. "The actresses are ugly. You can actually hear them talking in the background. In Binisaya at that."

The cover confronted Narita. Title in electric pink script: *Sweetheaven Girls*. It ought to have been "Sweethaven." She frowned at the misspelling. The rest of the cover was a blinding montage of close-ups — pink flesh, gray flesh, hairy zoological shapes.

From among these disembodied body parts a teenager stared. Narita's heart leapt, her blood ran cold. She thrust the DVD back at the vendor, wishing she had not seen that face, that thin, pale face with the full lips and dark eyes serenely raised above the flat chest spanned by a white sports bra. How divorced that face had seemed from the lower half of the body, the naked half, the thighs parted to expose the neat shaven cleft of its sex.

"Are you buying it or not?" the vendor said.

Narita paid. The video cost as much as a fast-food hamburger and Coke. She held her palm out numbly for the change. Her hand remained outstretched long moments after her fingers had closed over the coins. Then in embarrassment she shoved money and purchase deep down into her purse and stumbled off. The traffic was moving at last, she noted. Slowly, but moving. She would have to hurry, take the first available ride home — whether jeepney or Tamaraw FX; it did not matter — before another collision brought everything to a standstill. She struggled through the seethe of bodies, keeping her head down against the drizzle. Directly before her was the Church of the Black Nazarene — squat masonry, strings of Tivoli lights over its square towers, saints in grimy cement. But in the weird light of the rainy afternoon she saw it as a remnant of Spain, a fragment of Europe, and caught a fleeting glimpse of romance and escape. She bought a circlet of jasmine flowers from a ragged little child and held it to her face, taking deep, desperate breaths.

THAT very night she dreamt about her daughter.

She had not dreamt about Naia in a very long time, though in the very first months after she had been forced to leave, the girl had come to her every night as she slept.

It was a curious dream. In it, Naia was little again, and they were saying good-bye.

Words poured around them, not Tagalog, but Binisaya, the speech of Donostia, the speech of Narita's own childhood. The child clung to her, hair slipping out of the twin knots into which Tita Antonia had twisted it, and it was damp and faintly greasy, as though Naia had emerged from a fever or been splashing in and out of the waves. The lone runway stretched all the way to the sea. The passengers were boarding. Narita put the child down. The aircraft waited on the tarmac, the queue of passengers stalled momentarily, shielding their faces from the sun. At the metal staircase, Narita turned. *Don't*, she wept to her dream self. But her arm came up to wave randomly at the line of people pressed up against the chicken wire fence, people who had come many kilometers by decrepit bus to send off loved ones and witness the miracle of aviation — old men, drawn and leathery; their sad, ample-hipped wives; peasants; urchins. A score of brown hands were already in the air, waving farewell.

She could see her family: her father, Daniel, and her mother, Luth; her sister, Antonia, who held the baby up high in her arms. A tense knot against the terminal wall. Narita's lips moved, and it seemed a sound escaped from them and almost rescued her from the inevitability of the dream. The child's small white palm came up in the air, in a gesture that mimicked hers. Then, looking down, she found herself strapped into a seat by a window, and she found a book in her hand, a red book, a hymnal from the Sweethaven church.

The aircraft taxied to the extreme end of the runway, its nose pointing to the sea. With a start, she saw that the child had followed her, Naia's face blank with misery, a ghost child stumbling across the sun-flooded tarmac, moving too fast for belief, fifty feet away, twenty feet, beneath the silver wing now; in a moment she would glide through the carpeting at Narita's feet. In a great howl of engines, the plane flung itself forth, past ditches of succulent taro, tethered goats, a water buffalo, a tricycle loaded with palm fronds. A single, overwhelming moment of weightlessness, then the press of the entirety of sky.

Narita leaned into the window, toward the tilting horizon — corrugated blue of ocean, spindly outrigger craft of fishermen, the blazing zinc rooftops of the city, rapidly diminishing as the plane climbed. The enclave of Sweethaven University was indistinguishable from the rest of the city of Donostia — church vanished, elementary school any one out of a thousand specks, everything reduced to the same insignificance at this height.

She was gone, she was free.

And then, as half-dreams went, this one took a strange turn at the moment of exultation: the stewardess, emerging with a trolley of delights, began to travel in slow motion backward; the aircraft lifted, and Narita found herself looking up at her thighs; light poured through her skin; they fell silently toward the vast sea.

When the plane disintegrated she jerked awake, raised her head from the depths of the damp pillow. It was six in the morning and very hot and bright. She was alone in the flat, as always. A garbage truck churned and puffed in the street below.

She sat up and found herself, irrevocably, alive. Her clothes lay where she had shed them. The bottle of rum stood open on the kitchen counter. A spill of orange juice had drawn the ants. The empty video case was still there, where she had left it last night, by the computer in her living room. The shaven, stripped, serene-faced child was still there.

Nothing had changed. A breeze stirred the curtains. A vendor made his rounds in the street below, announcing his wares with a peculiar hooting cry. He was selling tofu bathed in syrup, his voice already fading as he strode rapidly away, covering as many blocks as he could before the early heat drove him to rest beneath one of the dusty mango trees.

In the bathroom, there were a few curds of vomit on the tiles, where in a blind panic, escaping the lurching images on her computer screen, she had missed the bowl.

She made herself look at the video cover. Not "Sweetheaven." Sweethaven. A real place, a place of learning, and for her first twenty years, the only way of life she'd known.

Two

"*LOLA* LUTH," Naia said.

The girl's voice was so quiet and deliberate that her grandmother looked up from the test papers she had been correcting, her heart thumping in fear.

"Lola, I can't go to school today. Don't be upset."

Luth saw eyes rimmed red from weeping, hair that straggled out of a slept-in ponytail. Her mind raced through the morning tragedies that a fifteen-year-old girl might face. The child bent to kiss her grandmother on the cheek. Then she handed her a creased white envelope.

"I fished it out of the mailbox last night. I didn't want you to see it. I'm sorry."

The envelope was addressed to her husband, Prof. Daniel Pastor, PhD. The seal was unbroken. With shaking hands — God, what had the girl done this time? — she drew a sheaf of paper out. The top sheet was a letter of expulsion. It was signed by the high school principal and several other worthies within the Sweethaven community. "With deepest regret we inform you that due to acts that prove bad moral character, to wit, her lewd performance in a sexually explicit, commercial movie, Naia Pastor has been removed from the roster of students of Sweethaven High School."

Swiftly, Luth read the details, and the pages slipped from her nerveless fingers.

"I had my graduation dress picked out," Naia choked. Then she turned away from the dining table and stumbled back to the room where she slept. Luth stared after her, the blood draining from her limbs.

The girl shut the door and slid the bolt home.

That was four days ago. She had not emerged from the room since, despite all manner of pleas and threats. The sound of water running in the bathroom, the disappearance of plates of food left outside her door — these were the only signs of life from within. In those four days, as phone call after mortifying phone call came through, Luth's worry turned to panic and then to a blinding, thwarted rage.

Her husband tapped gently on the varnished wood.

"Naia." His voice was barely audible. He sounded frightened of her. "Naia. Get yourself ready. A man is coming to see you."

"Just force the door," Luth shouted in his ear. "Drag that *demoñita* out."

Daniel did not answer. Ear pressed to the wood, he tried the knob one more time. His finger absently traced a pale set of lines scored into the varnish. Made with an ice pick, thought Luth, watching him with a twinge of pain. Back when their two daughters were young. When the girls fought, it was with a violence that she'd thought only testosterone could produce.

"Naia," Daniel persevered, in what Luth recognized as his counseling voice, reserved for the graduate students in crisis who showed up every so often on their doorstep. He taught English language and literature at the university, a daily ordeal that frustrated him and sapped his strength, but a piece of cake next to her job dealing with the rich brats at the elementary school every day.

Luth left him, lumbered to the kitchen. All this softness a sign of a weak man. She reached for a bottle of Spanish sardines, fumbled around in the bread box for salt buns, found a single crust. The house was a mess, the maid catatonic. No one had done any shopping in days. Coaxing scraps of fish out of the bottle with her fingers, she downed them still dripping oil. They had no taste. A frenzied barking from the front yard interrupted her nerveless orgy. The buzzer sounded once, twice.

A strange jeep was parked beyond the gate, in the cogon grass. A man stood at their gate smoking a cigarette, rather like one of those aimless types hanging around ten-peso variety stores waiting for prosperity to come and find them. The dogs growled, hind legs stiff, tails quivering, as Luth shuffled out to meet him, wiping her hands on her duster.

He ground the cigarette out in the gravel beneath his shoe and, with some embarrassment, introduced himself. Joel S. Fortun. Attorney Joel S. Fortun. He was the chief legal officer of Donostia, he said. His office was at city hall. And when she did not smile, he added, as if to smoothen things out, "I was a classmate of Narita's in college. She might even remember me."

Oh, she thought. He was about the same age as her elder daughter. And had he been one of her pupils as well? Her mind worked furiously, as it did nowadays when face-to-face with someone from a younger generation. One of the quiet little boys sitting in the front row of her classroom, copying down everything she wrote on the blackboard, to be memorized that very night? No, his was a face she was certain she had never seen before, and she could recognize many of them even today, though they looked careworn and disappointed, just as she did in the mirror, just as her husband appeared those afternoons when, as she hailed a tricycle outside the elementary school, he passed her unknowingly, steering their ancient sedan, his lips moving without sound through one of his old Men's Glee Club tunes. So maybe this Joel Fortun had emerged from one of the Catholic schools. That would fit, if he had found a post at city hall; political connections with the mayor. He looked a bit mestizo. This was a detail that automatically registered with her: a hint of European ancestry meant money, power, and the arrogance that went with them.

He extended a hand in greeting, a gesture that seemed foreign, that he must have taken pains to learn.

As he settled into the sofa his gaze took in his surroundings, quickly, professionally, sizing up the family with an awareness that shamed her. Her own eyes darted this way and that over the living room, seeking comfort in the familiarity of the place. The objects Daniel had spent a lifetime accumulating now seemed random, hapless, cheap. How we used to show them off, she thought, telling the story of each knickknack to our guests. How our friends must have snickered at that torturous living room tour: the Japanese masks, Balinese statuettes, engraved plates and souvenir teaspoons; four mismatched guardsman dolls from Scotland, their bearskins furry with dust, their sporrans and braid and blue-painted eyes eaten away. On one blazing, yellow wall, a bullfighter and a flamenco dancer, mock-posters inscribed with her husband's name and hers, which he had brought, as a present for the house, all the way back from Spain.

Around the time the girls were in high school, Daniel had stopped traveling — no more scholarships, no more grants, the funding gone to keener, younger men. And the junk stayed — why couldn't they ever throw it away? How they had clung to the status of the past. No wonder the girls of the family had gone crazy: Narita living from pay envelope to pay envelope in Manila in her so-called career, and Antonia running off to another country without her mother's blessing. And now Naia. The mistake, the child of bitterness. Now it was Naia's turn.

"Is this her?" Fortun said, pointing to a photograph that sat on the table beside him. "Is this Naia?" He picked up the beadwork frame, shaking his head.

Say it, thought Luth. *What a waste.* Just say it.

Her husband joined them. "I still can't get her out of the room, dear. I tried." She sat very still, hating his obsequious voice, the tacit plea that she put up a front for the sake of the visitor.

JUST one week before, they had been normal. Naia had come, without speaking, to Luth's fourth-grade science classroom, where the children were examining bowls of rooting yams. She wore her junior majorette's uniform but hadn't bothered to bind her hair — it fell like a black cape over her shoulders, making Luth's heart thud, it was so lovely.

The class of ten-year-olds fell silent as she entered. That is my granddaughter, Luth said to herself with pride. *Children, that slender, long-haired beauty is my granddaughter.* Naia made a beeline for the teacher's table at the back, where Luth sat writing the next day's lessons in her plan book. The delicate scent of green tea heralded her arrival. Luth had bought her that perfume for her birthday.

"My braids," was all the girl said, pulling up one of the well-worn wooden chairs and bowing her head. Luth reached into her handbag for the fine-tooth comb that resided there expressly for such moments. Deftly, she sectioned and pulled and twisted the silky black wings into the immaculate plaits required of each majorette. From the neighboring high school buildings came the squeal of a trumpet. A hundred and sixty pairs of boots thundered past the window. Seniors in their cadet fatigues, heading for the supply quarters of their citizens' army training unit. A few minutes later they poured out once more, in the opposite direction, armed with the school's ancient wooden rifles, en route to the Sweethaven quadrangle. Luth didn't have to ask: it was the elaborate parade and review held every March, just before high school graduation. It seemed an unspeakable tragedy that the bright youngsters of her science class would eventually grow up into those sun-blackened, crew-cut adolescents barking orders and playing at war.

Luth freshened the rouge on her granddaughter's lips and blotted a trace of oil from her nose. It was the last time Naia would wear the uniform, as she was graduating, too. The girl subjected herself to her ministrations with the faint disdain of a princess. Then she rose with a nod and strode off, thighs flashing, her hands empty but for the baton. She tapped one end lightly against her palm as though it were a truncheon. The casual gesture niggled at Luth: such a graceful child, and so naively assured. She had left her school satchel behind, with her mobile phone and all her money, expecting her grandmother to carry it home. Naia was like a boy, traveling light, perennially prepared for combat.

"How is the case coming along?" Daniel's voice brought her back to the present.

"Very slowly, sir," the lawyer replied. "Frustratingly slow. We have no witnesses. Plenty of rumors, and no hard facts. The mayor has put together a panel of investigators. I'm one of them. I was with him last week when a copy of this videotape arrived at his office. *The Sweethaven Girls*, or *Sweetheaven Girls* in some imprints. We put the video into the DVD player he keeps there, and I tell you, sir, all hell broke loose."

"Well, thank him for us. We are grateful that he cares so much for the university's reputation."

"How could he not, sir? Sweethaven U is an important part of Donostia. This school put Donostia on the map. If not for it we would be just another sugarcane town."

"The mayor's a good man."

"The problem is he demands sworn statements and arrests and trials and convictions, all due yesterday. He can't understand the delay. He has no patience, sir, with Filipina modesty."

They spoke rapidly, ignoring Luth, as though this were a matter too delicate for women's ears and they had simply willed her away

"Modesty?"

"We have been speaking to the families of the other two girls, sir," the lawyer replied. "I'm sorry to say they have not been taking the video with the same ... open-mindedness as you and your wife. But of course they are not as educated. One lady was a simple Bachelor of Arts graduate of the university. Worked as a clerk. The other comes from a family of roughs. She never even went to Sweethaven U, as I understand. Whoever made the video wanted to capitalize on the university's name."

"But will they testify?" Daniel spoke eagerly.

The lawyer hesitated over his next words. "We would be lucky, sir, to get them to cooperate."

Seeing the alarm in the older man's face, he fumbled for an explanation. "Think of it as a sort of rape, Mr. Pastor. In this society, a raped woman is damaged goods. We might feel sorry for her, she might even win a case in court. But no one will ever be able to look at her the same way again. With that to consider, it's no wonder these two young ladies just want to disappear. Or should I say, their families want them to disappear."

"How can you compare this to a rape?" Daniel spluttered. "Those two older women, they consented to it. How could they not? Who could be so stupid as to claim they didn't know they were videotaped having sex?"

"Sir, we don't know that. I have seen the video, and I tell you what they say is absolutely possible."

"We just want to clear our granddaughter's name," Daniel said. "Bottom line."

Luth found her voice, and it came out hoarse and unpleasant. "I've heard the rumors." The lawyer shot her a surprised glance. "They say the women in that video were really whores. They got paid for what they did, and had no reason to complain. How can you trust the word of a whore?"

"They say Naia is in the video, too, Luth," her husband said. "Please don't use that word on our granddaughter." He was smiling broadly, as though she were a precocious child. She hated his patient, utterly hypocritical tone.

"That's *not* Naia," she snapped. "You haven't even seen it. Why do you keep saying it is? Why do we have to go public with our problems? What good might an investigation, or a trial, do? Naia is going to Manila. Her mother's been making arrangements. Naia must disappear."

But she was so exhausted and confused she couldn't keep track of what she was saying. She didn't know what to believe anymore. The girls were whores — no, worse than whores, because they went for sex with an avidness that was beyond normal. What did you call a woman who enjoyed videotaping herself being used? A woman who gave it away for free? What words applied? *Even the little Pastor girl, who looks so innocent — yes, that was her, that really was her. I've seen the video and there were the most revolting close-ups.* She could still hear the voices of her co-teachers as they primped before the lavatory mirror, unaware that she crouched, holding her breath, her urine even, in one of the stalls. *Serves them right. Mahilig kasi!* Other voices: *Naia must vanish; leave town* — her daughters talking now, first one then the other, browbeating her from opposite ends of the world, over the phone.

And now her husband: *No, Naia must protect her honor, she is a Sweethaven girl, the only way to clear her name is for her to stand up bravely in court and condemn each of the men responsible for her shame.* Faith and prayer would give her strength. They would resume their evening rituals, as one family anew. The community would take her side, and never mind what the rest of the world said. The rest of the world was not Sweethaven, and had no influence whatsoever on Naia's future.

As for Luth, part of her was shriveling, dying slowly; another part would have loved to take up a broomstick and beat Naia with it until it broke.

On the morning that had changed their lives, she left her fourth-graders and their sprouting yams in the care of the student teacher and, telling herself that she was only going to the lunchroom, slipped out after Naia. She would never understand what had motivated her. Grandmother's intuition. Something in the sensual arrogance with which the girl had left the room, bouncing the baton's head in her palm. Luth followed Naia as she sauntered past the grade-two classrooms, glancing without much interest at the children within, as though they were so many Made-in-China sneakers on a rack. Not once did Naia look back. She did not run, but moved lightly and determinedly in the direction of the drumbeats. At the exit gate, Luth stood panting; the girl was too fast for her. Close by was a vendor selling bananas in caramel. Luth was hungry, and was distracted by the smell of melting sugar. The old man swirled the starchy fruit in a vat of boiling oil, fishing each piece out and spearing it on a bamboo stick. By her side three boys waited as well, seventeen or eighteen years of age maybe, but still clad in the crested white shirts of high school students. Boys from the free government school — "outsiders," as they were called — she could tell from the roughness of their speech, the pale fungal speckles on their napes, the lush odor of their armpits. And as they waited for the vendor to serve them, they talked among themselves. "I know that girl. That majorette." "Pastor? The one who just went past?" "She fucks for money." "I got a close look at her *bulog*. It's as black as the outside of a pot."

Luth knew about adolescent boys; she knew they invented stories about pretty girls, that a succession of boasts made those stories as good as true. Once a girl caught the eye of a rough boy, her reputation was finished. Perhaps Naia had smiled too carelessly at one of them as she marched down Felipe II Street. That evening, when the girl came home, Luth wrested the tasseled baton from her and in a rage that endlessly renewed itself, beat her about the buttocks and thighs. It was a fitting culmination to Naia's career as a majorette. Honor was something no girl should ever take for granted.

For a day or so it seemed that the spirit of wickedness had been expunged from the house. And then the obscene phone calls began.

LUTH watched the lawyer and Daniel negotiate. At least, they appeared to be negotiating. Their lips were moving. They smiled.

The blood pounded in her head. She could not hear a word.

"Luth," Daniel murmured, and nudged her. "Attorney Fortun asked you a question."

"No!" The word sprang from her lips. She had no idea what she was responding to.

It seemed to make sense, in the context, whatever that was, because the lawyer smiled and reached across the table, as though to take her numb hand in his. He hesitated, caressed the woven runner instead.

"We can move, all right, but only with Naia's cooperation. Think of it, ma'am," he said. "It will be over before any of you realizes. A few seconds of pain, like having a bone set. We will provide the anesthesia. What is half a day down at the police station, her signature on a document, maybe another half day in a court in order to convict the malefactors, which could be months and months from now, her trauma well behind her? She doesn't even have to speak, simply answer questions with a yes or a no. We will keep her name secret, her pictures away from the press. We do protect minors. This case is about child abuse as much as it is about obscene materials. A prosecution of this nature will go down in history. That's why it's so important that we do it right. So consider it, ma'am. A brief visit to the police station — tonight, or tomorrow even; there will be fewer onlookers on a Sunday. Or perhaps that might be too much. You are under stress. I shall try again some other time to talk with Naia. Is that all right, ma'am? Can we schedule our next appointment?"

Luth stared, uncomprehending, at the wall, at the twin Spanish posters, yellowed, put up even before her two daughters were born.

THE day that followed was designated for one of the ordeals of her life with Daniel: the Sunday service at the university church. Luth opened her eyes to gray dawn light. She turned over in the hope of getting more sleep and discovered her husband lying by her side. In discomfort she squirmed away. It was rare, nowadays, that they awakened in the same bed together. But last night he had crept in almost as soon as she had lain down. Perturbed from the meeting with the lawyer, she had immediately sought to lay a barrier between the two of them by means of a formal talk.

"How can you be serious?" she said in her normal voice now, picking up the conversation that had trailed off into nothingness the night before, when he had turned from her and lapsed into unconsciousness. "Why do you keep encouraging that man? Do you think I'm an imbecile, that I don't know we're being used?"

His eyes were wide open, too.

"You say you want to take her to the police station and then to court. Do you realize what that will do to all of us? The shame?"

She could not abide being next to him, the sweat-damp covers binding their limbs. Was he dead? she wondered suddenly. Had he had an attack of some sort, or was he asleep, like a frog, with eyes open? But she was afraid to drag herself up, lean over and verify, lest he, in this inappropriate moment, reach for her.

Her husband moved, stretched his thin limbs. He seemed to have gained ten years in the night. Luth escaped to the kitchen. In the sink was a used plate. An empty can of tuna fish sat on the counter, besieged by ants. Naia had crept out of her room some hours before to eat, and left the clean-up to her.

Luth breakfasted furtively, chewing and swallowing long after the hunger had been sated. Daniel busied himself in the garage. He revved the car engine a couple of times, humming in an annoying, joyless way. Luth knew he was casting around for something to do so he wouldn't have to talk to her. Why didn't he just turn his computer on? In the last year or so he, a sixty-one-year-old PhD, had discovered video games. Atrocious military fantasies were his favorite.

The door to Naia's room was closed, as always these days. Luth tried the knob anyway. The door opened without resistance this time. The girl was asleep, on her stomach, her breathing almost inaudible. The air-conditioner had shut down automatically hours before, but the atmosphere was chilly nonetheless. The drawn curtains kept out the harsh morning light.

She paused by the bed. Who was this creature? What was this horrible thing they had accused her of? When I was her age I was a good girl, thought Luth. Never went with boys, never read dirty books, never touched myself. There were *bailes* at the town plaza that the "ladies" could enter free of charge, but I never went to any of them. At fifteen I was a good girl — no, not a girl, a woman already. I had four siblings to take care of, and twice a month my father's two bastards came to the back door to beg. We had no maid; *I* ran the house.

Naia had kicked the sheets to the foot of the bed; her legs were long and smooth, without the damaging insect bite scars that so many lesser creatures bore, those pale round flaws, edged in black, that in Luth's childhood were called *diez*, after the ten-centavo coins. This perfect body, warm and breathing, submerged in the early morning light, had been host to God knows how many men, Luth grieved. The entire community had had her granddaughter. Lashed her and branded her with jets of hot seed. The Naia who lay there sleeping was irredeemably wealthy with experience.

Luth opened a drawer at random. It held the usual clutter a child cannot throw away: elementary school IDs, notebooks filled with messages from classmates, a grubby old Nokia phone. There was one photograph, of a baby. Luth squinted. Which one? It would have to be Naia, she thought; the photo was in color. The hand that supported the infant around the waist wore a white lace glove. Luth peered closer. It was not a glove. It was a bandage. The hand was Antonia's, then. The old injury. She shook her head to dispel sad memories — the appalling violence, the damage in its wake. *Where* are *you?* she mouthed to her younger daughter, always her favorite. *Why did you leave? Weren't you happy here?* Antonia had been gone two years. If she had stayed to guide the child, none of this would have happened.

A movement caught Luth's eye. It was the computer, still running, a screensaver — a woman with wild red hair — silently flipping through the same four images. Impatient with such modernity, she pulled the plug on the machine, banishing the hungry, knowing face.

Naia rolled over on her back, exhaled. She was no longer beautiful, thought Luth. She was used. What a waste, those long eyelashes, that lovely, tragic mouth with the droopy upper lip. A waste, a waste.

The lashes fluttered: the girl was awake.

"Lola."

Her voice was thin, as though from disuse. She sat up, smoothing down her T-shirt to cover her navel, the simple movements pained. "Lola, what are you doing? Those are my things." Her head snapped around, checking the room to see what else had been disturbed. "I was downloading music!"

"Waste of electricity," Luth managed, her heart thudding in her chest. She could not meet the girl's gaze. The dark brows, the crescent eyes that were no longer perfect, that were damaged, diseased.

"Lola, this is my room!"

"You don't own anything in this house. Get dressed. You should have talked to that man yesterday. He promised to save you from shame. But of course you're the one who knows best. All the time. Now we go to church. This is a Sunday like any other."

"Luth?" Daniel called from the next room. "Leave the child alone. Let her do as she wants."

Now it was eight and the sky was cloudless, the heat unrelieved. Luth took a shower to cover her weeping. There was a great void within her. The warm water sluiced over the hull that was her flesh. Mercifully her husband left her alone as she dressed in the bedroom. Occasionally he liked to surprise her by easing himself through the door, watching her movements with the diffident smile she had once loved. She hated their mutual nakedness, hated the casualness with which, nowadays, she could shed her clothes and converse with him, impervious to the nut-brown shriveled organ nodding placidly at his groin. This was all it came to — the lust, the dreams, the dance.

The maid opened the gate for them, her gaze downcast, her movements self-conscious. Afraid of getting yelled at again. Daniel had washed the car. Wiped the windows with a squeegee, scraped off the layers of dirt flung up by the wheels. She knew he would be pleased with himself, and expect a few noises of approval from her. Luth could muster nothing. She got into the passenger's seat. The backseat looked as always, a hodgepodge of books and student papers and, today, a crumpled supermarket bag. She gritted her teeth.

They chugged through the neighborhood, an enclave of fading wooden cottages sheltered by acacia trees. The Pastors had lived in a house rented from the university for nearly forty years, as did their neighbors, administrative staff and teachers like her and her husband. Luth had loved these unpaved lanes, their American names — Mercer, Dereham, Westbrook — the gardens bursting with bougainvillea and orchids and hibiscus, a riot of color all year round. Over time she had observed with chagrin the gradual decay of the houses. The university left maintenance to its tenants, but no one cared enough to spruce up their homes, not even with a fresh coat of paint now and then. It wasn't part of the culture. But it was standard practice to gripe about how Sweethaven U worked its employees like slaves. On paper, their salaries had increased in proportion to their seniority, but those wages had failed to account for inflation or the devaluation of the peso that began in the 1980s.

Luth saw no one, but fancied eyes peering through the grimy screens at the windows of each cottage, the inhabitants gleefully tracking their progress. At last they reached Urbino Road, city territory, a route that connected their neighborhood of faculty homes to the university campus. Here they were just one vehicle among several traveling the two-lane stretch. The houses and store fronts had kept pace with the times — they passed a restaurant opened not two years before, a privately-run kindergarten in a residential bungalow, and a handful of Internet stations, their glass doors papered with video game posters. Money from a generation working overseas. Luth and Daniel entered the university through one of the side gates, the guard on duty peering at their faces beyond the access sticker on the windshield. Small brown discs of acacia leaves, shed for the summer, spun up from their wheels as they drove down the avenue to the church. Luth cast a helpless glance at the edifice as they parked. Its concrete walls gleamed with a fresh coat of white paint, as in those early years, when she was a newly minted Protestant matron. The chimes sounded about their ears, calling to all of Sweethaven. Pretending to be searching in the glove compartment of the car, they waited until most of the worshippers had come up the walk and through the portals and been seated. Students mostly, dormers sent by alumni from the neighboring islands: boys and girls in shockingly casual jeans and flimsy Made-in-China cotton dresses. The old guard of Sweethaven would have arrived long ago and found their usual pews.

"Showtime!" Daniel said in that cheery performance voice of his, and together they marched up the steps and through the iron-bound winglike wooden doors and found an empty space in the center of the nave, just as the recorded chimes, broadcast from a speaker on the roof, came to an echoing end.

Luth sweated in her size-forty-eight silk dress, a gift that Antonia had sent her from Europe. The fabric that sheathed her was all wrong for this climate. Electric fans that stood in the side aisles brought the smells of fresh-soaped skin and a hundred different perfumes to her nose, but did nothing to dispel the heat. Last year she had sworn to keep her pain to herself — the humiliations of her marriage, the shock of her husband's betrayal — and show up at church by Daniel's side. Staking her claim. That had been in August. She had kept her dignity, put on clothes too fine for the lives they led, styled her hair. Above all, she had kept her face frozen and turned to the front. No one would ever catch her scanning the crowd for some foolish young graduate student face. The worst period of her life, and it was not yet over.

The scripture reading ended, and the minister claimed the pulpit. Daniel grunted approvingly by her side. He was always attentive to what was going on, or managed to put up a passable show. Wretchedly she pumped her palm frond fan.

Today the sermon was about listening. The minister used the patronizing, engulfing "we." Were *we* attuned to the voices of our children, could *we* discern God's word in the jumble of our mundane concerns? One could be an intellectual giant and yet remain a spiritual pygmy. Reverend Manguerra gripped the pulpit, glared at his congregation, looked directly at Luth and Daniel's pew. Smug from a scholarship at — what was that American school now? Wesleyan. A scholarship to Wesleyan. What kind of school was that? Had he been there on a minority program? In his day her husband had competed with the best of them, the best of those whites. In his day.

Now people were reaching for their wallets, and the soft strains of a guitar penetrated Luth's thoughts. In the center aisle, a man stood before a microphone, one foot up on a stool to support the instrument. He smiled as he sang the offertory melody, inviting the congregation to share in a moment of folksy intimacy, and at the sight and sound of him, Luth's heart thudded violently once more and she thought she might throw up right on her pointed leather shoe tips. It was Rinky Holland. In his mid-fifties but with a voice as sweet and seductive as a youth's. He wore a sports shirt and khakis, as though to mock the perfumes and embroidered *barongs* of the old guard. Two girls in the pew in front of her plucked at each other in delight.

Then Reverend Manguerra was praying for wisdom and courage, that dads and moms and, yes, grandparents, too, might gently guide the beloved among them who had strayed. Only God could condemn, and only God could forgive. Heads swiveled in their direction: the dean of women and her chemistry teacher husband, the head nurse at the pediatric ward, the grade school principal. There they sat, poor things, Daniel Pastor and his wife, Luzviminda, such a comedown, but oh, how they deserved it. How wonderful the Lord's justice was, in the end. Rejoice! How he managed after years of seeming indifference to take the proud among them down.

A collective mumble and clatter and the peal of the organ in the choir loft marked the end of the service. Luth would have bolted, first out the door, but her husband was in the way. They stood trapped in the pew, while the congregation inched through the aisle before them, men beaming at one another, reaching out to clasp hands, women calling greetings to friends. Nobody addressed the Pastors, but their every breath was marked.

Rinky Holland made his way up the aisle, smiling to himself. His wife, Emily, followed. She was the high school principal; her signature was first on the letter that had informed them of Naia's crime and punishment. They moved toward the rear of the church with a cat-clean confidence, the woman a beauty as she had been for as long as Luth had known her: pale, unlined skin; tiny, perfect figure; and dark, soulful Spanish-heiress eyes.

Emily stopped at their pew. "Dan, how are you? These must be terrible times."

"How are you, Emily, and congratulations to Rinky. What a wonderful solo that was."

Mrs. Holland frowned, took in his insane smile, then forged on.

"I know your present troubles are difficult to talk about. Our family has always been friends with yours. I would like to step in now and help you myself. Unfortunately it is not proper for a man to receive counseling from a woman. But your wife, Daniel, with all my heart I reach out to your wife."

Luth's eyes flickered warily from the upturned face. Emily had spoken as though she were not present. Her gaze fell on the young man who waited beyond his mother. His name was Brent; he was Naia's age and was some kind of cadet officer at their high school. The almond eyes that met hers were unpleasant, watchful. Sweat trickled from Luth's temples, down to her jawline and her throat. Her bosom heaved beneath the orchid-purple silk. She understood that he was laughing at her, laughing with his mouth in a perfect serious line, this dark, slender boy in trendy khaki trousers, fondling a late-model mobile phone, looking as if he came from a family of millionaire generals. Looking at her and laughing.

"Snake!" Luth spat.

The look of piety vanished from Emily's face. "What did you say?"

"I said, 'Snake.' You're vampires. Snakes. You feed off people's misery."

Emily's eyes narrowed. "People are in misery, Mrs. Pastor, because they bring it on themselves, in their solitude and pride."

Brent Holland nodded to a friend, smirked, and, pocketing his mobile, sauntered off toward a wing exit. Luth lunged after him, determined to grab him and shake the arrogance out of him as she might have done had he been a fourth-grader in her charge, but Daniel checked her, clamping a hand on her arm.

She surrendered to panic, turning this way and that to seek support from the other parishioners and seeing nothing but malicious glee in their faces. They could have been peasants gawking at a knife fight. Daniel was quietly leading her down the aisle. She tried to snap off the press of his fingers at her elbow.

Emily had quite recovered herself and pursued them a few token steps. "Luth, I know you are under duress," she said. "I cannot even imagine what pain you must be going through. You really, really must open up now."

"Tell that woman to shut up," she panted.

Daniel steered her out onto the lawn and in the direction of the science complex parking lot. A woman behind them gasped, "What happened? Who was it?" Another declared, "*Scandalosa*." She could still hear Emily Holland's parting shot: "You are more than welcome to come to our home for a cup of tea."

They walked rapidly away, heads down, two fugitives.

Three

LUTH SURVIVED the next few days by speaking to no one, outside the requirements for her classes. After thirty years, she knew the fourth-grade science lessons forward and backward and in her sleep. The only break in the routine was the appearance of Daniel in the car at exactly 11:30 in the morning. Lunch in the canteen with her colleagues was now out of the question. She would dismiss her pupils a couple of minutes before the scheduled time and, as thirty-eight children scraped their chairs back and donned their books and bags and slammed down the lids of their desks, slip quickly out of the room, down a hallway and over a gravel path to the auxiliary gate. She always went unnoticed, the teachers hollering last-minute admonitions to their charges. Precisely at the moment that Daniel drew abreast of the gate, the school bell would clang, and a torrent of children in white shirts and khakis and checked skirts would shrill out into the noon heat. And Luth, lowering her bulk into the front seat, would be spared the ordeal of greeting colleague after colleague as she pushed her way to the car.

Husband and wife would lunch together at the house, not speaking. From time to time Luth would glance at the telephone, waiting, unrewarded, for the peculiar two-note ring that heralded a long-distance call. Just moments before the afternoon bell sounded, Daniel would drive her back.

On Wednesday, the revised, silenced man who was her husband wore an expression grimmer and more determined than ever. He took the car in the opposite direction, between the university gates, through the main street a-growl with motorcycles and tricycle taxis, down a side way white with the uniforms of loitering high school boys, and out into the wide boulevard that ran the length of the seafront. She braced herself. They parked at the police station, next to the city hall building.

Luth had never been here before; there had never been any need. Men in uniform repulsed her, as they had since the Marcos days, since martial law, when the sight of a Police Constabulary uniform might have prompted her to hunch her shoulders and hide her face. She had lived in constant worry of being arrested and questioned about her younger brothers' associations with the Kabataang Makabayan, as much for their welfare — would they disappear into the stockade as had happened to so many other promising youths? — as for fear of being expelled from Sweethaven.

Now the Constabulary was defunct as a unit. These were simple policemen. Nonetheless, she tensed as, entering the shabby wooden building, she saw an expansive counter and, behind it, a massive creature in a blue uniform who registered no expression as she advanced. Deep grooves flanked his mouth. The nostrils, beneath Ray Ban aviator glasses, flared with each breath.

A chalkboard beyond the monster's head marked the station's efficiency record for the previous year: HOMICIDES, 12. ROBBERIES, 52. SOLVED CRIMES, 20. UNSOLVED CRIMES, 32. Unnerved, Luth turned back to Daniel, and realized that in this dim, humid space smelling of burst plumbing and sweat and stale smoke and engine oil and unlaundered denim, they were not alone. Men fell silent as she stared at them — men peering at her from between the bars of a holding cell just meters from where she stood. Men with skin the color of mahogany, roughened as though they had spent five lifetimes at sea, dark eyes starting from their faces, matching her stare for stare.

"The special panel?" Daniel said.

The policeman at the desk grunted. "Only those connected with the investigation, sir, ma'am."

He used the titles perfunctorily, without deference.

"We are," Daniel replied.

The aviator glasses swiveled to Luth, then to her husband, then back to Luth. A grunt came from the brown throat. "You are related therefore with the ... actresses?"

For one second she had no idea what he was talking about. Then her face flamed, and the more she contemplated his pronunciation of the word — the way he aspirated the first syllable, as one might speak, caustically, of a king — the more she burned.

"Joel Fortun, the lawyer, is expecting us," Daniel said.

"Second floor," said the man, indicating the direction with his lips. "Second door on the left."

Head down, almost running, she followed her husband up a sagging flight of stairs that magnified their every footfall. Behind one of the frosted doors on the second floor, the legal machinery was already humming. She had expected an air of silent shock, as in the hall outside an emergency ward, but the small room was filled with the noise and heat of men all talking at the same time. An air-conditioning unit thundered, futile, in a corner, sucking up rising plumes of cigarette smoke and spewing it over furniture and clothes and hair. She looked in one direction and saw a familiar face; it was the lawyer Joel Fortun. He looked grave and intelligent in his pale-blue *barong tagalog* — a handsome fellow, Luth realized, the sort her daughters ought to have married. He was speaking, she noted in dismay, with the dean of student affairs at Sweethaven. The dean did not acknowledge their presence. He seemed embarrassed by their arrival. A man, she thought. Why couldn't they have sent a woman? Hovering about them, eavesdropping and looking important, were a couple of uniformed police, the older one of some rank.

Two more men slouched slightly apart from these personages, on molded plastic chairs, squinting through the smoke of their cigarettes. They stared at Luth and Daniel, then turned back as if to a conversation, but their lips were clamped shut.

"The young man is married to Gemma Bulauan," Joel Fortun murmured, coming to them and bending over Luth as though to plant a kiss of greeting on her cheek. "She's taking a break from the questioning. She'll be back any minute."

Gemma Bulauan. One of the girls in the video now had a name. The surname translated to "wealthy, possessed of much gold." We'll see, she thought, if she lives up to that promise.

"Who is the other?" Daniel said.

"Gemma's father."

They wore thin collared T-shirts — one read, LAND BANK, the other, CENTRAL AZUCARERA. The husband, in his mid-twenties, sported a bracelet of leather cords. The father looked wasted, flesh drawn down to the bone — by years of labor or drink or methamphetamines, Luth could not tell.

And at a desk, before a gargantuan postwar typewriter, sat a clerk, face empty, gears in idle as he awaited the command that might bring his fingers to life.

Joel lingered before her. "This is a special and confidential proceeding, ma'am, with the special panel of investigators." Luth scowled at the slew of adjectives. Cops in the news were always referred to as special police officers — SPO 1, 2 or 3. She wondered if there were not-so-special police officers and what services they might be expected to render.

"The mayor himself brought us together. When the time comes, Naia will receive the same careful treatment."

The door opened behind Luth and Daniel, and the occupants of the room glanced up expectantly — Luth sensed the rush of blood, as in a beer house when a hostess clips through the swinging doors. It was a young woman who entered, chin high, slipping sideways and making for a chair beside the man with the rawhide bracelet. Luth stared. This was the victim?

Long hair. Such inherent beauty in smooth, loose black hair. But this girl had bleached hers, crimped it and singed it and God knew what else. It was the same color as her skin. And how did tall, well-built women get their midsections so tiny? thought Luth. The girl wore makeup, trendy shimmering gobs of it. Her forearms were covered with fine down; the sight of it made Luth's own arms prickle, as though she had entered a sitting room ruled by a cat. In between puffs of her cigarette, the girl cleared her sinuses with a staccato intake of air.

In the embarrassed, expectant silence, it was the clerk who moved first. He burst into an orgy of typing, so that the desk shuddered and the machine sung beneath his fists. He rammed the cartridge home, then once more lapsed into inactivity.

"Hey," the older policeman said. "Hey, Beyoncé, welcome back."

Nobody moved.

"Hey, Destiny's Child. Aren't you Destiny's Child? You look just like Destiny's Child, with that hair. Come over here. We've got to take your — "

"Take your temperature," the younger cop interjected. Luth could tell from his hard, native pronunciation that he had survived school by rote memorization of English phrases.

"Take the rest of your testimony," his senior finished.

In her platforms, the young woman called Gemma clomped to the desk and seated herself obediently beside the clerk.

"I don't know what else to say. I already told my story to you, sir." Her eyes slid pleadingly to Joel.

"Just a recap, please, madame," the older cop drew up a chair beside her. "As you can see, all members of the special panel of investigators are now present, with some guests. They would like to hear you air your side."

"My story is complicated, sir. I once had a boyfriend — "

"His name?"

"JP, sir. JP Torres."

It was the first time Luth had heard the name, had heard any man's name in connection with her granddaughter's misdeeds.

"So. You are still with this man?"

"JP and I broke up two years ago," Gemma continued softly, "and I met Tristan, who was very good to me, sir. Tristan and I got married last December. We are very happy — "

"So you had sex with this JP?" the captain said.

"Everyone does it nowadays, sir."

"Indeed. Well, where did you commit the act? How many times?"

"In his house. He told me it was his house. It wasn't really a house, just a one-room apartment with a bathroom, and a refrigerator, just like in a hotel, and not even a cooking stove, sir."

"And you had no idea you were watched?"

Luth cast a glance at Gemma's father and husband. A woman in her fifties now sat with them. A cheap old bitch, thought Luth: dry orange hair and a tight spangled tee that read, VERSACE, a thread of cigarette smoke winding to the ceiling. The mother.

"Why do we have to see this?" Luth whispered to her husband. Daniel shushed her. He was listening avidly.

"He did not pay me, sir," the girl was saying. "That I swear to Lord. But he was generous. He had a motorcycle, and the time that I knew him he was driving a Revo. And he had good manners, sir; his people are the Fortuns."

A general grunt of sympathy — or was it amusement? — made its way around the room. A couple of the men gave Joel Fortun the kind of long, challenging gaze they might issue a tricycle driver who had cut them off on the road, but the lawyer was carefully examining a sheaf of papers in his hands. The girl sobbed, affronted. A Coke was poured. The younger policeman handed Gemma a plastic tumbler.

"Here," he said, with mock brusqueness, as though she were a stripper tabled for the evening. "Ladies' drink."

The older policeman resumed.

"He was gallant — he paid for all your treats — and you allowed him to do anything he wanted, free of charge. You did not think it was strange that he kept turning you up to face the ceiling? You just let him pet your flower?"

"I don't remember. I wasn't thinking ... of those things."

"She could be telling the truth, Captain," the dean of student affairs cut in. "She herself says she had sex in that rigged-up bedroom too many times to count."

The men fell silent, examining Gemma inch by inch as they ruminated upon this thought.

The police captain went on. "The information we have is that hours and hours of footage were taken. What we see in the commercialized video are" — he searched for a phrase — "the prize cuts."

"What about the two other actresses?" grunted the younger cop. "You mean to say they also have hours and hours?"

Gemma spoke in an even smaller voice than ever. "I am not an actress, sir. I made no pornographic movie."

The captain stared at her in disbelief. "But you admitted just now that it was you in the video."

"Yes, but it was not my purpose to put a show. Please, sir, don't call it pornography."

"Did your flower appear in the video?"

"You have seen the video, sir."

"Did it appear?"

"Yes."

The police captain cleared his throat, looked peevishly around the room as though daring the others to cross him. "Then the video is pornographic and obscene. Because there is a flower that can be seen in it. That is enough. The law does not care about 'on purpose.'"

Gemma pressed wads of bathroom tissue to her ruined face. Her shoulders heaved with sobs. As she hoisted herself out of the chair, she seemed, literally, to be holding herself together, pushing in the edges of a mortal wound, but her voice, ripping forth, silenced the entire room. "Are you people through? Are you through with me? How many times do I have to answer the same questions? You have seen the DVD. Isn't that enough?"

Her mother grabbed her by the arm. "Shut up. You're not in a movie anymore."

"I can walk by myself," the girl snapped. Her husband and father-in-law rose and followed the two women out the door — deflated, refusing to look back at the roomful of men, the panel of special investigators assembled by the mayor of the city. Luth could sense the rage rising like sap in the two men. The girl's clogs resounded on the wooden stairs, the thumps soon blurring with her sobs and the footfalls of her companions. Holding her breath, Luth began to count, picking out Gemma's progress, monitoring her passage to safety. Four. Five. Six. On the eighth riser down, the rhythm shattered, the girl screamed, a fist thudded into the wall. "*Puta*," a man shouted. "I hate the way you cling to me."

The clerk resumed his typing.

Not once did Daniel speak throughout the drive from the police station to their home. Luth's spine, her limbs, gave out; she turned her cheek, gently, against the backrest of her seat and let it remain. Thus she rode home, in an attitude that would normally have made her bones scream in protest, and a single thought dominated all others: that it was over, that no way would she expose her granddaughter to that panel of tormentors, that as far as she was concerned the child was innocent, that the lawyer Fortun could dig up some other girl to shame. A sly tune wove itself round and round the monument of her resolve — it was the song she had heard rising from the holding cell of the police station as she and Daniel made their exit, a song from the throat of a dark-skinned fellow lolling upon a cot. "I saw a frog," the jailed man crooned, "a frog with hair," and though his main audience consisted of bars and damp cement and rancid fellow criminals, Luth knew he was celebrating the passage of Gemma, shrieking and bucking in her husband's grip as she fled the building.

AND when they got home it seemed, for a second, that here another attack was under way, because the gate was half open and an adolescent figure besieged the front door. Daniel parked the car among the roadside weeds. As soon as the motor was cut, the boy called out a greeting, in polite Sweethaven English. He carried a large white confectioner's box trimmed with a silver ribbon. "Our mother, our whole family, includes you in our prayers," he pronounced as Luth stumbled past, and she realized it was one of the Holland brothers, the older one, Adam. But she couldn't care about that now. Let Daniel deal with him.

The house stood in the yellow silence of the afternoon. "Naia," Luth choked, barreling against the girl's door. Unlocked, it gave beneath the full force of her weight. The bathroom door was ajar, and just beyond stood the girl, her face pressed to the tiles, her shoulders shaking. When Luth grabbed her and whirled her around she saw that her face, too, was a mess of tears. Weeping freely now, Luth ran her hands through the lank, acrid hair, mashing the tears from the girl's cheeks with her thumbs. "They will never get you," she moaned, embracing Naia. The girl sagged into her arms, and they stood there, unmindful of the odor of old urine stealing from the toilet bowl, of the stench of hair and face powder and sweat.

From the sunlit garden came the voices of men, an alternate reality, Daniel walking the boy to the gate, cheerily thanking him for the box, Adam wanting to know how they all were doing and that his mom was ready in case any of them might wish to unburden. Luth listened for the sounds of her husband at the front door, the bits of a tune and odd snatches of words that followed conversations with his Sweethaven peers. Visitors always got him excited.

She laid her granddaughter down on the bed and went to the window. Adam was still at the gate, all smiles gone, a mobile phone pressed to his ear. He wore a frown, seemed to be arguing with whoever was on the other end. His face was an odd blend of his parents' — his mother's doll-like features and the flat planes of his father's. Pacing over the gravel, he seemed a disjointed puppet, with his heavy shoulders and large skull and the childish curve of his forehead. As she watched, he mounted the bicycle and pedaled off, chubby but powerful, in khaki jeans and a wholesome sports shirt, as white of skin as his brother Brent was dark. She did not think he would be back. He would head straight home and report to that mother of his that the gift had been delivered. Luth was grateful, in that moment, for her husband's social skills, his determination to always show a happy, lying face to the world.

Then she left her granddaughter, to search for Daniel, curious despite herself to find out what sweet treat Emily Holland was offering them. She found the box on the bottom shelf of the refrigerator. Taped to the silver ribbon was an envelope, with a note, in the bold flowing hand of all who had grown up in Sweethaven in the 1950s and '60s, the elegant script taught by the last of the American missionaries: *Our hearts are with your family in this, your time of trial.*

It was a cake, a wheel of pure chocolate. Her stomach growled; tears sprang to her eyes; the glands along her jaw sang out for a taste. Poison, Luth groaned, and commanded herself to shut the refrigerator door.

Four

MORE AND MORE, Narita found herself catatonic, arrested in the middle of getting dressed, of sipping a cup of coffee, by the tremendous press of her thoughts. Today it was the e-mail that did it, the one from Antonia, short and taut, as all her younger sister's correspondence had become in the last year or so: "This is *your* shit."

There was a time, when they were small, when it was she, Narita, who meted out the tough talk, when it was *she* who made the rules. Antonia had been so easy to control. Any insubordination from the younger girl would be immediately dealt with by means of a pinch. The times Antonia fought back were rare, but she was vicious and determined enough, and on several occasions Narita had been constrained to grab both her younger sister's wrists and twist as hard as she could, staring her down with powerful dark eyes. Her father or mother whipped her often enough for bullying, but there had been times when Antonia did not tell. Times when Narita was sure the pain was unendurable, when tears sprang up beneath Antonia's lashes, when her wrists swelled and turned red afterward. But the younger girl always kept the worst fights secret from their parents. Through those private moments of torture, the sisters bound themselves in a tacit pact.

Now, hugging herself, nose pressed to a bedroom window pane, Narita tried to summon up the spirit of her childhood, that part of her that refused to be surpassed. Her shoulders heaved: strangely, the tears would not come. It was hard to cry when her primary emotion was not sadness, but a certain numb fear, a dumb resignation. Get up, she ordered herself. Get dressed.

It's your shit, so clean it up.

But she could not move.

It was nearly ten in the morning, and from this vantage point, five stories above the street, she felt removed from the life that went on about her, in the various cells of the apartment building and in the houses of the neighborhood, which seemed but a collection of irregular rust-colored roofs.

Home for her was a two-bedroom flat, expensive, eating up nearly half her monthly paycheck, and too large, really, for one person, when a rented room would have done just as well. But it was blissful to live alone; she could play all the music she wanted, walk around naked, eat breakfast at 2:00 p.m. The little paintings on the wall were all original, done by artists of some distinction: a few bright strokes of pastel on rice paper signified a woman, an underwater scene had been done with someone's fingertips, some bright red anthuriums meant nothing except that they were pretty. A former boyfriend had encouraged her to keep fish, in a couple of fifty-gallon tanks. He had said it would help her relax. She had a corner apartment, and there were lots of windows, and the air was fresher than down by the asphalt. Sunlight poured in through white canvas drapes. Her bed had a spread from the mountain city of Baguio, woven with tribal designs. It was a small life, neat and hermetic, and she could not bear to leave it.

A century ago this neighborhood had been a ritzy part of Manila. The sprawling three-story houses throughout the surrounding blocks were still owned by people with illustrious surnames. But the shadow of urban decay had crept across the white walls and narrow old roads. The houses were mostly empty now except for the household help. Their owners, well-to-do to begin with, were now comfortably ensconced in American suburbs — doctors and lawyers, she supposed, educated at the best Manila universities, to whom immigration had been an inevitable part of their career tracks. Now the riffraff that always seemed to accumulate in the shadow of the elite had taken over. Jobless men in frayed shorts lounged around corners, parked their buttocks on the curbs, rose when the sun was lower in the sky to join in a game of half-court basketball. In the afternoons, the sidewalks were a confusion of maids and youths and dogs straining at their leashes. Year-old babies, supervised by the entire neighborhood, stomped around in the span of concrete beneath the building where she lived, in novelty shoes that squeaked loudly with their every step, their audible progress celebrated up and down the street. Little boys flitted by on bikes, butterflies venturing in and out of the paths of cars. It didn't matter whose father was a dockhand or an accountant or a driver in Saudi, or who wore a starched white Catholic school uniform shirt Monday to Friday — in the hour before sunset, children acquired the same democratic layers of dust and roughness, they shrieked and cussed in the same hard voices, with the same wrinkled gray elbows and knees and the same penchant for young-coconut ice drops and rubbery ears of boiled corn.

At a quarter to six the wives started coming home, in their black stretch slacks and their dark tailored blazers, stepping resignedly around puddles and mashed dog turds, in the battered footwear they wore for the bus and jeepney commute. They kept their shiny new office shoes in drawers in their cubicles up in the older, dingier buildings of Makati, the main financial district. They drew their carefully budgeted paychecks every fortnight, while their husbands squatted muttering on curbsides, selling each other secondhand TVs and computer hardware, dreaming up schemes by which they might suddenly become rich. From the entrance to the fire escape in the hallway just outside Narita's door, the towers of Makati dominated the view, rising incongruously above red rooftops and a rash of palm fronds. It took a certain lofty distance to appreciate them: they were invisible from the street, concealed by the aging houses and pretentious pastel-colored apartment buildings like her own.

But at this hour of the morning there was little life in the street below, except for cars once in a while or jeepneys, progressing in explosive stops and starts over the asphalt, their drivers avoiding the perennial traffic jam on the main road by taking unlawful shortcuts through the neighborhood. All that to shave a minute or two off their travel time, thought Narita. Someone below her hollered an oath in Tagalog — an oath or a greeting, she was not sure. The words fell upon her ears but did not register. She had been thinking in English.

It occurred to her now that she was scared to death of going to the office, and that she had not experienced this sort of fear since the first year or so in Manila, when she had bumbled through the unfamiliar language that was Tagalog, and knew, from mocking remarks here and rebuffs there, that neither English nor Binisaya would pass. She remembered the remark made by the young woman at the video stall in Quiapo. "The actresses are ugly. You can hear them in the background, talking 'Binisaya.'" Then the sneer, the deprecating laugh.

But I'm Bisaya, too, Narita thought. Wasn't it obvious? After fourteen years, had she managed to blank out her origins? Had she ever been truly Bisaya in the first place?

In the train the feeling of remoteness continued. She was in the habit of taking the Taft Avenue line, getting off at the Manila City Hall, walking a distance through a network of tunnels before emerging close to the post office at Liwasang Bonifacio and flagging down one of the jeepneys that passed by her workplace. She had long been accustomed to the filth, to the odors, to the queer sensation of grabbing a handrail still warm from a fellow commuter's palm. All three lines of the railway system reserved the forward car for women. Still, it was impossible to avoid the men as she raced to the front end of the platform, trying to catch the train as it pulled in. For the first time in her life she hated them, the whiff of acrid sweat, the weight of a form that struck her by accident, their dirty, wilted rucksacks. In the front car she awakened, momentarily, from her trance, long enough to register the appalling proximity of the women, how they all sought to evade one another's eyes, the press of a breast on her shoulder blade, a hint of down on an upper lip, a mask of powder here, some lip gloss there, a student's glittering barrette, the outlines of a push-up bra, all the various devices of convention without which they were all naked. The train rumbled through a wilderness of sweatshops and dingy apartment buildings, fast-food restaurants and upper rooms converted to churches. Narita stared, mesmerized, at balconies from which drying clothes hung. In each of those places lived at least one person as unhappy as she, someone trying their utmost to negotiate the city while keeping true to some internal landscape.

In the Liwasang Bonifacio tunnel it occurred to her that her life had contained two trajectories, the second not a trajectory so much as a pathetic Brownian movement through her immediate environment. She shied away from a youth who advanced toward her with the small, hard eyes of a criminal, deafened her ears to the noise from a blind man's battery-operated guitar. Her efforts to collect a paycheck, the absolute necessity of learning to speak the Manila mélange of Tagalog and English — both had usurped immense reserves of energy and time. No one in this city was immune, she thought. It was a perverse collection of frustrated humanity, all dreaming of a better place, a few on the move to somewhere better. She thought of her younger sister, who had taken more than a decade to stage her great escape from Sweethaven.

Manila had not been good enough for Antonia. She had skipped the capital and fled to the other side of the world. At first she had been proud of her feat, but now she was lonely and caustic, carping about the long and dark winters, unable to negotiate the language of her adopted country even after two years. It was a relief to know Antonia was in worse straits. It felt to Narita as if she had kept her older-child advantage after all.

She had no clear picture of her sister's life at that moment.

She looked sharply at each person she passed: the boys in their billowy denims and stifling-hot hoodies, the girls in tight blue jeans and tacky jeweled sandals, the sightless man anticipating the chink of coins in his yellow plastic cup. Impervious, all of them, and ignorant of the world beyond their soap operas and their infuriating mobile phone shorthand. *She* read the papers, she watched the foreign cable channels, she knew the intricacies of life in another place — yet her mind was stunned, as though she had been whacked by a plank, like a dog destined for the fiesta cauldron, and the only image she could summon up was of Antonia shivering in a wilderness of snow.

The newspaper offices never slept, but the afternoon round of editing and story consultations had yet to commence, so the section where she worked was quiet for once. A television mounted above the editorial central desk was on as usual — she couldn't recall ever seeing it off — and a security guard and a couple of early-bird layout artists watched a hamburger commercial, their mouths slack.

The desks lay in that wide, high-ceilinged room exactly as they had been left the night before, strewn with faxed stories and press releases, each computer decorated with a paltry souvenir of its owner: a fortune plant in growth jelly, a blue plush dog. Otherwise there was little to indicate who sat at what computer — there were no name plates, no private space; the editorial staff chatted in the lavatories and smoked in the stairwell, and everyone could monitor everyone else. It was the life of her profession. She was used to it.

Down the dingy yellow-painted hall, the personnel department was open — the same confusion of papers as the editorial section, the same lack of privacy, the insular camaraderie of the staff. Journalism was not an affluent pursuit. With the usual high-spirited greetings and smiles, she procured herself a set of leave forms. Returning to the newsroom, she cast a glance at the editor-in-chief's cubicle; he had no office of his own, only a space partitioned off on three sides from the rest of the room. He sat at the desk, an elegant brown-skinned man in his early sixties, carefully dressed in a blue button-down shirt. A coat stand behind him held a dark jacket, still in its dry cleaner's sheath of plastic, and a couple of silk neckties. There was something about his dignity, his handsomeness, his small and dry smile, that reminded her of her father, or at least of the kind of man her father should have become.

"Well, come in," he said. "If it isn't the Donostia girl, the Sweethaven princess. How are things at the university there?"

"I wouldn't know, sir," she murmured, which was the truth.

The leave forms fluttered in her hands. He held out his hand for them, scanned them briefly, but did not sign them. "Personal reasons? And what might those be?"

"My mother's in hospital, sir," she lied.

"Not dying, I hope?" He chuckled. She smiled to show she was a good sport. "How long do you want?"

As long as it takes, she wanted to say, but answered, "Six days," unable to keep a humiliating quaver from her voice.

He shook his head and gave that same dry chuckle, and she felt her gut turn in fear.

"Well, perhaps you might help us with a story or two, then." He lifted the morning mail from his desk.

On the impeccable gray surface lay a copy of *Sweet Heaven Girls*.

Her extremities turned cold, and she felt a sudden and alarming urge to void her bowels.

"It seems a breath of scandal has perked up your hometown. It's more than a breath, actually. I hear your mayor has launched a witch hunt to rid Donostia of pornographers and various unsavory elements. You know about this movie, Miss Pastor?"

"Yes, sir," she said softly. There was no point in lying.

His voice dropped to a level so intimate it was almost sensual. "This is no ordinary sex scandal, it seems: even the Manila newspapers have picked up on the story. They say one of the women has killed herself, but they say that of every *puta* who unwittingly turns her *puki* into a screensaver. So are you acquainted with the girls? Personally?"

How much did he know? The video disc lay there, identical to the one she had so recently purchased, a shocking reminder once more of how close their profession was to the bustling and vulgar life of the street. No, she thought, we *are* the street, we *are* the masses, the whores, the market, we are no better than them, their exploits keep us and every other paper in this city alive. She flicked a glance up at him cautiously. Age had clouded his eyes over; it was impossible to see whether he was taunting her or simply curious, mildly concerned over the fate of three young strangers.

"Neighbors? Classmates, that sort of thing?"

Perhaps he sensed she concealed something, for he continued to scrutinize her, her jeans and Girbaud T-shirt, the misshapen, slept-on hair. She took off the glasses she wore for editing work and met his stare full on. It was the only way she knew to appear ingenuous. He had known her for six years. There was no way of telling how much of her he could read. In the newsroom beyond, the television blared. Applause and a hysterical announcer and a taunting drumbeat, one of the noontime variety shows.

"No, sir, I don't," she said indifferently, and wagged her cropped head.

He sighed and opened the drawer at his midriff, raking the DVD into it. She knew then she was in the clear. No one in Manila knew of the child she had left behind: all her personnel forms read "Single," and after "Dependents," she had always scribbled, "None." So he knew nothing, this crafty old man — he had not seen the resemblance, he had failed to make the connection between the fashionably starved, ironically smiling woman before him and the grainy teenage girl.

"Cheap porn," he muttered. "Dish of the week. Mustn't forget it's in there. Cora will have a heart attack when she comes to visit."

She waited for him to sign her leave forms.

He noted the direction of her gaze.

"Not so fast, Miss Pastor," he said, and one misty eye narrowed; the effect was grotesque. "Pull up a chair."

She thought, wretchedly, that now he would pick her brains for an editorial he planned to write, on morality and the depravity of the Internet and this generation's teenagers.

Before she could move, he tossed across the impeccable desk a copy of that day's Lifestyle edition, folded up until only the piece she had written was visible. It was now a crazy quilt of red and blue squiggles.

"The red," he said, "represents timeworn passages, outrageous clichés. The blue, Miss Pastor, are passages identical to some I found in similar articles in the *Gazette*, the *Globe*, the *Post*. I believe I hired you to produce journalism, my dear, not to stitch together press releases, which are there to inform us, not to be plagiarized."

"I'm sorry, sir," she said softly. "I've been tired."

"You began so well, Narita Pastor," he said, his face never losing its dry composure. "A talented writer, full of energy, a perceptive copy editor, and completely hassle-free. No husband. No children. A bit too active in the boyfriend department, but what young lady isn't nowadays?"

She knew it was not in her best interest to correct him.

"Your job," he said, "is the cushiest on any paper. All glamor and freebies, none of the shit that goes with putting the paper to bed, press kits and the Internet to help you along, and you give me *this*." He tapped the folded sheet of newsprint with the end of his pen. It was a Waterman, she thought detachedly. The accusation of plagiarism filled her with cold rage. Every journalist she knew derived material from the press releases that landed in their e-mail or arrived in little envelopes, often escorted by a gift. True, the lifestyle regulars were the worst, but the opinion and business writers were a close second, and any one of the editors was likely to print a feed verbatim, passing it off as a news story, as a favor to a friend.

"A fresh graduate could do your job," he grunted. "At half your price. So you better start showing some of that old fire, Miss Pastor."

She suspected some sort of personnel overhaul was afoot once more. Tenure was impossible in this profession. Was the lifestyle editor to be replaced, with some diva arriving with a retinue of her own? If so, this was a pro forma notice. Dismiss me, then, you old fart, she raged inside, though her face retained its usual mild, self-mocking smile. Once, at the very beginning of her employment, she had gone on a handful of dates with this man, married for thirty years to the same woman. Narita had been seeing someone else at the same time. The brief romance had been a mix of game and opportunism: rewarding him with nothing in the end, she had thwarted whatever ambitions he might have had of rejuvenating himself in her fire.

"Well," he said at last, "as your trip to Donostia seems hardly a matter of life and death, I will grant you six days. That, plus the day off. Any more and we'll have to find a permanent replacement for you, and pay you by the piece."

The other editors were arriving. She counted to herself, marking their laughter and the jocular taunts that came to her over the top of the wall divider. News, foreign, photo, sports.

Her own boss, the lifestyle editor, would not be there; he was on a press junket to Palawan Island. Poor old bag, probably making the most of his status before the management expelled him.

The chief editor signed the leave forms with short, dismissive movements and tossed them over to her. She turned to go.

"Oh, and another thing," the old man called. "Pay us back with a story. The scandal at Sweethaven. Send us a depth piece. Write about the girls."

THE STORY conference had begun, as it did every day at half past one, the editors planning the headlines, reporting the contents of their sections to make sure they didn't print the same story twice. Portly bodies and blocky heads, seamed faces and flabby stomachs. Veterans, men whose shoulders were humped and arteries slowly silting up from sitting at the same computers sixty hours a week. Two people were smoking. She herself had quit long ago, but the smell of secondhand smoke was not unpleasant. She heard nothing of the voices about her. Six days. Six days, nothing more, and the threat of losing her job. The years of careful work, of machinations, the prudent lunches with the paper's managers, had come to naught after all — she was in as much danger as any first-timer. The men listened in amusement as she took them through the lifestyle page lineup for the following day. The Chilean food festival at the Hyatt, the figure-skating championship in Minnesota that the Philippine team had won. It was candy; her job was to report on the candy. Over in the main room, the television blared on, ignored. She caught sight of a line of dancers in metallic shorts and matching thigh-high boots, now to the front, now to the back, the game show announcer squealing, whipping up the crowd, nine pairs of skinny buttocks winking in time to the drums.

NARITA stood in the middle of the living room, taking stock of her home. The nonfat milk had been poured down the drain. The houseplants were freshly watered. The lovely goldfish — the lionhead that looked like a newborn puppy, the triangular ryukins, the fat little pearlscales — were greedily sucking up the food pellets that speckled the surface of their tank. In less than a week they would be dead. There was no one she could trust with the key, no one to feed them and clean out their tank in her absence.

"Good luck," she addressed the small, quiet living things throughout the flat. "I'm sorry."

She drew the glass shutters on the high windows, saying good-bye to the sunlight that poured through the white canvas drapes. She cast a last look at the zinc roofs of the neighborhood: the expanse of summer sky, the billboards, and the eternal roar of the superhighway to one side, and to the other, Manila Bay, concealed by recent high-rises, evidenced only by the occasional scent of salt and rot borne on a hot breeze.

She had provisioned herself against the hazards of the return. For the flight, she had donned a pair of Calvin Klein jeans; at the bottom of her canvas bag was folded a second pair, DKNY. The blouse she was wearing was an H&M, and among her T-shirts was a Dolce and Gabbana, the real thing; she was ready to peel it back at the nape to display the label, if anyone were so tacky as to ask her for proof. Some of these she had procured through the gift checks that arrived regularly at the Lifestyle section, contained in innocuous white envelopes bound with strips of clear tape. She always knew when a freebie was coming, by the inordinate amount of tape. Otherwise, she filled her closet from export overruns and the secondhand shop a few blocks from her flat: off-season Tommy Hilfiger sportswear and wrinkled Ralph Laurens. She was proud of her labels, of her traveling exhibit. She would bring her laptop, too. In Donostia, laptops, even the huge ugly ones, still had a certain cachet. The native never returned a failure.

There was no point in delaying further. She took a deep breath, picked up her bags, locked the door behind her. She met no one in the hall, or down the four flights of stairs. Almost as soon as she stepped out into the street, a taxi lurched violently past, the cabbie escaping the traffic on the main road, eager to get to Taft Avenue, where the pickings were better. She flagged it down without thinking, taking a moment to assess the vehicle and what she could see of the driver. Behind the wheel was a man in his forties, a dark, shriveled man who set her nerves on edge. There was no backing out; he had already reached over to unlock the back door. At least the cab was clean enough, and she noted that all the locks on the doors were complete, as were the levers that rolled down the windows. Escape, in case he tried to abduct her, would not be a problem.

The antiseptic scent of lemon failed to relax her, and she cursed the masquerade of her clothing. Please take me straight to the airport, she begged silently, anticipating a holdup, watching the cabbie's every cue with suspicion — the direction of his eyes, the movement of one dark, powerful hand from wheel to gearshift. Please, please, she groaned. I am not the rich person I resemble.

But she made it to the terminal without incident, and after the customary twenty-minute delay, into the plane, where the armor of her clothing proved no help through the ordeal of the takeoff.

Are you afraid? she heard Naia say, for over the years she had kept the habit of conjuring up the child, when she was worried or quite simply losing it. It was good to have someone smaller and more vulnerable to reassure.

I'm always afraid, she replied.

Of flying?

Oh yes, flying in particular.

The plane tipped, shuddering as it continued to climb.

Why?

I don't trust the pilots. Human or auto.

And you think you can manage better than they? the child said, precociously, for the Naia of her thoughts had never quite grown beyond the cool, inquisitive age of seven.

Narita wanted to say that she couldn't even begin to imagine the efficiency of pilots, or of instruments, or the vigilance of the control tower — trapped as she was in a body strapped down and bullied by forces it could not understand. She was aware only of her heart thumping in her mouth, of her stubborn and undeserving self. All the silly rhyming prayers of her childhood descended on her then, evaporating just as quickly at the moment of landing.

I've never gotten used to planes. It was the long bus trips I loved. They gave me time to brood. And when I was little, I liked hanging over the rail of a stinking boat, musing over the blue islands on the horizon. I would watch the other passengers, how they tossed eggshells and the hulls of boiled peanuts in the wind. I was too naïve to recognize unhappiness, discontent.

I have not taken a sea journey since, oh, that weekend when I was very young and extremely confused and I decided to get rid of you.

Except something made me change my mind. I saved you. I installed you where I thought you might be safe, while I tossed myself into the air currents, to be wrenched every which way.

Five

THE TRICYCLE taxi would have taken her from the airport straight to her parents' doorstep, but Narita ordered the driver to stop a few blocks away so she could continue on foot through the neighborhood, past wooden frame houses that, after Manila, seemed so faded and small, so sadly provincial.

After the move, she had come back maybe once a year, staying no more than a week at a time, except for two whole months, in between jobs, when Naia was seven. Pet dogs had died, new ones had arrived to take their place. A pretty sort of vine with yellow flowers crept its way over fence posts and eventually took up residence over the garage roof.

Some things had not changed, she thought as she stood at the gate, waiting to see if anyone would notice her. The clutter in the garage had remained, and worsened. It seemed to her that the visible elements of the property could be sharply divided in two. Her mother's were the yellow flowers and the neatly clipped grass and the orchids that bloomed profusely to one side of the lawn. Her father's were the musty, oil-stained garage, the rust on the gate, the murky screens that covered the windows, the piles of newspapers and magazines that had fused through the creeping moisture.

As she hovered uncertainly, three muscular, enraged creatures charged around the corner of the house and assaulted the iron grills of the gate, barking and growling madly.

When she turned her gaze toward the garage once more, she realized her mother was watching, her bulk hovering just behind the screen door of the front entrance. It was a workday and yet she was home.

"Call the freaking dogs off!" Narita yelled.

Luth waddled out. She had gained a terrible amount of weight. The mongrels leapt and bounced, batting at her playfully. Luth cursed as their claws bit into the soft flesh of her legs.

Narita did not resist her mother's embrace. She turned her cheek to be kissed, and winced as Luth's lips left a smear of wet. The woman smelled of sweat and some other rich unshowered odor. Her body, engulfed in a shapeless print house shift, showed neither curve nor contour, and Narita shuddered at the dead, solid mass of her flesh.

"Naia uses your old room now," Luth informed her.

"That's okay." She hated the tight little voice that emerged from her throat.

As they threaded their way through the junk in the garage, she heard the shuffle of slippered feet. A thin and stooped man who she could not believe was her father appeared in the dimness beyond the screen door. Her parents stood there, just one meter apart, seemingly unaware of each other. Every time she came home she experienced this moment of disbelief: that in spite of their blistering differences they had managed to stay under one roof all this time.

"Hey, Pa," she said dutifully, squeezing through the door, which a box of papers prevented from opening all the way. He held out his arms to her with affectionate welcoming sounds. She held her breath as she pressed her cheek to his. She would never have guessed, by simply looking at him, how old and malevolent he smelled, of sweat and rot and unwashed shirt, like the forgotten wet gunk between the tiles in a corner of the kitchen counter, like a substance at the base of an old, sealed mayonnaise jar. She pulled away and cast her gaze over the living room. Every available surface held a pile of papers and letter envelopes and books. The piano stool; the music stand on the piano itself; the two chests, one inlaid with mother-of-pearl, the other carved with rustic scenes from old

China; the spaces between the knickknacks on the shelves; the top of the coffee table and the space beneath — she had forgotten this aspect of her home. This, the chaos of her childhood, which was simply mirrored in the clutter of her own apartment. As she looked around, incredible exhaustion and despair came over her. The life and habits of all who struggled to make a living through words.

HER first clear memory was of a night when water flowed ceaselessly in a bathroom, and just beneath that sound, the rapid tread of adult feet. Back and forth they went, through the living room, past her bedroom door, to the hall table where the telephone sat, to the bathroom again. A car engine exploded into life, violating the night, and she heard the squeak of metal, as if a weight had been hoisted into the backseat. Her mother groaned, a terrible sound. The car drove away, leaving behind the fragrance of burned gasoline.

There was a long silence that merged with the fuzzy warmth of her pillow.

She awakened hungry, to a desolate house: there was a strange woman in the kitchen, hauling steaming sweet potatoes out of a pot the family never used, and when Narita demanded to know where her mother was, she was told to come and eat.

But she couldn't — where was her mother? The strange woman wouldn't tell. Was she in heaven? Her father had told her about that vast, white space where loved ones went when they were old or ill, tired of bearing their mortal flesh. Her mother had often complained of being exhausted all the time. The very notion of heaven made Narita mad with terror.

The strange woman heard her shrieks well enough, but met them with an impassive face. Perhaps she did not understand. Perhaps she was mute. In Narita's distress it never occurred to her that the woman might have been too shy to attempt English, that indeed there was such a thing as language, as differences in language, which set insurmountable barriers between people.

But it couldn't have been a day later that she saw her mother again, very tired and pale, covered by a clean-smelling white sheet, in a room of glistening white walls. Her mother lay against a pillowcase of a pristine quality never seen in their home. She smiled at Narita with lips that seemed dry and odd without the color she normally put on every morning. She seemed to hear nothing the little girl had said. It was as though she had left part of herself in that heaven where she'd been.

Narita had no awareness of the journey to this room — she had fallen asleep in the car, as she was in the habit of doing, and had awakened here.

"Take her away," her mother mouthed, and her father took hold of the child's hand too firmly for comfort, and guided her out the door. Narita saw that they were in a hallway. It opened out into the atrium of a huge building flooded with blue sunlight from translucent panes set in the high ceiling. The space echoed with the wails of children older than she.

"Look, can you remember?" said her father. "We are in the mission hospital. It was here that, three years ago, you were born."

"This way, sir," said a pretty young woman. She wore a white dress and white shoes. A stiff white object with twin points was balanced upon her head. An angel. Father and daughter followed her down another hallway. Then he stopped and hoisted Narita up, awkwardly, his arm cinching her belly. She faced a long glass pane. Her reflection gazed back at her, vague and dark. Then she saw what the room beyond contained. Creatures, no bigger than cats, in their white-and-pink pods. She looked down suspiciously, to where he pointed — one of them was so near she could have examined it with her hand if not for the intervening glass. It had a tiny pig snout. She could see the sharp fringe of its eyelashes and the infinitesimally fine ridges across the back of its curled pink claws.

"Antonia," said her father. "Your sister."

Immediately she felt a flaming dislike.

The kitten came to live in a crib next to the bed where her parents slept. Though its mewling and burping filled her with dread, she couldn't keep away from it. At night, she climbed into her parents' bed, to keep watch over it, but also in the hope that they would remember her existence. But she was firmly banished to the other room, which she was now to share with the woman whose speech she didn't understand. The name of this woman was Murcia. She slept on the floor on a *petate*, a woven mat that, in the mornings, left a grid pattern on her skin. The permanent loamy odor of Murcia merged with the fragrance of strips of *buli* fiber. It was the hot, dense scent of sharing — the end of Narita's singleness, the death of her specialness. From that time forth she would be shadowed by someone young and demanding, someone who wanted to see, hold, and taste anything that was hers.

They grew bigger, and she looked after the baby called Antonia, and sometime in that year or perhaps the next or the one after that, she began to think of herself as an adult. She was gainfully employed. Her boss was Murcia, the maid, who washed diapers, scrubbed floors, snipped off tufts of Bermuda grass with a pair of rusty shears. Every morning, her mother and father left for work, which was something terribly serious, because they argued incessantly as they bathed and dressed, and then came home at the end of the day to argue some more about what had been said and decided in those eight unseen hours. But Murcia was quiet, methodical, competent. Narita imitated her. She learned to slice beans and pluck the odd-smelling *malunggay* leaves off their stems. She foraged in the ditches on the other side of the road for *kangkong*, and learned to tell the green shoots apart from those of the morning glory vines. She begged for the honor of cooking the day's rice from scratch. It was a game: Scrub the grains between her palms and fill the pot up with water a little past the second knuckle on her middle finger. Twist the gas tank ring, wrench the burner knob, and then, quickly, quickly, strike a match into life, before the smell of escaping gas overpowered her. Her fingers would fumble with the damp matches until one flared into life. The flames came roaring out of the burner, singeing her fingertips. Antonia, too small and useless for anything, would watch as blue fire tore up the sides of the pot. She had the kind of face that grew expressionless in the midst of rapture.

It was the same house, then as now, an artless half-wood, half-cement block structure, off a narrow road — unpaved for many years — that ended in the ocean. For as long as Narita could remember their home was cluttered, down to the last corner, with the bric-a-brac of years. There were bullfighter and flamenco posters, and a tiki god carved from what their mother said was sandalwood, and a row of seven-inch Scotsmen that she fancied were little girls, too, as their eyes were blue and guileless, and their plaid kilts and white knee socks were like her spanking-new grade-one uniform at the Sweethaven elementary school. There was even a funny silver elephant that Antonia couldn't stop staring at. It had wheels for feet, and a clock was set into its side. It was a present, their father said, from Ceylon, given by a visiting student of the ministry. Their mother hated it with a passion. It was more than exotic; it was beyond the pale. There were numerous such tokens from all over the world — in those years, on top of his teaching load, their father worked in Sweethaven's public relations office, where his beautiful English came in handy entertaining the foreign visitors, most especially the VIPs from the funding agencies. And of course their father had traveled. He had earned two degrees, an MA and a PhD, in England and America. They must never forget that. From time to time he was called on to attend something tremendously important called conferences, where his opinion was solicited and published afterward in real books. Their mother had never left the country. She rarely journeyed outside of Donostia, in fact. She needed to stay and mind the house, she told them when asked. But she was proud, very proud of him, and the girls were proud, too. There was no father in the world as clever and as laudable as theirs — if there were other fathers who traveled, they did it as deckhands on cargo ships.

There was always a gap between the Pastors and the world immediately beyond the hibiscus hedge that shielded their lawn from the dust of the road. "Out there," it was rough and vulgar, filled with sun-blackened boys and girls who stoned the house in the hope of knocking fruit off the mango tree. For years there was a hole in the hedge worn through the passage of limber little bodies. In summer those scruffy children would sneak onto the lawn, grab the split mangoes lying in the grass, and vanish. The Christmas that Narita was seven, she was declared old enough to hand out candy to the children who came to carol. Once, she counted out eight pieces, one for each caroler, as they watched, their eyes huge in their starved and dirty faces. She handed all eight pieces, reveling in her Christian charity, to the smallest boy, and in a flash he was off, grinning, leaving the other seven children to stare at her, closing zombie-like in on the gate, their palms out, that pleading, demanding singsong that beggars make rise from their throats. The selfishness of it, the opportunism of that stunted, crafty child, swamped her. She slid the iron bolt home and dashed back into the house, wailing for her mother.

Antonia was simply terrified of intruding urchins — one thing in particular filled her with horror: the round white scars, like loose change, that speckled their legs and arms, shining through weeks' worth of grime. Narita only had to say the magic words, "Hala, nuka!" pinching some random spot on the younger girl's legs, and goose bumps would break out all over Antonia, as though those blemishes had a life of their own, could crawl off their hosts and undulate over dust and floorboards, launching themselves at flesh.

Narita was terrified of the children for a different reason. While Antonia fled shrieking, Narita would peer from her bedroom window and jeer at them as they passed, daring them to pelt the house with a stone or a green mango. This they never did. They would hang their sun-bleached heads and shuffle guiltily past, toward the beach, sometimes swiping a hibiscus blossom just to spite her. She had power over them, as long as she remained in the safety of the house and of her half language, a collection of Binisaya insults that she had picked up at school. If they had turned around and shouted back at her, she would have had no words to reply. If she had called to them in English, they would have mocked her and barraged the house with stones. That was what worried her, each time she peered out from the potted asparagus ferns to taunt them — that her toughness was fake, and that sooner or later she would be found out.

But there was no shortage of language within the confines of home. She discovered her father's books early on: it seemed that, after his studies abroad, he had diligently shipped back every last book he had ever read or touched. Penguin classics, *Life* magazines, *National Geographic*, expurgated bestsellers from the *Reader's Digest*, and the anthologies of literature that he relied on for his teaching. Where had all these books come from? How could he have afforded them? He never explained. They simply sat there, like three-dimensional wallpaper. She had awakened from the sleep of infancy to find them already gathering dust. The family shelves were filled by the time she was in preschool, the year he came home with his PhD. That was the year her mother and father began to enshrine and gild the memories of his foreign studies. Perhaps the books had come from secondhand sellers in the various countries he had traveled in. She could not tell which ones he had read and which ones he had always meant to read, or which ones were there to make his friends envious. She could look at anything she wanted, but was forbidden to lend anything out. The collection was sacred. It had to be saved.

ANTONIA'S abandoned room had become a repository, like the rest of the house. Narita set her traveling bag down by the bed and took in the younger woman's leavings.

All around lay the evidence of Antonia's brilliant, ever-unfinished enterprises. Sketches, murky with dust, were taped, forgotten, to the walls. There were a couple of drawings of a pretty little girl, one in a summer hat, and Narita supposed the model for both of them had been Naia, though they were so idealized it was hard to tell. There were some drawings of dogs, the family pets, she figured; and even a watercolor of a seascape, with a blue mound of island on the horizon. She thought the island might be Marmol, or Pagong, but the painting was so runny and imprecise she finally decided Antonia had painted it from her imagination, a melding of vacation postcards and the back covers of issues of *Reader's Digest* from the 1960s. After an initial flaring of teenage brilliance, Antonia had lapsed into a kind of parlor art trance.

The basted pieces of a dress lay fading on a chair, untouched, it seemed, in the two years that she had been gone. When she peeled back a section of fabric Narita saw a label, Argenti, and understood that Antonia had bought the garment at one of the secondhand stalls at the market, and had tried, vainly, to remodel it. Why had she quit? For want of time? Or at the painful realization of the futility of her project? Where in Donostia would she ever wear a silk dress the color of emeralds? It was a hue that Narita herself had loved, as a girl, but which had been forbidden her, along with peach and pale pink and lilac, mint, garnet and purple, flaming orange and slate gray, lemon yellow and chartreuse, any sort of beige and any sort of white, for none of these colors — no color, in fact — went with her unlovely skin.

IN their childhood they had been known as the black Pastor girl and the white Pastor girl, but this stark distinction had less to do with race than with Binisaya, the language of Donostia, the language they spoke as well as English but that had been supplanted in their classrooms by Tagalog. The Binisaya they spoke was a language that made no compromises, especially not in the delicate matter of beauty. The word *itum*, for the color black, was the same word used to describe the dark brown skin that more than half the girls possessed. Anything paler than that was described as *puti*, which meant "white."

Whatever gradations there might once have been, indigenous words to evoke the color of sand or bark or summer leaves or the luscious promise of certain fruits, had all been lost.

Even now, though she was well into her thirties, the memory hurt. She understood, with the distance of years, that sisters could never be equals, and that no two would ever have the same exact shade of skin. It had simply been her fate to be the darker girl, just as it was Antonia's to enjoy all the privileges of being pale. She had not been pretty, and it hadn't been her fault. "But, still!" she thought. "Still, I would have been entitled to something."

She would never comprehend the imbalance in Luth's love — protectiveness of the younger daughter, perennial disgust at the elder.

For Narita, transformation was the promise contained in the pots and vials on their mother's dresser. These she pillaged with a fingertip, her ears ever alert to the sounds coming from the other rooms of the house. The creams and colors were of little use. Dark she remained. She'd sit, confronting the mirror, weeping in fear of punishment as the stolen makeup ran down her cheeks. Her mouth screwed up and her eyes puffed, the tears transforming her visage into something awful, mythic, a creature from the outlands, crunching up stalks of sugarcane and tearing wildcats limb from limb.

Antonia ran squealing around the furniture, pretending her sister was chasing her. Monster! Medusa! She stubbed her toe and tumbled, howling. Narita pinched her viciously, thinking, now Mother will kill me.

She could not recall a time when she did not fear her mother, hate her, feel useless and despised.

Man-hungry, her mother had called her once. Narita, at fifteen, was uncontrollable, one of her teachers had hinted — she was wearing makeup, her best friends appeared to be male, the high school and grade school teachers were in a tizzy over how the elder Pastor daughter might fall.

Man-hungry. The injustice of it lingered, stung. Narita had never allowed any of those boys to touch her. She had liked their company, their levity, the uncomplicated monosyllabic friendships, the occasional dirty joke. That was all.

There were other words her mother liked to use: *retrobada*, when Narita defended herself; *ingrata*, when she insisted she had rights; and finally *simberguensa*, "shameless," summing up the entire package of her character. She cursed Narita in Spanish, bastard Spanish, overheard by her ancestors from some Creole master over the course of four centuries. In her mother's mouth, the words became names of demons, black devils. She pronounced these epithets in the guttural accent of the sugarcane town where she'd grown up. As with her fellow schoolteachers, Luth's English was fluent but accented. She did not care how she sounded. There was no need to mimic the mannered accents of Sweethaven's professors, the accents from whichever country they had taken their postgraduate degrees. Her colleagues spoke the same way. They understood one another. The pupils listened to their teachers without complaint, without need for anything different.

All throughout their childhood, Luth scolded and clucked as she scraped under beds, dragging out rafts of dust and misplaced storybooks. On Saturdays, as she hung up the wash, her voice jarred the dust motes floating prettily in sunbeams, ruining the delight of morning glory flowers, their delicate fragrance and velvety throats. "Practice your piano," she would shout at the girls. When they were seven and nine, the unsavory instrument, a varnished mahogany upright, had arrived in a crate with no warning whatsoever. "Surprise!" their father had cried. Soon after that, the lessons began, on windless Sunday afternoons, the teacher drowsing in the rush of air from the Hitachi electric fan, Antonia and Narita banging out Hanon exercises and John Thompson ditties. Sweat pasted their thighs to the vinyl-covered bench. It was always "your piano," as though they had been personally responsible for the thing. "You are improving your piano," their mother might say, or else "You will never master your piano unless you practice; don't you dare look at me that way."

If they had company for the evening, their mother would pluck white ginger flowers and bird of paradise from the ditch across the road. She would switch off the fluorescent bar and turn on the lamps shaded in filigreed brass or coarse tropical fiber. She would sit one of the girls on the bench and order her to play — "any piece as long as it's recital" — for the arriving guests to exclaim over.

Neither girl had much passion for the music, but Luth kept both of them from doing housework just the same, because she'd read somewhere that it ruined talented hands. After Murcia took ill and went back to her barrio, none of the new maids could meet Luth's standards or stand her scolding longer than a fortnight. So she suffered the cooking and cleaning herself. Luth's sisters thought Narita and Antonia were spoiled, reading all the time. In the Character Education books, little girls were always pictured washing dishes and sweeping floors.

"A girl must be industrious," the aunts declared. But the aunts were lower class — Luth herself would be the first to say that. While her sisters had college degrees, none of them had studied at Sweethaven, so they had to be content with government jobs in their town. The Pastors enjoyed a certain patrician status, conferred by the shelves of books in their home; no town mayor, no lawyer even, possessed so many books.

As for Narita, the black-skinned one, she fell from grace when she was ten, the year she started combing through her mother's things. First were the old cosmetics, some already curdled in the heat. She puzzled over the fat, greasy pencils, one white, another the color of the sea before a typhoon broke. Then she dared open the perfumes, spiriting the bottles away from the stifling hot bedroom, releasing their fragrance out beyond the morning glory fence. Once a bottle tipped and spilled, assailing her with an odor of alcohol and soap; she did not recognize the odd name, Chanel No. 5, but knew it had been a gift from her father. She glanced wildly around, in case Luth was watching. She hid the empty bottle deep in her knickknacks drawer. She pilfered loose change from her father's trouser pockets. She stole his cigarettes, too, and borrowed his lighter; she filched her mother's cuticle nipper, her tweezers, the marking pen from her bag, a fountain pen from her father's pocket. The house had so many treasures lying around, and her weekly allowance was a joke.

Antonia took her scratch pads and flipped them open for their mother's inspection. "Look," she said in an affronted voice. "Narita's copying pictures. Here's Veronica, here's Wendy, here's the mermaid from *my* storybook. She's a bad girl. She cheats at everything."

"Never mind," Luth said tiredly, thinking, So she steals even those.

One afternoon when Narita was fifteen, she came home late and found her mother on the rattan sofa waiting, her eyes gleaming in the twilight. Luth grabbed her daughter's wrist and sniffed her hair. Exhale, she commanded, and made a face at the sharp fragrance of breath mints, the odor of tobacco underneath. Narita quivered. She had spent an hour behind the Practical Arts building with a boy. There had been no kissing, no skin contact. She was neither beautiful nor outrageous enough for that, and besides, there'd been another girl and two more boys present. Narita could not recall a single thing they had said to one another. As for the fellow she wanted the most, he had never spoken a word. Never smiled, either. Just took long, thoughtful drags on his cigarette, bending, proffering the end of it so she could light her own. His silky black hair had brushed her cheek. She had a thing for long black hair.

Probing her daughter's satchel, Luth found a packet of Winstons, a butane lighter, an eye shadow compact last seen on her own dresser top, and three joints. The boy had asked her to hold them for him so he could pass the security check unmolested. He was the kind of fellow who had his name and picture in the gate guards' log: number three on the list of troublemakers. The guards would draw him aside and pat him down for knives before they let him into the compound; leaving, he would be checked for school property. That afternoon, the boy had disappeared as soon as he'd exited the gate, and Narita had held on to his goods in ecstasy. They were so priceless and potent she was sure they would burn a hole through her bag.

Now the joints lay like shriveled bird turds on the crocheted table runner.

Luth leafed in silence through her daughter's Springback notebooks. She examined the notes scrawled to classmates. She gazed long and hard at the drawings of naked women in ankle-strap shoes that snaked, seventies psychedelic style, halfway up the margins.

"You are not to draw again, you man-hungry whore," she said.

That week and into the summer Narita lost her allowance. It left her no choice but to lie in bed picking through their mother's Harlequin paperbacks, glaring as her younger sister self-consciously opened a sketch book and began pecking away at it with a sharp black pencil. Antonia was given a mission: to report to their mother any attempts Narita made to break the no-drawing rule.

"Here," the younger girl said, more than once, not generous so much as placating. Across the bed, she would toss one of the notebooks she had been using the previous term. She had already sliced out the pages that contained her obedient schoolgirl script.

But Narita was no longer interested.

"I'm getting out of here," she muttered. "When I'm eighteen, I'm taking all my money and hiring a stud."

She sat up and swung her legs over the edge of the bed. She wore only a cropped T-shirt and a tiny pair of panties, and her legs were smooth and powerful. Her long wild hair fell hippie-like about her face, throwing her thin adolescent cheeks into shadow. There was murder in her eyes. "I'll find myself a tall man with a hairy chest and six-pack abs. He won't be cheap. I'll take him for a ride in my red Corvette and then I'll fuck him."

Antonia, tart and breastless, stared at her in awe.

Six

SHE WAS nineteen the year she brought her mother a durable and unforgettable gift: she was pregnant.

Luth was correcting papers in the living room, her bare feet up on a cushion because her cheap shoes pinched. Narita chose the chair opposite the sofa.

"Ma, I need an abortion," she said, and started to cry.

Luth did not speak. In the silence, Narita went on before she could lose her nerve, telling her about the sore breasts, her bladder bursting in the mornings, the period that had never come, though she had prayerfully pasted a sanitary pad to her underwear for seven mornings running. Deep within her a force had accelerated her heartbeat and invaded her throat with a new and constricting rhythm. She fell silent, and still her mother did not speak. "Look," she said, sobbing anew, "I have money." She produced a battered airmail envelope from her purse. There were several thousand pesos in there, culled from her allowance and borrowed from her younger sister, who that year had won a prize in a school painting contest. As the envelope sagged open, Luth turned her face away from the sudden wet-market smell of worn bills. "I have a doctor in mind. I know where to go. Antonia will come with me."

"What does your boyfriend have to say?" her mother said at last.

"He doesn't know."

But she was lying; she had told Zenon the week before, and he had walloped her across the face so hard that she toppled upon the dank bedspread in his rented room, her head hitting the plywood wall with a thud. If she went through with the abortion, he would put both his hands around her throat and choke the life out of her, he'd said, barring the door. In here she would stay until the baby was too big to be extricated without killing her as well. As she'd struggled to get past him, she'd called out for help, once, twice, and the radio in the next room had fallen silent, but none of his housemates had come to her aid.

"I'm going through this alone," she now sobbed to Luth, and put her arms to her face.

Her mother saw the blue bruises below her wrists. At this, her pain flared into anger. "But why did you have to do this? How could you. Whore. Liar!" Abruptly, she diverted her attention to the fourth-grade quiz papers. She resumed checking them as though her life depended on it, slashing red marks into their dingy surfaces with her pen. "I thought you had reformed. Shameless. That's all you'll ever be."

Her mother issued orders like the plantation overseers of centuries past, and never asked questions. She would never admit her ignorance. Or the possibility that she might be wrong.

"I cannot understand how you allowed this to happen to yourself," Luth stormed. "It is not the natural course of events, these forays into intimacy."

Shame checked Narita's tongue.

"First must come respect. Then, in the fullness of time, hope — and a proposal."

Her mother had never discussed the relations between men and women before, except to carp about the immorality of the world.

"Then, acceptance," Luth went on, her voice rising at the word, and Narita caught the ghost of an old excitement she had felt, or dreamed about until it was beyond real.

"Then love. And with the proper understanding between families, marriage."

The girl waited.

"And after marriage, then and only then: passion!"

"That's a crock of shit," Narita said.

Luth gave a profound sigh. The girl knew she had won. She felt neither triumph nor relief.

"You'll have to go to Cebu for it; I can't have you visiting a doctor in this city."

Always this need, thought Narita, to maintain the family image.

"And don't tell your father. That would only mess things up."

A COUPLE of days later, Narita packed a change of clothes and bought a couple of tickets on an overnight boat to the next island. Antonia was a silent, judging presence by her side — a small spare girl, hair scissored bluntly at the chin, her eyes focused on an inner landscape. They walked the interminable concrete pier, past crates piled twice the girls' height, keeping well away from the forklifts. Narita felt waves of disgust from her sister, and wondered how much of it was on account of the abortion to come, and how much was due to her own weakness, her weepiness, the inferior specimen of a man she had chosen for a lover.

Their cots were down in the hold, near the waterline. Sticky orange canvas affairs, never washed or wiped down. The odor of tar, an eternal feature of the docks, made her violently ill, and she clung to the railing where a thousand other hands must have rested. The vessel shuddered away from the pier, and as when she was a little girl and making this journey for the first time, she examined the black ocean, and the froth, green and white in the ship's lights, which slopped directly beneath her as the bow cleaved the waves. The thrill was in staring into that seductive glass green, envisioning a single, decisive leap into its warmth.

The aging ship had begun life hauling cargo in Japan. The toilets were porcelain trenches in a wet and muddy floor.

On the walls, the emergency evacuation instructions were in characters none of the passengers would ever crack; no one had bothered to change them. Dragging herself away from the railing, she stumbled over canvas luggage and great bails of egg noodles. The hallway space had been halved by a row of occupied cots. There were so many people on this vessel; there were too many people in this world. She found her place in the chilly compartment, where, like Antonia, fifty others were already prostrate, closing their senses to the thrum of the motors and the suffocating nearness of fellow humans. A steward went around absently tossing threadbare sheets onto each cot. He held her gaze for a moment, flirting.

That entire night she sat, looking caustically around at the men and women innocent in their sleep, scrutinizing their scaly feet, their worn denims, the precious purses they clutched to their chests. Walkmans soothed the lucky few through the darkness of their dreams.

The creature in her registered as a queasiness in the pit of her stomach. She sucked on one sweet after the next, but as soon as her mouth was empty, gastric juice and sausage garlic arose, grain on grain emerging at the top of her throat, invading her sinuses and nostrils. As it slept, tucked within the membranes of her abdomen, the thing fired bitter chemicals into her bloodstream. Tissues divided, flesh grew, with her every breath. Whose features resided within the bud of its face? It was as though Zenon lay clenched within her, his hands curling into the iron fists she had come to know.

Narita and Antonia stood at last on the concrete of the docks, trying not to show their trepidation. It was the first time they had been unsupervised in Cebu, this hot and sprawling city, so large you had to take a jeepney or a cab to get anywhere important, so affluent despite its beggars and filth. Packed with pretty clothes, double-feature cinemas, muggers, street vendors, bookstores, pickup girls, brand-new cars — and yet small and inferior compared to the unknown monster that was Manila.

They took a taxi from the docks to the abortionist, reading out the address from the slip of paper in Narita's hand. The office was in a block-long concrete building; there were elevators, and carpeting in the hall. The two of them glided wordlessly past these novelties, their hearts hammering — they had seen so little of the world. The tallest building in Donostia was the Sweethaven library, all of four stories — that and a crumbling bell tower from which lookouts had once scanned the horizon for Moro sails.

The doctor had gained some renown, through the whispered advice of women she helped, her reputation spreading beyond Cebu to the neighboring islands. The sisters found a waiting room that was as cramped and innocuous as a dentist's clinic — cacti in the window, and a secretary who chattered, her eyes never meeting theirs, as a cross-stitch bouquet emerged beneath her nimble fingers. "Which one of you is the patient?" she said, and a look of embarrassment passed over Antonia's face.

Narita gave her real name. She felt no shame. She felt as a novice might, on the cusp of a rite of passage. They sat down on the hard green cushions. Antonia fished out an issue of *Mod* from beneath the corner table and pretended to immerse herself in a fashion spread. Breathe, Narita commanded herself. This would be no worse than a root canal. She'd had a root canal in high school, had fainted, but survived. There was one other patient in the waiting room, a woman in her thirties who examined the two of them critically; stolidly Narita sat, refusing to meet that judgmental gaze. When she turned to check on her sister, she saw that the girl was drawing something on the thick sole of her deck sneaker. It was a fetus, in ballpoint, like a prawn with a domed head. Antonia's eyes met hers. Idiot, Narita thought.

And then the secretary motioned them in.

The abortionist couldn't have been very old, but she was as gray as her waiting room, and when Narita tried to smile, nothing registered behind the lenses of her eyeglasses. She asked the young woman if her periods were regular. If she'd had intercourse with anyone in the last three weeks. How often, and how many days, exactly.

There were no lab tests, not even one of those disposable-kit urine examinations that Narita had seen advertised in American magazines. "Well," the doctor said, shrugging after her recitation, having noted down a few dates. "You are pregnant. Now what do you want us to do about that?"

They wouldn't let Antonia into the inner room, where all the procedures took place on a rubber-shielded cot. Narita caught her sister's eye and shook her head, begging her not to leave. The receptionist took Antonia by the arm and pulled her, firmly, back out into the waiting room.

Narita undressed and lied down. On the wall above the cot was a framed poster, a watercolor, daisies and roses in a vase. She shut her eyes, whimpered as the doctor probed her with a couple of gloved fingers slicked with some clammy gel. "I haven't even touched you yet," the woman scolded. The fingers became an implement. Narita's vagina became a channel to mysterious chambers, one following the next, chambers she had never been aware of before, now clamped apart and explored with cold steel.

The doctor left her. She lay on her back, feet in the stirrups, until her nerves began to fray; instruments clinked, water ran in a sink somewhere. She had no real thoughts. It was silent, as though it knew as well — the creature whose heartbeat flickered at the base of her throat. There was no sensation in her gut, no sourness now at the back of her tongue. The secretary came in.

"There are no aberrations in the way your uterus lies," she said. She spoke in Binisaya. Narita gazed at her, waiting for what she would say next. The woman named a sum of money. It was bigger than they had budgeted — unless they sacrificed the taxi rides, she and Antonia would not have enough money for tickets to a movie theater, where she had planned to rest, for five hours if need be, until it was time to head for the pier and catch the night boat back to Donostia.

"That fee is already cheap," the secretary said, noting her hesitance.

"I will pay it," Narita said, adopting Binisaya, too.

The woman handed her a tumbler of water and a small cup of clear plastic. In it, three white pills rolled. There were no blister packs to identify them.

"They're Tylenols. Two are. The third will make you drowsy."

"And then?" Narita whispered. "Will I have to pay extra for the anesthesia?"

"They're all you need. And the antibiotics afterward. It's a small procedure. Only a blood clot. Don't worry, she does this all the time."

Narita began to cry. The assistant gave a quick snort and disappeared behind the curtain. It must have been the no-nonsense manner of the whole procedure — foolishly, she had anticipated a long lecture on proper behavior and birth control, as from a Christian counselling hotline, only face-to-face. She had never quite believed in God, but now she had her doubts — what if he was real, what if she would be found out? All her childhood she had been told that abortions were wrong, but on the wall of the hospital corridor where her pediatrician worked, there were stickers warning against having too many babies: she did not know which side was right. She knew nothing about babies. They were noisy, selfish little nightmares — but these three little pills in the cup, what was she to make of them, what if they were placebos and the assistant had lied? Once she swallowed them, there would be no going back. She had been pragmatic and emotionless, as she had imagined a frontiersman might be, shooting a dog torn apart by a weasel, but she was no frontiersman; she'd never even lived outside Sweethaven; she could never belong among the courageous men and women in the movies and in her books. She was only Narita. She had never made decisions. She was scared of her own red blood. She wanted her mother, she wanted her sister. She wanted to thrust the howling red bundle of her soul into their arms and be rid of it, absolve herself of herself.

The doctor stuck her face around the curtain

"How old are you?" she said. "Twenty, you said? Last week we had a girl in here. Fourteen years old. She didn't cry, and neither should you."

When Narita stumbled back into the waiting room, pale and shivering, shirt in disarray, she found her sister blinking back tears of her own. "Oh God, it's done," Antonia said. She put an arm around Narita's shoulders, to steady her.

In the taxi, escaping from that place, Narita told her the truth. "I couldn't go through with it. I put on my clothes and got out of there. The weird thing is neither of them stopped me."

"Shit!" Antonia threw her body into the air and landed, hard, on the upholstery, so that the driver checked his rearview mirror in alarm, thinking they'd been rammed. "Stupid girl!" she raged. "Stupid, stupid, stupid, stupid, stupid."

And then they shopped. They ordered the driver to take them to the largest department store he knew. They threw away their money, the contest prizes, months of saving from their allowances. Ripped, cropped tops were in fashion that year; they grabbed a couple each, and a pair of skinny denims for Narita, daring her body to wear them, and funky sneakers, and some ragged, lacy stuff for their hair. Antonia bought some fragrant oil pastels in a wooden case.

They were ravenous, drowning — girlhood's last gasp, or a frantic attempt to deny what was on its way. Their third sister, their daughter, only the merest flicker at the base of Narita's throat, a minuscule force, a riptide in her blood.

IN the old days they sent away girls who brought dishonor to their families. The convent girls of Manila were dispatched to their ancestral provinces, while small-town girls languished in thatch-roof huts in the depths of the coconut groves. Wherever one lived, there was always somewhere else more remote, more anonymous. Someplace where a young woman could spend nine months repenting at leisure, gazing at a cheap wall calendar, a freebie from the local rice mill, with Alpine meadows and Norwegian fjords saturated in unbelievable color.

The Pastors did not send her away. When she and Antonia got back from the trip on the overnight boat, Antonia rallied their parents for a whispered conference. Narita said nothing, simply lay down and faced the wall. She had a small cassette tape and a precious collection of cartridges recorded off the only FM station in town. She would listen to them for hours, those Top 20 hits from five or seven years back, songs and deejay ramble that over the years she had come to memorize. She clung to them as one might to a comforting hand.

Her parents had never met Zenon, though many times he had dropped her off at the house, after midnight, sometimes in a tricycle taxi, sometimes aboard a motorcycle he had borrowed from a buddy. They knew she had been seeing someone, but to them he had been no more than a voice and a shadow, smelled more than seen, in the residue of stale cologne and sweaty T-shirt that lingered by the front gate after he had driven off. She had always kept a key ready, but her mother, wise to her ways, would bolt the front door by eleven o'clock. Narita, giggling and cursing, would scale the chicken-wire fence, steal around to the back door, and wait until Antonia, alerted by the rustling and agitation of their dogs, unbarred the door to admit her.

In a sense, Antonia was at fault, too, for Narita's shameful condition, and scrambled to get back in the good graces of their parents. Narita would listen for her voice, emanating from the kitchen, the master bedroom, the garden, where her words blurred beneath the hiss of the hose.

"To think he would have lived in this house," she would sneer. "He's a loser, a gofer. Go fer this, go fer that. He's one of those pathetic little nobodies on the fringes of the crowd."

"I thought he ran for the student council," their father might say.

"He lost. He was last. Eight votes was all he got."

Inevitably, whatever tale she began about him evolved into invective that grew more and more hysterical as she spoke.

"He talks like a peasant; he mixes up his *o*'s and *u*'s. Wears the same clothes for a week."

"You don't have to like him, but you could at least respect him. He was your sister's choice."

"Oh, stop defending people, Pa. He used to hit her."

Her righteous anger comforted Narita, like hot chocolate, or a damp cloth pressed to her forehead. Throughout her childhood she had never been ill; not as often or as dramatically as Antonia, and she enjoyed her new status of moral invalid, of refugee.

She lay with relief on the soft, cool bedclothes burned with little holes here and there from her forgotten cigarettes. The sheets still smelled of smoke, an odor that would not disappear until after several launderings. She had taken up smoking because it was cool; she had given it up, cold turkey, for the baby, fearing the wrath of an Old Testament God.

From time to time the phone rang, and she would hear a door slam, her sister's rapid tread through the living room, and Antonia's voice, breathless, as she snatched up the receiver. Antonia was mechanical and unfailingly polite as she took wrong numbers and calls from their father's colleagues, speaking entirely in English, as though front-lining a huge and elegant corporation. A few times, Narita started out of sleep to catch the pleasant sincerity of that voice: "No, Narita's not here. She's out of town. I don't know when she'll be back." One afternoon, the words were sibilant and spaced far apart for emphasis: "No, she doesn't want to talk to you. I'm putting down the phone now."

She lay in bed, too depressed to rise, and allowed Antonia to protect her. Once, the younger girl asked, "What *did* he do to you? He's been all over himself apologizing. Why can't you entertain him just one time?"

She burst into tears. Her sister did not persist.

She cried off and on for three days. Sitting at the foot of the bed like a temple guard, Antonia watched over her, flipping through an art book from the collection of their father's father, the glossy color prints glued to the yellowing pages as they'd been in the days before offset printing. Narita kicked at her, hating her for being the pretty one, for taking her looks for granted, for always getting her way. She imagined grabbing the sewing scissors and shearing through the curtain of fine black hair that half-covered her sister's face until her scalp showed through in patches.

Antonia was enrolled at the College of Fine Arts, to the dismay of Luth: one daughter who was a dropout and another who wanted to paint. Their parents had willed her to become a doctor, but because they could never have paid for that kind of tuition, they hoped she might at least become a nurse. There was a nursing shortage in the States, and the hospitals wanted Filipinos, who were considered diligent and meek and genetically oriented toward nurturance. The summer before, Luth had taken both girls to the College of Nursing to meet the dean herself, who was hefty and imposing and the last person Narita would have cared to be nurtured by.

"My girls are interested — " Luth began, and a knowing smile spread across the dean's face.

"Why?" she demanded. "Because they want to go to the States?"

A few humiliating minutes later, they were out on the sidewalk, Antonia walking fast, her cheeks flaming, Luth struggling to keep up, Narita jeering to herself at the unexpected development.

"I don't want to go to the States. I don't *need* to go to the States!" Antonia spat.

"You think you are superior; you look down on people who earn an honest living," said Luth.

"Nurses do a shit job."

"You cannot say that about Dean Vergara."

"She's a bitch!"

Now they whispered, Antonia and Luth, as Narita lay quietly, listening for their voices through wood and the synthetic mattress: Who was to support the child?

"*Her?*" Antonia exclaimed, giving a short bark of a laugh. "She's heading to Hollywood. She's gonna have a grand career. She plans to be a screenwriter."

"Be serious."

"I am!"

One afternoon, Antonia came to see her elder sister, her face lit with pride. "I've decided," she said. "I'm going to be a nurse after all. It'll pay the bills."

"Shut up," Narita said, fighting nausea. "I know you. You don't fool me."

"You don't have to worry about anything," the younger girl said, gently gathering up the *sirigwelas* pits Narita had dropped to the floor. "I can do it."

"Go away." Narita could smell manipulation. Sure enough, the following day, Antonia burst into her room, tears streaming down her cheeks.

"I hate this!" she yelled. "This is the fucking end of my life. A nurse! All I'll ever be is a fucking *nurse*!"

All through the summer, Antonia sat humming to herself as her sister napped and wept. "Write anything new?" she would say to the older girl's swollen face. They knew it was farewell to their long childhood of spy novels and comic books and clandestine trips to the smelly cinemas downtown, of adventure tales scribbled out in twenty minutes flat, of postnuclear war stragglers suddenly emerging in the jungles of Vietnam, of erotic fantasies cribbed from the pulp fiction in Luth's stash.

Together they observed the old Narita dying slowly, the Narita who was reckless, loud, and brave, who leapt up at the throb of motorcycle engines outside the gate, the Narita who stole out after dinner in tomboy shorts and red geometric earrings to put in a couple of hours slugging beers at some beachside shack with boys who were not strangers and not lovers: just friends of friends who happened to be there for the evening, boys whom she had no reason to fear, boys whose eyes were permanently set on other, prettier girls.

One afternoon in late summer, Antonia brought up Zenon. "He's gone. I went to his boardinghouse, but they said he'd taken the boat back to Zamboanga. Flunked *totally* out of engineering."

"You went to the boardinghouse?" Narita said thickly. "Why didn't you tell me?"

"I wanted to square it with him. They laughed at me. Thought I was the new girlfriend. I didn't care." She kissed her sister. "It's wonderful. Now he'll never bother us, and you can come out of hiding, never mind the scandal. Is that the baby? I could have sworn it moved."

She indicated, with a toss of her head, the camera that sat on the bookshelf. "I'm taking that with me into the delivery room. I'm going to document all the gory details. You're gonna love me for it."

"I hate you," Narita said.

Seven

IN EVERY PAIR of siblings, there will be a good child and a bad. The good child — fair skin, winning smile, beloved by adults, virginal to the point of being frigid. The bad — she of the unruly hair, the dark complexion, the foul mouth.

Perhaps the tale of the overnight boat to Cebu, the abortionist's office that to our innocent eyes bespoke such affluence, rumors of how I smoked marijuana behind the high school buildings and in tumbledown beach houses with strange boys — perhaps these form the backbone of the Narita myth, the stories of origin that you received from my sister and my mother. How else can I account for the space and dead silence that grew between us over the years?

When I speak to you at last, I will take both your hands in mine and look deep into your eyes. "Naia," I will say, "I am not the demon they say I am."

"I am not a bad mother," I will say into the silence between us. "I left," I will press, as your lips tighten and doubt and disgust well in your eyes, "so that you and I could have a better life. There were no opportunities in Donostia. Manila was the only place to go."

In my fantasies you never speak. You listen, though, ever pliant. I can't give you a voice because I have never heard your voice, really. We do not write to one another. We talk once or twice a month, long distance, you dispensing the news in a choppy, noncommittal way, me brimming with goodwill, clutching the telephone receiver in moments of quiet when each of us waits uncomfortably for the other to speak.

What I'm really hoping for, in these dialogues that never materialize, is absolution. I want you to squeeze my hands in return and nod and say, "Mother, it does not matter."

"I didn't want to leave," I will confess, when it becomes apparent I have won your trust. "But they drove me out. Shamed me out. In the end it looked very much like my own decision."

See, even in my moment of imaginary connection with you, when all pretense supposedly drops away, I'm still looking around for someone to blame.

IN truth, it was Antonia's child. Narita was but the vessel. She could not get the hang of it, mothering. Maternity had nothing to do with instinct. Her fingers longed to find the switch on that slippery, struggling bundle — something she might flip, to instantly still its cries.

Luth and Antonia would snatch up the baby, and it would calm. They would rock it, glaring at Narita, at the book she had been reading when the creature started to scream, and after a while, she made no effort to conceal her relief at their competence. With the birth had come another mouth to feed, and Narita couldn't help feeling *she* was that mouth. In the past she had been worth scolding and arguing with. Now she was simply ignored, stepped around.

The week of the fight that changed their lives the heat was deadly — March heat, the kind that shriveled the leaves in all the acacias and browned the lawn and forced them all into the shelter of their dim bedrooms as soon as lunch was cleared. She carried the baby the half kilometer or so down to the beach, where the sand baked her feet through the soles of her rubber sandals. The child whimpered the whole time — Narita had forgotten to bring an umbrella against the glare. The light glancing off the waves was white. In the distance, against the looming shadow of the neighboring island, two fishermen bobbed up and down on the waves like children on a playground ride. She took the baby down to the water's edge and let the foam play about its toes, but it was no use; it fought her, wailing, and in the open-sided rest houses, strangers gazed at them, and some pointed with their lips — *Look, there goes that loose girl with her bastard; her parents are with Sweethaven, but little good that's done for her. Shame.*

Night was falling, quicker than expected from the intensity of the light. She considered the rank-smelling fishermen's *bancas* drawn up on the sands, and whether it would be easy to launch one into the current. Left to drift, how quickly would it sink? Would the wailing of a tiny passenger be detected from the shore? The baby hiccupped in her arms. What the hell was she thinking?

"What, are you hungry again?" she said. The baby was making a thin, unbroken sound. She walked as quickly as she could back to the house, joggling her child in an attempt to keep the mosquitoes from its face. The living room was dim; her parents had had dinner and were watching television stone-faced, she supposed, in their bedroom. Antonia was studying for a finals exam. Dinner sat on the kitchen table, a collection of bowls covered with saucers to keep the flies out. It looked to be the same food from lunch; the household was between maids.

"What do you want?" she said to the child. She herself would not eat. It had been months, and she had failed to lose the pregnancy weight. "You want chicken? You want some milkfish? You want Sky Flakes? Jesus, will you shut up for a minute?"

There was nothing a toothless mouth could cope with. She found an opened carton of milk in the fridge, sniffed it, made a face. Fresh milk was so expensive; the household saved it until it went rancid. It would have to be thrown out. Beneath one of the saucers was a half-eaten bowl of tapioca. Her father's culinary specialty. How long had it been sitting there? It didn't smell too good. Was it from a new batch or an old? What did it matter? It was on the table. She took a teaspoon from the dish rack and sat the child down in her lap.

"Here," she said brusquely. Her mother had scolded her some days before for her inconstancy, abandoning the child for days on end and then abruptly taking it up and carrying it everywhere, as though it were a new puppy. The baby began to eat. Was it happy? It had liked the tapioca before. She could not tell. Obediently, it swallowed teaspoonful after teaspoonful. It gurgled and farted and smiled. Narita wept. "I love you," she said. She held the child, and sweat made excruciating snail tracks down her sides. They were pasted together by the secretions of their skins. She did not know how long she sat there rocking the glutted creature. She thought they might catch on fire from this inexplicable wave of love.

THEN Antonia's door opened and she emerged, peevish, in the huge plastic spectacles she would wear only at night. It was finals week at the university, and for once Narita and the baby were not admitted into her bedroom. She was studying, passionately and on the verge of panic. The course in nursing was not going well — the exams were too objective; there were too many things to commit to memory: measurements and values and names of chemicals that were outside her sphere of experience. Still, her concentration was acute. She did not register her sister and the child as she entered the kitchen to fix herself a snack. A ferocious mechanism seemed to drive her, coupled with the bitterness of having to study something she loathed. She liked to remind Narita of this every so often — that she had shifted courses for her sister's benefit. Preparing for the day when the baby would be hers by merit. Narita's gut would go cold with rage. Oh that baby, that cumbersome, costly, insatiable child.

Antonia's was the only air-conditioned room in the house. Their parents had bought the unit secondhand, as an incentive for her to study, and for the baby to have a cool place to sleep when it was grouchy. Antonia had left the door open a crack, and the gentle wave of cold that emerged nearly drove

Narita mad. She slipped in, carrying the child. In here, it was a different country. Antonia's idea of home décor resembled something out of an American magazine. She'd found lengths of cheap ditsy-printed cotton down at the marketplace and sewn them into matching bedspreads and pillows and curtains, ruffled and quilted. There was a gooseneck lamp clipped to the headboard — an expensive and exotic thing in those days. On one shelf was a potted plant, some kind of herb, and a collection of varnished cowries of graduated size, the most common of shells, really, the kind the waves tossed up every other day on their stretch of beach, yet she displayed them with pride, as though she lived in some much colder hemisphere and saw the tropical ocean only two weeks of a year. The room smelled foreign, even, of Glade.

In the cooler air, the baby quieted at once. Narita laid it on the immaculate bed. Something was going on in that round stomach of hers; the baby frowned, gazed up at her mother, and emitted two strange grunts. Immediately the sweet stench of milk-rich feces spread through the room. Narita turned her over. The back of her diaper felt warm and mushy.

At that moment, the baby threw up, a great yellow wave, all over the spread. Narita grabbed the first thing that came to hand, a couple of sheaves of paper from the pile of notes on the bed. Working fast enough, she thought she might scoop all the vomit up and toss it into the toilet down the hall before Antonia noticed. But it was too late. The yellow dribble was rapidly soaking through the spread, to the sheet beneath, and into the mattress.

Then Antonia came in.

"Get her out of there!" she screamed. She saw the damage and began to weep. "My God, I'm going to kill you. Clean it up."

Narita clung to the child, dead certain her sister spoke not to her but to the baby. And strangely, she was relieved — now the pretense of sacrifice was finished.

"Clean it up!" Antonia screamed again, but she shook her head. Antonia began to rain blows about her shoulders. "This is your shit!" she wept.

She grabbed the heavy pillow, but Narita did not wait to find out what she would do with it; she wrenched it out of her grip and brought Antonia to a full stop, with a hand at the throat.

She did not throttle her. That was Antonia's version, later. But how was she supposed to react? Her sister had attacked her. Then it became immaterial who struck first, because she hit her sister hard, aiming for one of her breasts. Antonia landed against the desk, wrenched the gooseneck lamp free, and struck the side of Narita's face with it. "Slut," she panted. "Cunt."

Narita could hear nothing, not the baby howling, not their mother and father begging them to stop. Somehow she flung the lamp away and got a hand on her sister's T-shirt collar and slung her bodily out the door. She had to keep Antonia from the child. Her head throbbed, her skin burned; not even Zenon had aroused such a storm in her cells.

It ended in the kitchen, with the paring knife Antonia had left on the counter to cut a guava. Her palm came up in a plea for mercy, and that was where Narita gashed her, clear to the bone — gave her an extra line, a change in her fate; leave it to the fortune tellers to figure out what.

SOON after that, the distance she craved was granted, and she acquired a space of her own. The space was a long rectangle, just wide enough to turn over on her side in the night, with a limp pillow and a striped sheet borrowed from her landlady. She lived with seven other girls in an apartment, in a dingy corner of the state university campus.

This was her last chance, her father told her. Thank goodness they had had the foresight to make inquiries. Now she must complete an undergraduate degree, in the relative anonymity of Manila. After that, she would finish a master's degree. One could not get a decent job without an MA, he said doggedly. She need not worry about the baby's welfare. Antonia had sworn to sacrifice for the child — she was younger, she had more time; and wasn't an aunt's nurturance the next best thing to a mother's love? They fully understood Narita's need for a career, he droned on in that stern yet kindly way he had, impervious to the tears welling up in her eyes. There were a few more words about realizing her full potential. She was truly his daughter — how happy he was that she had chosen the intellectual track expected of a Pastor. The family would pay for her tuition and expenses. They were not poor, but neither were they rich — they just wanted a dignified conclusion to her education, so she might get on with her life. For her, his neglected, misjudged elder daughter, they were willing to sacrifice.

She had listened dumbly to his words, trying to fathom the logic. They were kicking her out. "You can always come back," her father had said magnanimously, as though he were talking to one of his students in crisis. "You know you will always be welcome."

"Which will it be, Narita," he had pressed her. "European languages? Tourism? Library science?"

She'd considered her choices in silence, too depressed to feign delight; they both knew these were low-prestige courses at the state university, but at twenty-two she was too old, and her marks too poor, for anything better.

She shared the room with three of the bed-spacers, as the boarders were called. They were all college freshmen, all sixteen, all taking A.B. Tourism. The course was open to any and all: there were no grade requirements, no limits on the number of students who could get in, no competition. "Because we want to travel," the girls would giggle. They had no idea that a tourism career would consign them to years of slaving in the government bureaucracy, that travel would be by bus from one dusty provincial city to the next, that the so-called training trips abroad, lasting all of four days, would go to the family and friends of whoever was top dog in the hierarchy. Their fantasies stopped at meeting foreign men, Tom Cruise look-alikes in shades. They didn't even have passports, Narita thought with a shudder. They spoke, as though from experience, of the nasty officers behind the glass windows of various embassies their aunts and uncles had been to, in the perennial quest for work overseas. Any kind of work: one could support a whole family by driving a truck, mopping floors. If you want a visa, never wear a red blouse, they would hector one another. Wear blue instead. Red is painful to the eye — it means *Denied!* And never, ever wear perfume.

They studied in chorus, learning their notes by rote. Taking breaks, they'd extricate high school boyfriend photos from their wallets and pass them around, pretending not to brag.

Drained, she let them chatter about her ears. She lied; they were so gullible. She told them she was a school teacher in a graduate course, adding five years to her age. She was their *ate*, their big sister, plain in her too-large T-shirts, hair cropped and frizzing past her ears. They must have felt sorry for her: girls would pour out their secrets to those who posed no threat. In the beginning, she couldn't speak Tagalog too well, which heightened their pity, though she heard them giggling, in the next room, about the Bisaya spinster who shared their lives.

Her landlady slept with her husband beneath the stairs. They were both clerks. A four-year-old boy lay between them. The adolescent son took a cot that in the daytime folded up against the kitchen wall. There were three other children who every night chose a spot on the living room floor beside the maid. That maid — even in that cramped misery, there was someone whose status was lower. In the other bedroom on the second floor were four other students. Eight persons above, eight below. That was her Manila.

Insomniac, she would feel her way down the pitch darkness of the staircase, wondering where the children were sleeping this time, trying to detect, through some primordial radar, the twin lumps on the linoleum breathing heavily and steadily like drugged animals. The bathroom light, when she switched it on, was yellow and cruel, the bulb naked — the kind glimpsed in the windows of one-room nipa shacks. It awakened the sleepers, all of them stirring, blinking, resentful. But the bed-spacers put food on their table, and so they could not complain.

She hated those midnight trips. She couldn't help them. Her bladder had a mind of its own, screaming for attention as soon as the whole house had settled down, as awful as in the first months of her pregnancy. The ghost of Naia lingered in her pouches and tubes. Childbirth had damaged her somehow, permanently.

The bathroom — she thought of it as a latrine. A shower fixture and a faucet sprouted from one tiled wall. A piece of looped wire fixed the rotting door in place. With the door shut, the room was so cramped she could not wash without water raining onto the porcelain seat. The toilet wouldn't flush. Bathwater was rationed to one pail per person. A strange odor seeped through the drainpipes and pervaded the kitchen. It wasn't fecal, or ammoniac. It was the smell of fungus on a corn cob. It was the smell of yeast, of perverse growth.

She felt constipated all the time, stoppered up and bloated with cheap cafeteria food. A lump of meat, a cup of rice, a few spoonfuls of limp gray plant matter. The food gleamed in a requisite slick of flavored oil. No matter what it was called, it tasted the same.

She thought she might walk the campus after class, to shed weight, purposely choosing the darkened paths, her sneakers squelching on the damp mat of flame tree flowers, eyes dully seeking out pinpoints of lights in the foliage where fireflies survived. She marched to the raunchy creaking of bullfrogs. In the monsoon rains of July and August, stretches of the campus grounds turned into shallow ponds. September came, and with the rains came the chilling drafts. She was a dumpy little figure stealing through the dark, stopping at the library some nights to stare, dully, at the students who tripped blithely down the concrete steps to drive off in late-model cars.

THE first year alone would be the hardest, her father had said. But it would be the trial from which you emerged the stronger.

She found she didn't care. Time carried her along, from one classroom to the next, from rented bed to rented bed. The following semester, she found another boardinghouse, along the road to one of the business districts, in a tenement of concrete occupying half a block. The food, served in the kitchen on the first floor, was still awful, but by then she had discovered the benefits of starvation.

Her housemates went to the nearby Catholic women's college: they spoke the Tagalog-English patois in that chiming, half-singing fashion of Manila's private school girls, clumping up and down the narrow metal staircases in their white-and-green uniforms, hugging books to their chests with bony arms. She listened to their speech and copied it, knowing a proper disguise would be her ticket out. The *colegialas* regarded her in puzzlement, then probed in their artful, delicate way. Who was her father? What did her mother do? Had she lived in the States? What was the reason for the slight but unmistakable American accent? "I have a *tita* in the States, too," one of them might volunteer, in condescension. Still, they kept her at arm's length. They knew all too well of Daly City, Venice Beach, various communities on the West Coast overrun by Filipinos of the totally wrong sort. Anyone could pick up an American accent these days.

They belonged to an exclusive club, these girls — outsiders banned or simply ignored. Four of the housemates wore braces — not the disfiguring metal bridles that the occasional kid in Sweethaven had worn, but expensive ornaments sported with pride. The brackets on each tooth were jeweled in pink and amethyst, so that whenever they smiled, the wearers appeared to have masticated flecks of their own gums loose. They never ate. They would stare in longing at the plates of macaroni and cheese congealing on the kitchen Formica, then sniff delicately and, stomachs rumbling, ascend to their rooms. She supposed it was too much of a bother to pick flecks of food out of their braces. As she studied their speech, she copied their diets. Her hips shrank. No one could tell, by looking at her, that she'd ever borne a child. The stretch marks on her belly, smooth white and gray waves that she idly passed her palm over at night, were invisible beneath her jeans. As the fat leached out of her, so did the shame.

ONE DAY she answered an advertisement in a newspaper, and found herself, after a long and dusty jeepney ride, in a part of the city where container vans rumbled ceaselessly through the narrow streets and hawkers sold cheap goods — stuffed toys, fishing rods, cassette tapes and clothing, all copied from some designer ideal. She entered a long, low-ceilinged room of arctic temperature, and the first thing she saw were the computers. She had never seen so many of them at one time; she counted twenty before giving up; each topped a desk at which a nondescript person of advanced years tapped away. She had never seen an office so messy — piles of papers on each desk, the waste bins overflowing with more paper; long paper ribbons emerging from a fax machine as she stood there.

Two televisions blared overhead. She had no idea TVs were allowed in a workplace. A doughy, effeminate man in a black silk shirt plowed into her and went on without an apology, in one hand, a wine bottle; in the other, a gaily wrapped present that drew her hungry eye. She followed the man's progress over to a room at the far end of this huge communal office, a room with an outsize viewing window through which she could see all that took place. At a desk sat a wizened lady of clear importance, her makeup dramatic, her waved and layered hair carefully lacquered into place. As the man approached her with a skip and a cry, the lady nodded imperiously, and was greeted, and she rose to receive her present and her bottle of wine. In that moment, Narita resolved to take for herself whatever it was this personage had for her to deserve such wonderful gifts, borne with such arrogance. Over the din of activity she caught the rise and fall of their voices, their *dah-lings* and their *mahals*, and to her longing ears, filled for the most part by the staccato vulgarity of street Tagalog, they sounded impossibly posh. Someone, somewhere in the vast room, was bellowing about a lost dummy. The televisions blared on. She stood there, unnoticed, exactly where the receptionist had bidden her, and after a while, the person for whom she had been told to wait arrived, an oily, impatient old man, his sports shirt faded, the stench of cigarette smoke attending his person. He sat her down at an empty desk and shoved a piece of paper at her.

"Edit this," he commanded.

Narita turned confused and outraged eyes up at him.

"I need some paper, sir," she stammered. "To write on."

"What kind of school did you go to? Didn't they teach you proofreaders' marks?"

"I'll rewrite the article on the back," she said. She rummaged uneasily in her shabby denim shoulder bag. She needed a pen, a good one.

"Here," the man said, drawing his own fountain pen from the collar of his shirt. "A tip, Miss Beautiful, from the news editor, yours truly. In this profession, you don't get anywhere by taking your bloody time."

She nodded, wondering how she was supposed to feel at the name he had called her. He didn't seem unkind, just old and overworked, his skin blackened as she imagined a fish might look strung up over smoking twigs for three days. Her fingers began to shake with anticipation at the thought of taking a test, under time pressure, a test that required no academic reading, no wretched theory, surely only a matter of putting in a comma here, a matching word there. She scanned the piece of typescript the news editor had handed her. It was an excruciating little piece about the darling buds of May, though the May they knew in Manila was a month of deluges and drought. Someone had headed it "Lifestyle/Sir Ivan Borja's Column for Sunday." She had never seen such awful English in her life. She scribbled and scribbled, lost in the effortless joy of asserting her knowledge. This was fun. She had never trained for anything like this. Her mind drifted to Antonia; it was like the stories they had written years and years ago, adopting the voice of some lovelorn small-town adolescent swain. She chuckled, the dull resentment lifting for the first time in months, and before she knew it the piece was done. She looked up gaily to find the news editor assessing her with his sharp, cynical old eyes, eyes that flickered rapidly over the piece she had rewritten.

"Bachelor's degree? Sweethaven U?" he queried.

She nodded. No use in telling him she was a dropout.

"A throwback you are, Miss Pastor. A throwback to the grand old days of letters."

As she shook his tobacco-stained hand, she could barely believe what was happening. She was hired. Her job was to correct the galley proofs that came fluttering, loose-edged, from the paste-up department, where the aging personnel eyed any computer with derision. In addition, she would be on call to rewrite the Lifestyle columns — but gently, lest she offend their authors. She would work from twelve to seven, six days a week, minimum wage, to start the following day — she need never see the inside of a classroom again. Her heart leapt. She was through with bed-spacing. She would get her own room in a boardinghouse. The humiliating monthly audits of her family were over. She glanced around, at the novel new Macs and their deferential handlers, and every cell in her body crackled with energy. She listened in a daze as the lonely old news editor with the mannered speech gleefully voiced his congratulations, and then issued her a series of half-joking warnings about the newspaper life. But she didn't understand. She was part of a word factory at long last, the culmination of her dreams, where academic degrees didn't matter, where the only things that counted were language and style and wit. She didn't care how many hours she worked without overtime pay, how many weekends she would have to give up from now on, how overstaffed the paper claimed to be, how little room for advancement there truly was. At that very moment she didn't care how they bled her. No matter how hard she labored, she was certain her passion for stories could never wane.

IN THE years that followed she fought the city, the traffic, the three-hour commutes, the men whose eyes consumed her body on the street, the paychecks that came late, the newspapers that closed and reopened at the end of every election. She had no notion of goals, of graduation, of commencement, no way of grading herself, no common standard against which her life could be measured. The vocabulary of achievement, which she'd grown up with, lapsed into irrelevance.

It was lonely. For the first time she did not have a younger, clingy person at her side, to yank along, to serve as sounding board for her thoughts. Her sister didn't need her. Antonia was independent now. She had taken on the burden of caring for Naia with a sigh of resignation, and this martyrdom was a precious victory in the war for Luth's grace.

Ten years. Ten years of struggling for her space; of rented beds, rooming houses, up-and-downs shared with grudging officemates, studio flats with the single window kept shuttered against the fumes and dust of the city. There was the apartment in Cubao, a few steps away from a major jeepney route, where water flowed from the taps for only a couple of hours each evening, after the landlord had tripped the booster pump, noisily sucking other households' water supplies through the surrounding network of pipes.

One year the pump drew nothing. In a bucket, she collected rain streaming down from the eaves, fishing out leaves and hunks of rotting iron with her hands. She bathed with Eskinol and a face towel, washing her hair with rainwater that she boiled in the bucket, using a plastic heating coil. A rash of pimples erupted over her arms and back. Fearing an uprising from his tenants, the landlord uncapped the rusted artesian well that stood in one corner of the property. She cooked, brushed her teeth, like the rest of her neighbors, with water that had come up through depths of rain-soaked clay. It was the color of diluted termite spray. The fact that it was contaminated — cracked sewer pipes and open-pit toilets leaking their effluents into the earth — did not hit home until the morning she awakened and found herself struggling for breath. A thick wad blocked the back of her throat. She hacked it loose and spat. It sprang to the floorboards and writhed, blindly — rubbery and dark pink, alive. She screamed, once in terror, then a second time, out of despair. But there was no one to hear. And so she sobbed, wanting to plunge a knife down her throat and scrape herself inside out. After a while she stopped crying and sat, knees drawn up beneath her chin, afraid even to breathe. There was no point in moving house; Manila pulsed, blind, around and in her.

Eight

THEY WERE killing time, Luth and Narita, over the remains of breakfast. The maid, Cecilia, puttered around the counter, washing plates, lighting a fire on the gas range to boil a pot of beans. Luth's mug of tea had grown cold. She had phoned in sick for the day.

In the master bedroom, her husband talked to himself. Disjointed sentences boomed out through the half-open door as he tapped delicately away at his computer. From time to time Daniel read, with great brio, a sample of his own wit. He was working on a book. For the past twenty-five years he had been engaged in some book project or another. The most recent Luth knew of was a history of Sweethaven University in which the contributions of his father and grandfather were prominently catalogued. Once, there had been a six-hundred-page novel about philosophy students during the martial law years. He had written three different endings, postmodern style. If he hadn't promised her its immediate success, respectability beyond the confines of the university, a spot on the bestseller list — but which list? And where? Who read books in this country? — she might have found room in her heart to be sorry for him. But he could never find a publisher. The ones he had approached, on his visits to Manila, praised his language but advised him to find a definitive conclusion to his characters' agony. "Bunkum," he said. After all those years spent in front of his wretched typewriter while she did his laundry and laboriously drew up the weekly budget and made sure his children were decent and clean — after all those years, he could not tell when enough was enough.

Sometimes he called her name out loud. He said, "Luth, Luzie, Leth, Lith," as though praising a goddess — a youthful goddess with a '60s beehive and a painted fan; a goddess he could keep in his shirt pocket and pat reassuringly from time to time. Her skin crawled with loathing; he had no awareness of what escaped his lips. He might as well have been a child crying out to its mother about some wonder wedged between the floorboards.

"Forty years I've known him, and all he ever speaks is nonsense," she murmured. When she glanced over at her daughter, she saw with surprise that Narita's face reflected the same raw disgust. She had never perceived her elder daughter as an ally. And then she grew sad — though the family had closed ranks, they remained divided along the old patterns of anger and blame: she, as distanced from her husband as possible; the children, in between.

From a practical perspective, his lectures were just that, nonsense. Educational philosophy, John Dewey, the morphology of the English language — she had heard enough over the years to deliver her own miniature lectures, so filled with high-sounding utterances that no one would discover for at least a minute that she hadn't the faintest idea what she was talking about. Did any of his students care? Did his colleagues?

I do not want a new car, she thought. I have no need for a stylish new house from the ground up, or a Pierre Cardin bag, or a shopping trip to Hong Kong. But it would be good to live with a little bit more dignity than we do today.

It would have been good, for a change, to drop the fortnightly ordeal of drawing up a budget from their meager paychecks, and splurge as the wife of a doctor might splurge. She had often wondered at their lives, those former pupils of hers, now doctors and lawyers and engineers, who turned up at the elementary school on Parents' Day — "Ma'am Pastor, you're still here!" — to point out their robust offspring from the tangle in the playground. Men and women who were confident, affluent, impeccable, in the way she had never been — while her husband was scruffy and apologetic, his eyebrows untrimmed, hairs straggling out of his ears.

She had stopped hoping for the big career move that would change all their lives. She had come to terms, at long last, with the fact that her husband's knowledge would never be marketable, that no university, in California or the American Corn Belt, would ever hire him, not even for a semester. His politics were all wrong, Antonia had pointed out once. He insisted on teaching Shakespeare, year upon year. He had never been a political detainee; never carried a gun in the hills; his entire career had been founded on Sweethaven's neutrality, which Luth took to mean its imperviousness to fashionable schools of thought, such as Marxism or national democracy or whatever it was the foreigners wanted. Instead, he had maintained his total commitment to English language and literature, which he doggedly taught in its purest possible form. She did not see anything wrong with that, but Antonia claimed this had been the death of his career.

Luth sipped the last of her coffee and looked with some trepidation at Narita. Antonia had behaved like a typical younger child: a strong sense of entitlement, confident enough to chirp bits of cutting wisdom at the dinner table, but sweet, sweet. Narita was different, Narita had great reserves of venom, steeped in the resentment of a lifetime. Luth scarcely dared admit it to herself, but she feared her elder daughter.

This morning would be even worse than yesterday, as Naia's door remained implacably shut. Narita had found it locked when she arrived from Manila yesterday afternoon, and throughout last night it had stayed barred, faint music seeping through the walls. At first it did not seem conceivable to Luth that several hours could go by without their seeing each other, without the girl emerging to greet her own mother as a simple expression of respect.

See, you big shot Manila career woman, now you reap the results of your neglect, she had crowed to herself, knowing she was being unfair. The night had worn on, and admitting defeat, Narita had finally gone to bed.

And earlier this morning — oh, the awful confrontation in the hall. Narita ambushing Luth as she stepped out of the bathroom.

"I've unpacked my bag. Here it is, mother."

It was one of those video DVD things, wrapped in a brown envelope; Luth drew it out — *Sweet Heaven* something or other — and recoiled immediately from the images on the cover.

"What is that thing doing in this house?"

"I want you to look at it."

She thrust the plastic case back at her daughter, her face averted. "I do not believe any of their lies. How many people have actually seen that thing? Rumors spread because people are evil; they will take hold of any means to bring a good, hardworking family down. That is not Naia in there. It's just someone who resembles her. People will say anything."

Narita looked stunned.

"Have you viewed it?" Luth challenged her.

Narita could not lie. "Only the beginning."

"There, you see!" Luth stormed. "What is your proof? So stop talking about it." She cocked her head in the direction of the kitchen, where Daniel was stringing a series of unrelated syllables to form one of his happy breakfast tunes. "And I wish *he* would bear that in mind and stop shooting his mouth off in front of his colleagues."

AND yet, here they were, mother and daughter, at the breakfast table, sitting companionably, each waiting for the other to speak. Now Daniel joined them, fresh, it seemed, from a literary victory at the keyboard, and smiling as if they were both strangers.

"Do we have anything to eat in this poor house?"

Luth's gut churned at this dramatic affectation.

"Only that chocolate thing your friends brought around," she snapped. "You know we have no money."

"Cecilia," he called grandly. "Bring in the cake."

The maid took three steps to the refrigerator, hauled out the confectioner's box, and placed it, still covered, on the table in front of them.

"Spoons," said Daniel, and added to Cecilia, his tone lowering intimately like a minister's, "Please take a slice. Take as much as you want." He took a teaspoon and a dish and began to cut Narita a piece, over her protests. For Luth, he proffered a black sopping chun topped with two candied cherries.

"Our hearts are with you in this your time of trial," Narita read out from the card.

Luth picked out a cherry, crushed it against the roof of her mouth. More, her salivating mouth ordered; her stomach rumbled audibly, and Daniel beamed, as though he had personally provided them with this bounty.

"These must be the hearts," Narita said, eating a cherry.

Yes, thought Luth, eight of them. Topping each slice. Delivered up in their bleeding glory. One from Emily, one from Rinky, a couple more from the boys, this hard little one from stuck-up Tabby, that awful middle girl of theirs. Three more from, oh, the Father, the Son, and the Holy Ghost; but we've scarfed them down already, we're such pigs.

"The Hollands must be trying to kill us," Narita said. "This has seven hundred calories to the slice."

"It's lethal only if you eat all of it," Daniel chuckled.

"I can't fight on those terms," Luth growled. "We can't afford a cake like this, and she knows that, and she rubs our face in it. I hate the way women fight."

Daniel kept his face to his plate. He cared a great deal for the Hollands. He and Rinky had much in common, he pondered, married to the same type of woman, though one might never have guessed this from looking at Emily, that sweet thing. Besides, Rinky had been his friend for more than half his life. Even when Rink began taking his religion a bit too seriously for comfort, breaking away from the Sweethaven church for a few years, their bond had remained firm. When Rink had left for the States on a generous two-year study grant, taking his wife and their three kids with him, he had felt no envy. As students, they had both sung in the Sweethaven men's glee club; he in graduate school, Rinky as a charming young college freshman. That choir was the closest he would ever get to a fraternity. They had reunion parties every few years, and on these occasions he and Rinky would call each other "brod," short for "brother." Unlike in regular fraternities, upperclassmen did not beat up neophytes over the course of a clandestine weekend. No, the initiation, conducted with utmost civility, lasted a lifetime — members fell away over the years, and the social ordeals, the hoops to be leapt through, extended to the wives.

In Luth's case, Daniel thought, church had been that hoop. She'd been raised a Catholic, and he had certainly never forced her to convert. He told himself she had been happy with her choice.

Luth, too, was thinking of religion, which was where her mind invariably swung, prompted by mention of the Hollands. When their marriage was new, she had embraced Daniel's faith, for it went with her status as the wife of a rising professor at the university. The church building had impressed her, emerging clean and white from the sheltering acacias. And such simplicity within, so few people, so unlike the Catholic church of her childhood, packed with peasants and the flagrantly devout. The latest of Sweethaven's American missionary families sat with their fascinating pale-haired offspring in the rows closest to the altar. They reminded her of the drawings in the Norman Rockwell book in the elementary school library, the lovely color plate book only teachers could take out. If she had known, in those early years, that the Americans would vanish one by one, child after child entering their teens and packed off to proper high schools in Virginia or Kentucky, the missionary couples themselves growing faded and arthritic and then flying home for good, if someone had told her that the church and the university that had sprung up about it would someday be replaced by the missionaries' ambitious Filipino pupils, who squabbled incessantly among themselves, she would not have wasted her time. She was sure of that. But deluded, she had followed her husband dutifully, like a carabao with a ring in its nose.

Eventually she had understood. Only a handful of Filipino families could play tennis with the Americans, and chat with them on the lawn after the service. In this preposterously small academic community, there was a hierarchy. There was an elite, just as in the dusty towns strung out on the highway that ringed the island, where all the top dogs could trace their ancestry to Spain. Sweethaven University was Donostia in miniature, though attending a separate church, observing slightly different customs, looking to a different country for inspiration.

Presbyterians had built Sweethaven shortly after the revolution against Spain. So Luth would proclaim to a fresh batch of pupils every year, though she had always known that, in actuality, Spain had never left. This was something she would never teach those wide-eyed, trusting little brats. Faithfully she read out from the textbooks — the Spaniards were overthrown in the revolution of 1898 and soon afterward the American administrators came, with democracy and education for all.

She had memorized the appropriate words. She had even read Daniel's manuscript, the history he had been laboring on for years.

But the dream of Spain — or rather, of mestizo life in the white mansions at the end of long driveways set into sugarcane fields — this was something no revolution could ever pry away. As her daughters had sought to be American, so Luth's mother had sought to be mestiza. Luth herself had been caught in the middle — that is to say, in the worst of both worlds. She could still recall the parties thrown in the gracious homes by the town plaza, sitting silently with her friends in the shadow of the bougainvillea so old they had sculpted themselves into trees, watching the long black cars drawing up by the grilled gates. At the time, she knew that a girl's worth in the classroom or at a party was determined by how much Spanish blood she could claim. She herself had none.

In the beginning, the city of Donostia had had nothing to boast of but the sugarcane fields hacked out of the strip of land between the chain of mountains and the long coast. Sweethaven changed all that — put the hot, dusty agricultural outpost on the map. The earliest Holland, from Ohio, had been a teacher here, and when his wife died childless, he had married a local girl. Daniel Pastor's grandfather had been among his first students, a distinction the Pastors could never forget.

When Luth had married Daniel, a man four years her junior, she knew she was entering Sweethaven's upper crust. Not a bad move, she had thought, for the daughter of a handsome, promising but very dead municipal judge and his struggling schoolteacher wife.

What she realized only later was that Daniel's grandfather had been a barefoot pupil when the school was but a collection of rude huts beside the sea. The disenfranchised must have been among the first to convert — those without land to their name, the lame and ugly, the bastards. They quickly became

Sweethaven's chosen, an inner circle of quiet, hardworking young men with an aptitude for the Americans' language and a talent for humility. Even now, she groused, three generations down the line, the Pastors still deferred to the Hollands — though, if you compared the two men, grant by grant, doctoral program by doctoral program, her husband had had the better education.

What was it, in fact, that I married? she thought, frowning. A British accent? But that had come later, after the years of scholarship. The friendly, energetic charm of the perpetual schoolboy? That, maybe. Her husband had kept his youthful looks, losing some hair, gaining little if any weight. Girls and boys both sent him meaningful letters at the end of each term. They claimed that he had changed their lives. Luth kept careful track of the missives from his graduate students that purred with cryptic sexuality; every few years she'd locate a note slipped casually where he presumed she would not look — beneath a sheet of anti-tussives atop a bureau, maybe, or between the pages of a Penguin classic. This she might jeeringly read out loud while he stammered his apologies: none of these courtships had ever amounted to anything, he swore, and the poor creatures had certainly not received any encouragement from him.

At mealtimes, jaws moving in a rhythm as easy as breathing, she watched him. He kept his head bowed as though in shame. He had been a handsome man; he had needs. For years he would reach for her one night a week. Had she less respect for her body, he might have gotten away with more.

His daughters, he could hardly touch. A few times a year he might kiss them — when they won ribbons at school or saw him off on a long trip — and they would stiffen and pull away. They sensed his pathetic need for contact, in the grasping fingers, the soft grunt of delight when he caught them. They struggled to distance themselves.

She hated it when he tried to caress her in front of them. She had never once seen her father kiss her mother. That man, he died of a heart attack the very year he was appointed a municipal trial court judge, leaving his wife not a legacy of ease and respect, but the task of fending for five school-age children. Luth had been in high school. She could remember staying up long before her siblings had gone to bed, helping to steam small parcels of sweetened rice to be peddled to her mother's colleagues. Mother and daughter had worked doggedly, in silent annoyance with one another. No words of love, no touching. Boyfriends led to early pregnancy. Even the shyest admirer was off-limits. No one ever kissed. Kissing was what the Technicolor *artistas* did, to the strains of orchestral music, in the single cinema in town — "lips-to-lips" it was called, with a fillip of discomfiture: it was a luxury, an affectation, a pleasure reserved for those whose foreign blood ran hot in their veins.

But she had enjoyed the warmth and smoothness of her little daughters. They were her reward, after those lonely years. She left wet lipstick stains on their foreheads and in their hair. Narita would struggle, embarrassed, out of her grip, echoing Luth as a girl — no time for extravagant hypocrisy. Antonia had been different — sweet, pliant, surrendering herself to Luth's embrace, rubbing her nose into the cool plumpness of her mother's arm. Luth knew that from the very start she favored the younger one, the pale, sensitive one who seemed to need so much more care. Early on, she had quietly admitted the truth to herself, and justified it — Narita had simply been too difficult. She had not been a pretty child. Her hair was too wild, her skin too dark. Her scent, a deep and oily musk, had always discomfited Luth, collecting in her palms and the folds of her clothes, hinting at a certain carnal precocity. Narita had bullied her sister mercilessly, to compensate, and Antonia had fought back with appalling violence. Still, there was a space in her younger daughter's soul where Luth could never go. Narita's power over Antonia saddened her.

If she had any regrets, it was that she'd given them too much freedom. Her work as a teacher went beyond the 5:00 p.m. dismissal bell, and there were the chores and the marketing besides, which she had sought to spare the girls. In the evenings, Dan would insist on a movie, something easy and stirring like *Cleopatra Jones* or *Walking Tall*, and they would bring the children to one of Donostia's movie theaters — there were five or six when the girls were small. The children were admitted without fuss, to *Shaft* and Disney alike. In the darkness that smelled of old steamer trunk and bedbug-ridden mattresses, Antonia would nod off uncomprehending in her lap, while Narita sat unblinking through lynchings and car chases, Luth too exhausted to care. Dan always wanted to make a little love afterward, his imagination fired by what they had seen.

In the days that followed each film, the girls dealt with the mysteries they had witnessed in whatever way they could. "Let's discuss!" Narita would start, and they would choose a bedroom and lock themselves in. It seemed harmless enough at the beginning. It was that period in her life when no maid could please her, and it was a relief to note her daughters babysitting each other while she ran the house. Simply inseparable, those two. From early childhood to adolescence, thick as thieves, giggling, shrieking, playing their father's records on an old turntable, poring over movie star magazines, emerging hours later flushed with delight, exchanging glances at the dinner table. She knew they had created a world somehow, in which a go-go dancer from one movie might start a new life with a bionic athlete from another, but when she begged admission, mentioned a name, pretended to be in on the game, they clammed up and stared. Parodied her words. Made her look like a fool.

When they were about ten and eight, they started speaking in American accents. Was it a favorite teacher, a *balikbayan* classmate, their wholehearted immersion in rented Betamax movies? Luth never figured it out.

Suspicious, left out, she raided their rooms every few days, searching Narita's in particular — under her sour pillow, the places between bed and the wall. She dredged up stained Harold Robbins paperbacks borrowed from God knows where, and once, when the girl was in high school, a whole copy of *Penthouse*.

"Do you think boys will respect you, reading this trash?"

Silence. Those flinty eyes, those flaring granite nostrils, nostrils that she recognized to be a smaller, more delicate version of her father's and brothers' and her own.

Once she found a fragment of a comic strip, in ballpoint, on the remaining pages of an old school notebook. She recognized the confident strokes to be Narita's, but felt no pride in the almost-proportional human figures, only a bitter dread that she was drawing like a boy, about war, and men in webbed helmets toting ArmaLites. The snippets of story she discovered a few pages farther on plagued her even more, because Narita did not write poems for peace, as she supposed a fourteen-year-old in the honors section of her class ought to write, but tough, manly passages about recon patrols and grenades lobbed into machine-gun nests. Was this the fundamental flaw in her daughter, then? Was Luth unknowingly raising a tomboy, a war freak, a (God forbid) lesbian?

"You are living in a fantasy!"

Narita had neglected her Social Studies exam and spent three hours with her sister, plotting adventures for some person called Sergeant Rock.

Silence. An exchange of amused glances, one girl slouching toward the kitchen, the other contemptuously flipping open a Tagalog textbook.

Barely breathing, ear pressed to the wall, she followed the crests and troughs of their laughter. It alarmed her that they could speak so casually of men, for it was certainly men they were discussing, judging by the names.

"I get to molest Gunner. You can have Captain Turner," Antonia said.

"We tie them up by the north gate, and see to a small matter of discipline — "

"And then we switch."

As lightly as that, as though speaking of puppies. They discussed men, in fact, with the same sense of entitlement that men could speak of loose girls. Their precocity infuriated her. Who were their friends? Who else from Sweethaven knew what violent, perverse nonsense filled their minds?

Nine

THE LAWYER Joel was not what might be called old money, though he bore an esteemed family name. He wasn't from the branch of the Fortuns that had sent upstanding men to the National Assembly or to the cabinets of presidents past. In Donostia, there were Fortuns *kawayan* and *cemento* — Fortuns of bamboo and Fortuns of cement. The cement Fortuns had built the mansions by the waterfront promenade that had been downgraded to restaurants and bars. Most of the *cementos* had kept their money but now resided in the gated communities of Manila. The bamboo Fortuns were sons off the left testicle, born in thatch-roof huts, scattered here and there. But Joel had gone to the best law school in Manila, on a scholarship financed by a local politician. He had acquitted himself well enough at the bar examinations and found work as a legal researcher at a decent-size law firm in Makati. The pay had compensated for the monotony. There had been a woman, sleek and well-bred, whom he had endeavored in vain to satisfy; they had lived at an enviable address; he had driven a late-model car. He himself wondered why he had chosen to come back and slum it at city hall, for no matter what honors he brought home, people would always mention his origins when his back was turned.

He had been conscious for days of being watched. The stalker was a gallant cavalier, a young man in sunglasses atop a dirt-track motorcycle, in jeans and a muscle T-shirt. Sometimes the T-shirt was white; sometimes it was black. The sunglasses never left the face.

He couldn't remember when he had seen the stalker first. Donostia was rife with mounted Don Juans, all younger than he — he felt ancient, and could not be bothered to tell them apart.

The stalker hung around in the rearview mirror of his jeep. At night he was a yellow headlight that time and again came blindingly close, then receded, peeling away at an intersection or disappearing behind a procession of tricycle taxis.

A few days into this surveillance, Joel came home, to a bungalow so new that parts of it still smelled of fresh cement, and, trembling, turned on all the lights, tested the doors to see if anyone lurked behind them, stomped over to his bedroom. From the bottom of the wardrobe, beneath an unused pair of Florsheim shoes, he drew out the felt-lined case that contained his father's gun. For a long time he crouched there, staring at the gleaming metal and the row of cartridges — not touching them, only looking. How the hell was he supposed to defend himself with it? He had never carried a gun. He put the weapon back, where it had lain all these months since his return.

He occupied an air-conditioned office at City Hall now, with mock-velvet drapes and a mahogany desk as large as an altar. There he had constant company. The notary publics and secretaries, a whole pool of them, were in the habit of dropping by to chat, seeking his exalted opinions. He was so new, not more than three months in office. Refined to their eyes, Manila-soft yet worldly wise. It did not seem possible he could screw up. The clerks served him coffee and confections of sticky rice.

He had built a home in one of the newer subdivisions, formerly a farm and just a fifteen-minute drive to his office: he had intended it for retirement, but removed as he was from the life he had built in the capital, it would have to do. He made it a point to drive the jeep that had once been his father's, to maintain a low profile and remind himself of where he had come from. He felt completely alone, going through the silent house, turning off the lights, ruing the absence of a wife and children — loved ones to call the authorities in case of his disappearance. There was only a senile dog, and a houseboy. His fingers stole over to the mobile phone in his pocket. This, he thought, was the one true means of civil defense. In the event of his murder, yeah, sure, he would notify the authorities himself.

On Friday, two days after the mayor's investigators had met at the police station, he took the jeep to the outskirts of town, to a neighborhood where the houses were of bamboo and wood and held off the ground by stilts. Swarthy pigs rooted happily in the shadows underneath them. Where the path broadened out to become a tiny square, stood a pump marking an artesian well, and he slowed his step, negotiating earth slippery with laundry detergent. In his wake, he collected children — two, three, four; tattered, underpantsless — who neither spoke nor smiled. Once, twice, he stopped to ask directions — "Do you know a couple called Bulauan? Gemma and Tristan? Which one is their home?"

At last he found himself before a little bungalow, its walls of raw hollow block, its door decorated by a crucifix woven from a palm frond. It was not the kind of place he would associate with a young woman with bottle-blond hair. The door did not open no matter how loud and long he called "*Maayo*," politely offering his well-wishes to those who dwelt within.

The wooden jalousies were shut firmly against probing eyes, but from inside the house a radio played, on and on.

"Gemma?" Joel called, and hammered on the door.

"Oh, they're home," a neighbor said from behind him. "Try a little louder."

Joel did. The jalousies next to the door opened an inch or so. He saw a pair of eyes — irises fierce and black, the whites bloodshot.

A man's voice told him his wife was out.

Joel persisted, fighting to control his anger. Gemma had sent him a string of text messages. She had said he would find her at this house. She would not be out; she had no money, no means of getting anywhere. Her husband had burned her clothes.

The woman spoke then. She was all right, she called softly to Joel through the wood. She sounded as though she was just inside the door, pressed to its very surface.

"This is a matter between man and wife," her husband snarled. "I have friends. With the police. The military. Now leave."

Joel had no choice but to obey, stomping angrily past the knot of men and women who had gathered behind him. Blind, abstracted, he crossed the road and sat for a span of time in his jeep, starting the motor only when he realized that the neighbors and the urchins with the naked buttocks had made their way over the rutted path and were now within touching distance of the jeep. Behind him, another engine spurted to life. The stalker had been waiting, parked beyond the overhang of a *sari-sari* store. The motorcycle winged past his vehicle, the rider casting him a long, meaningful glance. Bastard, Joel thought, and gave chase.

They left the city limits and sped up as they gained the national road, setting a course, it seemed, for Usurbil, the next town. The landscape consisted of coconut palms on their left, sugarcane and mountains on their right. From time to time, between the loose palisade of trunks, he caught glimpses of water — not the blazing summer sea but something sullen and gray that heaved seaweed and rotting timber upon the volcanic black sand.

The motorcycle took one of the unpaved roads that meandered past nipa groves and huts and half-naked children until it terminated in a public beach. Joel's wheels hit sand. The bike was nowhere to be seen. His heart racing, he parked the jeep where the ground was firmer, bought himself a San Miguel at a nipa-roof refreshment stand, and settled down on a bamboo bench to wait.

A pair of Nike sneakers appeared in the black sand before his own. A new odor overrode that of rot and wet bamboo — a blend of cigarettes and menthol candy, of sweat and designer cologne.

"Winston Lights, two," the newcomer said. Accepting a few coins, the old woman minding the store handed over a couple of cigarettes from one of the open packs on the counter.

The stalker chose the bench opposite Joel. He took off his sunglasses.

"JP Torres," Joel said in realization.

"Uncle," the stalker said. "You've got to help me."

"I THOUGHT you'd forgotten," the stalker went on. "I am Juan Pablo, the son of Pedro and Auring. We have the white house by the plaza in Monroy. *Tito*, all this time you acted as if you didn't recognize me."

But he hadn't, Joel thought. He honestly hadn't. There'd been something familiar about the face in his rearview, but time had erased that face from his memories — this boy whom he'd seen only at Christmases and fiestas some twenty years before. Joel could remember a fetching youngster whose Spanish blood emerged in the curly hair and huge, long-lashed eyes, eyes that bore a false melancholy. Youngest child of a faded mestiza, following four disappointing girls. At age seven, he'd been lighting cigarettes for his older cousins; at age eight his father had put him behind the handlebars of a motorcycle and given him his first exhilarating lesson.

"You changed. I knew you by your nickname. Pabling."

That name had been bestowed by the boy's own father. In Donostia slang, it meant "Playboy." Pabling. JP. Two images — the wispy little boy sucking eagerly on a cigarette until the tip flared to life; the motorcycle rider, superlatively cool. Two images, irreconcilable.

"That was long ago."

"What do you want?"

"Tito Joel, I know you are a good man. You've been driving around town for more than a week, talking to people. You even interrogated that crazy woman down at the station, with all the police watching, so I heard."

"Say what you mean," said Joel.

"Tito, you are diligence itself. Yet you haven't come after me. You have asked no questions. Why?"

Joel felt fear in his bowels.

"I've been biding my time. That is all," he said, knowing how weak his excuse sounded. "Sure, they pointed to you — Diana Rosales, and that poor Bulauan creature back there. But there is nothing in the final video that identifies you. You know that. We can't see your face. There are no scars, no tattoos on your skin."

But JP was not listening, or did not believe him. "I know I can count on you," he repeated. "Because you're giving me a chance. You know we are family."

"What do you want?" Joel said.

The young man reached into a pocket of his jeans and pulled out a mobile phone.

"Here," he said. "I have been getting these. Three just last night."

Gingerly, Joel took the phone, avoiding contact with JP's fingers. He squinted at the screen: *Tang na mo hayop ka we just warn 4 u b redy ur life only cost 5thou*

There were more messages, in a similar vein: threats on JP's life tapped out in the same patois. There was no point in tracking them. They would have been sent from an anonymous prepaid number. He handed the phone back.

"It's the families of those girls," said JP. "You know what kind of people they are. They're brutes. They're peasants. They live by the machete. You are powerful, Tito, you are even closer to the mayor than my father could ever be."

No, thought Joel, he could not escape the curse of family after all, not in Donostia or its satellite sugarcane towns. How could he respond, except to order another drink and contemplate the smooth sun-browned face, the soft moustache, the wince and frown as the boy drew on his cigarette? Fine hair covered the lean arms. Every move was self-conscious, theatrical; JP was the hero in his private Western.

"You brought this on yourself," said Joel. "What do you want, police protection?"

JP gave no sign that he had heard. He sat there, a corner of his mouth deepening, head bobbing as though in time to some private rock anthem. Then he said, "Tito, how are your hectares in Usurbil? Have you kept the bank away this year?"

A reference to a debt of gratitude Joel's insolvent father had owed the Torreses. He'd known it would come up soon enough: emotional blackmail. He knew Pabling's family and their heirs would continue to collect on that debt well into the next fifty years.

Joel was on the defensive — from now on his moves would consist of parrying and giving ground. *My father is dead. Leave him out of it*, he could have said, but JP would not have understood. How could you reason with such a deeply ingrained sense of entitlement? JP would have chuckled softly in his face. In the middle of his third bottle of beer, he could no longer stand the young man's crafty appraisal, or the soft stream of flattery from the nicotine-stained lips. *My Tito is a lawyer now, with a degree from the best school in the country. My Tito Joel knows how to get his sad cousin out of this mess.* He paid the storekeeper and walked away before the startled old woman could hand him back the change. It was not a tip and not a bribe, simply an offering, so that in future, should she remember this meeting upon the bamboo benches of her stand, and recognize one man as the lawyer from the mayor's office and the other as the amateur pornographer, she might be discreet.

He strode to the water's edge, knowing that JP would follow.

"I cannot save you," he said.

"You need me," the younger man said. "You know you can't arrest me. Our mayor would sooner die than have his favorite nephew thrown into jail." He snickered to show he had made a joke. "But you have to come up with something soon. You know the Bisaya mind. People will think you've been taking bribes. And you'll start getting messages like these."

He tapped the phone in his pocket.

"Are you finished?" said Joel.

"I wasn't working alone," JP grinned. "You think me, a poor unemployed farmer's son, would have come up with enough money to print all those DVDs? The family name is really all a Fortun has."

You son of a bitch, Joel thought.

JP regarded him with a sly look. "Who handles all the business in this world? Not the *Kachilas*. Not anymore."

"You tell me."

"The Chinese," JP said with a measure of triumph.

Joel's heart sank. He thought of the economic power that rivaled that of the mestizo planters. The Chinese community, businessmen all, in their high-walled homes, their warehouses and granaries protected by four stories' worth of masonry.

"Supposing I tell you about an old friend. Harrison Co. A friend ever since I got kicked out of Immaculate Conception and they put me in Sacred Heart. Harrison, who manages an Internet shop for his mother."

Joel knew the Cos, all right. The family owned a huge appliance shop in Santo Domingo.

"Harrison has proven to be no friend in time of need," JP said. "I run to him, and he closes the doors of their house in my face."

The tide was going out, Joel noted bitterly, and exposing a depressing surface of muck that seemed to stretch all the way to the next island.

"How about it, Tito? We give these Chinese a taste of the law. They think they can run Donostia from their dingy little hardware stores in the market."

"Enough!" he said.

"I can help you," the young man pressed. "I'll bring you to the house that we rigged up."

Joel sighed. As though this had been the sign he'd been waiting for, JP laughed softly and put his sunglasses back on.

"Why are you doing this?" Joel said.

The young man faced him with a wide and meaningless grin. "My conscience, Uncle. I can't sleep at night. I want to do the right thing."

Ten

"LUTH," DANIEL said. "Dear, are you all right?"

Luth found herself at the dining table, the television on, ignored, at her back, the breeze from the electric fan giving her a measure of relief each time it swung in her direction. Dinner was on the stove, she could smell it, and Cecilia was laying the table. It seemed only an eyeblink since she and Narita had sat here over their late-morning coffee. Where had the day gone?

"Luth, isn't it time we talked?" Daniel said in his gentle minister's voice.

Her eyes focused on him with difficulty.

"I have a plan," he said. "I will go and speak with Emily. She is our friend, no matter what you say. I will persuade her, Luth, to readmit Naia, perhaps even allow her to graduate from high school this year. The poor child has finished all her final exams. She has a term paper just waiting for the teacher to accept it. Emily will listen to me, Luth. She isn't the type to end a girl's future just like that, with one stroke of the pen; she is a caring, wise person at heart — "

When she heard the word *caring*, Luth snapped. "Go away!" she screamed. "Get out of my sight. I don't care, I don't care what you do, you fool. You betrayed us, you brought that wretched family back into our lives!"

Daniel started. What was that look in his eyes, was it rage, was it hatred to match hers? Then he turned away, muttering, "All right, I'll leave, woman, and you'll be sorry."

LUTH SNATCHED a tumbler from the tabletop and hurled it at him. It was a tall plastic Coca-Cola giveaway, the one he liked to have his *kalamansi* juice served in, and it bounced lightly and uselessly off his back. Cecilia froze in the act of laying spoons, not daring to pick up the tumbler as it clattered about the floor. Luth began to cry. One moment she was standing there, in stark and righteous anger, and the next moment she was slumped in a chair, her mouth making loose vowel sounds. She cried alone, abandoned by her husband and the maid, avoided by the granddaughter she had raised. She rose on creaking knees and made her way to the refrigerator. The last three slices of cake sat on a plate, waiting, daring her. Her cholesterol count had shot up in recent years; her doctor had warned her about diabetes. But in that moment, all her resources focused themselves on drawing out the plate, easing a fork out of the dish rack, cutting herself a dark, rich gob. The tears rolled through the corners of her mouth and mixed with the chocolate.

Someone was standing in front of her, a narrow form dressed in black, despite the summer heat. It was Narita, chic and strange in her pixie haircut. Narita leaned over, tried to take Luth's hands. "No, no, no," she said, shoving her daughter away. The plate of cake clattered to the floor. Narita stooped and began to gather up the pieces. If only she had been this good as a child, Luth thought bitterly.

"Tell me," Narita said.

Luth tried to say no, but the single syllable emerged distorted from her mouth.

Narita, on her knees, fixed her with a gaze that was stark and practical and entirely devoid of judgment. "Tell me," she said again.

WHEN she thought back, trying to discern the beginning of their troubles, Luth's mind inevitably stopped at that lunch with the Hollands in August, though she supposed the disease had begun, festering unrealized beneath the surface of their lives, long before that day. For weeks Daniel had been restless, temperamental, coming home long after dinnertime on Mondays and Thursdays, the days he met his graduate classes. It had grown increasingly difficult to get him to do things around the house. His behavior was erratic: the piles of term papers remained unsorted, but the car gleamed, washed and waxed. Luth ought to have suspected *something* — he'd taken to a very youthful tobacco-and-vanilla-blend aftershave — but a certain melancholia had gripped her, consumed as she was with worry for Antonia, who complained in bitter e-mail bursts about her adoptive country and the language lessons she had been pressed to take. Naia, too, had been difficult as of late. Bristly, secretive, flaring up violently at her grandfather. "Stupid old fart!" she would scream. Luth once heard him shout back, "I can disinherit you!" recalling the caustic words he had flung at Antonia and Narita when they were girls.

It was Daniel who had sprung the lunch invitation on her. She had not had anything to do with the Hollands for ages, and her first thought had been to turn it down. Rinky and Emily had had three whole decades to make her honest acquaintance — what had taken so long? The only thing her husband would say was that it would be an introduction to family counseling, which they and their granddaughter were in need of. "What counseling?" she had demanded. It sounded suspiciously religious. She had known Daniel long enough to discern an agenda of some sort. What it was, she could not be certain this time. But he had persisted, and exhausted at the prospect of another argument, she had said yes.

The Hollands occupied one of the two-story wooden homes on the Sweethaven campus, homes originally built for the American missionaries. Rinky had inherited the right to that house from his father, who had inherited it from his; thus, the grandson of that first Holland enjoyed the rootedness of a plantation heir, treading the floors and staircases of his childhood, parking his Toyota over flagstones where he had once hidden baseball cards and a secret agent diary.

The house was patterned after the homes the Spanish lords had built in the nineteenth century. Guests were entertained on the second floor, where the family slept and where all the official business of the household took place; the ground floor, a dank space where once carriages had been kept, was where the servants slept, where the household laundry was dealt with, where the cars and bicycles were sheltered for the night. As Luth ascended the polished outdoor staircase, Daniel ahead of her and Naia in tow, she could not suppress a traitorous feeling of delight. She had not been invited to eat at the Hollands' in years, and had always come with a group of Sweethaven colleagues, for some fellowship gathering or other. She was prepared to note down every detail of the experience, from Emily's choice of curtains to the varnished conch shells that sat at every second riser, all the way to the top of the stairs. Wasn't this practice vulgar? It had been a fad on campus in the 1970s — the native look, it had been called.

And at the top of the stairs, in a porch completely screened against the infernal insects, the welcoming committee waited, husband and wife, falling over each other to greet the guests, one picking up as soon as the other had spoken, to stave off the long, awful silences between Daniel and Luth. "Oh, it is *so* good to see the two of you together. Luth, you never come to our parties!" "Isn't she slim?" "Slimmer!" "And this must be Naia." "Oh, this is Naia? What a big girl you are now, Naia." "Naia, speak up, don't be scared of me; today I'm not the principal, I'm only Ms. Emily." "Haha, she's shy."

"Shy" was what strangers concluded when they met the child for the first time. She had small, precise features, and at that stage in her life she rarely smiled.

"How old are you now, Naia? You've certainly grown into a beautiful young lady!"

"She's fifteen."

"Fifteen? How interesting. You are in the same year level as our youngest, Brent."

In a dull voice, the girl spoke at last, "I've seen him around."

"You've seen him around," Rinky says, taking over. "Hahah, yes, your son certainly gets around, doesn't he, Emily?"

Laughter, Daniel joining in, Luth managing a smile.

Naia was unmoved. In manner, she was what unimaginative people called demure. She looked from one adult to the other, and they sparkled and twitched in their attempts to impress her.

A door opened, and a teenage boy emerged. This was Brent, thought Luth. She had a hard time remembering their names — the girl was Tammy or Tabby, the middle child Noah or Adam. The boy stood there, his face blank and his spine very straight, like a cadet on the parade ground. Something flickered in Naia's eyes. She raised her head and, rather expectantly, wet her lips. The boy came toward them and, without warning, took Daniel's hand and raised the back of it to his forehead in the traditional way of greeting one's elders.

"Brent," said Rinky, furious at the gesture.

The boy's face broke into a beautiful smile. In an instant, all was forgiven. "Good to see you, Uncle Dan." Smoothly, he took the hand Daniel held out and clasped it in a firm and sincere handshake. He greeted Luth the same way. He did not touch Naia, but nodded to her — "Hi."

"Where's your brother?"

"Downstairs, in the bathroom. Tammy-Shalom's in the kitchen. Shall I get her?"

As the boy strode off, Rinky said, "I apologize for that. He's going through a phase."

"He was just trying to be funny," Daniel said.

"He thinks all native practices exist to be mocked."

"Youth is a time to make mistakes," Daniel persevered. Rinky smiled. The two men shared a moment of conviviality, united by cliché.

"Naia, what's the matter?" whispered Luth. "Do you need to urinate? Do your shoes pinch?"

The girl shook her head. Her gaze was fixed stolidly on a potted plant.

"Well, now *here* they are!" exclaimed Daniel. "What did you do, Rink, to deserve such children?"

"I don't know, I guess I was just lucky."

In the pleasant living room with its potted ferns and book-lined walls, they stood awkwardly, speaking around Luth in an easy, perfect English that belied the tropical landscape beyond the picture window, their teeth bared in smiles. Four adults and four young people: "children," as the campus kids were referred to in Sweethaven, a fiction that tactfully ignored puberty, bad skin, and the first inklings of real-world failure. The Holland three were undeniably handsome, thought Luth grudgingly. Though Tammy-Shalom was suffering the consequences of an American college diet, and Adam was chubby from Jollibee fries, no one could fault their white complexions and the sharp angle of their little noses, and even though their eyes were identically small and almond-shaped, this enhanced, rather than detracted from, their Eurasian appeal. Brent was a scrawny, dark thing, but there was potential in his face as well: the lines of his nose were clean, and his skin was shining and flawless.

"How are you finding Wesleyan, Tammy? You like the winters? When do you return?"

"Oh, don't get my daughter started, Dannie, you'll regret it."

Laughter, Daniel turning to her brother: "What about you, Adam? How do you find Manila?"

Rinky's smile wavered. "Manila is an acquired taste."

"It sucks, to be honest," the young man said.

Luth frowned, unseen, at the unfamiliar expression.

"You're only saying that because you flunked out of the world's easiest course," said Brent.

There was a painful silence. Luth cast a glance at the elder Holland son. He stood awkwardly, hands jammed into the pockets of his khakis, one sneaker-clad foot stabbing at the polished wooden floor. His jaw was hard with rage. He was in his early twenties, old enough to marry, actually, and instead here he was, obliged to suffer his parents' rituals for as long as he lived in their home. She thought him quite capable of breaking his brother's neck.

Emily stepped in: "Well, that's all over now. Adam's a businessman."

"I have an editing service with an Internet shop," the young man mumbled. "I help the communications students with their theses. Visuals. Graphics."

Brent rolled his eyes.

"Wonderful!" cried Daniel. "You will be the next Silicon Valley millionaire."

An intriguing aroma wafted out from the kitchen.

"Shall we sit down to lunch? We must not disappoint Sebia. Her pot roast will get cold."

"Pot roast?"

"Oh yes, no adobo in this house, at least not today. Today is special. I hope pot roast isn't too heavy for you, Dannie, Luth."

"No, no, it's perfect."

"It's a hot day, after all. We thought there might be some rain, a bit of a breeze this morning …"

"No problem."

"We can send Adam downstairs for the portable air-conditioner. I'm afraid it's a bit low-tech. Runs on ice cubes."

"This electric fan is excellent."

"Dannie, would you like to be over there? Luth, you sit here. Tammy-Shalom and I like to stay as close to the kitchen as possible. Naia, sweet, you sit on my right. I want to get to know you. Perfect. Sebia? Let me help you, Sebia. There, everybody, doesn't that smell wonderful?"

"Oh my."

"Tammy-Shalom has made us her signature salad, with real lettuce, and those are pieces of feta cheese — have you tasted feta before, Naia? — and these are mashed potatoes, and some buttered vegetables, and cucumbers, and try some of these cheese fingers."

It was one of those excruciating meals where Luth had to constantly figure out when to use her knife. Why couldn't these people eat with spoon and fork like everyone else? She switched utensils from hand to hand, lost a forkful of peas. The simple act of eating, of taking her cue from one or other of the Holland children, involved all her concentration. The voices of Tammy and Emily surrounded her like gentle sparkling rain. Rinky and Daniel could barely get a word in. They complained out loud in a manner so smooth Luth knew they were joking, and as soon as coffee was served, rose bearing their cups and entered Rinky's office. The two boys excused themselves and disappeared. Luth nudged Tammy, whispered, and was pointed to the guest bathroom, which turned out to be done up in ruffles and potpourri. One could tell a lot about a family by their bathrooms, she thought. Her face in the molded-frame mirror looked startled and gray. She was in a charade, she fretted, borne along by the glib voices about her, the only one — with the possible exception of Naia's — with no concept of the objective.

When she returned to the table, determined to tell Daniel she was ready to go home, she discovered it completely cleared of dishes, of food, of people.

"Tita Luth," Tammy said, appearing at once at her side. "Let me show you my Grand Tour album."

She had a child's voice that belied her age and her education and her size, and a manner Luth thought of as pert — attributes that had probably driven more than a handful of young men crazy.

"Where's Naia?" Luth demanded, refusing to be charmed.

"Oh, somewhere in the house. With my mom, I expect."

"She's supposed to take her throat medicine now."

"We went to Europe last spring on a school trip. Go on, Tita Luth, you can turn the pages, I used superglue on the leaves and twine and stuff, and the glitter won't come off of the page, I guarantee. Isn't that cute? I'm teaching myself layout. This is Sammy, Sammy Park, he's my best buddy, and you can't really see it in this picture, but this is us at the *Mannekin Pis*. Do you know what that is? Oh, okay, no problem, I don't blame you. Yep, Tita Luth, that really is a bag, it's this Louis Vuitton thingie just sitting in the middle of the sidewalk, like five stories high — but you're jumping; you've skipped the red boudoir ..."

And this was Tammy, thought Luth, Tammy-Shalom — this chubby girl in her mid-twenties with skin bleached pale as a radish and hair cropped and dyed a color that she insisted was auburn — laughing, chatting, distracting Luth from the business that was taking place in unknown corners of the house. This was Tammy in the Thalys, which was apparently a high-speed train between Paris and somewhere; these were Tammy and Sammy and a geranium and a houseboat; this was Tammy channeling Anne Frank. And over in the extreme left margin of the picture was the cute Frenchie who served Tammy at the Relay in Charles de Gaulle ...

But what was "channeling?" What was "Relay?" Luth had no idea, but was mesmerized by the laughing eyes, the tinkle of the practiced American accent. Minutes dragged by, and gradually she realized that she was listening to another sound: the rise and fall of a male voice beneath the girl's monologue, coming from the direction of Rinky Holland's office. Tammy, too, seemed to be listening, making a deliberate effort to ignore the voice as it broke into harsh and stretching sobs.

"Enough, hold on, enough," Luth ventured, and as the rhythm of the young woman's words intensified, she roared, "Will you *stop*?"

Tammy slammed the scrapbook shut. Her face was tight and dismayed.

"I am not interested in your Europe," said Luth. "I don't care."

In the sudden silence, the man sobbed on. It was none other than her husband.

Luth fumbled, misplaced her English, dropped a clutch of photographs. She stared at the girl, and Tammy stared helplessly back.

Other than the incredible sounds Daniel was making, there was nothing to be heard. It was as though everyone else in the house were eavesdropping on them, with baited breath.

"Where's Naia?" Luth demanded, gaining her feet with an effort. She looked around with fear at the closed doors that led off the living room. The certainty began to build that the child was in trouble; no, worse than that. Making trouble. Getting herself into a fix. Life was moving too fast for Luth to control: one night the previous week, Naia had come home late, long after she and Daniel had eaten their dinner and the six o'clock news had segued into the nightly *telenovella*. Luth had watched in astonishment as the girl banged through the front door and headed straight for the bathroom, and in those first moments it did not occur to her to ask why she was empty-handed, where her bag and books were. And where was her blouse? As Naia emerged furtively from the bathroom, Luth saw that her singlet was damp and streaked with dust. Her skirt was crumpled and wet as well, as though she had rinsed something out and put it in her pocket. As the girl brushed past, Luth caught the smell of sweat and dust, and mud somewhere on her person, as though she had been running in the *cogon*, but there were no cuts on her skin, or grass seed on her clothes.

"I got into a fight," Naia had mumbled, and shut the door to her room. Luth's suspicions grew until she felt her head was going to blow, but just as she was priming herself to storm Naia's bedroom, the girl's voice, weak and sad, called from within, and she found her granddaughter curled up on the bed, her cheeks flushed from a forty-degree fever.

"What fight? Where?" Luth demanded. This was exactly what she'd been dreading. The girl had collided head-on with jealousy, violent and female, the wages of being a majorette.

In the yellow light of the bedside lamp, she fancied she saw a red mark on the girl's cheek. Naia shivered and burrowed into the quilted spread, resisting Luth's efforts to pull down the covers and investigate.

"I'm so cold," she whispered. She had taken a shower; her hair was wet. She had neglected to comb it out. Luth made scolding, clucking noises as she smoothed out the tangles. Where was Daniel? In his office, wasting his time on the Internet, no doubt. Never there when you needed him. He ought to have been here by her side, taking down the facts, so he could draft the necessary long and angry letter of complaint to the girl's teachers. This had been their standard means of dealing with trouble, when Narita and Antonia were in school.

Now Luth stood and stared into the face of Tammy-Shalom, this carrot-haired creature who had surely been planted in the living room to distract her, forestall the possibility of Naia's rescue.

What had her granddaughter said, that night last week, when annoyance was the only emotion Luth had allowed herself and she had demanded to know whom the fight had been with.

Naia's lips had been bitten, swollen, her voice a husk. "The girls," Luth had caught, and then "held me down."

And then, a few unintelligible syllables later, what sounded like "demons."

SUDDENLY Emily was back in the room, face white and eyes sparkling with what looked like triumph.

"Mom," Tammy said, a plea for help.

"Go now, dear," said Emily. "Go sit with Naia."

Tammy rose and, her eyes worriedly on Luth, left them. Emily took Luth's hand. When she spoke, her voice was professionally calm, and her words were about Daniel.

"Your family is in crisis, my dear," she said. "Dannie was in to see my husband the other day. They talked for hours. Rinky wouldn't tell me why at first. But I managed to get the story out of him."

Luth fixed Emily in her stare, the glare that had brought fear into the hearts of a generation of fourth-graders. Luth tried to tell Emily this was none of her business, but her tongue would not obey her. The other woman was simply too beautiful, too perfect, with her large and solicitous eyes and that air of utter confidence in her superiority.

"Luth, Dannie has sinned. He took the love of a young student and used it to satisfy his basest desires."

Now that it was laid out so bare — the reason for her husband's short temper, his sudden enthusiasm for grooming, his unaccountable moments of good humor — Luth felt hollow, emptied out. She snatched her hand from Emily's and averted her face.

"You're silent," Emily went on. "It's as if you already suspected."

Luth felt it safe to nod.

"But he's sorry, very sorry. He has accepted that he sinned. At least we can be thankful for that. The important first step."

What? she thought. What was Emily talking about? Once, when Luth was young, a woman had put two bullet holes through her husband, and his mistress, too. Caught *in flagrante*, and the whole town had cheered. The wronged woman had gone free, because that was the law.

"It was one of his graduate students," Emily offered.

They stood there, listening as Luth drew deep, measured breaths.

"It seems, *Manang*, that one of the biggest issues in Dannie's life is the absence of intimacy. Not physical, which of course we all know about, but spiritual, a soul connection. He has said to us that, over the years, you seemed to turn away from him, and toward Naia and your daughter Antonia, creating a home in which he, as man of the house, was excluded."

Now was the time, she thought, to turn on her heel and leave. *I told her off, the meddling bitch*, she would boast to her co-teachers on Monday. Then it occurred to her that she had no friends, no intimates among her colleagues in whom she could confide. Antonia had been her sounding board. Tears came to her eyes at the thought of her younger daughter. She abandoned me, Luth thought. I am stranded.

"But the victim in all this is Naia, Luth. She's been getting into fights. Acting out. I'm afraid the boys have noticed her, and not without encouragement; it seems that majorette's uniform has gone to her head. And such a sweet, loving child; how she and Brent used to play after Sunday school. I could hardly believe what happened last week, how she fought her classmates like one possessed."

Luth started, alert, suspicious, remembering.

"She attacked her teacher, and some missionaries who had come to heal the class."

"Missionaries?" Luth croaked.

Emily hesitated for a moment, then proceeded with the same self-assurance. "We believe in academic freedom at the high school, dear. For me, the Social Studies class could only have been enriched through their input."

Luth, uncomprehending, waited for what would come next, but apparently Emily had more on her agenda.

"My dear, how long since Antonia left? Nearly a year, isn't it?"

"She left a year and a half ago," Luth said, automatically supplying the answer she gave to all those inquiring about Antonia's whereabouts. "She lives in Europe. She is a landowner." She did not say "farmer." It did not have the proper cachet. Antonia driving a tractor! She was damned if she would give Emily more reason to laugh.

"It must have been a major change for you. She must have been a very important person in your life."

Who had told her this? Daniel? Naia? How dared they?

Emily was searching Luth's face. At the indignation there her voice grew gentler, even more subtle. "Antonia isn't really Naia's mother, is she?"

There'd been no legal turnover of the child. There had never been any need. Luth didn't reply.

"We never acquired a habit of gossip in our family. So I thought I'd make sure. Naia's mother is Narita, your older daughter, isn't it? The one who went away."

She hated the way Emily was walking her through what was common knowledge at the university, as if to spite her.

"I suppose Antonia did most of the parenting. It must have been traumatic, for Naia to be abandoned all over again, and right at this crucial age. A teenage girl needs a mother, desperately."

Antonia had never explained. Not to her, nor to the child. Perhaps she had thought the choice was obvious: a woman past her first youth takes whatever opportunities come her way. And hadn't it been a settled fact, in their family, that Antonia was too good for Donostia, that it was incumbent on her to seek a better life someday?

If I let loose one word, I will hang myself, thought Luth.

"Come," Emily said then, beckoning with a graceful and magnanimous hand. Luth cast a glance at the door to Rinky Holland's office, which had remained closed all this time. No sound emanated from behind it. Emily moved, through the screen doors, from the living room and out into the porch. She stood waiting for Luth, lit from behind, against lush Boston ferns and mounds of decorative asparagus, perfectly turned out, her tailored blouse and Capri pants and sequined slippers in complementing shades of pink. Luth stomped toward her, followed her through the porch and down the gleaming outdoor staircase, then through a white-painted, though humbler, door. The ground floor of the Holland home was distinctly shabbier, as with most of the older faculty residences close to the center of the campus. The concrete floor was cold and uneven, and the walls were of woven bamboo slats, though here a plywood layer had been established all around, for privacy. Luth caught the comforting odor of detergent, of drying laundry, of bleach, but there were other smells, too. Boy smells, she thought. Musky sweat. And expensive recreational smells. An atmosphere of old tennis rackets and softball mitts, Nike trainers and golf clubs.

The Holland brothers were bent over a billiard table, examining a configuration of three balls. Brent, the dark one, was stretched over the cue. Adam's expression, as he watched his younger brother, was at once vacant and intent.

As she stood in the doorway, Luth heard one of them say, "Hang out? That's all they do, hang out?"

The other replied, "Yeah, they've got this mansion in Almagro with two PlayStations and a pool."

"Think we might get a ride in that Cessna someday?"

"Fat chance. It's a couple of thousand bucks a pop. Aviation fuel."

In the corner, completely ignored, was Naia. Perched on the edge of a revolving office chair, her body twisted in indecision, half-facing a running computer, half-turned to the boys. Her legs were askew, her feet in their cheap kung fu shoes restlessly scraping the concrete. On her face was an expression of annoyance and misery. Luth knew a small tantrum was in the works, but that the girl was too uncertain of her position to let loose even a hint of what was going on in her chest. Naia's eyes rested hungrily on the cue, on the balls. She wanted to join the game. She wanted to handle the forbidden: billiards was not a pastime for ladies. Luth watched the changing expressions on the small, hard face. What Luth felt was dread, that young girls could crave the impossible with such passion. She thinks she is a boy, Luth marveled. No, she thinks she can deal with them as an equal.

She would never be their equal. They might have all grown up on the same university campus; she and Brent might have both been seniors — he a cadet officer, she a majorette second-class, dressed all in white. Stars in the microcosm of high school. But with a Yankee ancestor on one side and a Spanish one on the other, with their mother's pineapple fortune and a sister on scholarship on the East Coast, the brothers were too good for Naia. It boiled down to class. Everything boiled down to class.

"Come on, Naia," Luth said. "We're going home."

Something in the girl's face closed up. "I can't, Lola. I start my first session with Auntie Emily today." She cast an anxious look over Luth's shoulder, at the Holland woman, who smiled in response.

And Luth felt the enemy scrambling up the walls, knew her fort was being overrun.

"Very well," she said. "I shall leave you, then. Be back in time for supper."

"Maybe," Naia said. "It depends on when Lolo wants to go home. I'm riding back with him in the car."

"Naia," Luth murmured. "You don't have to do this."

The girl sighed, and her eye fell once more on the brothers, one of whom had just dispatched several of the multicolored balls. "But Lola, I do. It's part of my punishment. Auntie Emily and I made a deal. After six sessions of counseling they'll allow me back into the band. On glockenspiel. If I do six more, I get to be a majorette again. You want me to be a majorette, don't you? You paid for the uniform."

Luth did not have time to mull over the logic of this deal. Emily was gently steering Naia back up the stairs. In the living room, the two husbands were sprawled. Tammy was diligently pouring them Cokes. She cast Luth a glance inexplicably filled with malice, then disappeared into the kitchen.

Luth sat numb. She listened to her husband as though to a newscast in a foreign language. She observed him crying.

Eleven

SO IT WAS not until several weeks had passed that she found out about the woman called Mother Martha and, for the moment, understood. It took that long to dig it out, for almost at once, the patter, the transactions of everyday life, restored a measure of normalcy to their home. Fish or chicken, which would it be; check the piano for termites; get the dog to shut up, please. Through the mundane, she had found it possible, not to forgive, but to forget the very real presence of Daniel. That was what she said to herself, many times a day, with exaggerated emphasis — Oh, my *husband's* still here, I hadn't noticed.

There had been the unpleasant business of sharing a bed with him. At first she slept in Antonia's room, the spare room now, lying on the narrow bed with the blankets about her throat. For three nights she stared up at the shadowy ceiling, the dark startlingly relieved, in places, by tiny paste-up stars that glowed. She lay there and listened to the rain. Unable to sleep. On the fourth night, she came home from the school exhausted and, without bothering about supper, entered the master bedroom out of habit and fell across the bed in her day clothes. She was unconscious, dreamless, for hours, and then, awakening before daybreak, realized that her husband was curled up on his side, at the very edge. She had not heard him come in. She understood at once that to avoid him she need only retire an hour before normal. Tormented by conscience and the ups and downs of a midlife crisis, he might stay in his study smoking until half past one, to rise long after she had dressed and left for the 7:00 a.m. flag-raising ceremony. She took to going to bed earlier and earlier, sometimes at 8:00 in the evening. Her body had never craved so much extra sleep. She would get up before five and, shirking the kitchen or living room, lest the servant find her, seek refuge in Antonia's room, the only private space in the house. She chose not the overhead fluorescent light, but the ancient reading lamp. In this hot circle of light she wrote out her lesson plan for the day to come. This was a ritual she had never reneged on, not in the forty years she had taught school. Sometimes she surprised herself with a wetness in the eyes that fell upon the neat, upright letters of her script. She wrote with such intense and deliberate pressure that, on occasion, the ball point ripped through the page.

One cold, rainy morning, coming back from the kitchen with some ginger tea, she realized that Naia had crept into the room. She and the girl had not spoken much since that day at the Hollands'. She had let the girl know, through her implacable silence, what she thought of the betrayal, and of Emily and Rinky's religious talk sessions, simply an elaborate way of trawling for gossip. Now she knew that the time for reconciliation had come. Her granddaughter lay on the bed, knees drawn up, eyes wide open. Her breathing was audible, through her mouth, as a child might breathe who has just been crying, but there were no tears.

"That day I came home late without my blouse," said Naia. "I didn't get into a fight."

"I know," said Luth.

"You can't know everything that I do, everything that I think. You're not that powerful." The girl looked at her with an expression she had never seen before. What was it? Contempt? Pity?

Luth thought about her own daughters, how they had approached a confession tangentially, dropping a hint one day, another a couple of mornings later. Something was not right — this deep and resonant sadness was out of place in a person so young.

"Why don't you tell me what really happened, Naia?" she said carefully.

"That old witch," the girl began. "That gospel teacher. She wanted to kill me."

THE missionaries had materialized one afternoon outside the Social Studies classroom. The blonde one was in her twenties, short, apple-shaped, and broiled pink. The other was maybe four decades her senior, thin, tall, with a severe mouth and a stiff white hairdo.

The old one called herself Mother Martha. She wore an unfashionably long gray skirt, a thin cotton blouse with a collar, and high, heavy black shoes with a T-strap for support. The other was called Valerie. "*V-a-l-e-r-i-e*," she spelled carefully, as though they had never heard of the name. Her tank top revealed the shocking expanses of her upper arms. Her breasts and belly bulged through the spandex fabric. She was not even ashamed. Until then, Naia had always thought religious persons covered their bodies up as much as was practical in the heat — that was certainly the case with the old one, the important one, who waited regally while her fat sidekick spoke to the Social Studies teacher in nasal tones that made the class giggle. Naia thought the young woman's demeanor arrogant, as though she expected Mrs. Galvez to stop the Social Studies class there and then, that they might claim the space before the blackboard and preach whatever gospel it was they were peddling. Naia was used to having sessions interrupted with neither warning nor logic, the weary teachers giving the floor to guest speakers and college student politicians beseeching the class for votes. She was aware that there were different sorts of Christianity, each claiming to be superior to the next. She had already concluded that, with their thin noses and Southern accents, the women were there to convert the class en masse — it was what Americans did. Besides, word of these preachers had spread among her classmates. These women had already done the rounds of Donostia public high schools and, invoking the Holy Spirit, performed true-life miracles on the shabby adolescents.

No one could describe in terms precise enough for Naia what those miracles had been.

The final bell for the day rang at last, and without being summoned, the women, one fat, one spare, entered the classroom and stood, backs straight, examining the rows of fifteen-year-olds as Mrs. Galvez explained what they had come for. Mrs. Holland appeared in the door and lingered for a few minutes, as though to make sure Mrs. Galvez got everything right, and at the sight of her, Naia bowed her head, feeling a burning guilt.

Neither of the white strangers smiled. The effect was unnerving. Naia had never met a foreigner who did not immediately smile down at her. She turned her head as surreptitiously as she could to survey the class, trying to envisage her peers as the two strangers might. She looked at Marvin and Alan, Iris and Irish, Honeylet, Rommel, Ian, Paolo, Maite and Jazzmeeh. There were twenty-five others, but she dared not twist around to account for the entirety of the class.

She perceived her classmates, suddenly, with new eyes, with the eyes, she fancied, of the visitors. She saw them as a collection of wilting white shirts and quizzical expressions, of transfixed faces that were clear-skinned or pimply — faces that were in many different shades of health but always described as brown. She saw black hair that was bobbed or braided, scraped back with a colorful band or shaved close to the scalp, straight or curly, fine or wiry — but black anyway. She smelled them: a strong, healthy odor of vinegar with a sly base note, the scent of certain mysterious plants her kung fu shoes crushed when, en route to the parade ground, she took short cuts through the brush at the back of the school.

Naia, gaining her bearings, realized the foreigners were staring, not at her classmates but at her. Heat suffused her face. All other persons in the room had been transfixed by the visitors. Mother Martha caught her gaze and continued to hold it long after regular folk would have politely glanced away. Her eyes did not match her blouse. The blouse was a mousy shade of gray, but the eyes were a blue Naia had never seen before, not in the summer sky nor in the tropical sea nor in the bolts of cloth down at the Sunshine Mart. They were a subtle hue from a colder, more complex universe, and though pale, they glinted with menace.

She bowed her head in confusion, for she was ashamed. Her hands came up to smooth the plaits of hair on either side of her head. She could smell the lotion that her grandmother made her smear over her arms and face as protection from the sun, for it was crucial for a drum majorette to have pale skin, to be beautiful and distinct from the hordes who ogled her snappy booted progress down Donostia's streets. The lotion smelled of candy. Of night blooms. It was not a clean smell. It was an odor that might hang around a loose girl in her twenties. Naia felt that Mother Martha, who looked into her so intently, could discern even this.

"Boys, move the desks," Mrs. Galvez said.

The air was rent by the noise of wood scraping over gritty concrete as, one by one, the long tables were dragged to the back of the room. Each row of displaced students joined the restless company waiting alongside the wall. No one dared venture into the space created in the middle of the room. Naia was among the last to stir. She stood half a head taller than the girls on either side of her. She was often picked out of lines for this fact.

"Boys, you are dismissed," said the teacher.

There was a momentary silence, born of confusion. Then, in a great hooting, shoving, guffawing wave, the youths quit the classroom to stride off down the central quadrangle to freedom. Someone bolted the door behind them. Someone else began on the windows, slamming the old-fashioned wooden jalousies shut. Both tasks were performed by the teacher's pets, thought Naia, who had never been one herself.

"Girls," Mrs. Galvez announced. "This afternoon you will be slain."

No one could explain exactly how the experience had gained that name. All Naia had heard was that the miracle began with an impassioned prayer. And now this was exactly what Mother Martha and Mrs. Galvez and Valerie were doing. She looked nervously about. All the other girls had closed their eyes, as bidden. Lips were parted, bodies swayed gently to keep balance. The whispered words of one classmate came back to her: "They pray over you, and then you cannot help it: you fall over back, as though a spirit had thrown you down, and then you are slain."

"*Which* spirit," Naia had hissed back, and the girl — she was called Irish — had flashed her a frightened look: "Don't say things like that, Naia. You are not as strong as you think. They have mighty powers on their side. They will have you speaking in tongues, like that girl at Central."

"And who translated?" Naia had forged on. "How do you know what she really was saying? And if they're all that holy, why is their terminology so *criminal*?"

Abruptly the prayer broke off. Mother Martha scanned the room. The young girls continued to sway, their faces calm, their arms relaxed, palms open at their sides. "I feel resistance," the old woman said. "The Devil perches on the shoulders of the proud and beautiful one."

Naia squeezed her eyes shut. Clothing rustled. Heat and three separate human odors came and went. The foreigners and the teacher were pacing, deliberately, between the girls. Naia's nostrils quivered — someone had stopped directly in front of her face. She fought the urge to open her lids. Not even a fraction. After a long, long moment, the person moved off, and the prayer began again.

"Children, clear a space," the old woman said. "The Spirit has come in this room. He shall triumph over the Horned One. Come to me, one by one. Come and be cleansed by my touch. The rest of you, open your eyes now and observe the handiwork of the Lord."

A shout came from one corner. "I am ready, o Lord, take away my sins." There was a thump. The girls leapt. It was Jazzmeeh, on her knees, tears already streaming down her cheeks.

"Foolish child," Mrs. Galvez said. She grabbed Jazzmeeh by the armpits and hauled her back to her feet. "Not there. Not yet." They stumbled to the center of the room, where Valerie and Mother Martha waited. The girl's nervous giggles subsided, and she shifted her weight from one foot to the other, her smile sheepish and expectant, as though she stood in line for a free and long-promised ice-cream cone.

In a movement at once firm and tender, Mother Martha took the girl's head in both her hands, staring searchingly down into the square brown face. "Oh yes, something lurks," she said pleasantly. "Down in there, down behind those sweet little eyes." A hard and urgent voice came suddenly from deep within the old woman's frame: "By the power of the Holy Spirit, I command you, *leave*."

A gasp rose from the watchers. Jazzmeeh's eyelids fluttered, and as her knees buckled, Valerie caught her and, with surprising agility, laid her down on the concrete floor.

There was no need for Mrs. Galvez to appoint another volunteer — the young girls began to crowd the missionaries, each hoping to be spotted next. By the power of the Spirit, Mother Martha slew Honeylet, Maricor, Theabel, and Daisy in quick succession, holding their faces steady as she gazed into their eyes. Her fingers, long and deft, traced the soft hair at their temples, the fine skin at their jaws, as though they sought some secret point of contact, and then they fell still. But Naia noticed the woman's fingertips turn even paler as, lightly and surely, she pressed the young girls' flesh against their skulls.

"The Lord works miracles for those who surrender to him," Mother Martha said. "Examine yourselves, children. Are your bodies healing? Is there some action the Evil One prevented you from performing all your lives?"

"My keloids are fading," Honeylet called out.

"I cannot run," volunteered Theabel, for one of her legs was shorter than the other.

"So *run*," said Mother Martha, but there was no warmth in her voice. Nonetheless, Theabel picked herself up and did an awkward lope around the room and down the corridor, reappearing a few moments later with a sheepish smile, rolling her eyes expectantly toward Mother Martha.

"Good girl," the old woman said, but Naia could have kicked her, for she had known Theabel since kindergarten, and they had played tag and jumped rope all the way to the sixth grade, and she knew for a fact that the little bitch was as competent as the rest of them. The truth was that Theabel was a toady and *that* was one flaw that would never be fixed.

One by one, the girls were lowered to the concrete, into a random quilt pattern of white-and-red checks. Some lay stunned and rolled their eyes to the ceiling, and some moaned and thrashed their limbs, so that their pleated skirts rode up over their thighs. One or two wept and arched their backs, bracing their heels against the floor, their moans so affecting that soon more of the girls had joined in, sighing and crying out like twenty R&B singles played at the same time.

And then only three girls were left standing, and it was Naia's turn. Someone caught her by the elbows and propelled her stiffly a meter or so toward Mother Martha; she had not realized how closely she had gravitated.

"I feel defiance in this one," Mother Martha murmured.

The teacher replied, "Ah, yah, she misuses God's gifts."

The cold fingers explored either side of Naia's face, the area of her throat beneath the curve of her jaw that she had never been conscious of till now. She jerked her face from side to side to dodge the probing touch. You could slit a fellow's throat from ear to ear, she thought, recalling the crime novels on her aunt's bookshelves. There's a special artery below the jawline that transports blood to the brain. Sever it, press down gently on it, and you interrupt that flow of blood. The body goes into a faint.

"Look at me. Look at me," Mother Martha said. Surely Naia had never seen such eyes so close before. So blue, such a true color, nothing like the flat images in magazines. Tears sprung to her own eyes at the gaze of this old, ruthless woman. And then she felt herself going under. The room darkened, and a pair of huge breasts loomed over her forehead. Valerie the assistant was bearing her down. In the haze of her near faint, she kicked blindly, lashed out with one of her famous high-stepping legs, and connected. She was shod, today, not in her shabby kung fu shoes but in a beautiful pair of ankle boots her aunt had sent in the mail, and one scandalous stiletto heel caught the unsuspecting Mother Martha in the shin. The old woman crumpled to the floorboards. Through the fog around Naia's mind came a harsh cry and a thump and a scrabbling sound. As she fell, a thick knee that she recognized to be Valerie's clubbed her in one ear. Now she, too, was on the floor, on one hip, her palm scraped where she'd flung out a hand to break her fall.

The old woman lay on her side, her groans of pain gaining vigor as it became evident that Naia was scrambling to her feet, shoving at the fat assistant who lay stunned on her back. Fighting the teacher now, hurling herself this way and that as three of her classmates ripped at her hair, snatched at her skirt, whirled her out of her blouse.

"Serpent, serpent!" Mother Martha rasped.

"A devil!" some girls cried. "A devil's possessed her!" and others wailed, "Catch it! Do something!" as they miraculously came back to consciousness.

In a trice, Naia broke free of them all, wrenched the door open, and hurtled down the corridor pursued by screams.

"Bring her back!" the old woman rasped. "Don't just stand there, you monkeys, bring her back!"

The wooden boards thundered beneath her feet. Her heart thumped in her chest. She skipped down the sagging wooden steps, hurdled a low plant border, made a snap decision and headed for the basketball court, where a group of students her age were undergoing their afternoon ordeal at the hands of the senior cadet officers. They were training to be officers next year. Some were struggling through squat jumps and others sweated through push-ups and still others circled the court with wooden rifles slung across their shoulders, as their fifteen-year-old superiors harassed them like pit bulls. All activity ceased as Naia plunged into their midst, leaping nimbly over several prostrate bodies. Behind her, her pursuers collided with plebes and officers alike to a great roar of outrage. But she was not free, not yet. The cries of "*Demonyo, demonyo*" continued behind her and seemed now to be coming from all sides and she punched her way through a knot of faceless boys who grabbed futilely at her arms. But another sort of cry was rising in counterpart, a sniggering, mostly male, athletics day chorus — "Go, Naia, go! Go, Naia, go!" She turned a corner, saw doors, a flight of stairs, a corridor, a waiting boy. The boy caught her; he was her height, wiry, and very strong. He whirled her into a dark space, slung her gasping, too shocked to scream, against a wall. He shoved the door shut, hanging back on the knob at the last minute that no slam might be heard. He locked it with a key from a massive ring. She trembled, gasping for breath, for life itself. They were in the armory. The wooden rifles were black columns in the gloom. In the hallway, running feet, confusion, hysteria, laughter. Fists pounded on the door. Someone tried the knob.

"What are you doing," she cried as the boy advanced on her. "Shut up," he said. Fists assaulted the door once more. She whimpered. He stood behind her, trapping her legs in his own, and clamped a cold, nervous hand over her mouth. Sweat slicked every surface of her shaking body.

"Shut up," said the boy again. "Shut up, don't move, shut up."

Twelve

LUTH HAD DIVULGED all she knew. Or so she said. It was plenty. Now she fell silent. Narita fetched her a glass of water from the refrigerator. She drank it down without thanks, without comment.

Narita felt nothing, not even surprise. It seemed nothing about her daughter could astonish her anymore.

What time was it? It seemed she had been listening for hours, here in this bedroom that had always been Antonia's and, for several months after that disastrous lunch at the Hollands', her mother's haven, and now hers. Here they had retreated, to get away from the kitchen where Cecilia hovered, listening with huge ears and an expressionless face as the household groaned in various degrees of misery. Here, too, they were safe from Daniel, and his monologues and his mindless habit of calling out their names as though they were saints who might save him in his hour of need.

They looked at each other in what was almost understanding. Mother and daughter, and tentative friends.

"So she was raped," Narita said.

"God," Luth exploded. "Don't you dare use that word. It was not rape. *Nothing* happened to her."

LUTH had probed, fixing Naia in her glare, as Mother Martha had done.

"Did you know the boy?"

"No. *No.*"

"Had you seen him before?"

"Maybe?"

"Was he another senior? A classmate of yours?"

"I told you I don't know his name."

"Listen to me carefully, Naia. Did you see this boy at any time after that afternoon?"

"*No.*"

"Did you tell Emily and Rinky Holland about him?"

"No, no, no." Sobbing softly now.

At that point, Luth's mind became absolutely clear. Daniel would never find out. He did not deserve to know. And this would have to be kept secret. The scandal would destroy Naia's chances of a good marriage. No boy in Sweethaven would deign to approach her. She would end up one of those awful young whores arched on a motorcycle behind some *haciendero* playboy, lazily sweeping up her hair as they rocketed over asphalt.

Gently she asked the girl if the boy had had his way with her. Naia did not seem to understand. "Did he take your maidenhood?" Luth said. "Did you bleed in some way?"

"No," the girl said again. "But he made me hold his thing."

With a shudder, Luth banished the image from her mind.

"MOTHER Martha!" Narita said in awe. "What a creature she must have been. And Emily Holland allowed her in. An old hag from the Bible Belt most probably."

"Who thinks we are monkeys," said Luth.

"Huh."

Their eyes met and immediately lowered, for the label, the very sound of it, shamed them. Discomfiture made the corners of their mouths flutter in the beginnings of two smiles, though there was no one in the room they needed to defer to, no one to placate. A lifetime of fretting over the color of their skin, the shape of their noses, tempered their feelings of outrage.

"That is Sweethaven for you," Luth said at last, in a low murmur. "This is a community of hypocrites."

Narita sighed. For as long as she could remember, there had always seemed to be people like Mother Martha, if you lumped together the Evangelicals and the Pentecostals and the Mormons. Americans who dressed in dowdy clothes and always seemed on the brink of poverty — perhaps that was because of their willingness to associate with the poor and the riffraff, as though they saw no difference between social stations. They would set up chapels in little rooms above storefronts, or in rented houses in the subdivisions around the city. The Mormons, of course, had their pretty white church with the manicured lawn. A cloud of suspicion had hung around these proselytizers — Narita had heard they were CIA spies, endorsed by Ferdinand Marcos to keep people's minds off the various failings of his administration. And of course they had been yet another pathetic group of people for her and Antonia to jeer at.

"Those missionaries can't be Sweethaven, Mother," she now said.

"Not Sweethaven when they've got the ear of Emily Holland!"

Narita shook her head slowly. "I majored in psychology in college. I had tons of friends. They took zoology, medical technology, chemistry. Zenon was studying to be an engineer."

"What is your point?" snapped Luth.

The point formulated itself slowly as she groped for words — that the Sweethaven she had known, that had formed her, had been soundly grounded in the quest for knowledge, in scientific inquiry. It did not proselytize. It was not a seminary, not a theological institute, despite its origins. Something was amiss for it to be so easily breached by the fundamentalists — something had gone wrong down the line.

"Jesus, why are you so afraid of these people?" Narita said at last. "How can you take them seriously?"

"They would take over Sweethaven if they could. They already have."

"I don't believe you. Not Father. Not the faculty down at Humanities. Not the gay organizations. This is still a university,

Ma. We're *educated*, we're not desperate. We're not like Brother Mike Velarde's followers, rallying by the millions in Manila every Saturday."

But Luth was shaking her head. "No, no, no, no, you do not see. You have been away for so long, and you come back with all these superior notions of yours, diagnosing the way we live."

Narita flushed. A retort rose to her lips, as of old, but she bit it back.

"It doesn't matter what a university is supposed to be," said Luth. "The important thing is what it *is*. 'Quest for knowledge.' What are you talking about? Sweethaven is a glamorized nursing institute. Even doctors are studying nursing now. The peso has been worthless for decades. Everyone dreams of going to America."

Narita was silent. She wanted to see if her mother would leave the room. She couldn't move from where she sat, awaiting the next words. She was certain Luth knew more than she was letting on, that revelations were forthcoming.

"Monkeys. I was your father's monkey for a long time," the older woman said at last, in a tone that was beyond bitter. "Worked so hard because he felt he had to entertain the whole university at home. Get-togethers every fortnight — all his colleagues and his graduate students and those foreigners that had to be impressed with local food, *kare-kare* and *escabeche* and chop suey, and what went into each dish, and what was the reason for each pest of a name. Cleaning and cooking, no maid, keeping track of the conversations, making sure everyone had a Coke refill and cashew nuts at hand. I loved cashews, did you know that? But I never got much of a chance to taste them."

"At least we helped you," Narita volunteered.

"You would serve the peanuts, give them all away before the party had even begun. Then the two of you would vanish to your room, carrying all the chips."

Narita pondered this. This was not the childhood she remembered. She had thought they had done their part. And she had loved those Jack n Jill corn chips. She had assumed no adult would ever want them. She'd had no idea of her mother's misery. What would Luth say next? Without the figure of Antonia to complicate matters, some connection with Luth seemed wholly possible.

SHE could not share Luth's suspicion of foreigners. The Pastor kids were not like ordinary Filipinos — growing up in Sweethaven, they had not been ignorant of the world. Foreigners were fixtures in the landscape of the living rooms and front lawns of their childhood. At least for a few years in the 1970s and early '80s, the family could look forward to an outing, piling into a vehicle driven by some thrilling, knowledgeable white man, down into the hinterlands or to some desolate beach. They telescoped their great bodies down to her height and, looking pleasantly at her out of odd pale eyes, taught her a song or made her a very special sketch of carabaos and trees. They informed her that Manila was the capital and that José Rizal was the national hero and told Antonia that the name of the red flower was hibiscus, though the girls knew about Manila and Rizal, and hibiscus flowers, which were really *gumamelas*, were everywhere in the landscape.

The foreigners' lawns were always trimmed, and they served strange stuff the children never knew existed: mouthfuls of oily pink fish and little round things called olives and once a little sip of a sour, burning colorless liquid out of a stemmed glass. They drank from plastic tumblers of canary yellow and hot pink; ate off superb little plates of fire engine red with a border of flowers. They had separate rooms in their sprawling, low homes for laundry, and in these laundry rooms sat machines especially for doing the wash. They owned vans, off-road jeeps, entire boats, even. The girls tread gingerly in their lovely homes, to which being invited was a privilege for which they wore their Sunday clothes.

No one ever said to Narita, "Look out, that creature coming at you is a foreigner; be very careful and keep answers to a minimum; you can never be sure what he wants." Stunted village urchins goggled at her as, at seven or eight, she tramped self-importantly over a rutted road, alongside a tall, lumbering fellow in shorts and sandals — a coral reef expert spending a term at the university, or a translator or student of hill tribe languages.

They still kept photos from those years, faded to a cold, reddish hue. In these images, Rinky Holland played a prominent role. There he was, an arm around her father's shoulders, mouth stretched in a devilish grin. His long hair was feathered back Shaun Cassidy style. In another shot, he was off to one side, his head half-turned to address someone outside the frame. In his hand was a small glass of some dark liquid; it could well have been one of those exotic European potions, though it was probably just Coke. He was always laughing, talking, posing, flirting with the camera, exhorting others to loosen up. Daniel, who owned the camera, appeared in these photos only occasionally, and if he did, his smile was always sheepish, his head dipped. He always seemed abashed.

A whiff of scandal hovered about Rinky Holland in those early days. His youthful exuberance, his movie star grin, filled Narita with a shy excitement she was too young to recognize as sexual. Her childhood had been laced with grown-up gossip about his numerous girlfriends, but as if that hadn't been enough, there came one day the horrendously delicious tale of how he had seduced one of his students — an heiress, it was reputed, from a neighboring province. There were tears, tragedy, furious parents, an inheritance embargoed. One day in church, Luth had pinched Narita's arm, and then just as quickly followed it up with a loaded glare. Narita understood there was something of deep interest in the vicinity, but she would have to be subtle if she wanted a glimpse. Thus she was introduced to Rinky Holland's new wife, sitting in the pew across the aisle: tiny, perfect, and pale with the embarrassment of a first pregnancy. Narita, at age eleven, did not understand pregnancy. All she saw was a young lady who bore all the trappings of glamor, wealth, and Hollywood. At once she devised a name for this new being: Elizabeth, after Elizabeth McGovern. All the pretty mothers were named after movie stars.

One day Mr. Holland showed up on their doorstep. He spoke quietly and frowned a lot, as though he had come on a matter of utmost urgency, and in his hand was a toolbox made of real wood. In his checkered shirt he looked like a lumberjack; he even had pale-ish hair and the right shape nose. The girls were delighted with that tool chest, from which emerged a metal device like a gun, which he plugged into the wall. It made a horrific whining heard all over the house. "Black and Decker," he said, in a tone of satisfaction, and Daniel repeated, "Black and Decker," in exactly the same manner. And then Mr. Holland bored a pair of holes in the wall of the kitchen. Antonia gaped at him. He had violated the wood — what would their mother say?

Pretty soon the reason for this performance became apparent, as he fixed a hard plastic stump to the wall. The girls had never seen anything like it. It was a metal arm equipped with saw teeth. Mr. Holland plugged the device into a black box that must have been heavy, for he, the lumberjack, actually grunted as he hefted it onto the counter. This box he plugged into the wall socket. The teeth whirred merrily. "You even get a free transformer," he said, and the two men laughed. The girls didn't understand; it was an inside joke. The procedure took a whole hour, for Mr. Holland had a glamorous, unhurried way of doing things, taking care to explain the process to their father every step of the way.

But when their mother came home she demanded to know how much Rinky Holland had asked for the thing, and when Daniel told her, she blew her top. "Who pays their entire salary for an automatic can opener?" she screamed.

The children were mortified — this would be like the other time they had come home from an outing with their mother to find a thermometer clinging to the wall, some newfangled contraption that showed the temperature inside the house as well as out.

"Is this how our life will be from now on, a life of receiving your best friend's castoffs?" Luth raged.

He wept: "It was a gift on their wedding! It took so much out of him to part with it. They need our help badly, it's the least we can do!"

"Come on, Antonia," Narita said, to distract herself from their father's shame. The girls went to the cupboard and collected all the cans they could find — Alaska Evaporada, Ma-Ling luncheon meat, Del Monte fruit cocktail, Gita peas. Antonia lined them up on the counter, and Narita fed them all to Mr. Holland's wonderful apparatus, so that in minutes, disks of metal glinted on the countertop like giant fish scales, and Antonia was sucking a mix of milk and sardine sauce off her fingers. The sad thing was that can-opening would be over so quickly from then on — no more moans and groans from their father as he pretended to have lost a thumb, no more theatrics with tomato juice.

"Worthless secondhand toys," said their mother, and Narita saw that she was weeping as well: two adults in tears; the day had turned upside down. "Made in Germany!" The phrase sounded like a curse. "They must be desperate, penniless; *she* must be selling her jewels, too."

AROUND that time, Mr. and Mrs. Holland got religion, simultaneously and with much drama, from the fundamentalists who came to infect Sweethaven every few years. That was how Daniel put it, "got," and "infect" — their faith being an affliction, like the measles. Emily, recently converted, was volunteering to teach Sunday school; Rinky was testifying, vigorously, about how his acts of contrition had led him straight back into the fold. Perhaps, in time, they might lead his wife back to her money.

"Well, that gives the campus something new to talk about," Luth said. The Hollands remained a hot topic at the Pastor family dinner table, the mood shifting from amusement to concern to dislike. There was a perverse single-mindedness in the way Emily and Rinky went about their faith.

Thirteen

IT FELT LIKE they had lingered by the seaside for hours, Joel and JP Torres. Joel smoking as casually as he could manage in the driver's seat of the jeep, and JP leaning his weight on the motocross bike as though passing the time of day.

Most of that span of time had been spent on a ritual of reacquaintance that the lawyer found surreal. JP had taken him through a roster of aunts and cousins he had wished to forget. Lola Mimay was not well, confined to her bed by arthritis, her heart broken because Manolo, her favorite nephew, had burgled her jewelry box. Tia Clara was very happy, happy to be leaving for the States next month, as Beatriz, her eldest, had petitioned for her at last. And as for JP, he thought he might try his hand at flying Cessnas down at the airstrip. There was a new school, populated with Pakistanis and Indians looking for cheap flying lessons. "Terrorists," chuckled JP.

Joel wanted to wallop him. Instead, he laughed expansively and said, "'*Tang ina mo*, I've always wanted to do that myself," noting that JP wasn't short of money then.

"It takes balls," JP said.

"Like it takes balls to do that to a high school girl."

JP shrugged. "I have no idea where that Sweethaven girl came from. Ask Harrison. I never knew her. Maybe I saw her at some parade, but she wasn't my type."

"How many were you?"

JP ignored this. "So don't be a hypocrite, Tito. Fifteen is a grown woman. My own grandmother was married at fourteen."

"Those were the 1930s. It was a different time."

"Do you know how young a girl can be before they charge you with raping her? Come on, Tito, which of us is the lawyer?"

"Twelve," Joel said unwillingly. "Twelve years old in this country."

"You see?" JP gave a snort of a laugh.

And then he mounted the bike, kicking it into life and surging forth in the manner of someone used to calling the shots. He looked back only once, an easy, amused tilting of the head. Joel, fuming at the game, started his own engine and sped after him, heart in mouth, vision focused on the red taillight that grew smaller and smaller in the darkness. There were no streetlights on this rutted stretch, flanked by brackish swamp and nipa palms that led away from the beach. By the time Joel had gained the highway, the motorcycle had disappeared. Taking a chance, Joel swung the jeep in the direction of Donostia. Just within the city limits he found the motorcycle waiting by the roadside. JP put up an arm in a lazy wave and led him for a couple of intersections, turning at last along a two-lane road, past sari-sari stores and walls of whitewashed hollow block, then what had once been farms, parceled up in Joel's childhood into residential subdivisions, interspersed with stretches of land planted with coconuts. JP shot forth again, as though playing a game. Soon enough, though, the jeep's headlights picked out the motorcycle, pulled up beside a rusting iron gate and leaning on its kickstand.

Joel peered through the darkness beyond the grilles. He knew where he was. To the denizens of this Donostia barrio, this compound of four or so bungalows was Villa Milagros, named after JP's mother, the long-suffering wife who had brought the Fortun inheritance into her marriage. At some point Joel remembered that the individual houses had been rented out to young marrieds — bank tellers, low-level highways engineers — "nice people," as the clan liked to repeat.

He cut the motor, noting, in the second before he killed his lights, how decrepit the gate now looked. In the silence, he realized that the compound beyond was completely dark.

Something had happened in the years since he had divorced himself from the Fortuns.

A shadow sauntered across the road. JP Torres had been waiting under the thatch overhang of a variety store. He thumped the hood of the jeep as he drew abreast. Joel swung himself down with a grunt.

"Where are all the tenants?"

"Hard times. They left owing us rent, the bastards, every last one of them. My father refused to repair the plumbing or the roofs until they paid us what they owed. But they packed up and left anyway."

They stood beneath the streetlamp, a white fluorescent bar beset by wriggling winged insects. Its light turned their faces into skulls. Each examined the other's morbid visage; each challenged the other to speak.

"Who lives here now?" Joel said at last.

"I do. I did. I had one of the bungalows to myself. Since my name got dragged into this mess, I've been sleeping on a couch at my mother's."

The youth was struggling with the rusty padlock, cursing, dropping the keys. The padlock yielded at last, and he shoved the gate open just wide enough for the two of them to pass.

"So you've been the caretaker."

"My father decided I needed a place of my own. One of the units had been promised to me from the start, so we evicted the people living there, and I moved in."

Joel decided that caretaking had been the least of the young man's concerns. He wondered how long the lodgers had had to endure JP as neighbor: intoxicated strangers weaving between puddles, caroming into doorways; the whine and explosion of motorcycle engines all hours of the night. And in the morning, JP the *haciendero* himself, pockets empty, sweet-talking the lodgers for a couple of pesos to buy a cigarette.

"All right," Joel sighed. "Which bungalow was yours?"

But JP cast a glance into the compound. "*You* go in, Tito," he mumbled. "I can't bear to. It feels like it might be haunted."

Joel shot the young man a look.

"It's the scene of the crime," JP said, the phrase spoken a shade too jauntily.

In disgust, Joel entered that dark space, moving gingerly over the packed earth, noting a gleam of reflected light that indicated a large rain puddle. The first two structures were locked, their windows boarded up. Against the third, some scaffolding had been erected, fortifying JP's tale of repairs his father refused to carry out until it was too late. A fourth structure was intact.

"That was my place," the youth said. "It's still filled with my things." The fifth and smallest house was a single-level bungalow with a terrace.

"For lady lodgers," said JP.

Joel ignored the joke. He glanced up at the roof, which was peaked, with space enough, he supposed, to accommodate a man.

"This Chinese boy you worked with — he sampled the girls, too?"

JP laughed out loud. "Harrison? No way. He was in charge of distribution, that's all. His family owned a big video rental shop for years. The pirates put them out of business, but they were smart: they started selling pirated videos themselves. He knows a few syndicates in the industry. He gets around."

"How many others were there?"

The youth was grinning nervously, shaking his head. "I've already given you the Chinese."

"I don't see a fellow like Co crouching up in a ceiling for hours watching *you* hump a girl."

JP looked away, into the darkness, avoiding the weight of Joel's stare. "Tito," he said. "The family believes me to be a good boy. And I want to spare them the truth. It's one thing to confess to the act and beg forgiveness. It's another to rub their noses in the proof."

"What do you mean?"

"Out there is a mass of footage of me, some of which I haven't even seen, doing things to women that no mother could stand to watch. Footage with my face in it; I know that for a fact. If you crack down on the cameraman, Tito, if you make just one move, one inquiry in his direction, that footage could go straight to the Internet. I can't inflict that on my family."

He had been holding the keys, jouncing them tensely in his fist, and now he dropped them squarely into Joel's palm. "Here, Tito, they're yours."

Fourteen

THE BEST PART of Narita and Antonia's childhood was the surfeit of paper in their home. At the start of every summer, their mother would clean out her classroom and take back to the house whatever notebooks the pupils had abandoned in their desks. Their father, too, had tons of unclaimed term papers, perfect for recycling. Without the annoyance of school, they were free to travel wherever their fantasies took them.

There wasn't much they could do to entertain themselves in summer anyway. There was no tennis, no hiking, no boating, no skateboarding — not that they had the money for any of that. Besides, in that climate, all the outdoorsy things that fantasy American people did were impossible. The burning April sun kept them in their rooms, and in May, the threatening monsoon, combined with the humidity from the ocean, soaked them in sweat. Their father liked to joke that May was the month when no one was worthy of human company.

One year their mother found a treasure in a corner of her classroom. It was a book about the size and thickness of an old *Life* magazine, and it was called *How to Draw the Head*. There was a name scrawled in a margin or two; nothing she recognized, but she knew well enough that she had stumbled upon an object of extreme value, an object certain to be missed. The girls begged her to keep it a bit longer, say, a week, before turning it over to the principal's office, and when she wouldn't relent, Antonia suggested that they bury it, deep down in their closet, so that their mother would eventually forget.

It was Antonia's book. In the span of a fortnight, she made the leap from doodler to portrait artist, slouched over the study table, her fingers making minute and patient movements over the paper. She invented faces of people she had never met, chiseled Nordic faces with by-the-numbers proportions.

Sometimes Narita stole through her sister's sketch pads, wondering who these people were who seemed so genial — on the verge, it seemed, of speaking. The Caucasian faces embarrassed her, being so different from hers and her sister's and those of the people around them. As there were no suitable boys and girls in the neighborhood, Antonia seemed to be inventing her own friends. The depth of her loneliness was chilling.

Narita wasn't too bad with a pencil, but she didn't see the point in making pictures unless they told a story. It was that summer that their paths diverged. Antonia was simply the better artist. To cover her frustration, Narita went swimming at the university pool and hung out at the faculty homes where there were kids her age. She brought home Stephen King paperbacks, cassette tapes to copy. But Antonia lost all interest in these treasures. She drew; Narita read with headphones on. And then, one day, she flipped through a sketch pad Antonia had left lying around and found the creature.

The face was half human, half horse, with broad, flaring nostrils and thick chapped lips. There was a name: Ramon. There was even an arrow pointing from drawing to name. Surely a high school classmate, whom Antonia had never told her about, and this by itself was a revelation: Antonia was getting crushes on *real* people. No more Ice Cream Soldiers, no more Captain Dwyers. It was a miracle.

Antonia must have realized Narita had been going through her things because, the following day, she called her sister over as if seeking official approval.

"What the hell have you been doing?" Narita said, feigning innocence.

How to Draw the Head was over. The younger girl had broken free of the book's prescriptions and had drawn six men, one after another, six imperfect men. The first bore a striking resemblance to Humberto Manguerra, the reverend, who was often at the house and who used to sing with Daniel in the men's glee club. The second looked like their uncle Policarpio, their mother's younger brother, who'd gotten himself stockaded during Martial Law. The third looked like their father's father, an elegant man with deep-set eyes that the Pastors maintained were Spanish. And the fourth was unmistakably the meanest security guard at the high school gate, who had never let her through until he had thrust a varnished baton into her schoolbag as though to inspect it.

"Portraits!" Narita said.

Antonia fixed her with a withering look. "No. Templates," she corrected, in their father's lecturer voice. "Filipinos are a homogeneous race. There are only a handful of faces in this archipelago. What you think constitutes individuality is just a matter of age, degree of wealth and nutrition, factors impacting the same basic features." She flipped through the pictures again. "I've been practicing. I've been looking around. I never take the sketchbook out. I fix the images in my mind. I think I've isolated most, if not all."

She tapped one of the drawings with a pen. "This is maybe the most common. It's broad in the cheekbones, very Malay, very flat in the nose. It's a nose like a palm frond laid on its face. It looks like a rowboat turned upside down." She snickered. "This face, this face isn't true Filipino. It looks like it came from Amoy a hundred years ago with only a loincloth as baggage. Look at the lips, how the teeth behind push them out, like *so*. We won't shade this one. Pale yellow doesn't translate so well in graphite. Now look at this specimen. It goes with a big belly and a shark's tooth on a piece of twine. It's the kind of face you would see paddling a canoe in the South Pacific."

Narita began to giggle. It was brilliant, all of it. "But they're not human!"

"Oh, they are. Very lifelike. They'd recognize themselves if they were real."

She thought she might make a token protest. She was, after all, the family rebel.

"You've made them ugly, Antonia, like you weren't one of them, too."

But her sister shook her head. "You only think they're ugly because you can't accept the way we look. The way *you* look."

"How do I look, then?"

"Polynesian?" the girl shrugged. "Negroid?"

Narita's face turned hot, for her cousins had flung similar insults at her when she was small, and yet their father had taught her, by way of consolation, that there were no ugly people in the world; specifically, that everyone was beautiful regardless of their origin.

"You're not a scientist," she shrieked. "You're a racist. You pick out the most shameful things about a human face and fixate on them. What do you take yourself for, an *Americana*? You're only Filipino, Antonia Pastor."

And she ripped the sketch pad from Antonia's hands and flung it across the room.

THAT was the summer they followed mixed-race couples down the main street of Donostia, ducking into doorways if the man or woman turned around, and examining the magazines or knickknacks or roast chickens that had caught their attention some moments before. Antonia was working on a new project: a study of the Filipino female face. She was convinced that the average Sweethaven face was inauthentic, diluted with Chinese and Spanish strains. To get to the ultimate face, one had to get down to the ultimate poor: the squatters whose huts sprawled over the swamp that came almost to the dockside, the wives of the sugarcane cutters in the vast plantations beyond the city, even the madwoman who wandered through the marketplace naked but for a skin of filth.

One morning they were at the Philippine National Bank closing out their kiddie savers accounts when a woman swept grandly through the doors. It was high summer, but she wore a long shiny coat of black with a fuchsia lining. Beneath it peeked a red tank top. Her legs were encased in red capris. On her feet were high-heeled black patent leather slides. Her hair looked like it had been washed in artesian well water all her life, including that part of her life spent in whatever land had inspired her to sling on her finery. She tippy-tapped her way to the teller's booth and somehow one of her stiletto heels caught their mother in the toe, right where an ingrown nail had been making its presence known for weeks.

"*Ka-arte, murag si kinsa!*" their mother snapped.

"*Ikaw nang gabalabag,*" the woman retorted.

Their mother didn't leave it at that. "I have every right to be here," she said.

"*Kinsa ba kang mag-Ingles-Ingles diha,*" the woman spat, mocking Luth for speaking English and putting on airs.

"Dried-up old monkey," Luth said. "A mail-order bride."

Antonia was staring.

The dried-up monkey face translated well to graphite. It had small eyes and a button nose, not a flat nose. Between that nose and the upper lip of the rather wide mouth was a substantial expanse of face that, Antonia explained, was stiff from the effort of looking superior, giving it a distinctive, simian effect. She thought "mail-order bride" was too good a name to waste, like "Maid in Hong Kong," but she could not decide which of her facial templates it belonged to. She finally figured out that it could apply to them all. One was not born a mail-order bride. It was a choice, a condition one worked for.

Antonia was fifteen. She could not accept that a woman might send her address and photo to an agency, that a man elsewhere in the world might send letters to that photo, and if the correspondence went well, they might marry and come to live in a better place.

"It's cheating," she said.

"Well, who can blame them?" Narita said. "Who wants to be stuck here forever?"

"Would *you* do the same?" Antonia badgered her. "You once said you would hire a stud to sleep with the moment you turned eighteen. And then you'd run away to the States. What if the studs all wanted a Pontiac? What if you couldn't raise the airfare? Would you hire yourself out to some old turkey like those women did?"

They were beginning to realize that their father had no desire to leave Sweethaven, no matter how hard their mother nagged. Without his ambition, the door to America was closed. That was something else they would have to accept, that they were Filipinos, and access to the places they had been bred for was denied.

They saw the black sateen coat one more time that summer, entering a cheap restaurant escorted by a white man. Their mother had taken them to the seamstress to be measured for new uniforms. Although both of them knew she had no spare change, Antonia begged her for a snack. "Ma, could I have a fruit shake, please, I'm burning," she whined, and so they entered the restaurant, on the couple's heels. They followed them to the counter, watching the twosome point to the pans of meat and vegetables behind the glass, and Narita suppressed a deep sense of inferiority, at the reminder that there were people in the world who could eat anything they wanted on a whim. Two women accompanied the couple, of the same slatternly extraction as the girl. Their mindless chatter filled the air. The man was a pink-skinned fellow of Nordic proportions — his companions barely came to his elbow, despite their stiletto heels — and she noticed that he paid for everything they ordered. A spark of mischief appeared in Antonia's face. The restaurant was quiet except for the hum of a blender from the kitchen. From up in his aerie, the Nordic man rumbled impatiently — "Stop complaining, or we go home." The dried-up monkey woman winced to her friends, but when she craned her neck to look up at her man, she was all smiles.

"No, no, no, darling, I am not complaining, I am enjoying, I am enjoying," she said.

THEY were galloping into womanhood, the two of them, smart and wicked and boyless, despite their accomplishments. Narita suspected it was because they hung out together too much, but she couldn't shake her sister's clinging need for approval, and she supposed she needed her sister as a sounding board, for her cold-hearted opinion. She worried for Antonia. The girl was clearly talented and so brilliant, but only in the fields that interested her, such as drawing ugly people, and resurrecting dead orchids, and making complicated slipcovers out of scraps of cotton cloth. Narita didn't dare think what she might grow up into. Her grades were good enough, but Narita couldn't see her working in an office, getting along with regular people. It wasn't that she couldn't speak the vernacular of the place — no, her problem was that she couldn't bear to listen to it, to anything that was said in it, to the individuals who used it. She was people-proof.

The strangest part was Antonia's duplicity. She had a pretty face and a responsible smile, and left new acquaintances with the most positive of impressions. She knew, instinctively, the recipe for pleasing people, giving them what they wanted to see. Her success at school poster competitions, for instance — she would begin by choosing a central image, a seedling perhaps. She would add a hopeful child, a man in a hardhat, a wife in a housedress, a factory or an airplane or a ship. A tame dog would materialize by a knee, for cuteness. All faces would be oriented heavenward for emotional impact. Tribal weave-work would be appropriated to fill any inadvertent space. In this way she was always rolling in minor wealth. Not a semester went by when her artist fingers didn't win her some sort of medal. People Power had come and gone, but if anything, New Society imagery was alive and well, and she had imbibed it all, by osmosis, poring over the art at the back of telephone books and their parents' old Marcos-era magazines. Everyone thought she was profound, and would move on to greater things.

NARITA HAD gotten her looks from her mother's people. She hated her face: it was tolerable only when she grinned. She had spent the entirety of high school grinning at people to win them over. Smiling hurt, but she kept it up. She had realized, the hard way, that when her features relaxed, unguarded, they resolved themselves into a scowl. Her brow was heavy, her lips thick. She looked like a cattle thief or one of those indigents down by the waterfront, scraping the rocks at low tide for mussels. It seemed, while she was growing up, that everyone at Sweethaven was beautiful and refined — and cruel, too, for unless she smiled and spoke out, they always seemed to assume she was stupid.

The cruelest of all was her own sister, whose forays into anthropology had culminated in Narita's face glaring out one morning from the sketch pad propped on the piano. Narita Tadhana Pastor was a native. She didn't belong.

SHE supposed the turning point, the moment when she emancipated herself from their childhood, was that March night when, driven mad by the summer heat and the demands of the baby, they fought, and she cut Antonia with a paring knife. It was no ordinary cut — the neat little instrument slashed into Antonia's palm, severing a tendon, and on top of that she had bled, mightily but without a whimper. Their father had to drive her down to the mission hospital in the middle of the night, and the morning after, he had stripped the seat cover from the passenger side of the car, rolled it into a ball, sealed it into a garbage bag against the dogs, and buried it in a far corner of the yard. No sense in the scavengers finding it.

The hand had required an operation, which healed badly, and only after a very long time. Antonia, quick and impatient and believing herself indestructible, couldn't keep the bandages dry, insisting, after a couple of days, on looking after the baby, changing her and feeding her and picking her up when she cried. Narita didn't know how much of this was for dramatic effect and how much was Antonia's own neurotic belief in her saintly competency.

She wore the bandage a long time. In the pictures taken from those days, she appeared to be wearing a white lace glove as she cradled the baby, a white glove as was the fashion among brides. They traveled to Cebu a couple of times that summer, Antonia and her father, to have the wound looked at by specialists. They assured her that with proper exercise she would regain full use of all her fingers; that the scarring was minor and did not in any way detract from her overall beauty, and that she would be well advised to keep the hand placidly at her side and refrain from broad and unwomanly gestures with it.

It was the hand she used for writing, so the exams she had been ferociously studying for were out of the question. The injury set her back an entire semester. Maybe it was then that she lost her zest for competition, for trying to prove that she was the smartest person in the room.

Narita didn't know if the two of them could ever have been cleanly and symmetrically healed, for she herself left for Manila that May. There was no Internet — did anyone remember what it was like in those days? There were no DVDs for burning high-resolution documentaries of a baby's progress, no digital cameras, and no mobile phones. There weren't even any pagers. If they'd been invented, no one she knew made use of them, not even in Manila. A stranger to the city would have been lucky to find accommodations with a phone line, and that phone would have to be shared with the landlady's kids, who could cling to the receiver for hours.

So as they stood grimly side by side in one corner of the airport terminal, Narita holding the baby, Antonia cradling her bandaged hand, they knew, without a shadow of doubt, that this was the end, the absolute good-bye. They did not talk. They avoided each other's eyes. As little girls, they had once exchanged letters over the course of a year, pretending to be two different people, narrating adventures that each one had made up, getting together each evening to review the course of the tale and agree on which personages were to be married, divorced, cuckolded, jailed, or dispatched. Now the thought of writing, with the same humor and the same desperate intensity, seemed repugnantly intimate.

A security guard called an announcement into the terminal. Everything was very loose in that time: no PA system, no metal detectors. The flight to Manila was the event of the day. The plane was ready for boarding. It was time to leave. Narita's parents were talking, laughing softly to themselves: a rare moment of solidarity.

Their mother said, "Remember when you were small and your father had to leave us for conferences abroad, how you waved and waved at the plane from the wire fence until it had taken off?"

"And I would wave back," said their father.

"And Antonia would squeal and jump around in my arms," their mother chuckled.

"You waved a book from the window, so we would know which of the hands was yours." Narita said. "It was a red book."

"I don't remember," said Antonia, adamant.

"This is for you," their father said, and handed Narita an object. She looked down. It was a hymnal, bound in red, the kind they sang from at the Presbyterian church. It was so typical of him, such a sentimental thing to do. She held on to it, not wanting to offend him, and Naia twisted around in her arms, trying vainly to see what the flat, red thing was all about.

The security guard called out again. At last she eased the baby into her sister's arms. She remembered how warm and smooth and damp Naia was, how soft her cheek felt, how precious her skin looked: as pale and fragile as the inner layers of an onion.

At the foot of the stairs, she looked back. Her family had moved to a spot by the terminal wall, almost lost in the confusion of well-wishers flush up against the wire fence, and they were all waving good-bye, Antonia with her bandaged fist, Naia with her jasmine hands.

Fifteen

"YOU HAVE BEEN home two whole days," Daniel said. "It's ridiculous for you and Naia to be acting this way."

"I'm not the one carrying on the cold war," Narita told him. "Naia avoids me. I've had glimpses of her, once, twice. She slips out here to get some food, then goes back into her room. What does she do in there, anyway?" She stared at her father, trying to visualize him as a stranger might. He was a sad, slow-moving man, with a smile she'd grown to think of as apologetic, though perhaps *diplomatic* would have been the right word to describe his smile and his nature all these years.

He used to lecture to his students wearing the benevolent expression of one of those plaster saints at the Donostia cathedral. At other times, as enthusiasm got the better of him, his voice would rise in a tenor almost painful to the ear, then boom out in release so that, true to his surname, he seemed to be preaching hellfire from the pulpit. A fair amount of theatrics was demanded of Sweethaven's professors. It impressed the students. It communicated authority. Narita and Antonia had themselves absorbed hours of those lectures. That had been in the span of time when they were too young to stay home by themselves but the family was between maids. Their father would babysit them by plunking them down at the back of his classroom. Once the picture books had been leafed through, the seed pods collected from the flowering weeds on the walkway outside, the sheets of paper scribbled over, there was nothing to do but squirm in the worn wooden chairs. No matter how closely Narita listened to Daniel's words, she couldn't crack them. It was hard to believe this was the same father who produced animal sounds and farting noises at dinner to make them scream.

She wondered whether he had believed in God at all. He had always gone to the Sweethaven church, that white edifice facing the harbor, a space that echoed with the chitter of nesting birds. She wondered how often her mother accompanied him there nowadays. Luth had grown up Catholic and converted for his sake, but for as long as Narita could remember, she would cross herself and mutter under her breath before embarking on a journey, even a half hour's drive to a friend's house, on the feast day of a saint.

It was close to midnight now. They were in the kitchen, the coolest place in the house, shielded from the sun most of the day by the mango tree. Insects beat at the fluorescent bar over their heads. Narita had showered three times that day, but was perspiring again. April! She held her breath every time her father came too close. He had grown odoriferous over the years, like an old dog sloughing off skin, nursing a mouthful of bad teeth.

A cellular phone chirped from the direction of Naia's room. The girl's in-box had received a new text message. She got plenty of those; they annoyed Narita. Who were these friends, this unknown support system of hers? They seemed more plentiful after 11:00 p.m., when the house was supposed to be asleep; Narita had an image of scrawny, effeminate boys crowding round the drum majorette to pinch her and giggle and squawk good-natured obscenities in her ear.

"I *would* cut the Internet connection to her room," she went on. The household subscribed to broadband, and Naia had appropriated the modem for herself. A trail of wires led from the living room to her bedroom. Someone had duct-taped them down to the floor, so now the hallway resembled the stage of a dingy Quezon City bar when some band or other was performing for the evening.

"We thought of taking away her cell phone," Daniel replied. "And the Internet connection as well. But none of those gadgets are ours, Narita. Antonia pays for them. Antonia bought her that computer, too. Pays all her bills. Every luxury Naia possesses, every gadget, was arranged for by Antonia. The Net, the phone — they're the only ways those two can communicate. We didn't have the heart to cut Naia off. We figured the state she is in is enough punishment already."

Enough punishment. Narita couldn't fathom the contradictions in him: beloved by his students, henpecked by his wife, outrageously fire-and-brimstone in his values, despite the tentative little smile.

"You know," he said — he was smiling now — "out of all the people in the world, you are the one she wants most at this very moment."

"Don't be stupid, Pa," she snorted.

"You share a bond that cannot be replaced — "

"She hates me. She only wants Antonia."

" — because you are her mother."

Narita sighed. "Look, it's late. Why don't you go to bed? I don't need you to play middleman."

Fortunately, he did not protest at this; he could be quite tiresome when he felt slighted. When he had shuffled off, she lifted the lid off the bowl of hot food he had left behind. It was stew made of mongo beans with a couple of soup bones in it, simple fare that he had said was Naia's favorite. Every night since she had been expelled from school he had assembled a meal for her.

Narita cut the light in the kitchen and lay down on the living room couch. Twelve o'clock passed. She felt herself dropping off. A door opened. Behind closed lids, she sensed a change in the light. The kitchen was illuminated. The refrigerator shut with a muted thump, a chair squealed on the floor.

Naia sat at the table eating great spoonfuls of her dinner. She glanced up in astonishment as her mother entered, then shrank into herself, like a mimosa folding up its leaves when touched.

Narita hadn't meant to look so implacable, or to stare so hard. When she drew up a chair opposite the girl's, Naia took off, leaving the food.

She was maybe five foot four — taller than Narita, at any rate — and already possessed that slender roundness that happens to a woman's figure for a span of a few years in adolescence, never to return. She wore a pair of cotton shorts and a little T-shirt decorated with a heart in pink studs, right over where her own would be.

In the hallway the girl paused, weighing her choices, then came back to the kitchen. She hunched her shoulders, as though to protect her prettiness — naturally pale skin, a hint of down over the arms — from her mother's gaze. As she paused directly under the fluorescent bar, Narita realized that the buoyancy she'd been expecting, the glow that came with good health, was absent from Naia's face. The white light from overhead brought out the heavy shadows beneath her eyes. Her hair, long, black, and so fine it looked wet, fanned out over her collarbones, too limp to hide the rash of tension pimples at her jawline. Pimples, thought Narita — and they had always been flawless of skin in their family. Her chin was a little *v*, startling on a face her mother had always remembered as round.

"What are you doing here, Ma?" she said. "How long are you staying this time?"

She had a tough, gravelly voice, like a girl who spends a lot of time cheering at basketball games. She had always sounded that way, even as a child.

"I've come for you," Narita replied. "I want to take you back to Manila."

Naia laughed, short and disbelieving. She did it with her mouth open and twisted, tossing her hair over one shoulder. Narita cringed from the sound, for it was a whore's laugh, and the little trick with the hair was something the fast girls used to do back when she was in high school.

"Fat chance," she said. "You've been promising me that for years. You said that to me in grade two."

"This time I'll do it."

"What are you going to do, kidnap me?"

In the next unlucky moment, Naia's mobile phone chirped. She drew it out of her pocket and examined the message on the screen. Her contempt for the sender was obvious, but nonetheless she turned away from her mother and began to tap out a reply with her thumb.

"Hey," Narita said.

The girl ignored her.

"Hey!" she repeated, too harshly. "We're not done here."

"Well, I am," Naia snapped, storming back to her room, and this time she didn't return.

NARITA sat, too numb to cry, and her thoughts turned to her father. Why did he persist in his pathetic efforts to reconcile them, telling her good things about Naia, giving her false hope? The girl had blanked out all memories she had had of her mother, ignored all sacrifices made for her as she grew up.

Whose daughter was she, really? Narita thought. She resembled Antonia, truly, but in her face her mother could clearly see the features of the boy who had betrayed her. It was said in these parts that if a baby looked like its father, the mother's love for him was greater than his love for her. Only the women of an earlier society could have devised that rule, Narita thought bitterly. Such malice, so typical.

The first time she set eyes on Zenon she was nineteen, a college senior. She was minding the English department office over lunch break. Her dad was the chairman. This gave certain privileges: she and Antonia could come in when the place was deserted and read with the air-conditioning going full blast. That day, Narita was alone, her dad at some faculty meeting, and she had left the door unlocked. In came a slender but strong-framed boy in jeans and a white T-shirt. He went straight up to the desk where she sat, moving in a way that was rapid and a bit alarming. She was annoyed rather than menaced. He stood over her and fixed her with a very intense, direct stare and then asked, in the roughest Binisaya accent possible, "*Ma'am*, are you open?"

In retrospect, he must have been frightened and desperate: he was flunking a literature course that term. She didn't yield, or make things better for him. "No. Students not allowed. Wait outside till one."

Of course she was a student herself, and not authorized to mind the office, but she and Antonia considered the university their home, and their dad's workplace an extension of their living room. She didn't think much of the young men and women who came to Sweethaven from different parts of the Visayas, and this one's sense of entitlement and superiority got under her skin. *Are you open*, indeed. Ha. Well, for eyes like that she would always be open.

It wasn't until the following semester that she saw him again. They were taking a literature class together. It was the same course he had flunked. Zenon sat in the back, in his plain white T-shirt, among the older, shabbier boys, the ones who were taking the course a second or third time in order to graduate. She came in late and proud of it, taking the seat next to him. The class tittered. He didn't notice her entrance, intent as he was on what he was writing, and she saw at once that he was left-handed. He had laid his notebook on the armrest of the empty chair beside his, and he wrote in so confined and intense a manner that the whole chair shuddered with each stroke. The notebook was made entirely of graphing paper. He was going to be an engineer. She loved that immediately, his competence, his diligence. He was always punctual, always took notes.

And yet he managed to flunk pretty much everything that came his way. Maybe he had smoked too much marijuana and his wiring was shot. They read bits of Shakespeare that semester. Standing up in the center of the classroom, she was Juliet and he Romeo, meeting for the first time, the coy lines forming a perfect sonnet. Zenon turned a delightful shade of red. Each time he opened his mouth, the class shrieked with laughter. It was his accent. His vowel sounds were unsophisticated — in fact, he could make only three. It sounded nothing like English. Beneath the gale of hilarity, no one heard her speak.

Possibly, he was just stupid.

He rode a motorcycle to class, which in a private school like Sweethaven was not special. He didn't own the bike; he borrowed it once in a while from a friend, and it was a humble Honda 70, poor relation to the Vespa. It didn't matter. A motorcycle meant freedom, aimless joyrides around the city. She thought she might seduce him. His speech annoyed her, but she made herself deaf to it. He had read so few books, though she was glad to learn that he liked the same adventure movies, more or less. Antonia was appalled when she found out. "*That's* your boy toy, that *Rambo* fan, that's your stud?"

He kissed like an animal. Without preamble, without apology. A tongue-sucker: he made the back of her throat ache from the strain. He said he was a virgin, and she wanted to believe him but couldn't, because he was too good-looking and too cavalier about the claim. He'd gone to a Catholic boys' high school. His whispered love talk was straight out of the Betamax movies he had spent his boyhood watching. They went all the way at long last during midterms week, in his boardinghouse, where the residents could do as they pleased. He had his own bedroom, and his own cassette player, useful to mask the sounds they made. He was turning eighteen the following day. "Advance happy birthday," she told him. She thought she might remind him that it was her first time, the best present any teenage boy could ask for, but she didn't want to rub in the fact. When she opened her eyes she found the sheet streaked with her blood.

"Oh, shit," he said. "Who's going to wash this?"

So they declared themselves in love. They talked about the future, passionately; kicked around the notion of having children; dreamt aloud about the things they would have someday. He wanted a bigger motorcycle. She wanted her own computer. They rode down to the beach by the airport and watched the jet from Manila come in, followed an hour later by the propeller plane from Cebu. He mentioned, idly, that the city could not stay backward forever, that the airport must expand. Or he himself must advance, haul himself out of the sinkhole that was Donostia. He was the exact opposite of Antonia, who wanted everything to stay just as it was.

They imagined what it would be like to run away.

Four weeks of that, and then he changed. He was handsome and never easy to control to begin with, and she began to perceive that he was no longer attracted to her body. He was done with her. When she called him at his boardinghouse, it took him ten minutes to come to the phone, and throughout the wait she fancied she could hear his housemates snickering. She began to suspect the woman teachers of ulterior motives; she set her eyes on girls who were taller or shapelier or fairer-skinned, and began to imagine each of them pursuing Zenon, though he had never laid eyes on them. She supposed it was she who hit him first, a wide, theatrical slap to begin with. But then they began to hit each other on a regular basis, making up just as violently afterward. One afternoon they fought at the beach, pelting each other with handfuls of sand. He had unearthed some tale of her wild high school days. "You weren't a virgin," he accused. "I bled!" she said, weeping. "Hymens grow back," he said obstinately. She snatched up a stub of coral and, clamping his hand to her thigh, scored his forearm with it. Blood welled up along the cut. Zenon blinked back tears. They waited, in conspiracy, for darkness to fall, and then he dragged her across the sand to the rest house they had rented, and he had her up against one of the bamboo posts. He was out of condoms; they were tempting fate. Zenon was actually crying. "You don't know how much I adore you." The sex was explosive, of course, given the buildup. "I love these rape games," she said.

FOR years after she'd moved to Manila, she dreamt of him, allowing him to sneak under the covers with her, late at night, when the world was asleep and she had only herself to account for. At first the thoughts filled her with guilt, then she resigned herself to them, and then he became an old and familiar lover, who forgave her every pore and stretch mark. They had known each other for the span of a single semester, had lain together for less than that. So she used this irrevocable absence to get to know him better. She didn't know how many times she created the moment when they would see each other again. Sometimes she stumbled after him, pleading, a romantic heroine: tears and streaming hair — the works. At others, she rolled him beneath the sole of her hobnail boots. Each encounter ended in sex. When one fantasy had exhausted itself, she turned over in her narrow bed and started on another. She tracked him down to an apartment in Marikina; she met him in the kitchen of their empty house. She encountered him at the funeral of her parents; he came to the funeral of Antonia; he showed up at *her* funeral, gazing into her casket while bouquets of red roses opened simultaneously about them, filling the chapel with their scent.

PERHAPS if she'd devoted more of each night to sleeping she would have done better at her jobs. She alternated between the newsprint women's magazines and the daily papers, editorial assistant here, writer there, staying no more than a year each time. One year, right after an election, the paper she was employed at closed. The candidate who owned it had lost his bid; no funds were left; the paper's reason for being was no more. She came straight home to Sweethaven, armed with gifts.

"Are you really staying this time?" her mother said cautiously, as she set up her computer in her old bedroom.

She wasn't sure; she'd left her résumé in various offices around Manila; in a couple of weeks she would be making a stream of long-distance calls to follow up.

"Well, think your decision through," she said. "This confusion can't be good for Naia."

Ah, Naia. What miraculous transformations had taken place in her absence. Naia was a restless, long-legged little girl with huge eyes and a deep, scratchy voice. She made boats and kites out of paper, stole every roll of tape in the house, had stamped her name on five different pairs of scissors. Entering a room, she left it in shambles: cushions on the floor, wads of paste on the sofa, doll limbs and hair ornaments and colored felt-tip pens on every available surface. She and Antonia had made up a series of nonsense melodies, one for each of the dogs, it seemed, and whooping and gazing into each other's faces, they would sing at the top of their lungs.

She, at seven, had the most amazing whiskey laugh, sensual and adult, filled with promise, heard in every room of the house.

Antonia she called Tita, and nothing else after that; it made sense, for she knew of no other aunts.

Her mother she called Narita.

"That's Mommy!" Antonia exclaimed, scandalized.

"No," Naia said, frowning. "She's not a mommy. She doesn't even live here."

"Give it some time," Antonia said when she and Narita were alone.

One evening, as Narita tried to work, laughter and a scandalous splashing from the bathroom intruded on her thoughts. She leapt up in annoyance, her chair thudding back against the wall. Distractions in the news room she could cope with — the explosions of temper from the direction of the editor-in-chief's desk, the boys from layout arriving with pages for her to check. But this — this low, vital child's voice, the squeals and giggles from Antonia, the snatches of meaningless words in their private language — all these sent a wave of pure jealousy through her, and the sentences curdled in her mind before she could even tap them out on her keyboard.

She had been writing a feature on Donostia as it faced the coming millennium. It was a feature she hoped to sell to one of a score of magazines that had cropped up with the desktop publishing boom in the capital. And now, suddenly, she realized she did not care about the new Internet café that had sprung up outside the Sweethaven gates, nor about the mobile phones that more and more people were brandishing like phasers in their own private blockbuster movies. In the same moment she realized that no one else in the world cared, either. Technology was advancing at the same pace all over. There was nothing enviable or indeed distinguished about the little city where she had grown up.

Enraged with herself, she flung her bedroom door open, in time to catch a small, pale figure as it flashed down the hall, wet hair flying, sturdy thighs pumping — leaving a trail of water drops and wet footprints all over the living room. Investigating, she found it had balled itself giggling and naked in a corner of the couch. Antonia stood over it, wielding, of all things, a toothbrush. As she watched, her younger sister unfolded Naia, parted the strings of wet hair over her face, and slipped the business end of the toothbrush between the unprotesting jaws.

"That's the weirdest thing I've ever seen," Narita exclaimed.

"What?" snapped Antonia, jolted out of the ritual. "That I brush my child's teeth for her?" With a sure hand Antonia maneuvered the instrument over Naia's molars. "I just want to be sure it's done right."

My child's teeth, thought Narita. Antonia hadn't realized what she'd just said.

Give it time.

But there was to be no further time, for, a week later, a news daily called. The new owner was replacing the entire central desk to avert future mutinies, and could she start at once?

"It means more freebies." She shrugged, packing up her gear once again.

"We have enough exotic soap," Antonia said.

Sixteen

BUT IT WAS unfair. Narita *had* taken care to remember them, every few months and at birthdays and Christmas, in envelopes stuffed with money, and boxfuls of clothes and toys. Like a secret disease, Naia had sapped her, prevented her from choosing the kind of jobs she would have wanted — she would have liked a nest egg somehow, to rely on while she waited for a good position, one in Makati or Ortigas, to open up. Instead, she had always been a paycheck shy of being turned out of her apartment.

With the years, Antonia became caustic. She had long abandoned all hopes of working abroad; her life, as she wrote Narita, revolved around her surrogate daughter. She was so busy, she admitted, that she had no more time to paint.

Then she was a secretary for one of the Sweethaven administrators, a terrific strain on her; she was by nature such an introvert, and accustomed to being served. She strove to be pleasant and memorize everyone's names and titles. She made coffee. The determinedly wholesome chatter, the watchful humility that pervaded the culture of Sweethaven — all were a torment.

When she was deemed to have gotten enough education, she started teaching basic humanities courses, following a track that was well beaten by the time her father had first set foot on it thirty years before. It was a life that pleased everyone, a dignified and low-risk life.

And then came the day when she surprised Narita with a phone call at work, saying she was in Manila and could they meet for coffee? The hotel Antonia named was cheap and rather disreputable, in the Ermita district. Narita passed it often, those days when she walked partway to work for the exercise. She had never been inside — she'd marked it as a place where malnourished women in animal-print leotards had profitable sex with their towering Caucasian escorts.

Antonia was seated at a table off the lobby. The younger woman had gained a little more weight, and because her hair had been lightened to an odd tea brown, her complexion seemed a bit dusky, an adjective that would never have applied before. She looked ... well, like a schoolteacher who, after the milestone of thirty, had started to let it all go. In a few more years she would be a minor version of their mother.

What was going on? People who worked in Sweethaven didn't just step into airplanes. They couldn't afford it, not even the budget fares. She must have been planning this trip for weeks. It occurred to Narita that Antonia might be ill, that she might be in the capital to see some specialist. Her mind leapt, fleetingly, to breast cancer, heart disease.

The mystery was solved in a trice.

"I'm leaving the country," Antonia declared. "This time it's for real."

At this revelation, relief and the old envy swamped Narita, and she realized she would always greet good news from her sister with ill will. She knew that several times Antonia had sent out to various universities in America for brochures on graduate programs. So she had won a scholarship at last. Narita hoped, for her sake, that it was a long-term, generous one.

"Congratulations." She smiled to cover these shameful thoughts.

Antonia leaned in, as though the people at the next table might be remotely interested in her life, and whispered, "I'm getting married. He's from Finland. His name's Lasse Hakkinen."

Narita's mouth popped open. "Lasa?" she said.

"I guess." Antonia grinned self-consciously. "I suppose. I can't really pronounce it myself."

Narita sought desperately to conceal her shock. Shock, and something else: a treacherous flicker of satisfaction. A white fiancé was *not* good news. She hoped her sister would not notice. She knew she was being prejudiced, but she didn't care.

"How did you meet him?"

"On the Internet. We've been corresponding for years."

"For God's sake, Antonia, please don't tell me he's some old — "

"Oh, he has children," her sister said, having anticipated the question, it seemed. "He has a handsome son."

"Oh Jesus. Finland — and I suppose his son's called, what, Nokia?"

"Urho," Antonia said pettishly. "It's a very famous name."

It was too much: the news, the situation, the very opaqueness of the language that had spawned those strange syllables.

"Why didn't you tell me?"

Antonia shrugged. "What good would it do? I knew you would have done your best to discourage us."

"Why a *puti*, for God's sake?"

"Why not?"

"What did Mother say?"

From Antonia's silence, Narita realized she had come in on the tail end of some dire family drama. She was furious. How could her sister have kept her engagement a secret? How was Naia taking it?

But part of her anger had to do with the sheer surprise of it. Antonia was not a people person. She wasn't supposed to get married — certainly not before Narita did. That was an accepted fact that went all the way back to their childhoods. Narita was the wicked rebel; Antonia the grim introvert. If the latter confided anything lengthy and intimate, it was to the safety of a diary — increasingly, scathing dialogues with herself. As she learned the formulas for pleasing teachers, collecting As with minimal study and a smile, Antonia curled herself inward, selecting her friends from the books she read and the movies she saw. Even now, her letters, so self-absorbed, were a torture to read.

"Do you *love* this guy, Antonia?"

The younger woman acted as if she hadn't heard the question; and perhaps she hadn't, because it was at that moment that the waiter arrived with Narita's order and another slice of cake. And when the sisters had settled down once more, Antonia began to talk about other things.

"Father's been diagnosed with diabetes. His cholesterol levels are way up. To look at him, you'd never suspect it; that's one benefit of having a skinny frame. Mother's cholesterol's up, too, by the way. They're so stubborn. Won't exercise. He sits in front of his computer for hours. She vegetates in front of the TV."

Narita didn't know what to reply. She refused to feel guilty.

"They're old, that's all."

"They're ill. That's that. And they're expensive."

"What are you saying?"

"All I know is that one of us had better start earning in foreign currency soon."

This was too much. Antonia had no right to judge Narita's life and career, especially since she, wasting her talent, had made so little of hers. Narita very nearly got up to leave, but something — pity, or curiosity — kept her silent and in her chair.

"When are you going?" she managed to say.

Antonia clamped her lips together and averted her gaze to the entrance of the hotel, where a couple had just entered. Narita wished she could honestly say that in that moment her sister looked dreamy and hopeful, walking on air, but her expression was the same one their mother had worn, at cash registers, digging into her purse for stray peso coins as the counter girls waited. She turned to look at the couple that had seemingly caught Antonia's attention: a little Filipina and a white man, much, much older, holding hands. They were speaking to one another, their words lost in the rumble of street noise that entered the lobby with them. It was plain neither was comfortable with the language they had chosen; it was also plain to Narita that the transaction was temporary, a few hours or a few days at most. But to humor her sister, she said, "There goes another lucky lady, preparing to ship out."

"Lucky, sure, with that face."

"You could sketch her on the tablecloth," Narita quipped, but Antonia wasn't biting.

"Some get sent back."

"Some do."

"In a box."

"Good God. Why think of those things at this time?"

Anyway, it was the maids in the Middle East, Narita thought distractedly, the Ginza district entertainers, who came back in caskets. The Internet brides, the mail-order women, they did return, eventually, but with their clumsy husbands, their yellow-skinned children in tow. It was amazing what powers of transformation a half-breed toddler wrought. A brown woman accompanying a white man was nothing but a whore. Add a child, and suddenly the union was legit — suddenly he was a devoted husband and she the affluent, deft, and generous wife.

HER ordeal did not end there, for just then the elevator doors opened and out strode a man. He was of average height for a white fellow and was somewhere in his late fifties, which seemed a very unsurprising age for a white fellow in this part of the world. He wore shorts and sandals and an appallingly patterned cotton shirt. At least, she thought, he still has all his hair. What was so alien about his appearance? Meeting a foreigner, she did the usual spot check — pink skin, blue eyes, impossible height. And of course, the nose, but she'd be damned if she admitted to her colleagues, let alone her sister, that she coveted a tiny triangular nose, sharp enough to open mail with.

But the eyes were a safe enough fetish. Few could refute the rarity of blue. Even caustic teenage Antonia, constructing the husband she would have someday, had wanted blue eyes. But what color? Cornflower, Prussian, cobalt? They searched their memories of their Crayola boxes, those pure hues that they had held over the stove, for the thrill of watching them melt. "Gas-flame blue," Antonia had giggled at last. "Burning bright."

Lasse Hakkinen stood there in his tallness and his pinkness and in the preciousness of his eyes. He was looking in the wrong direction, toward the entrance, and then he spotted the sisters and came toward their table. He was not smiling. He seemed displeased, actually, or maybe the air-conditioning wasn't strong enough. Antonia introduced them. Narita shook the sweating hand. She didn't remember what any of them said. The softness with which her sister spoke seemed forced, and the smile wavered at the corners of her mouth. She realized that Antonia was ashamed. Or was she — didn't she seem, after all, to relax, to gaze up at her fiancé in bliss?

But as Narita bade them good-bye, Antonia leaned over as if to kiss her sister's cheek, and whispered, "Oh, darling, I am enjoying, I am enjoying." She giggled. Narita felt sick.

TWO MONTHS later, her visa approved, Antonia flew. She stayed with Narita the week of her departure, as though guilty for having kept her life a secret from her sister for so long. Perhaps she had been hoping for connection, some rekindling of that bond from their childhood, some mention of the teenagers they had been, even. But Narita was at work for the better part of the day, and six days a week at that.

But they did have the mornings together. Narita would awaken at ten, as people who work on newspapers often do, to find that Antonia had laid the table for breakfast and that the rice was warming in the cooker. She would make tea and cook some eggs and garlic sausages, and she did all this professionally and without spilling anything. Narita kept up her token protests about the food, saying she would gain weight, and each time, her sister would chuckle and say, "What's a couple of pounds?" And then they would sit down to eat. Afterward, the meal cleared, they would linger over more coffee, as their parents had done every Saturday when the two girls were children.

Narita pointed this out, thinking it might draw one of her now-rare smiles, but instead Antonia snorted, "Huh," sounding exactly like their mother.

"You don't know what they've become," she said.

OVER the span of a week Narita came to understand this need of Antonia's to get away, get as far away from the house and Sweethaven and anything to do with being a Pastor. It was a sense of shame, of being past thirty and still living at home, husbandless and without much of an income. She did her part, Narita supposed, paying the utility bills and such, but it was not enough; to be honest, she was not a showpiece anymore. Their cousins on both sides, and many of the Sweethaven kids, were working abroad. They were nurses. They worked in old folks' homes, they taught school in inner cities where no American teacher cared to go. Antonia had tried to be a nurse, but failed; after that, their mother had dared her to be the artist she had always threatened to become; and at that, too, she had failed.

"I am like a dog," Luth would brag, "a dog who keeps silent and then, without warning, bites." Their mother had a way of talking, of spacing her words (with a glint of malice in the eye) so that her victims, powerless to walk away, could only listen for the words that they knew were coming. At last she had informed Antonia, "You live here on sufferance." Except she said it in Tagalog, to cheapen the younger woman — *Nakikitira ka lang dito.*

"The fuck with you," Antonia had screamed at her. "Why don't you go to America yourself?"

"And then I saw how frightened mother was," Antonia said. "I saw that for all her bossiness and bullying, that was all she was, an old woman balanced on the Pastor family pedestal, afraid of tipping over."

"WHAT'S going to happen to Naia?" Antonia said on one of those mornings, and there was such grief and regret in her voice that Narita couldn't speak, and sat there stirring her coffee and hoping that the moment would soon pass. She thought of the younger woman packing the battered overnight bag she had been carrying at the airport, trying to decide which of her clothes might be worthy of a Finnish summer, knowing at last that whatever choices she made would be irrelevant. Turning a book over and over in her hands, and then a watercolor set that had never been opened, and then an album of photos. Take nothing with you. Leave everything behind.

Naia had been impatient to get to band practice the morning of Antonia's departure. It was her first year in the band, and although she wasn't particularly talented on any instrument, they had given her one of the glockenspiels, mainly because she looked so cute in her little white uniform. "Give me a hug," Antonia had said, and Naia had torn away, frowning, not wanting to be late. She'd set her sights on being a majorette, and perfect attendance at practice helped a great deal.

"I'll write you a note," Antonia had promised her, with a sigh.

"You'll be back in three months!" Naia had snapped, and banged her way out the door. Separation anxiety, Antonia reasoned.

"How could you have deceived her?" Narita said, glad for a chance to pass the buck. "She's not a child anymore. She would've understood."

"No, she wouldn't. She'd have given me hell. I had to do all my surfing in secret. She thinks women who marry foreigners are all mail-order brides."

So did you, at that age, Narita thought, but held her tongue. It was all very strange.

"But she does know about ... the Finn?" she said instead.

"She thinks I'm going on a scholarship. It's better this way. She'll brag to her friends, and I'll keep my reputation." Antonia hunched her shoulders in a sheepish manner. "Lasse and I are soul mates. But no one will ever understand that. They'd all think he was some wife-beating drunk no countrywoman of his would look at. It would break our father's heart to have that kind of gossip circulating about me."

"My God, you *will* marry him."

"As soon as I'm off the plane. And then I need to file an application for residency. Don't worry, I'll come back as soon as I've raised the money."

"And now you've left the explaining to Mother."

"I think it's time you did the explaining. You are Naia's mother, after all."

Narita accepted this rebuke in silence.

Antonia's fingers closed over hers.

"Narita," she said. "I cannot tell anyone about *this*. Until it's *there*. Until it's *happened*. For luck. Luck. Do you understand?"

TWO years had passed since Antonia left. She had wanted to draft a proper letter to Naia on the flight from Donostia to Manila, but her handbag, with pen and paper, were in the overhead luggage rack. Every change in the sound of the engines had filled her with terror; she hadn't dared move.

Narita did not know when Antonia had at last summoned up the courage to write the girl, to tell her she was never coming back. She would have played safe, Narita thought — secured the bond between herself and the Finn before cautiously writing home. And when at last she made up her mind, when she knew for sure that the loneliness, the incomprehensible language, the culture of indifference, were all worth it — had she been strong enough to tell Naia outright? Did she send the news in an e-mail, an electronic greeting card, a long scrawled poem? Or had she, unable to shed the all-too-Filipino trait of vacillation, continued to give the girl hope? Narita did not know. How different their lives might have been if she'd come clean, Narita thought. A small note, a true good-bye that Naia could have kept in the bottom of a drawer or in a wallet. Or even a phone call from Narita's apartment in Manila, when toll charges would not have been an excuse. Closure. "Here," Narita might have said, picking up the receiver and forcing it into Antonia's hand. "Tell her now." But in her own distress at her sister's leaving, she had been all too eager to fill those last days in ridiculous pursuits. Shopping. Restaurant dinners paid for with her gift checks from work. "This is something you can't enjoy in Finland." The confusion of the capital city, the pollution, the murderous buses on EDSA, and Antonia's frequent embarrassments in the language, Tagalog, which in Sweethaven she had had little occasion to use.

The malls had humbled Antonia, from Shangri-La to Star, as did the scrawny well-turned-out women glimpsed behind the wheel of a late-model car. When Narita tried to explain how everyone in the city lived from paycheck to paycheck, deal to deal, their desires upgraded in proportion to their income, she gave a small lopsided smile, half of superiority, half of disbelief. They went shopping in bazaars for clothing, used and new, and although it was high summer, they found all four seasons and more among the export overruns — cheap, because in that climate few people were interested. The highlight was when Narita dove into a bin and pulled out a pair of sheepskin boots in the younger woman's size. The clothes were more than mismatched woolen seconds from China and Dri-Fit jackets off the garment mills of Luzon. They were raiments. They had power: they conferred upon Antonia an identity that was rightfully hers.

ON THE transcontinental flight, Antonia did not sleep. She sat in the twilight of the cabin, among the forms of her fellow passengers huddled beneath airline-issue blankets, and a few times thoughts of Naia crossed her mind, but her immediate reality was too exciting to ignore. She looked at the Filipino passengers, and what she felt for them was contempt. It annoyed her that she who had always been respected, an honor student and a teacher and a Pastor, was now the novice among these experienced world travelers. On her left was a seaman bound for the Middle East, on her right a loquacious janitress at a fast-food restaurant. These amiable brown-skinned folk knew the codes of this new world more thoroughly than she did. She gazed at the European passengers, and they frightened her, and fascinated her, and angered her at the same time. You have no idea who I am, she thought. You think I am like these small, hopeful forms that have finally fallen asleep to each side of me; you pass judgment on me because of the features of my face. She thought of the time she and Narita had journeyed together on the night boat to Cebu, and they had scrutinized the slumbering passengers, whispering, "Equus!" "Scabies!" "Mail-order bride!" Now she knew how it felt to be on the other side.

Her life of precariousness was only beginning. But no matter what, she was escaping, and she swore to herself she would never, ever forfeit this chance.

Seventeen

INTO THE SILENT house, the madman was speaking. Daniel was pouring his heart out to empty air, his voice rising in waves of despair and oratory.

"My dearest friend." A pregnant silence while he shot several puffs of air through his gritted teeth. "My longest and most esteemed friend and colleague. Dear friend in Christ."

There was a long pause, followed by the clack of a keyboard.

"What a day."

Luth knew this phrase. It was a refrain he might sigh out at any hour, even at eight in the morning, the syllables beautifully pronounced — a snippet of a conversation from decades before maybe, or an exclamation carefully rehearsed for some blond girl, on some warm afternoon by a brook, carefully rehearsed but never articulated.

"'What-a-day,'" he said. "'They'll-wish-they'd-never-been-born.'"

A line of dialogue from a movie perhaps, or from one of the Penguins on his many shelves.

"'I'm a stickler where right's concerned. I'm a stickler where right's concerned.'"

The syllables trailed off, then suddenly reshaped themselves into a cheerful song. Luth tried not to listen. She was bent over, her wet feet braced against sudsy floor tiles. The reek of bleach made her vision dim, but slowly and surely the mold was disappearing from Naia's bathroom walls. The wreaths of black hair obstructing the drain had been gathered up and tucked in the garbage pail.

This ought to be your job, she silently berated Narita. Of course, she could easily have handed the task over to the maid, but there was a certain comfort in her martyrdom. It strengthened her moral authority over the household.

She washed her hands and feet. Time to take a break, to give the cleaning agents time to work their way through all that organic debris.

Naia was sitting on the unmade bed, watching her forlornly.

"Thank you, Lola," she said.

Luth nodded, sat on the edge of the bed and began to towel her water-wrinkled feet dry.

"What is Mother doing here?"

She frowned, trying to decide on the best answer. It was imperative that the family cohere. "She wants to see that you are all right. Aren't you happy that she's back?"

"No. She makes me nervous. It's as if she expects some kind of performance from me."

Luth decided to ignore this. "Would you like to take a trip to Manila?"

"What is in Manila?"

Escape, Luth thought. A new life for you, a second chance. You will be sixteen in a few months. And she knows better than me how to handle an adolescent girl, or if not, it is time she learned. Yes, I am sending you away. Because I cannot go on taking care of you. For a time you helped me. You were the buffer between me and that sad, crazy man in the far room, but now it feels as though *I* have to perform for even you.

"I want to go to Aunt Antonia." Tears rolled down Naia's cheeks.

"You cannot go to Finland. There is no room for you in their house." For some time after her aunt left they had gone through this awful, rending ritual, every few days, Naia pleading, Luth explaining, until eventually the girl seemed to subside into a stony sort of acceptance. Now it was all coming back.

"Then I want to stay," sobbed Naia.

The very thought of your stealthy, treacherous life ravages my heart, she thought. Aloud, she said, "You cannot stay. You are ruined."

"Lolo says I must be brave and take my punishment."

Daniel was declaiming again, his voice, surprisingly full for such a narrow chest, booming through the wall.

"Crazy man."

"He's not crazy," Naia said.

Pain shot through Luth's left breast, so sharp and unmitigated she had to hold still, suppressing her breath until the spasm had gone.

"I know," she said gingerly, not daring to relax until she could be sure there were no further twinges. She knew the next bolt of agony could start in her head. "That's the way he's always been."

"I remember. I grew up on that." But Naia was still a child, not a grown-up. "Why is he that way?"

Luth did not know what to tell her. She had never discussed Daniel's nature outside their family, so she had no euphemisms to dignify him with. How could she explain that loquacious, vain, pathologically insecure man? He was the son of a respected Sweethaven teacher. His brothers, whom he loathed, had become doctors and moved to other cities: they never corresponded, and he was too proud to ask them for money, they who had disparaged his ambitions, saying a writer died with eyes stark and staring in an emaciated face. He had proved them wrong, he liked to crow. He'd had his moment of brilliance, of being educated overseas on several scholarships, and from the way he told it, describing what seemed to be black-tie dinners and brilliant debates in lecture halls, he had championed his countrymen admirably. Pleased with himself, he had allowed the university to lionize him, to dull and soften him. It was a haven, true to its name, where he could be certain of a modest but regular income. Where Luth's co-teachers habitually praised his brains and his education to her face, in a tone that she now suspected to have been humoring all along. Where all the young people he knew called him "sir." His daughters were the exception. She supposed he had never gotten used to the demanding way they addressed him as "Pa." At Honors Day exercises each year, he sat onstage with his colleagues in the stifling hot gymnasium, a flock of black birds in their togas and caps, each perched on a folding metal chair. The gowns were banded in velvet and satin, in the colors of emeralds and rubies and sapphires. Each swatch represented a doctorate degree from overseas. The keynote speech was always rendered by a successful alumnus, never a politician, so there were no superlatives or empty kudos, only an abstract, ascetic idealism. Leadership. Excellence. Service. Sacrifice.

What sort of life would they all have had, had he been a banker, or a rice merchant, or a prosperous farmer, shoulder to shoulder with his own laborers at planting season? Other girls were protected by a small army of husky bodies at the paterfamilias's command. But Narita and Antonia had had to fend for themselves. Just as Naia would learn to, without brothers or uncles, without henchmen on call. Had Daniel been a stronger, more awe-inspiring figure, the wall that had separated them from the rudeness of Donostia would never have been breached.

"He's like a spurned suitor," Naia said. "He can't accept that he's been dropped by his friend."

"Who do you mean?" Luth said, but in her heart she knew: Daniel had only one friend. "Why would Mr. Holland abandon your grandfather?"

The girl shrugged. "Because Rinky thinks he's superior to normal people? Just like his sons?"

Naia's eyes were huge and still, but the corners of her mouth quivered as though she were suppressing an abashed smile, the kind that begged for forgiveness and approval. Luth remembered how the child used to gaze up at her, her face angelic but with mischief at the back of her eyes, daring her to figure out what she'd been up to. The bank book stained in lipstick, the new cushions crusted over with glue. A lovely collage made from fabric, and holes cut on the fold lines of a length of pink dress cloth. Holes in the shape of hearts.

Naia's secrets, so awful and monstrous they excited her to a point beyond shame.

"What is it?" Luth said. "What else haven't you told me?"

"That day that Mother Martha came to our school. The thing that happened afterward, in the armory."

Luth felt sick.

"He wasn't a stranger."

"All right, you might as well tell me."

"I'm sorry!"

"Tell me the truth, Naia."

"It was Brent Holland." She began to weep, her eyes screwing into slits, her mouth stretching like a frog's. Runny-nosed and red-faced, she had never looked so ugly. "And he didn't rape me."

"Because you let him."

Luth realized that she had always known.

THE phone rang. Luth jumped. It was a sound that had not been heard in the house for days.

"Cecilia," she bellowed. "Who plugged in the telephone?"

There was no answer from the kitchen. The instrument kept up its nerve-shredding noise, temporarily drowning out the tune that Daniel was hissing between his teeth as he typed away. A door slammed somewhere. Narita cursed, charged out into the living room.

"Are you deaf? This thing has been ringing for one whole minute."

"Don't pick it up!" Luth warned, straining to reach the phone before her elder daughter did.

Narita glared at her. "Hello?" She was silent for a few moments, and when she spoke again, it was in Binisaya and in a high, tentative tone. "Yes, this is Naia."

Luth stood, waiting for what would happen next, her heart racing.

"My cell phone is off."

Nothing good would come of this.

"I can't be friends with someone I don't know."

"Put that thing down," Luth hissed, reaching for the hand that held the receiver, but Narita twisted out of the way:

"A *special* friend? What does that mean?"

Then an expression of astonishment came over Narita's face. Luth caught hold of her daughter's arm and wrenched the receiver from her limp hand. Poised to slam it down, she stopped — What *did* it take to be a special friend? — and allowed her own wretched curiosity to get the better of her.

It was a young man. The voice was thin and crepuscular, and an image came to her mind, an amalgam of schoolboy faces, what must have been hundreds of faces by now, all those who had exited her care and gone the way of all children.

"You can suck it," the voice was saying. "You can suck my cock. I know you're good at that. I saw what you were doing to your boyfriend. Your tongue went there and there, like a lizard's."

Luth slammed the phone down. They stood there, mother and daughter, feeling the heat creep up their spines and spread through their scalps, averting their eyes from one another in their shame.

Luth thought of the stream of messages arriving in Naia's in-box, each one heralded by an annoying two-tone peep, and how, addicted to technology, the girl could never seem to turn off her mobile phone. In the first days of the siege, Luth had assumed the calls, to the landline as well as the mobile, came from an army of peers, supporting their fallen friend with love and understanding.

THE instrument rang again.

"Answer it," Narita said.

"Don't answer it," said Luth.

"Answer it. This is your house."

"I won't. That's why it's disconnected."

"It's stupid to keep a phone you never use."

"So it was you who put the connection back on. When your father told you not to. This is your fault."

"For God's sake, Ma, you're acting like a peasant."

It hit home, whatever Narita had intended by that. Luth snatched the receiver up and tossed it at her daughter.

"*Bahala ka*! Have it your way."

"You dick cheese, you uncircumcised piece of shit," Narita hissed into the phone.

Then she went limp. "I'm sorry," she said, in a subdued and educated voice, a voice that seemed to belong to another person. "Yes, this is Naia's mother. Let me apologize again ..."

It's a lawyer, she mouthed. *Joel Fortun*.

Eighteen

HE STRODE UP to the gate like a young swain from Sweethaven's 1950s heyday. He was in khaki trousers, a button-down striped shirt, and polished loafers. He looked as if he were headed to a well-appointed office, with air-conditioning and a sweet, soft-voiced secretary to fix coffee, so that when Narita looked beyond him, to the vehicle that was parked across the road from the gate, she felt a flicker of dismay. He was driving a battered jeep, the exterior unpainted and seemingly made of beaten tin, the kind of vehicle a policeman might drive.

Her eyes met the man's. She held his gaze a moment or two longer than necessary; it was not deliberate: he had such large and sad eyes. The smile wavered at the corners of his mouth. She glanced away quickly. Her heart thudded; she swallowed hard to calm herself. It was not good to look a stranger so clearly in the eye. It led to expectations; it promised agreements that she was not ready for.

Narita let him through the gate, conscious of her mother's suspicious gaze from the safety of the house. Give it a rest, Ma, she thought. I'm an adult, I can have sex with whomever I want, but that doesn't mean I want it all the time, at the first opportunity, and with strangers, no questions asked.

The man was older than he had seemed. His hair was shot with bits of gray and he had a small paunch. There was no wedding ring, she noted briskly. He smelled good, a subtle fragrance she could not identify. She was sensitive to the way men smelled, and partial to expensive odors — they made a fellow more civilized. Had he chosen that scent for himself, or had someone given it to him in expensive black tissue paper wrapping?

As he smiled and took the hand she offered — a dry, firm grip there — she saw her mother's scrutiny in the proper light. Luth was simply desperate for one good match. For Chrissakes, Narita thought, he's *not* for me; we live in separate cities; he's left-brain; he's provincial; my English would scare him off. And Ma, the *circumstances* of this meeting — how could you even think what I know you are thinking?

"We were classmates," he said.

"Of course!" she cried, calling on her cocktail party ebullience. "In college. I remember you."

As he advanced down the driveway, she turned around to view the property, trying to see it as he did, conscious of its run-down quality. The garden seemed decent enough, the lawn mown not too many weeks before, most of the orchids in bloom. She did not know their names, saw only charming clusters of burgundy and peach floating above straplike leaves that looked like palm fronds. In the center of the lawn was a set of newly painted metal furniture. No one could accuse the Pastor family of being poor.

Naia had curled herself up in one of those metal chairs, her back to the gate, her face bent over a magazine. It was a twenty-year-old copy of *Tiger Beat*. Narita had done what she could, years ago, to improve the girl's reading tastes, sending her the Harry Potter books and a couple of Tolkiens, but there had been an unspoken rejection in Naia's shy promise to read them when summer rolled around, if and when she would have the time.

Out there in the pale house dress she had outgrown, she looked pathetically small and vulnerable. How many days had it been since she had gone out of this enclosure? She was absolutely forbidden to go downtown, out of the gate even.

"Naia, get in the house; people will see you," Luth called from a window.

Narita heard footfalls in the dust and turned. Several women were shuffling past the gate, heading toward the seashore. Two were in their forties, one in her teens. Inhabitants of the shanties close by the beach, from their clothes and the dusty quality of their skin. Their heads were turned toward the property, and their faces bore uniform expressions of curiosity at the sight of the girl, and the lawyer in his preppie clothing. When they registered Narita's challenging gaze, two of them lowered their eyes in mock deference, whispering to each other, but the third gave her a slow, knowing smile.

"Hello, Naia," the lawyer was saying, choosing a chair at a right angle to hers so she would not have to face him.

The girl regarded him as though there were nothing extraordinary about the circumstances of this visit. Then she looked away, her eye caught by movement among the orchids: a cat was perched on one of the supporting tree stumps and was eyeing her with malice.

"I'm Joel," he said. "We haven't met, but I've been here before."

She nodded. After a few beats she opened her lips. He leaned forward to catch the faint words that emerged from her throat.

"I saw you from my window," she said.

"Okay," he said in reassuring tones. "Well, Naia, I'm here. You sent me a text message, but when I called the house it was your mother who answered, and we had a short ... exchange."

Narita, taking the lawn seat opposite the girl, flushed.

"Now I'm here, in the flesh."

"I think I can help you," Naia said softly. "You want a personal account from one of the ... actresses in that video, don't you?"

"I don't want you to use that word, please, Naia. You don't have to use that word, no matter how often you hear it about you. But yes, personal knowledge from a witness is exactly what we need. So please, tell me how you came to know the boys ... Tell me about Harrison Co."

The girl's eyes widened for a moment in bewilderment.

"You don't know the name?" said Joel.

The look she shot him was one of suspicion. She shook her head sharply once, as though in annoyance.

"Tell me what you know, Naia."

Her eyes flickered up and down his person, as though she were weighing several possible outcomes if she replied.

"If I cooperate," she said at last, "do I get a reward?"

"What do you mean?"

"Do you watch crime shows? They have this thing about a witness getting some deal in return for testifying."

He gave a tight smile. "I don't think that applies to your case. A defendant in a criminal case might possibly get a lighter sentence in exchange for testifying against his co-defendants. But you're a witness. Not one of the accused."

She mulled this over. "So, no deal?" she said at last, softly.

"Not in the sense of a plea bargain ..."

She seemed disinterested in the technicality. "But you need me, I think. What I know is important to you. You don't really have anyone else."

She sat back and waited for this to register with him. His face was a mask of professionalism. This might have disappointed her, for she pressed on, "Fine. I will testify, Mister Joel."

He was silent for a few heartbeats. When he spoke, his voice was gentle, the words slow and evenly spaced. "Your decision makes me very happy, Naia. But are you sure you have come to it of your own accord? Has anyone forced you? Are you aware what testifying will demand of you?"

She shrugged. "It will be a great scandal. Worse than it is already. But we'll get used to it." She glanced rather challengingly at Narita.

"You will be seated in a room filled with men," said Joel. "The video will be played. You will be made to point out which of those … lascivious images are of your body. People will make insulting remarks. They will be looking at you to see if you show any shame."

The girl, though she sat easily and spoke in a gentle voice, had never seemed more stubborn. "I won't be, sir. Not in the least bit."

"That won't be good, Naia."

She frowned at him in puzzlement, a good child who had, up to that moment, been doing her utmost to be cooperative.

"'It is inconceivable that an innocent Filipina girl, modest and traditional in her values, would fabricate a rape charge, thus exposing herself and her family to ridicule,'" he quoted. "That's a line from our jurisprudence, Naia, but I would say it would apply here as well. It means that the braver you are, the bolder, the more casual about your horrible experience, the more scheming you will appear to a judge."

She didn't seem to understand. "I'm a majorette, sir. I may not be the prettiest, but I'm never shy before a crowd."

"You will be asked whether you were … turned on. They will demand that you describe how sexual arousal feels, to check your references. They will sympathize with you only as a victim, and you cannot be a victim unless you were forced." The strain was showing in his voice now. "If you are cross-examined, the lawyers from the other side will question your credibility. They will try to paint you as a dishonest woman, a loose woman, a whore."

"I never received money for what I did."

"People never stick to the dictionary definition of a word, Naia. You know that."

They stared into each other's eyes, the man's jaw tense, the girl's face bland and implacable.

"You are so young," he said. "And you have grown up among such intellectual, sophisticated, Westernized people."

He glanced at Narita, to see if the flattery met her approval. Naia, too, shot her mother a sidelong look, as if for explanations.

"So you probably don't know that there are men out there, lawyers like myself even, who perceive the enjoyment of sex … by a woman … as unnatural, as something humorous, something to be mocked."

He was sweating profusely, his face dark with embarrassment. Narita felt sorry for him. He looked so handsome, so distinguished, that he couldn't possibly be a jerk. But she knew from experience that the well-turned-out men who had clawed their way up from obscurity were the worst.

"Once you submit your testimony, Naia, there will be no backing down."

"My grandfather says this is the one honest way to get justice, sir," the girl said.

"I hope you're not doing this to please him," Joel said.

She ignored him. "But in return, sir, may I have something? I need a visa to join my aunt, sir. Can you help me? Or maybe the mayor can. My grandparents tell me he's a very rich and influential man. Could he lend me the money for an airline ticket? I can pay him back when I start to work."

"Yes, yes, of course," said Joel. He sat there — waiting, it seemed, for Naia to begin her story, his mouth stretched into a tentative smile.

But the girl refused to yield. In the same unruffled tone, she began to outline travel costs and immigration procedures, step by objective step. It would be important to reserve her ticket well in advance, taking advantage of off-season rates, she asserted. Narita realized that she had been doing tons of research online.

First of all, a passport, came the soft, steady voice. Then a letter of invitation from Tita Antonia. She was confident she would get this; but if the Finns didn't think Antonia was a credible enough sponsor, then her husband, Lasse, must be persuaded to sign one. Did Joel have a contact at the Finnish embassy, someone who would move her up the line a little? The mayor had said, on TV, that he would do anything he could to help the three girls involved, rebuild their shattered lives. Naia's life *wasn't* all that shattered, but she did intend to collect on the mayor's promise, and she missed her aunt, who had promised to send for her as soon as she was settled.

The lawyer's throat worked. "I'll do my best," he said at last.

"Thank you," Naia smiled. "Mother," she addressed Narita for the first time. "Will you remind Mr. Joel tomorrow?"

Then she rose, folding up her magazine.

"The boy — " he said, but she had already slipped into the house.

Narita and Joel gaped at one another.

"The mayor didn't actually say that about the tickets," she said at last.

"Oh, he did," Joel admitted. "Sort of."

"How sensitive of him," she sneered. "Where does he plan to get all that money?"

"He's a very rich man. And he has his pork barrel fund."

"What did he say — get these cunts out of my city?"

Joel's embarrassment was obvious; his face turned a definite shade of purple. It did not help that their eyes chanced to meet once more. He dropped his gaze at once.

She felt sorry for him then. She wanted to tell him that she knew what it was like to work for an impossible boss — to be a scapegoat, a whipping boy. That she had no idea who Naia had taken after, that this cunning child was a stranger. Instead, she said, "She had an encounter of sorts last year."

"With whom?" said Joel, alert again.

"Oh," she sighed. "Someone from Sweethaven. A classmate, a teacher, a coach maybe. Someone from the high school. It was my mother she told."

His expression was one of surprise, dismay.

"Look," she said. "If this is the first time you're hearing about it, don't blame my folks. This happened months ago. They're old. They're blurry with details."

"Narita," he said. "What exactly did Mrs. Pastor tell you?"

For one moment she wondered whether she ought to play games with him, as the girl had done. But her life was complicated enough. "Joel, I don't want to get anyone innocent into trouble," she said. "You ought to ask her yourself, though I doubt she would tell you outright." She wanted to add that Luth was strange, bitter, apt to let the oddest things fly. "Ask around. I'll bet you know who Naia's classmates are already. Talk to her friends. Ask them if they noticed anything around the time last year that Naia was suspended from the marching band."

His eyes were shining with fresh hope.

"Maybe she had a secret boyfriend. If you can find the man, find the connection, you won't need my daughter. You can prosecute the case, and I'll get her out of the way for you, bring her to Manila; it won't cost the mayor a cent." She knew she was torpedoing Naia's plans, taking away something the girl had staked her whole future on, but she was desperate. "Get your hands on some evidence. Raw video," she went on. "E-mails. The insides of a computer. Anything."

They fell silent. Joel drew out a small appointments book from his trouser pocket and made a note on a corner of one page, with small, precise strokes.

"I will look," he said at last.

"Thank you very much, Attorney Fortun," she said.

There was a pause. Joel did not get up.

"You don't remember me, do you?"

But of course she did. She knew she had seen him before. She faltered, embarrassed, hating moments like these. The truth was, although she could put up an outgoing veneer, she cared very little about strangers, unless her sustenance depended on them.

"We were classmates one semester. Literature, world literature."

"Oh well," she said. "I've seen a lot of faces in my life. I'm a journalist, you know."

"I was a skinny, miserable boy," he said. "I was poor, very poor, or so I thought at the time. And you, you had such a full calendar, and a real social life."

She tried to laugh it off. "I was always tardy." With another sort of man she might have embarked on a triumphant reminiscence of how she had never studied, had rarely come to class for even the best teachers, how not even a finals exam could persuade her to come to school on time. But something in his melancholy checked her. He would not have understood why, despite her indifference, she had collected an A-minus average over the three years of her education. He looked to be a man who had strived, who had never taken success for granted, who had pored over *How to Increase Your Word Power* far into the night in an effort to better himself.

"I sat at the back of the classroom," Joel said. "With the drug addicts, with the smart alecks. I was a smart aleck, too, a moron quoting Guns N' Roses. You talked to me two times that semester."

"Oh?" she said politely.

"You had your eye on my seatmate, Zenon Cuaresma."

At that moment his phone rang. He rose, moved in the direction of the gate, almost as though it were some secret lover on the line. She was grateful for this; it gave her time to get over her surprise.

When he returned, she could tell his thoughts were elsewhere. Her life had ground to a halt upon his visit, and for the past half hour, he had been the single most significant person in it. But the reality was she was but an appointment on his engagement pad, one of many throughout the day. "It's my father's birthday," he said with some embarrassment. "My mother always makes a big family dinner on the day itself, never mind that he's passed on."

Then came the self-conscious scramble to exchange contact data — the totality of numbers and addresses that made up their various selves — hauling out their mobile phones and keying in what the other dictated.

She scrutinized him with a new wariness as he crossed the road to his jeep. So Zenon had been his friend. Which one had he been? She wished she had paid more attention to the people he used to hang out with, but after she and Zenon became lovers, he seemed to lose all interest in male company. Had they discussed her, Zenon and this man? How much did he know?

Nineteen

SIESTA HOUR. The house is still. The world is still, an airless summer day, the leaves on the fruit trees shriveled. The household lies exhausted. I am the only one up and about. In your aunt's room, I lay my laptop on the desk and let it boot up. I take the video of you that I bought in Quiapo, contemplating the cover for a few moments. Why is it I feel nothing at the sight of your face? Then I slip it into the machine.

There are no credits, no cheesy shout-outs. The video opens with a young woman lying on a bed. I do not know her name. I suppose I might ask my mother, or Joel even, but cannot imagine myself doing so. Is it a bad thing, to participate in a woman's humiliation and not care to know her name? It is a round, pleasant face, certainly pretty, but not beautiful. Her naked breasts are round as well, larger than mine — when will a woman ever escape these kinds of comparisons? She lies there alone, her arms behind her head. The camera is on her face. She looks down, at someone out of the frame, at her lover, at her lover's hand as he strokes her. She wears an expression of bliss and expectation.

Do you know this girl? Have you seen the footage, too? It was wrong for the men who did this to leave that moment in. There is a tenderness to her gaze that no professional can have evoked. For me, the theft of this moment is the true pornography. It is the moment at which the camera's eye and our eyes begin the rape.

Or perhaps you are like everyone else I know who has seen this video. She disgusts you because she is not beautiful enough, and you do not care to see, or know about, the sexuality of someone as dark as she, as native and as provincial and as unexceptional as she. Look, there is a constellation of moles over one breast, and there are patches of dark skin between her thighs — or would you rather not look: accustomed as you probably are by now to the red-carpet perfection of celebrities, you must be repelled by these marks of her individuality.

She speaks, murmurs something in her language. In the background a radio plays on. A man's head rises from the bottom of the screen. It is impossible to see what he is doing, though the girl's response is clear. She arches her back so her breasts point at the camera, and a series of small cries comes from her throat. Perhaps this is too tame. The Internet voices I have found all refer to this video in derisive terms. Boring as hell, someone has written. Third-rate production values and fourth-rate actresses, another remarks.

Then the girl is gone from the screen, like an aperitif whisked away after a single taste. I suppose that would be one interesting way of putting it. My professional vocabulary, my storehouse of imagery, has revolved for the last months or so around the act of eating. At the newspaper, one of my assignments is to attend the various food festivals and restaurant inaugurations around Manila. It is my job to shield my boss, a tempestuous linen-wearing older gentleman, from any harm food might do to the waistline. I read nothing nowadays except press releases and the occasional erotic tale downloaded by a coworker. Hence the inadequacy of my words — "a series of small cries" indeed.

But here is another girl, in a tailored blouse that must be part of a uniform. Of what? Donostia has a culture of uniforms, as you know, and it is mostly the powerless who wear them: this new girl might be a pharmacy assistant or a student teacher or a room girl at one of the better hotels. She is not beautiful, either. No one shot in natural light, through an aperture in the ceiling, clothing dragged off her piece by piece, can look beautiful. Beauty is in the stillness and the careful oblique gaze, the explosion of white studio light that blanks out pimple, pore, and the offending curve of nostril. This is a face for that bygone anthropology project of your aunt's — a plain Malay face with flat cheekbones and lips that protrude. The girl spreads her legs; the man she is with — he is little more than the back of a head, a pair of hands — has eased her panties off. Such an unruly ruff of pubic hair, momentarily captured in the exact center of the frame — no stylish Mohawks for this woman, who bares herself, and then touches herself, for her lover alone.

This is not the first time I have seen this footage. Like a doctor experimenting on his own system, I merely want to see how far I could go. I am aware, scientist-like, of my response: that I am calm, breathing normally, that I feel neither disgust nor anxiety, only a dull desire to experience the next twenty-four minutes through to the end.

But now you appear, you emerge from what seems to be the bath of a cheap hotel room. For a moment it is possible to deny the identity of this uniformed schoolgirl whom I see, blurry as she is, standing just beyond the bed as she strikes a pose, smiling, her arms at her side, fingers linked below her belly. But the image sharpens. And it is indubitably you. And it is alarmingly clear that rules can be broken and new rules made to supplant them. Because the camera has descended from its cage in the ceiling. The camera is in someone's hands. You welcome its presence, you smile and pose for its eye. It is mobile, intelligent. There is nothing it won't disclose.

But I am a coward, because I can't bear this, I am cold to my fingertips, shaking; this is the way I feel every time. I deny this is you. My mind leaves me, my thoughts spiral up into the summer sky. I leap up and begin to pace, wearing a track in the dusty floor with my bare feet. Why do I think of the lawyer at this moment? Why do I evoke his huge sad eyes, the trailing sweetness of his cologne? I keep the movie running but ignore the screen. When I return, they have finished with you, for the moment, because it is the first girl once more, the one with the speckled round breasts. I hoped that at least she might be spared, for she seemed so pitiful in her sexual confidence. These men, whoever they are, know the format all right — slow, then fast, then very fast. It pains me, it grieves me, it angers me, it makes me want to lash out with my fists. There is her cunt, in the lower edge of the frame, stretched and compressed

with the movement of a disembodied hand. The sounds from her
throat are real. The camera zooms in.

IT TOOK hours of agony to arrive at the decision, but by
dawn, the answer was clear. She would not allow Naia to go
public. She was, after all, the mother; her word still carried
weight. She would tell Joel so at once.

In relief, she slept, unwittingly. When she awakened, it
was noon. As she lay in bed cursing her sloth, she understood
that something else was at play. That this was part of her
strategy to see the man again. From the phone call onward,
they might negotiate.

As she dialed his mobile she wondered if she had gone
crazy. She pictured him saying, "All right, as you wish," and
hanging up, caught unprepared in the midst of a hearing that
had absolutely nothing to do with her life, impatient to be rid
of her, thinking only of his next appearance fee.

He answered on the second ring. Was he on the road,
at work already, at the breakfast table half undressed? Her
announcement about Naia was met with a long, uncomfortable
silence. When he spoke again, he sounded deferential, very
much the shabby boy at the back of the classroom, but she
caught a note of amusement, as though he were humoring her,
as though he had seen past her ploy at once.

"Of course it's vital that we have a meeting of minds," he
said. "But, Narita, I'm engaged all of today. I simply can't see
you." She caught the whine of a tricycle taxi in the background.
So he was out in the field. "Tomorrow? What say we discuss
your issues tomorrow, over lunch?"

He would try to get away from his morning affairs as soon
as he could, he added. Oh yes, oh yes, she said magnanimously,
wondered whether he, too, craved excitement and adventure to
fill his days, or whether the mayor had ordered him to drop all

commitments except those relevant to the three young women who now linked their lives.

The day dragged by. Lightheaded despite her long sleep, she thought about her boss, what he had demanded. Write about the girls, he had said. She could not. She wandered about the garden, played with the dogs for an hour. She opened drawers in Antonia's room and shook out the clothes left behind. Procrastination was one of her talents, as was nonchalance under pressure. She wondered what Joel was doing that was so important — perhaps it had something to do with the tip she had given him. Tomorrow she would find out. Everything would turn out fine tomorrow.

In the morning, Joel called her mobile. Would it be alright if they met on the city hall steps? he said. He apologized for the rudeness of asking her to come and meet him halfway on such a hot summer day, but she laughed off the sun, told him she didn't care whether she turned dark or not, and said she would be happy to spare him that extra half hour's drive to her place and back. When he had hung up she told herself that their behavior — his self-effacing mien, despite his rank in the city; her gregarious and immediate assent — was modern and professional and aboveboard; it did not compromise them in any sense.

Joel was wearing a loose-weave *barong tagalog* this time. It was standard provincial lawyer's getup. He seemed exhausted, though he brightened as soon as he saw her. His eyes dropped quickly from her face to the low *V* of her jersey top. This little evidence of his vulnerability assured her.

"Please don't ask me to suggest a place," she said convivially. "I've been in town less than a week."

"Chicken or seafood?" he said.

"Oh, I don't care," she said, resisting the urge to chew on a fingernail. "Anything as long as it's quiet. I hate music. Is there any place in this country where you can have a meal without music? And why does it have to be dance music all the time? We spend all our waking hours in one great big fucking nightclub. Or in one great big R&B-slash-pop ... orgasm."

He looked so serious as he maneuvered the jeep out of the parking lot that she thought she had offended him. Maybe he stocked his CD rack with Beyoncé and nothing else. Or was it her manner? How was she supposed to speak? And in what language? She lapsed into a rapid, *Cosmo* girl English when she was nervous. It was a turnoff. Men ran.

"Is the beach okay for you?" he said.

What did he mean by that? she thought. Good girls didn't ride down to the beach with men they barely knew. That was an old maxim of Luth's generation.

"The beach is fine," she replied.

They left the city, driving through a landscape of coconut trees and scrub, and he was silent for such a long time, it seemed, that her Manila instincts began to kick in and her nerves began to fray. There was no lunch, no restaurant. He was in league with the men who had violated Naia. Their destination would be a bunkhouse deep in a coconut plantation, where a steel bed and plastic ties awaited. This was the last day of her life. It was a beautiful day, blue range of mountains rearing up on one side, cloudless summer sky. The only vehicles they met were the long yellow buses, packed to the rooftop with baskets of produce, that menaced them in clouds of stinging dust.

Just as she was contemplating a decisive leap onto the asphalt, the jeep slowed and her driver made a sharp turn off the road, into what at first seemed to be a gravel driveway. But there was no house in sight, and they went on, over a rutted track so narrow that branches scraped their windshield. "Sorry," he said more than once. Then the path came to an end and she found herself staring at clipped Bermuda grass and a border of flowering plants. Beyond, a collection of deliberately rustic bamboo-walled bungalows, with hot water, no doubt, and a minibar in each. Some people might refer to this place as a resort, others as a motel. Now she understood why he drove the derelict jeep. A more elegant vehicle would have been wasted on Donostia, which, beyond the provincial exterior, seemed to keep a few lively secrets.

There was a splash, some distinctly Germanic roaring, a series of high-pitched screams. Two ladies, and at least two white men, she thought. She clambered down from the jeep self-consciously, feeling superior and shamefaced at the same time. The pool was small and kidney-shaped, and the bikini-clad girls frolicked in the water, holding out their arms, coaxing their elderly escorts to jump in again.

The restaurant was in the pavilion by the pool. They seated themselves at one of the polished wooden tables. The Bermuda grass went all the way to the beach, where a chicken-wire fence secured the property from outsiders. The usual band of scruffy children drifted past, casting disinterested glances at the world in which she sat. A breeze ruffled the fronds of the golden coconut palms. It was all very manicured and pleasant. She had had no idea places like these already existed here. A waiter came with a menu. The food was not expensive by Manila standards, but most of the clientele would have to be foreign to afford these rates. She chose from the pasta menu, playing it safe, not sure if she should insist on splitting the bill at the close of the meal.

"What do you think?" Joel said. "Is it a nice place?"

"You don't own it, do you?" she said nervously, trying to flatter him — the instincts of the good lifestyle journalist, nosing around for freebies.

He shook his head. "No connection at all. But here they don't play dance music."

Embarrassed, she thought she might as well get to the point. "Why have you taken such an interest in Naia?"

He blinked. "I'm doing my job. I feel sorry for her, yes. But I assure you I have no ulterior motives. I've been seeing a lot of your parents. They may have told you. But that's because they have opened up to me. They are educated people. They're not angry, they're not unreasonable."

"Unlike …?"

"Unlike the families of … of the other two."

Narita shuddered, suppressed the memory of the video. No, she would not go there. Not yet. There was silence. She chewed on a handful of peanuts from the tray in front of them.

"Zenon didn't tell you," she said at last.

"Tell me what?"

"That I'd gotten pregnant."

Was that surprise, sudden fear in his eyes? Well, hadn't he known about the pregnancy, then? She'd assumed the entirety of Sweethaven had eventually found out. Well, if not, surely he could count back from Naia's age, surely he had been smart enough to draw the appropriate conclusions.

"Well, I figured it was him, on my own," Joel said at last. "Who else could it have been?"

Thanks, she wanted to say.

"How well did you know him?" she asked.

"Not very well. We hung out, like regular guys. That was all. Believe me, you had a powerful impact on our lives. On Zenon's life in particular. The moment he set eyes on you, the first day of school, it was all over with him. I guarantee you, he spent weeks agonizing with us over what to say to you before he managed to make his move."

He was looking past her shoulder now, as if hoping that her daughter might peer palely from a window of one of the bungalows. He seemed to have a hard time meeting her eyes. She had thought he might be interested in her, sexually; that early face-to-breast once-over had told her that, and she had thought she might build on it, gain leverage. Now she wasn't so certain.

"I wouldn't have known she was his," he said, shifting his weight as though in discomfort; he would be the kind of man for whom talk of a child's paternity, any child, would be grossly impolite. "She doesn't at all look like him. She resembles you, through and through."

Was this flattery? She couldn't think of a single thing to say. If only the circumstances of this meeting had been different.

"I pity her," he said. He did not sound condescending in the least. "I want justice for her, that's all. I'm not here to clean up after Zenon. It's not up to me to make right the ... things that he put you through."

Things? she thought. Which things? It had been so long ago, and she had harbored her private Zenon for so long that she could no longer quite distinguish between fantasy and what had really taken place. What had Zenon told this man? It occurred to her that the woman he thought he was speaking to was far different from who she was.

"I haven't kept in touch with him," Joel said. "I guess we had very little in common. But I thought about you a lot. I hoped you were okay."

The meal was over. They lingered, left the table to walk on the grass, sought the shade of a young guava tree. Joel asked her if she would like a glass of wine. She couldn't remember anymore whether that was appropriate to have after lunch. What did it matter, she thought. Who was there to correct her, point out the embarrassing residue of provincialism? The Europeans goofing around in the pool were too enamored of their brown girlfriends to notice, too working class to know the difference, too old to care. The wine made her skin burn; it was the wrong thing to drink on such a hot day. They took the last few steps to the seashore and sat at a weathered bamboo table beneath a thatch parasol. The sea breeze, though sticky with salt, brought relief. There was a jetty a hundred meters down from where they sat. It was a private one, Joel said; the owner of the place, a German, he had heard, used it a few months a year for his own boat. It was not a pretty beach, she thought. The sand was volcanic — brown, not black — and rimmed with decaying seaweed, coconut fronds, whatever flotsam the tide had tossed up. Beyond the brown waves, the water was a deep and forbidding blue. Antonia would have rejoiced in this ugliness, she thought. She would have gone to work at her sketch pad at once, laboring over the details until she owned the whole scene and could tuck it away, defused, into her black Rotring carrying case. Narita wished she could encapsulate the past in the same way. She wished she could shake this compulsion of hers to evoke what had been, redrawing it, rewriting new versions of it. The truth was, Antonia had cast off their brilliant Sweethaven childhood as though it were a shabby and outgrown skin, had reinvented herself as a sweet-tempered brown-skinned Internet bride.

In the sky beyond Joel's head, metal flashed. A little Cessna was taking off from an invisible point within the fringe of coconut palms.

"I don't believe it," she heard herself say.

"What don't you believe?"

"That there's so much money in this world. Look at that plane. A flying school in the middle of nowhere. And this hotel, and a man who owns a boat that he uses only a few months out of the year."

The Cessna, so like a little boy's plaything, turned inland — a vanishing strip of metal in the sky. Joel smiled sadly and shook his head.

"Who's making all that money?" she pressed. "How is it being made? Why didn't any of it ever trickle down to me? I work so hard; I always have. Six days a week at the newspaper, closing pages, chasing after stories, talking to socialites about their wretched hobbies. Every day. Even today I'm working. I'm supposed to make a feature out of this video scandal, you know that? In payment for my weeklong break."

He was looking searchingly at her.

"They expect you to write about your own kin?"

"They don't know she's mine."

This astonished him, she could tell. It took him a while to speak again.

"I'm sorry for that. Certain things are beyond our control." He sipped the last of his wine. "There's plenty of money going around. The *haciendaros*, the grand old plantation owners, they no longer rule as such. There are the Chinese. As ever. But the European investors have come in, and our countrymen haven't done too badly for themselves in America. I know one of the men who run that flying school. I helped him with one of his deals."

She wished she hadn't brought up the subject of wealth, of work, of compromises. Her family — rootless, anonymous until the moment each parent had gravitated to Sweethaven — embarrassed her. *He* could trace his roots to some bearded horse-riding, whip-cracking Castilian pioneer, whereas the university was now no more than a glorified institute to train nurses: hundreds of young men and women whose futures hinged on a labor shortfall abroad.

"Narita, what I really want from you right now is your trust."

She jumped. It seemed he had an agenda as lengthy and involved as hers.

"What do you want me to do?"

"Are you comfortable with me?" He frowned. "We get along, don't we?"

She shrugged.

"Then come with me. I am taking you to a place. Whatever you find there, whatever you feel, must remain a secret between us. Just don't leave for Manila without giving this a chance."

Twenty

ON THE DRIVE back into the city, she was positive she had said yes to an afternoon tryst. She supposed he was claiming a small advance on what the Pastors owed him for his help. Men had different ways of expressing their need. Some were up front. Others waited slyly until the air crackled with unreleased lust and it seemed stupid not to lean over in, say, taxicab or foyer, and crush her face against theirs. When things went wrong it was these kinds of men who retreated and let her take the blame. But she herself kept a small storehouse of tricks. She liked the ambiguous hug that drew mutual surges of blood. She never went for the mouth, only the soft, warm point below their cheekbones, the better to slide her own lips to earlobe or elsewhere, or to retreat forever with a chaste and pleasant smile.

They sped up the narrow, palm-flanked road that edged the bay. Every travel article about the city included a stock helicopter shot of this blue expanse. Joel kept up the conversation, telling her he had been a second-grader when he learned, from a nun, of the other Donostia, the city in Spain that the conquistadores and priests must have been thinking of when they weighed anchor, rechristening the heathens and their settlement. The *real* Donostia, the nun explained. Over thirty years later, he still mulled the meaning of that phrase.

The city was changing, she thought; she could barely recognize these roads that she had once traversed, with long-forgotten friends, on the back of a scooter, riding in the dust of cornfields and getting her Converse sneakers wet as they churned through streams that spilled right across the asphalt. Everywhere, houses had sprung up, and with them came the tricycle taxis parked by the roadside, the Toyota Tamaraws rigged up for passenger use; the vulcanizing shops staffed by skinny, shirtless men who moved around seemingly without aim. Joel stopped at a compound that looked embarrassingly like a small motel — four or five bungalows, their windows closed against the summer heat, a grille frame over the gate that read "Villa Milagros." There were weeds everywhere; the place looked neglected. He drove the jeep right in — an experienced patron apparently — and, producing a bunch of keys, unlocked one of the structures.

They were at the threshold of a one-room apartment. It had a weary, professional look: a toilet and shower to the right of the entrance, a closet to the left. The bed stood against one wall. It was the focal point of the small space. Behind it, a tall window with dusty glass jalousies. The ocher drapes gave the room the necessary touch of glamor. The foot of the bed faced a wall with an expansive mirror set in a stylish frame of iron bars and rivets. The bed itself was covered in a duvet of masculine tans and russets. There was an air-conditioning unit to one side of the window; it was dead now, unplugged, and the room was stifling. On the side opposite it was a mini-refrigerator, just large enough to stow a weekend's supply of drinks.

"This isn't where you live, is it?"

He shook his head, his smile sad and abstracted.

"Who owns it, then? A friend of yours? You pay him to use this place?"

She walked to the bed and lay down on the spread, knocking off her shoes, keeping her eyes on him. Joel did not touch her. He drew up the lone chair and sat with his elbows on his knees.

"This is where the videos were filmed."

She froze, went dark with embarrassment. But her instinct for self-preservation kicked in. She remained where she was, as though all her life she had been in the habit of entering strange, suffocating rooms and artfully lying down supine. It was likely he had had no idea of her prior thoughts.

Then the realization struck her. He had taken her here, and he had had a key.

"Don't get up," Joel called. "Don't leave. Not yet."

"You're one of them."

"I am *not*. Whatever you think of me, however bad it looks, I am *not*. Trust me."

"How can I? *Talk* to me. Why weren't you more forthright? Why do you claim to help my daughter?"

"Be still," he said. "Please be still. Let me talk. This was not the work of one boy, but of a *barkada*, a group of friends. Now one of them is trying to cooperate. With me. But the situation is tricky, as he has powerful backers."

"Is this the Torres boy my mother told me about?"

"Yes," he said, and sighed. "Your parents were present when we ... interviewed ... one of their victims."

"Well, charge him, then!" she said, the residue of embarrassment sharpening her voice. "What are you afraid of? I can't let you have Naia."

He got up, as if to give himself time, and bending, plugged the air-conditioning unit into its outlet. The hum of the machine filled the room. Almost immediately the atmosphere became bearable. Joel came back to his seat.

"I know it is your prerogative, as her family, to decide. I know you want what's best for her. But Narita, I brought you here because I want you to see how close we are to achieving something. That we have evidence, that we have hope that her testimony will put some people behind bars."

She was not placated. "Well, if this is evidence, where's your crime scene tape? Why can you come in and out like those pornographers did?"

He sighed. "It's so complicated. This is Donostia. Things are not very formal around here."

Narita rose, keeping a sharp eye on him. He was way out of line, and she couldn't quite forgive herself. The air-conditioner thundered in its niche by the wall, blocking out all sounds from the outside. Climate-controlled, this would have been a pleasant and private place, anytime of the year. Any young girl would have been happy to hole up here for a few hours, away from the dust and heat and the aimlessness of Donostia. She was not in a position to condemn any girl for trying her luck with a young man she did not know.

The studio had a secret, underground quality, like an animal den. There were no books, or shelves for that matter, but there was a low, dusty table where a sizable television might have sat, or a complete entertainment system, or perhaps a computer for games. She took in the ceiling over the bed. She knew the adventures that ceilings could promise, from tales relayed to her in childhood. There were always crawl spaces between the paneling and the iron roof. Some means of trapping heat and conveying it away was crucial in a tropical climate. People stashed their fortunes overhead, as well as their bags of marijuana and *shabu*. Little boys trembled atop a beam, observing, through gaps in the plywood, the systematic slaughter of their families. Narita recalled a story she had heard in high school, from the boys she had smoked with behind the Practical Arts building — how they had climbed into the ceiling of an uncle's house to spy on his concubine as the woman lay on the bed, ankles straining against the footboard, alone but for a blue dildo and Van Halen pounding out of the tape deck.

There was a light socket over the bed and it was empty.

"The camera came through there," Joel said.

She had guessed that. Gemma and Diana had had no idea. The last place a human ever checked out was the space above its head. Even when lying supine, neither girl had ever imagined that her ruin might come from above. One or the other had, in the throes of pleasure, stared directly into that cold, probing lens.

"They must have stationed a man above the bed," she said. "Who was that man?"

"Yes, above the bed." He left the other question unanswered. "The ceiling is accessed through a hinged door. In the bathroom."

Joel retrieved a wooden pole from a corner of the room. He poked at a couple of points in the dimness above the toilet bowl, and a square of board swung down. He went to the closet and emerged dragging a folded painter's ladder, which he positioned carefully over the floor tiles. The ladder rocked. Narita mounted it, pausing nervously at every rung.

"There is a light switch to the right," he offered.

She had never been inside a ceiling before. It was an oven. Tiny leaping specks greeted her hand as he reached for the switch. The bulb was weak and yellow. As she straightened up, she saw that she was on a gangway, wide enough to accommodate a man lying prone. Electric wires, thick with dust, disappeared over the panels. It was a hiding place, she realized, from one's enemies, for stashing contraband. She edged over the planks, hunched over, flinching when her forehead brushed the sun-heated galvanized iron sheeting above her. Her toe brushed a ball of scurf: a rodents' nest. As she inched forward, the electric bulb died without warning. She pulled out her mobile phone and navigated by the blue glow of the screen. A circle of brightness marked the empty light fixture. She took a deep breath and, leaning over, put an eye to the hole. Through it, she saw the earth-toned pattern of the spread. Insects assaulted her face, wriggling, chewing. They were fleas, drifts of them, in her ears, between her fingers, burrowing into her trousers.

"I'm sorry about the vermin," Joel said, when she was safely down, her horror screeched out, her clothes brushed off. "I ought to have warned you. It's the cats. They get in somehow."

She tried to block out the memory of the flea attack. His eyes, he noted, flickered involuntarily to the region above her breast, which, like one eyelid and parts of her arms, felt hot and swollen.

She could not stay. The longer she remained, the more she became a participant in what had taken place here. In the span of a half hour, the room had become a familiar space; she recognized the bathroom door as the one Naia had emerged from, in her footage — glimpsed only for a second or so, but certainly the same one. The tawdriness oppressed her. A faint oily sweetness, an imprint of the men and women who had lain there, rose from the sheets. She was compromising the investigation by staying. She supposed it was his problem, primarily; he was with the impotent prosecution, but its failures affected them all.

"Why haven't you filed charges against Torres?" she said. "He's one of yours, isn't he? You're still looking for a fall guy."

Joel was examining her carefully, weighing the risk of what he would say next. "JP Torres calls me uncle, but we're barely related; I am a poor relation to the Fortuns, as you may already know."

She waited.

"But JP ... his mother and the mayor's wife are sisters. What happens to him will have an impact on the mayor's future happiness, I tell you."

"So screw the mayor."

"I serve at the pleasure of the mayor," Joel said. "His family paid for my education, from Sweethaven to law school. I'm his man." He considered this last statement. "I'm his *boy*."

She felt sick. It was time to leave. She found her bag and let herself out the door. Behind her, she heard him switching off the lights and air-conditioner, like a good caretaker. She wanted to put distance between the two of them. If only a tricycle would happen by. But it was the wrong time of day; they were all downtown, or at the schools, where the first of the elementary school sections were letting out for the day.

Joel came up to her as though to beg an apology. She could hear his mobile phone ringing in one of his pockets, a maddening noise. Finally he pulled it out and answered. She scanned the road. She was aware of his breathing, long and measured, and his short bursts of speech. "Yah? When. Now? Okay."

"What's going on?"

"We have to leave now," he told her. "I suppose you've seen a dead body before."

THE young husband himself had raised the alarm. A hoarse and incessant keening from deep within their dingy home brought the neighbors on the run. Two men burst themselves through the barred doors, splitting wood and hurling the barred bolt to the raw cement floor. They saw all they needed in an instant: just off the living room was the cubicle that housed the water-sealed toilet and shower, and in the doorway to this dank space the young man crouched, cradling his wife in his arms and begging forgiveness. The house filled with neighbors. In the frantic and curiously mute rush to see the body, someone remembered to call the police.

When the jeep stopped, it was at a point on the asphalt road beyond the airport, north of the city limits. The police jeep and the ambulance were already parked at the roadside; they must have arrived some minutes before.

Narita turned to her companion. He was looking at her too. Something passed between them: an understanding, an imperative. Then they clambered down. A dirt track wound away from the asphalted highway, into a screen of coconut and banana trunks. It looked dry enough to negotiate on foot, no that they had a choice: there was no way a vehicle could get down the short embankment, let alone propel itself down that twisted rut of mud.

As they stood there, two men in civilian clothing appeared bearing a stretcher. A hospital sheet concealed the body that lay upon it. A motley group of neighbors formed a procession as the men came toward them, grunting as they hoisted their burden up the embankment, gingerly locating footholds on the cracked concrete steps. A branch of low-growing Bangkok frangipani caught a corner of the sheet, disclosing painted toenails, a pale narrow foot.

Her journalism had kept Narita within hotel ballrooms and mall boutiques: she had had no experience whatsoever with the raw dead, the dead with all organs intact, the dead minus flowers and makeup and expensive funeral dress. She stared at the girl's foot, feeling nothing — no sympathy, no sense of outrage, only a clinical surprise at how lifelike that foot still looked, that it had neither suppurated nor withered in the span of an afternoon. And yet how inert it was. The stillness of that outline beneath the sheet — that was the part she could not accept. Huge black flies alighted on the rough cotton, rubbed their forelegs together in glee and flew off.

She drew back as the men loaded the dead girl into the ambulance. The crowd of neighbors followed them up the embankment, milling around the shoulder of the road. No one touched the stretcher; no one wept; not even the handful of women who were there, and it occurred to her that Gemma Bulauan, whoever she might have been, had been a newcomer without relations, a stranger in this neighborhood.

Narita picked her way down the track, past houses on stilts where animals rooted in the mud beneath. The house where the girl had died was a small one-story bungalow, with walls of unfinished hollow block and a rude porch of cracked red tile. The Palm Sunday crucifix on the door must have been tacked there for years. Joel stood in the doorway, talking to a policeman. She yearned, suddenly, for him to touch her, put an arm about my shoulder, make some silly little gesture to stake a claim.

He seemed to have forgotten about her, though. The policeman gave her a searching look.

"Media," Joel said. The cop only nodded.

At their feet was a grimy mat of woven rags, and resting on this mat were two pairs of sandals, a man's and a woman's, misshapen and dusty, the woman's studded with cheap beads.

The husband was still in the house. He looked about twenty-five: clean-skinned and healthy-limbed. If he had been blessed with a handsome face, there was no way of knowing, for his features were red and swollen from continuous weeping, and there was a crusted splotch on his forehead. He had doubled himself up against the wall, and as they ventured over the threshold, he began to moan and to bang his head against the concrete. The abrasion at his temple left a rust-colored imprint on the surface. He shook his head against the alighting flies.

"How did she die?" Narita muttered to the policeman.

"Asphyxiation."

"What did she use? A belt? Clothesline?"

"She didn't use anything," the policeman said. "He choked the life out of her with his bare hands."

The young husband brought his palms up to his face. There were handcuffs about his wrists.

On a table covered with a printed swatch of cotton, a few photos lay helter-skelter, half out of their gilt frames. In the struggle, something or someone had barreled into them. Narita pushed aside a pink soft toy and a copy of *The Upper Room*. The young couple smiled up at her in their wedding finery, a fine-looking barong tagalog and a limp satin dress, the neckline high to cover what imperfections there might have been on the woman's skin.

Narita turned and walked out of the house, half-running, putting distance between herself and the place. The sun beat down on the pale blooms of orchids lashed to the coconut tree trunks. She told herself she did not know the girl, that it was not her concern. She was just a name and a dead foot and some grainy video footage that had kept her up half the night.

After a while, Joel found her. They stood there, not saying anything, brushing off insects. Around them a few teenagers hovered, waiting for something to happen, hoping a clue or two might be tossed their way, some hook to hang the next episode on. Finally he looked down at the mobile phone in her hand.

"Have you called your folks? Best that it come from you."

She shook her head. "In due time. I don't think I want to see or talk with anyone right now."

"I have asked the police for pictures, in case you want them," he said.

"No," she said. "No, I don't. I can't play journalist with this; there's a limit."

Her head throbbed in the heat. She needed to lie down. "What happens now?"

"I'm going home," he said. "Do you want to come with me?"

Twenty-one

LUTH SAT, devoid of energy, unable even to rise and turn on the lamp, in the twilight of the living room. It was that time of day that always filled her with melancholy, as cooking smells drifted from the kitchens of the houses on either side of them and young people made their way past the gate, coming back from the sea, their ribbing and laughter jolting her nerves. Sociable little animals, she thought, without a care in the world, like ... monkeys. The comparison made her uneasy. It was hers, but it also belonged to Mother Martha, the woman who pronounced herself a missionary.

"Monkeys," the charlatan spits. The wild blue marbles of her eyes galvanize the girls; they stare at each other in disbelief — Could she really be talking to *us*? Then someone giggles and they are off — *Monkeys, monkeys!* — pursuing Naia, shrieking and teasing each other. No one gives a thought as to what might happen when they catch the girl. A wild, exhibitionist spirit possesses Naia. She has no idea where she is headed, but she runs.

In a deserted corridor she comes face-to-face, chest-to-chest, with the boy. He is Brent. She has known him all her life. They have played hide-and-seek and Three Billy Goats Gruff after Sunday school, concealing themselves under foliage and within sections of brightly painted concrete pipe, taking turns napping while they await discovery.

Elated at the prospect of rescue, she lets him take her by the arms. They whirl into the armory as though in a dance.

He locks the door: the keeper of the keys. He is a cadet officer, she a majorette; they belong together; there is no need to struggle. Brent clamps a hand over her mouth anyway, gripping her wrists firmly in the other — moist, trembling, adolescent hands. In the close air, they stand like that for a long time, feeling the heat of each other's bodies through their clothes. In a little while he lets his hand slip and rest on the neckline of her singlet, and she glances down in astonishment, realizing for the first time that her blouse is lost.

He pulls her about, his sex a hot questing lump against her skirt as she arches to him, his hands on either side of her face. He touches her gently, where Mother Martha gripped her to demonstrate the consuming power of the Lord. Into this sweetness she lets herself fall.

IMAGINATION was Luth's curse. Her reading habit had fueled it — a thirst for stories that, with the years, had had to be sated with borrowed copies of the *Reader's Digest*, and then of Harlequins and Mills and Boons, until at long last she gave up books altogether, blaming her bad eyes and the household chores that used up all her free time.

Her job had never afforded her much leisure. For nearly forty years she had worked from the 6:45 flag-raising ceremony to the five o'clock dismissal bell, and then in the evenings and weekends, checking papers, recycling exams, writing faithfully in her lesson plan book. When she was younger, what a torture it had been not to yield to whimsy, not to record some silliness observed at the school canteen or the sour faces at the PTA meeting. She wished she had, now that the names and events all ran together, but she had been mortally afraid of a random check as the principal paced the corridors of the school. Those forty years of lesson plans now formed the diary of her life, but what a meager record it was, how inert its entries, what an ultimate waste of time.

She thought she remembered Brent, though, or perhaps Adam — could conjure an image of a somber child, very pale, with distinctive light brown hair, standing alone on the blacktop while his darker schoolmates tore about him. A child who looked this way and that, as though lost, or recently deprived of hearing, or unable to comprehend the language of his peers.

There was one other memory — of a knot of boys glimpsed at recess, and the lonely, pale child in the center, shrinking between two of his peers as one of the bigger boys shoved a set of knuckles into his face. She had thought they were beating him, but saw that the large boy wore a ring, the stone made of some greasy green substance, like dried Play-Doh or nose dirt. "Kiss poo-poo, kiss poo-poo," the big one coaxed, whatever that meant, and at that moment the persecuted child had caught her eye, but for some reason she had not been able to summon the energy to break up the knot. Let nature take its course, she had thought.

By dumb luck, or clever machination, the Holland three had never been among her pupils, not in all the years of their elementary education. She knew only that they had vanished from the school for a couple of years while their father worked on a PhD in some American state, and when they returned they were chubby, short-tempered, irreversibly transformed.

INTO the dusk of the living room, there came some tentative movement, and Luth drew a deep breath and mechanically began to give instructions for dinner.

But it was not the maid. It was Naia.

The girl stopped a couple of meters short of the sofa, as though afraid to draw closer. Luth saw that her face was horribly swollen from weeping. She was clutching something in her hand.

"Have you heard from him?" she whispered.

"Who?" said Luth, taken aback. "Brent?"

"No," Naia choked. "Have you heard from the lawyer?"

Luth understood then. The girl had built up her hopes, hanging on to that halfhearted promise to get her out of Donostia and to her aunt.

"No, Naia," she said. "He hasn't called."

"Where's mother?" the girl persisted. "Is she with him? Are they discussing me?"

"I don't know."

Abruptly Naia whirled about and headed back to the bedrooms. Luth braced herself for the sound of a door being slammed. When nothing happened, she rose gingerly to her feet and felt her way over to the hall.

The girl was not in her room. She was huddled upon the bed in Antonia's, sobbing, an object by her limp hand. It was her mobile phone.

"He's never going to call, Naia," Luth said gently. "There's no way they can get you to Antonia. You know that."

Behind her she heard Daniel's tread. She cast him a quick glance of warning, but there was no need. Something else had caught his attention — Narita's laptop, sitting quietly atop the desk beside a recent drift of papers. She saw him brush the top of it, furtively glancing at something lying there.

"We can't help you unless you tell us how it happened," Luth said. "You cannot handle this alone, Naia. Tell me."

The girl's lips quivered as she struggled to speak through her sobs. Luth told herself that she must wait, that something important was about to be revealed. There was a point, she now knew, at which a human being, young or old, gave way, broke down, came crawling out of itself sobbing for help.

Sounds came from Naia's mouth. "I did not know."

"What didn't you know, child?" Luth said. She noted the edge in her own voice. Her body started to shake with the effort of keeping herself in check, for strangely she felt no pity for the girl, despite her distress. She felt only the same tired exasperation she felt when having to explain a lesson for the umpteenth time to a roomful of stupid children. Only the same dread, rapidly masked with anger, when long ago Narita or Antonia came to her with a lovelorn face and a circuitous confession. And she was grateful to be whole and in control, while everyone around her had reached breaking point and dissolved.

"I didn't know he would show the videos around," Naia said, with an effort.

Then Daniel was hovering over them, trying to touch the girl as though solace might travel through skin. His voice was soft and kind in a way Luth's could never be. "Who are you talking about, child?"

The girl shook his hand off with a cry of rage. *Get out*! Luth mouthed to him. He was a man. What did men know?

Daniel retreated a couple of steps, over to the desk.

Now, thought Luth. Now was the time to get at the truth.

"So it is really you in that movie," she began.

"Of course it is," Naia spat. "What did you think?"

"You lied to us," Luth started to say, but checked herself. The girl had not lied. She had said nothing. It was she, Luth, and Daniel, who had lied — to themselves. Instead, she said, "How did it happen, Naia? That is all I want to know."

The girl was crying, infuriatingly, again.

"A to B to C, Naia." It sounded, appallingly, like a fourth-grade lesson in science, reduced to its key points, to be regurgitated for a periodical test. Luth remained by Naia's side, loath to touch her, but unable to get up or even shift position. She sat and waited, calling on all her reserves of patience, until the girl's sobs dwindled once more.

"He said the videos were private," Naia said.

"Who did?" said Luth. No reply. She could feel herself on the outer reaches of sanity, but when had her instincts ever been wrong? "Was it Rinky Holland?" she shouted. "My God, Naia, it isn't enough that you give us clues here and there and expect us to come up with our own version to believe. You must tell us the truth. We raised you like parents. You owe it to us to give us the truth, Naia. You owe it to us."

"You are so sick," the girl screamed back. "You are filthy. It was Adam, okay? Just Adam. I wanted to tell you, but you weren't listening. Now shut up, Lola, shut up. Just shut up."

THE girl lay with her face buried in the spread. Her sobs had gradually diminished until she was silent, asleep maybe, indifferent to the effect of her words. Luth sat, frozen, as though at the bottom of a dark lake, breaking surface only at the feel of something creeping down her cheek. As she shrugged the tear away, her eyes focused on Narita's laptop, and she wondered what had caught Daniel's attention so. There was nothing there now, she saw as she rose. Her husband, stumbling out of the room at Naia's words, had taken whatever it was away with him.

She went tiredly back to the bed. Absently she put out a hand to smooth Naia's hair. In a few days she would be bundled off to Manila, her clothes given away or shipped; there would be little left in the house to remind Luth of her pain. It would be possible to heal.

But the prospect of a future minus the girl petrified her. Who would be left to receive her ministrations then? Not Daniel. Oh, she loathed him. She still found excuses to be out of the room when he was around. In this half-light, one hand brushing mosquitoes from her sweating limbs, she felt the monster of resentment rising within her — her dark twin, swollen and black and soft. What might she do, when she and Daniel were alone? He had not had her in years. Thank God, that pounding at her gate, the begging, the humiliation of yielding to him, was long over, by mutual agreement.

But with Naia gone, would his old urges be awakened? And what excuse might she use? *Quiet, you fool, you don't want the maid to hear us.* Oh, he would gladly have performed for Cecilia's benefit, halting and stupid though she was.

What delight she had experienced with him had been minimal, had come mostly at the beginning of their marriage, when he was tall and willowy, with soulful eyes and a baritone voice, and her body had been novel even to her. Somewhere in the piles of test papers and laundry, that flame of awareness had guttered out. In later years, she had consented, once or twice a month, to a brief and itch-inducing encounter in the darkness, which amounted, eventually, to a few minutes of pleasure, for him, she assisting him with her hand. He always embraced her afterward, with a gratitude that rose from the depths of his soul — it made her feel heartless, petty. She would lie numb, listening to his snores, sleep gone.

Whatever else those visits to Rinky Holland had accomplished, they at least had marked the end of her battles. Perhaps Rinky had prescribed celibacy. A veritable hair shirt, to atone for the surge of libido that had — if Daniel's confessions were accurate and not the product of a fevered imagination and a perverse drive to impress anyone who listened — led to hour-long, straining, weepy encounters with that graduate student. In the back of the family car, at an unnamed hotel on the outskirts of town, and even in the faculty comfort room at the English department, after office hours.

That graduate student. Candidate for a PhD. That by itself meant nothing; there were scores of universities in the country that annually churned out PhDs. Diploma mills, they were called, and Sweethaven, for all its airs, was fast becoming such an institution. Luth shuddered in revulsion. She could not even bear to think of the creature's name. The woman had been Narita's age. She imagined an obsequious little voice: "Dannie Pastor, why do you refuse love that is given to you?"

But divorce was not possible under the country's laws; Luth's home and her position would forever be secure, as were her children's inheritance and Naia's. The little slut had dumped him. She had pulped his heart. Luth felt the same debilitating satisfaction that infused her when she thought of her husband's literary enterprises. He had not been good enough, not virile enough, not wealthy enough, even for a thirty-ish spinster with a thickening waist. You had best stay with me, old fool, she thought, I know your quirks better than any other human being; we are the same, two old losers who have lost our energy and our sheen, keeping up appearances to maintain our self-respect.

She supposed she would never kiss, let alone sleep with, another man; it was too late. There were honey-haired Florida retirees on television who mated like baboons, but there was no possibility of such behavior in her world. From time to time, if thoughts of beauty and fleshly desires intruded, she satisfied herself by watching the Fashion Channel: slender, belligerent young models advancing down the catwalk, then retreating, always new, never changing.

And of course there had been Naia, and the joy of watching her grow, shooting up to a height never before seen on her side of the family or Daniel's. Praying anxiously against the first crop of pimples, having her devoutness rewarded by a face that never lost the freshness of babyhood, of features that had grown in all the right directions and at the same even and balanced pace. In a way she had never admitted aloud, Luth had thanked Narita for snaring such a wonderful package of genes while young, before experience and cynicism quenched any aspirations she might have had of having a child. And she had thanked Antonia for staying, albeit for what might have been too long — of growing into the role of the playful, intelligent young mother, unencumbered by marriage and the job of pleasing a husband.

LUTH heard a door open. She stood up and moved on cramped limbs out into the living room. Daniel was heading for the front door, moving with rare energy. There was some change in him; she strained to see through the gathering darkness. He had replaced his house singlet with one of the *barong tagalogs* he sometimes wore to morning convocations or meetings with university officials.

"Where are you going?" she said.

He started; he had not seen her in the dark.

"Just for a short drive."

"To where?"

He murmured a reply. He smelled of Tanduay rum.

"You're going to the Hollands, aren't you?" she said. She could not let him out on the road in his state; he would surely mow down a bicyclist, if not wreck the car.

He ignored her and shuffled to the door. His keys jingled in one hand, the other clutched a square of plastic that she realized was a DVD case.

"Dan!" she called after him, her feet sweeping the floor in search of her step-ins. She heard the squeal of the gate, then his feet crunching on the gravel of the driveway. She ran out to stop him. He was about to get into the car, swaying back and forth drunkenly — how much of this was feigned? She grabbed at his arm.

"Let me go," he said in a heavy voice. She ran to the other side of the vehicle and, wrenching the door open, threw her weight into the passenger seat, so violently that the breath was knocked out of her. With an effort, she wriggled, adjusting her buttocks on the seat, her right leg still outside the car until she hauled it in with both her hands. She slammed the door shut and locked it. Further movement was momentarily impossible. She sat there, panting and sweating.

Daniel started the motor and drove the car backwards straight out of the gate. He screeched to a stop, spun the wheel, gunned the vehicle down the lane.

They sped down a road devoid of traffic for the summer, past the mission hospital, past the Sweethaven power station, past the gates that led to the residential section of the campus. She tried to keep calm. She had no idea what she might say to Emily and Rinky Holland, for unlike her husband, she was not one to rehearse her confrontations. She would let her husband do the talking, at the onset — whatever it was he needed to say. She only hoped he would not humiliate himself in the process of saying it. Was there a comb, some Eskinol, a travel pack of tissues in the glove compartment? Whatever. She would be silent, and only when he began to repeat himself, and to smile and — this she knew only too well — to simper, would she come to his rescue.

A series of violent lurches threw her almost to the dashboard. Their wheels had gone over a part of the sidewalk where acacia roots had thrown up thick sections of concrete.

"Stop!" she screamed. The motor died. "We're not going further until you calm down. I won't allow it. You're completely crazy!"

Daniel clutched the steering wheel in both hands. Tears streamed down his cheeks. He began to sob and wail, horrible sounds, the noises made by a man who had never learned to weep for sympathy. He bellowed like a prisoner condemned to a lit oven. Frightened, she made no move to touch him, scrunching herself up on her side of the car.

Finally, he was exhausted, and sat there with the fingers of one hand taut over his heart.

"I ran this on the computer," he said, and passed her the DVD Narita had brought from Manila, keeping his eyes averted from the images on the case.

She shuddered, refused to take the thing.

"I couldn't finish — it *is* her. I hadn't ..."

"I know," she said. The sight of the cover would have been enough for him.

"I'd been running on this hope, this vague hope, that all we were talking about were *model pictures*." At the ridiculousness of the phrase he began to sob again. "I can't breathe properly; I cannot think. All I ask of God is *why*."

But "why" was pointless now, she thought. What next — that was the significant thing.

"You shouldn't have done what you knew you couldn't handle," she told him, trying to sound dry and calm. If he began to cough, to turn purple and to choke, she didn't think she could run fast enough for help.

"You are so strong, Luth, you are so strong."

"Yes," she said. "Now please, turn the car back. We mustn't make a scandal. Please, Dan, for the sake of the family."

"He betrayed me," he moaned. "He assured me Naia would be safe in his house."

"That's right," she said. "But his sons will pay. That's what the case is for. The authorities will prosecute them, with or without Naia. Let's just go home, lock the house and go to sleep."

"I want Rinky to talk to me. I want him to look me in the eye. I want him to say that he is sorry."

That was it, then, she thought. No violence. It seemed reasonable enough. She might go along with him, wait for this valiant surge of masculine aggressiveness to exhaust itself. He might even turn the car back to the house, no harm done.

"All right," she said aloud.

"Please hold me, Luth," he begged.

"I can't," she said. It was too much to ask of her; she wasn't a martyr.

"Hold my hand. Please hold my hand."

Gingerly, she reached out and, with the tips of her fingers, touched the ridge of his knuckles where he gripped the steering wheel. He did not start, as she feared he might. His skin was papery, gray, like the frightening husk she had discovered one day as a girl fluffing back the soft fur on a rabbit's foot that her father had given her.

She laid her soft old palm over the back of his hand.

"Thank you, Luth," he said heavily. "That's all I want. That's enough for me."

Tomorrow, she would divide the cattleya orchids. It was too dry for the task, but she would hang them in the shadows of the mango tree. She needed the small, repetitious work, the delight in discovering horns of new growth. The affirmation of it. She longed for a haven free of any reminders of the Hollands, free of any reminders of Sweethaven, for that matter. This semester, she would retire, a bit earlier than expected, but at the school she was not irreplaceable. She would clear her shelves of PTA minutes, ancient Green Revolution brochures, biographies of José Rizal, of *I'm OK, You're OK*, three decades' worth of typewritten quiz bee questions in science, math and *Araling Panlipunan*, various dust-covered wedding souvenirs, and, finally, her lesson plan books. Her lesson plan books. These she would burn. After that, she would wear loose dusters, watch the Fashion Channel all afternoon, see no one for weeks at a time. The maid would do her shopping. Her retreat from the world would be complete.

DANIEL slid to a stop at right angles to the Hollands' driveway, blocking it.

The house was dark, except for a small light shining through the screened porch on the second floor, its source somewhere in the dining room.

"They've gone to bed," said Luth.

The ground floor, walled in a lattice of whitewashed bamboo strips, seemed completely empty: no sound from within, no trembling flashlight beam, no clandestine movement glimpsed through the high screened windows.

The Hollands' Toyota was missing from the driveway.

Daniel got out of their vehicle and advanced without hesitation to the steps.

"Rinky!" he bellowed.

Luth followed, more slowly, lest it be necessary to call him back.

"Rinky!" he called again, and rapped on the door.

Luth thought she heard breathing from deep within the ground floor. She did not know if it was her imagination. Her instincts told her the house was empty. Maybe it was ghosts, the ghosts of those still living; that seemed possible.

"Rinky!" Daniel bawled.

A door opened deep within the house. Footfalls on the wooden floor, a shuffle of slippers.

The bulb above their heads clicked on. No, every light bulb beneath the eaves of the house, and even in the yard, came on, a signal to the campus guards walking their beats, as though burglars had come to call. Luth felt no embarrassment, no fear. Let the public see.

They heard the sound of the main door being unbolted. Tentatively, it squeaked back. Luth peered through the screened outer door, at the small shape that stood just beyond, trying to discern its features. The light from the bulb above them dazzled her eyes.

"Let us in, Emily," said Daniel.

The catch on the screen door slid back. Daniel wrenched the door open and stomped over the threshold. Luth followed to avert further tragedy. The living room had gone completely dark. Someone had extinguished the last lamp in the house. The woman shrank back against furniture with a small scream. The light from the eaves, falling through the porch screens, momentarily striped her face. It was the maid, Sebia. A small hammer was in her hand.

"Where's your employer?" said Daniel. "Where are his sons?"

"They're not home, sir," she stammered. "They left this afternoon."

"Where'd they go?"

"I don't know," she said. "They must have gone to the golf course. It's a long drive."

"You're lying."

The maid backed away, making a few futile jabs with the hammer in the air before her. She didn't know whether to threaten them or beg for mercy.

"I don't know, sir. Don't ask me, sir. I don't know."

Luth sensed, before she saw, the new presence in the room, the woman who emerged from the depths of the shadows and said, in a taut voice, "Go away, Sebia, I'll handle this."

The maid shrank against Emily Holland, the hammer now firmly in the air, poised to strike at the intruders should they advance another step.

"These people should have been dealt with long ago," her mistress said. "Give us some light."

A fluorescent bar sprang to life. Luth had not seen Mrs. Holland since that Sunday at the church. She had been smiling and confident, powdered and coiffed, exactly as she had appeared in public every day of her life. Now the figure that confronted them, in a sagging cotton duster, seemed a ghost of itself, the hair in greasy tufts, the face devoid of makeup, sallow and wrinkled, like an old piece of garlic. But the eyes were livid and rimmed with red: vengeful spirit eyes.

"Goddamn you, Emily, your boys are going to jail."

"Daniel Pastor. How dare you come here. When you promised never to harass us again."

Daniel had not foreseen a counterattack. He stood stunned before her while she drew herself up. She was shaking, but not with fear.

"A man was here yesterday. A lawyer from the mayor's office, a Fortun. Our boys weren't home, thank God. We had to face him, Rinky and I. The questions he asked. We had nothing to hide. I told him all about your granddaughter. How many weeks I tried to help her. He wouldn't stop at the answers we gave." She shuddered violently at some memory. "And in the morning the police were back with more questions. Demanding to see my sons. They couldn't arrest Brent; he's only fifteen. But Adam, he turned pale at the sight of their jeep. My Adam, pale and trembling, jumping out of a window and running away in his shorts and sandals."

"Where is Adam?" Daniel demanded.

"I don't know, I don't know! Brent's gone, too. One moment he was here, and then he was gone."

"He left before noon, ma'am," the maid volunteered. "With a knapsack."

"They could be anywhere. They could be lying in a gutter, hurt. Rinky's gone out to find them; he's been looking for hours. This is what you've done."

Emily started to weep. "My sons. My eldest has a girlfriend in America, a Christian girl. They've sent each other promise rings, they've made vows. My youngest is starting college in Manila. They had their whole lives in front of them. And you did this to us."

She must have been well admonished, in the convent school of her girlhood, against any attempts at violence, and now she stood, her small face raised and twisted by real tears, her fists clenched on either side of her wretched housedress.

"You son of a whore, how dare you do this to us. What have we done to you? This after all our help. You were nothing, Daniel Pastor, you had nothing left when you came to my husband for help: no dignity, no morals, no courage — worthless."

She turned to Luth, seeing her for the first time. "And you, what are you looking at? Are you happy at last? Your mother sold rice cakes at the St. Joseph canteen. You've come up in the world, haven't you?"

She took a stiff-legged step in the direction of the woman. Emily took a stiff-legged step in Luth's direction.

"That Naia," she spat. "She was a joke. The girl who'd spread for anybody given half the chance. She tempted Adam, led him to ruin. Rinky confronted him as soon as the lawyer left."

"What else did Adam admit, Emily?" Dan said. "Did he show you the footage, too? The footage he took up in that ceiling, of those two other women, and God knows who else? You damned hypocrite, I'll sue you. You ruined my granddaughter."

"Quiet," Emily screamed. "There is no footage. Our sons are clean. Watch that porn video. You can get it anywhere. See for yourself. Are my sons in it? Do you see their faces? You tell me. All I see are those two prostitutes and that filthy little girl of yours, touching her body and posing. Baring herself without shame. If you're too cowardly to look at that wretched video, do so now, because *I* have, in my capacity as principal I *had* to. It was the worst, the dirtiest, the most pathetic thing I have ever seen in my life. And I pray I forget it soon."

Luth stood her ground, though her body shook uncontrollably, rot and fear and hatred rising in her gut until she felt them battering against her clamped jaws. She felt something snap in the back of her head — it could have been a capillary; it could have been a bone in her nape unlocking after being held rigid for so long. When she opened her mouth she thought a torrent of black fire might pour from her bowels; she felt a great singing energy along her arms and back, as though a pair of shivering membranous wings might burst in that moment through her skin.

But instead, a string of small, precise sounds issued from her throat: "No, Emily. It is you I pray we forget soon. Your eldest son is no artist. He is a pornographer, and you and your family are the dirtiest, most pathetic set of hypocrites Sweethaven has known. You are your own worst punishment. Mark my words."

Daniel took her arm, exactly as he had done at the church, that day when she had been so afraid, so choked with shame and rage that she had wanted to slash every last one of the smirking faces turned toward her. Firmly and surely he guided her to the door, guarding her back, protecting her from the wrath of the other woman. They made their way down the stairs, each descending step a challenge, for Luth's entire body was shaking so badly she thought she might collapse in a heap upon her husband. She could barely feel her extremities, they were so cold. Don't run, she admonished herself. Do not hurry; there's no need anymore. A flame of triumph leapt in her breast. Had she ever felt safer, ever felt stronger than in this moment, picking her way down the shadowy steps of this storied house in the very belly of Sweethaven? Above them, within the screened enclosure of the porch, flowerpots shattered and books tumbled to the polished floorboards as Emily wailed and wept.

Twenty-three

JOEL LIVED BY himself in one of the new subdivisions on Donostia's outskirts. In a corner of the *sala* was a table with a lamp and a wedding picture. In the photograph, the bride and groom looked ridiculously happy. Her waist was long and pinched — no impending infant to conceal. Joel was young and slim and looked as though made of porcelain, not in the fineness of his skin but in the fragility of his happiness. Narita noticed that he wore no rings on his finger, not even a class ring or one of those atrocious carbuncles other lawyers might match with a gold chain.

There was one other framed picture of his wife, against a snow landscape. Narita didn't know how distant his wife was from his heart. For that matter, she had no idea whom he may have invited, no matter how temporarily, to take her place.

The houseboy fed them a heated-up supper, glancing at her before disappearing into the darker regions of the house, presumably to eat his own meal, and then to feed the dog she could hear off the garage moaning and rattling its chain. She wondered where the boy slept, if he cared who she was, if he knew anything about his employer's life.

There was a report of the homicide on the local news, and photos of Gemma and Tristan Bulauan. No mention was made of the porn video, let alone Gemma's attempt to speak to the authorities about it. The announcer only said the husband was being detained as a suspect. But the announcer's voice was loud and engaging like a sportscaster's, and his ringing tones exhorted his listeners to crude speculation. She cringed, hating this aspect of the evening news: it was the same here as it was in Manila, information as entertainment.

"A man who lays his hands on a woman needs to be punished at once," Joel said grimly. "Otherwise he'll never stop."

"How do you punish him?"

"Thrash him. Dose him with his own medicine."

Your good friend Zenon used to beat me. How would he react? *Zenon looked like an angel, but his hands were light, as the old folks say.* What would happen if she told him? Would he put his arms quickly about her shoulder and give her a squeeze, would he embrace her in sympathy the way a woman might, a fellow veteran of pain? Would revelation be the key to sexual congress? They were sitting side by side on the sofa, thighs touching lightly, his skin warm through the material of his trousers. Either of them could have edged away. She needed to urinate but was afraid to ask where the bathroom was, lest the intriguing contact be broken.

This was not the first time she had been alone in a strange man's home. There had been plenty of that in Manila, so she was familiar, more or less, with the trajectory of events. Under any other circumstances, they would be approaching the moment of reckoning; all he needed was a little push. But why? she thought. Why disturb the ecology of his life? Why him, of all people? Once she had wearied of the phantom that was Zenon, she had granted entry to a variety of men, and gotten all the affirmation she would ever need.

Joel broke the contact with her body at last. The news had segued into the nightly soap opera, and with an exclamation of disgust, he got up to surf channels, holding the remote a yard from the screen, outlined, tense and impatient, against the glow of the box.

Finding nothing of interest, he turned the television off with a snort. "Would you like coffee?" he said. "I have a sack of *barako*, and a machine that's gathering dust. I'm sure I kept them in the hope of company such as yours."

Gallant man, she thought. *Mambobola. Bolero.* Offering her a cup of genuine *barako*, the brew with the name that meant "stud." Fitting enough, she thought.

She paid him back with a smile. "I need the bathroom."

"You can have both," he said. "And whatever else you desire."

She turned away quickly, perturbed, avoiding his face; was he being flippant, or was this an awkward attempt at courtship? She and the man had been in each other's company for nearly half a day. This was not Manila; this was Donostia, and every moment she spent here compromised her, and her family's battered reputation. It was late, too late in the evening, too late in her life, to engineer intimacy. She wished she weren't so tired, that she had the energy to launch herself from the sofa, instead of burrowing into these pillows, watching his movements like a hapless puppy. What did she want? She wanted her own connection, her own dose of oblivion, she needed someone to embrace her and rock her a bit — she wanted a tiny carnal reward, because she was *spent*. Those months and years in Manila of nonstop work that paid in peanuts, the hours stuck in traffic every day, the press of moist human skin in the jeepneys, the void at the heart of it all.

There was a bathroom off the living room. It was so fragrant and perfect, towels matched to soap, that it was obvious he never used it; he must have another one in the room where he slept. In the mirror, the public Narita confronted her. The same woman she had known and come to terms with over more than a decade. You like him; accept it, she told herself. You don't really *want* him; not yet. You've known him, what? Three days? Excluding that single college semester, half a lifetime ago. You *could* wreck his life. You could make him weep. But why, Narita? Why bring another truckload of shit upon yourself?

She wondered how his career as city attorney would fare. One witness was dead; the other would be banished to Manila.

There was the third girl, the one called Diana Rosales, but Narita knew little about her, only what Joel had provided: that she had taken up the mayor on his offer and was now temporarily housed at one of his homes, in Bacolod or Cebu, weeping and ruing her foray into what she called premarital sex. Good for her, Narita thought; she'd had the sense to repent, to grovel, to swallow what scraps of mercy Donostia might toss her way. And she was still alive. In a little while she might even venture out, under a different name. "Diana Rosales," the shameless whore, would be dead and gone, but at least the poor girl still had the world, or what thin pleasure she might extricate from it — the taste of mangoes; the blind, stupid love of a pet dog.

Narita was sorry that her decision to protect her daughter would be the instrument of Joel's undoing. Without Naia to attest to the identity of the young man in her footage, there would be no scapegoat, no choice but to prosecute his own cousin.

But the case would go on. What was she worried about? Joel was determined to pursue it. There was too much buzz about it in the press; it had reached the national dailies. Yet when he spoke, darkly, of his determination to bring Torres and his friends to justice, she thought he sounded a shade too theatrical, as though he were convincing himself of the wisdom of his plan. What was he so afraid of? He had evidence enough. There was the video itself, to begin with. There was the small bungalow he had brought her to that afternoon. There was the boy called Harrison Co — Joel would simply have to labor a bit more, talk to a few more people. Young men never kept quiet. Surely there had been someone: a disgruntled servant, an enemy of the family, a drinking buddy he would have bragged to. No community in Donostia was ever watertight. It was up to the police now to find the rest of their witnesses, even if the entire merchant population closed ranks and rallied about their black sheep.

Then she thought of the confession Joel had made to her that afternoon, at the bungalow. He served at the pleasure of the mayor, he had admitted. He was the mayor's *boy*, giving the word that particular Binisaya inflection that called to mind not the smiling, clean-scrubbed protégé, but the silent, dusty household retainer who, every so often, might be counted on to cook a meal or drive a mistress home or inter some unpleasant business in a sugarcane field.

She massaged her temples in misery. Naia alone mattered. Naia was above everything now, even these feeble attempts to vindicate her honor that, deep down, Narita knew would never prosper. Daniel Pastor was simply not powerful enough. Not within the microcosm of Sweethaven U, and Sweethaven's power quailed before the numbing reality of Donostia. If she had learned anything from her years in Manila, it was to live and let live. People smarter and more well connected and infinitely stronger than she could ever be decided matters in boardrooms and on golf links to which she would never gain access. Go with the flow — that had been her motto. Accept your paycheck with a smile of gratitude, greet the graying, distinguished boss a pleasant good day as he passed you in the halls, and quietly accept the occasional bit of lucre that fluttered your way.

So, smile, she told herself. Show him your excellent nacreous surfaces. Smile, damn you. The mirror image obeyed: the result was painful, her face broken up into a dozen planes, none of which was connected to the others. Mustering that buoyancy and goodwill that had sustained her from adolescence, she grinned and embraced her fear.

He was not in the living room when she crept out. A single cup of coffee rested on a coaster on the glass tabletop; there were small packets of sugar and creamer as well, the kind a cheap hotel might offer. She glanced sadly down at the fragrant brew. No one had ever made coffee just for her. And she wouldn't even enjoy it. Now was the perfect moment to grab her bag and leave. He would not miss her. She might take a small sip to honor his hospitality, then get herself out of there before trouble developed.

Still, she did not fancy picking her way to the main road in the dark. There would be few tricycles about at this hour. The memory of Gemma Bulauan was still fresh; when she closed her eyes the image of that still, bloodless foot came to life behind her closed lids. She did not fancy having *that* for company in the darkness. Perhaps Joel might drive her home. In any case, it was only polite that she thank him and bid him good-bye.

Several doors led off the living room. One was ajar. She approached cautiously, his name on her lips, and fell silent when she realized the space was empty. It was his study; she was conscious of bookshelves, a narrow bed half-covered in stacks of plastic binders, a document open on the computer. She moved toward the paper-strewn desk, aware that she was trespassing, holding her arms stiff at her sides to curb the impulse to disturb his things. A printout lay among the papers. From the format, it could have been a search warrant or some such legal brief, but as she drew closer to investigate, something else caught her eye: a spill of objects by his keyboard.

They were videos. The topmost was the one of with Gemma, Naia, and Diana Rosales — identical to what she had purchased on the side street in Quiapo just a few days before. She picked it up, perturbed; the ones underneath were of the same genre, paper liners shoved carelessly into their scuffed cases, all of them most definitely used. Local and foreign, glossy and rough. Pornographic videos.

She felt his presence in the door even before his soft exclamation of surprise. She whirled around, confronting him, the videos in her hands.

"What is this? Research?" She laughed.

In a single moment, Joel saw and understood. The flippant, indulgent expression drained from his face.

"No, Narita, it's not research," he said tiredly, and looked away. "I own them. I watch them."

"And this?" she said, holding up the square of plastic with her daughter's image. "You watch this, too? For what, for inspiration? To profile the enemy? To wrestle with your sense of outrage?"

"Here," he said, moving in on her. "Let me take that from you. It's not the time to discuss this."

She clung furiously to the video. They struggled, silently, a contest reduced to the tension in their fingertips.

Abruptly, she relented, flinging her arms violently in the air. But the sudden movement offered no release; the rage, contained for so long, began to build, fueling itself; she felt more awake than she had in years.

"What does it do for you?" she confronted him. "Porn, I mean. How big's your collection? Don't worry, I'm not judging you. I have my own stash, I tell you; porn's a good thing."

He put up his hands helplessly, as if to beg "Peace," but she was determined to have it out with him, if only to untangle her thoughts.

"It is not the same," he said. "I know the girls. I have talked to each one of them. This footage — it was made without their knowledge. It was something stolen from them. How could I possibly respond ... naturally, to something like that?"

"Naturally," she jeered. "What is 'naturally?' Is that your prerogative as a man?"

"What do you think?" was all he said.

She stared hard into his face, appalled at the change in his features, the absence of expression; trying to gauge the degree of his helplessness, of whatever desire she had thought she had detected, trying to determine where the lies, the pride, the greed left off and genuine decency began. He seemed, as they stood there, to shift shape before her exhausted eyes: toadie, gallant, coward, angel. In reality he had not moved a muscle in his face. He simply stood there, an old hand at the game, watching her, knowing his edge, aware of her needs, waiting to see how far she was willing to come.

"That happened to me, too," she said. "Your good and wonderful friend Zenon Cuaresma. He ran a private peep show from his boardinghouse room. His friends used to watch us. Through holes in the wall."

But he did not react. It was as if he hadn't heard, or her words had made no difference. He just kept staring into her face.

"They took turns, don't you understand?" she raged. "He decided which of them to invite. To look at us. To look at *him*. Using me."

Joel said, "I know."

She began to cry. "You knew what Zenon was doing in that house."

"Yes."

"You knew. Why didn't you stop him, then."

He held out his arms.

"You knew what Zenon was doing to me. Why didn't you — " She left the sentence unfinished.

He said nothing, merely closed the distance between the two of them. They had reached the end, the wretched end of it all. She wrapped her arms tight about his shoulders, as she had done too many times to count, with too many men, too many reckless conquests. She stretched the length of her body up against his, testing him, barreling into the wall of his reserve, punishing him. He did not push her off, or stagger backward with a feigned apology. His cheek burned against hers, his breath was hot against her hair.

THE ritual of boyhood. For Joel it begins with what they call the snake crawl, a term they have borrowed from Citizens Army Training. Flat on their bellies, propelled in the darkness by the tortuous movement of their elbows, over mud, grass, twigs, animal turds.

Snake crawl is not absolutely necessary; one may dart from bush to bush, bent at the waist, sharp buttocks in the air, and if truth be told, a boy might straighten up to his full height and amble unnoticed over to where the action is taking place, to stand tactfully behind a banana trunk and, perhaps, release a few hoots of encouragement now and then.

But snake crawl brings with it all the filth and discomfort of adventure. The front of Joel's T-shirt is furry with detritus. He scrapes his elbows, his knees. He is a ninja, a commando. He is fourteen.

What is this place? A pitch-black grove. Bamboo. Coconut. Mango. Each of these. None of these.

Where, then? The border of a vast estate, over where the hog-wire fence has been trodden down to the ground and it is possible to hoist oneself over into the adjacent hacienda, where it is rumored armed guards patrol night and day, ready to shoot or lop off the heads of lurking thieves or adventurous young boys.

No, really, where is he? Perhaps he haunts the cemetery, creeping from tombstone to whitewashed tombstone, drawn by the sound of voices, daring himself to witness a revelation biblical in its import.

He could be by the river, in a stand of aging banana trunks, some reputed to bear tunnels the circumference of a penis, set at approximately the height of a young boy's waist. No one has actually seen these scars. Joel thinks he spotted one, only one, the afternoon he took a shortcut through the trees, hurrying home lest it be discovered he had gone boating on the treacherous river. The scar was a round hole, sure enough, weeks old by its color, and surrounded a splotch of brown tissue, standing out from the firm and living green. But it was on a level with his chest — some anomaly there.

What exactly is Joel doing? He is creeping up on a friend. The friend is with a girl. The friend is getting laid.

There are other boys in the bushes, hearts pounding and skin aflame, though the breeze blows cool on this summer night. Yet as he gets closer and closer to the goal, he feels totally alone.

Where is the light coming from? Starlight. A fluorescent bar, pasted with dead insects, atop a distant lamppost. The moon.

This is the first time yet this has all happened to him before.

There is no light. It is pitch black. He sees nothing. He has lost out. All he can boast of, if he dares open his mouth tomorrow evening as his buddies gather at the corner store, is the brown muck that crusts his good Lacoste sports shirt, acquired just last Christmas.

No, there is a glow, from a lighter, and his friend Andoy, on hands and knees, is revealed. In all his stupidity — for upon this ignominious carpet of banana grove filth, Andoy is completely naked. The youth has taken off all his clothes, as one might do with one's girlfriend, as one might do on one's wedding night, as one might do with a woman who is worth it, with a woman one swears to love.

Andoy — now on hands and knees, now crouched like a frog, the grimy shins of the girl on either side of his arse. Who is the girl anyway? The one who haunts the plaza in the evenings, voice loud and rough, traveling round and round the perimeter fence with a pack of urchins. Of these urchins, the oldest is no more than eight — they are the ragged retinue that shout obscenities at the girl in between taking experienced drags on their cheap cigarettes. They are sellers of sweets and boiled peanuts and ice water by day, besieging the minibuses that pause for a few minutes at the marketplace in between runs among the sugarcane towns of the coast.

They call the girl Lala. Joel remembers that detail, but not her true name nor where in the town she slept nor any feature of her face. You would think after a childhood of peddling menthol candy to carsick travelers she would have learned the business of buy-and-sell, but no, the sex she renders is completely free, and yes, a few of the neighborhood youths take, with alacrity.

The rest of them, Joel included, watch. Snake-crawling through the brush or darting from slab to slab in the cemetery. They fear eczema, scabies, pubic lice. They fear venereal disease most of all. In the language of the town, all varieties of VD translate to "the disease of woman." The thought of being laid low holds them in mystic thrall. To descend into that sucking well between Lala's thighs, to emerge unscathed, if shrunken and wobbling and slicked with protoplasm — this is an experience granted only to the boldest of corner store warriors.

Because they watch so much, and discuss with one another even more, they have developed a unique vocabulary to describe one another's exploits. Andoy is the fool who goes naked. Mikey's specialty is rape style. Jik wastes precious time talking to the girl. It is reputed Jik likes to get to know the girl first, for between these unparented, perennially giggling females there are certain differences: one hopes for a little baby someday, another's father was a negro GI, and so on. Poor Jik. But what does "rape style" mean? Joel does not know Mikey, not personally, but he conjectures it has something to do with force applied, with the drama of wrenching someone's thighs apart when they have already been widely and resignedly spread.

As for Kiddo, he is the uncircumcised one, the pathetic coward whose penis wears a sweater in the tropical heat. They call him the paper bag. Wrinkly and brown.

SOME of his friends marry young, settle with a pregnant new wife in a hollow-block hovel, and there their thirst for knowledge ends. For others, the shy, misshapen ones hampered by buckteeth and pimples, the adventure goes on, well into their womanless college days, where they are crammed into boardinghouses in Donostia, two boys to a room, or three or four. Vacating their bed spaces for an afternoon to watch, a single eye plastered to an aperture in a thin *lawanit* wall, as a housemate performs on an unsuspecting girlfriend.

Joel and Zenon pay several hundred apiece for their rooms. They occupy a single bedroom divided into two by a *lawanit* wall, share a bathroom with the rest of the house. They take most of their meals at the *carenderia* over on the next street. When they are broke, which is often, they stretch a little can of sardines over the course of the day, pouring tomato sauce and slivers of fish over heaping plates of rice. They can't live without rice, or cigarettes. Zenon borrows everything: smokes, money, a motorbike. Joel has stopped keeping score, but knows his friend has probably cadged a month's rent from him in small change.

Joel spends his free time at the library, and the weekends in the town he calls home. He can't bear to be alone in his room. The odor of Zenon penetrates the wall, of sour sweat, cheap cologne. Lying down, he finds it takes a tremendous effort of will to get up again. Some days he is rudely shaken awake by one or two of the other boys, who bundle into his section of space, hiss, "Wake up, your buddy's back. It's showtime," and cut the lights.

He pities the girlfriend who enters in a jingle of earrings, a sweep of skirt. She had seemed such a vibrant, indestructible personality when he had met her for the first time in World Literature class. What would it take to know a girl like that? She will go far, he thinks — all the way to America, or at least Manila, where she will be an advocate of some sort, and wear business suits and give interviews on TV. She is not pretty, but she comes from a good family, and is clever and fearless and articulate, strong and blunt in her opinions; she has every advantage on her side. He is not worthy of her, which is why he refuses to peer through the gaps in his wall, one of which a buddy has designated "Narita's hole" in pencil. His housemates tease him, calling him faggot, thinking that the rain of insults will build up his nerve. He doesn't watch, but many times he listens, sick at heart, as her voice rises, wave upon joyful wave. The boys pile around the peepholes. They are all virgins in that house, but for Zenon. They enumerate the many strange things they have observed about her body; they point out various moles and irregularities on her skin, then dramatically spit in the dust of the tiny courtyard, as if to get rid of her aftertaste. The more she visits, the less worthy she is of their respect. Joel knows that, if he ever dared speak to her, look her in the eye, be the recipient of her wide and unknowing smile, what esteem he harbors for her would vanish as well. He is aware he is stealing from her, but lacks the courage to warn her, to shake her equilibrium with a small, secret note or a cough from his side of the wall.

One afternoon there is a struggle from the next room. The girl cries out in surprise and outrage. Zenon shouts back. There is a thud, as of a body thrown backward against the bed, a series of alarming thumps upon the wall. The girl begs for mercy. Zenon lets her go. "You'll be back," he snarls.

She's pregnant. The word rips quietly through the boardinghouse. It fills the teenage boys with consternation: they have an instinctive fear of babies, of misshapen bellies, of mothers and the mysterious power they possess. But unless Zenon confirms it, the news must remain a rumor, and the girl's status in the house goes unchanged.

The following day, there she is indeed, knocking plaintively at the front door. She interrupts a poker game being played atop the bed spread. The boys are galvanized at the prospect of another show, but Zenon is merely annoyed: they have been playing for stakes and he is winning. "Get under the bed," he growls to Joel. Joel shakes his head, rises in disgust, leaves. Anton follows. The fourth, Manny, giggling, gets down on his hands and knees. "Hurry up!" Zenon hisses. Obediently, the boy hunches himself up among the dusty shoes and forgotten socks: he is an ugly youth, with a big head and a mouthful of large teeth.

In a little while, the girlfriend enters. Zenon takes her, soothingly, in his arms, and she melts. Joel, his heart broken, does not stay to hear the rest of Zenon's performance. Nor the moment of discovery, and the girl's scream, of disbelief, of realization, as her innocence comes to an end.

BUT they are good boys; in every sense they are simply exercising their prerogative. They are the youths who, on summer afternoons, go riding about the plaza of their hometowns on rented bicycles, the luckiest ones on the dirt-track motorbikes that are hand-me-downs from uncles and fathers. Few of them are old enough for driver's licenses, but all have learned, or are learning, to control their wheels. Often the talk centers on motorbikes rather than women. They guide the vehicles past the two-story frame houses about the plaza, craning their necks when they pass a significant balcony. Their eyes flick left and right, already experienced, after a summer of two, in the art of filtering, dismissing the peasants and town hall clerks who plod through the town's streets after Mass, tuned only to the sight of a mysterious and unreachable female face.

The boys, they part company around eleven at night, surrendering the neighborhood sidewalks and the corner stores to the real men, the tough guys in their twenties and thirties who do, occasionally, make genuine trouble. What a relief it is to Joel to leave the summer day's filth from his body, making a great splashing in the dim and tile-less bathroom as he pours water over himself again and again with the plastic dipper, leaning on the artesian well hand-pump to fill up the bucket. His grandmother croaks, in complaint, from an upstairs bedroom. She is widowed and cannot sleep unless her maid is in the room. Joel, on summer holiday from his parents and siblings, paces the darkened *sala*, reveling in the freshness of his skin. He treasures these midnight moments of solitude, for he is fourteen and his world is intact, and yet perpetually and excitingly threatened. He knows that at any moment the tale of his activities down by the cemetery might reach his father, twisted by adult histrionics. He will be branded a pervert and a rapist, a marijuana addict, or a pusher, which is the worst of all.

He comforts himself by padding up the pitted wooden staircase, taking care to avoid making unnecessary sounds. The doleful image of the Sacred Heart, adorned with red electric candles, presides over the head of the stairs. Joel genuflects without excessive thought. He is more interested in his grandfather's law books, which occupy the horseshoe cupboard that crowns the stairwell. Gently he slides open a glass door and reaches inside for a volume. Like the wood of the risers, it is riddled by the action of small chewing insects. He begins to read, about murder. He appreciates a good paperback now and then, but these ancient tomes, elegantly annotated by a hand long dead, enthrall him. He reads the penal code, puzzling at the convoluted sentences. Beneath the weak yellow bulb he may peruse these legal reports until the breezes of predawn dry the fresh sweat from his armpits and the back of his knees.

In the morning, he rises at six to the metallic rhythm of the church bells two blocks down, and dons his rubber sandals for the walk down to the baker's. He takes the handful of coins that his Lola has left for him on the kitchen table. Where he passes storefronts and eateries still boarded up from the night, his sandals crunch over shattered beer bottles and cigarette butts.

Occasionally he chances upon a slip of rolling paper pasted to the sidewalk by rain. Beauticians use the paper to fasten hair to curlers, but Joel knows that furled around a teaspoonful of marijuana, it makes for a pretty good smoke.

When he returns, it is with a bag of warm *pan de sal*. His grandmother is awake, smelling of lipstick and powder and old person's armpit and some mentholated Chinese balm. She embraces Joel, and he twits her for her vanity. He is strong and healthy and can function for three days without sleep. He is the talented and beloved grandson; he can do no wrong.

Twenty-four

THE PEAL OF a phone, very close to her head, woke Narita, and in that unfamiliar darkness, dominated by the hum of air-conditioning, she had no idea where she was. When she reached out foggily to silence the instrument, she touched the man. He was firm and warm, and at the contact with his skin she sighed and tried to snuggle closer. She felt him leave her side. He had taken the call, his voice terse; he was already in a world to which she was barred. The door opened and closed behind him. She rolled over, tugging the blanket around her shoulders. The air-conditioner shut down with a thump, and in the quiet, she thought she heard a siren in the distance: a fire engine or an ambulance.

As a child, she fell asleep to the wail of the alarm from the firehouse, a most comforting noise, for it told her that the day had ended and it was time for all fathers to come home, time to lock the doors and slam the shutters to, time to light the mosquito coils and crawl into bed. The siren hurtled up over the darkened city every night for years, for there was Martial Law, and the sound signaled the start of the curfew hours: woe to anyone stumbling into some police constabulary officer in the darkness.

She might have slept a few minutes or so, because the next thing she knew the overhead light was on and Joel was bending, fully dressed, over her.

"Bad news."

The rush of powerful vehicles made her heart thud. The sound was coming from the main road not far from his home.

"What's going on?"

"Villa Milagros is burning."

They let themselves out of the house and boarded the jeep. Toads leapt in consternation away from their headlights. The roads were empty; the night's quota of drunks had yet to get behind the wheel of their cars, and the rest of the world was fast asleep. Life was suspended at that hour. They barreled through the empty marketplace, taking a route through the center of town.

"Did your team get to document the unit?" she called to him over the rush of the wind.

She didn't catch his reply.

The flames had been quenched by the time they got to the compound, but the air, as they approached, bore the acrid stench of carbonized wood. It was impossible to drive all the way to the gate, with three fire trucks taking up most of the street, and in addition there were police jeeps and a thick crowd of neighbors and gawkers, amazingly alert for the hour. A skinny man and his wife slipped past the jeep, muttering, lugging a bundle of what seemed to be clothes wrapped up in a bedsheet. Across the street, it looked like a garage sale was in progress. Three electric fans, a television, a set of monobloc chairs and more sheet-wrapped bundles stood on the sidewalk, ready to be whisked out of harm's way, and guarded from thieves by a sleepy-looking teenage boy. "Of course, the fire trucks got here after it was all over," she heard the woman say to her companion. "A waste of time, getting us out of bed like that," he groused back.

"You should be thankful the fire didn't get your house," Joel snapped at them. It was his City Hall persona, coming to the fore at last.

The crowd wasn't thinning in the least. In fact, motorcycles were arriving, discharging their curious riders in twos and threes. Young men, young girls, even a sleepy child or two. "Anybody dead?" they said, to no one in particular as they sauntered past, and in the streetlights they seemed to be grinning, ghoulish, desperate for excitement. The night wind changed direction, rewarding them with the stench of smoke and a wave of black ash.

Narita stumbled after Joel. The fire trucks had turned the side of the road into muck that sucked the shoes right off her feet. Joel had reached the gates to the compound by the time a man in uniform stopped him; another took Narita not too gently by the arm: members of the public not allowed. She could have flashed this fellow the press pass that she always carried in her bag, but in case he knew something about Naia, she didn't want any questions about her surname. Through the ironwork fence she peered at the unfamiliar buildings: they were still standing, and it was hard to tell, through the darkness and still-rising smoke, which had burned and which were intact.

"Was it the Torres unit?" she said to the uniformed man who had accosted her.

"We know nothing about that," he said, in dismissal. It shut her up. One fire truck, the one manned by the Chinese community volunteers, was still at work; the predawn wind, when it turned, sent stray droplets into their faces, through the belches of smoke. At last, her eyes tearing up, she called to Joel, who was still talking to the police, that she was heading back to the jeep. She wrote about flowers and cuisine for a living, not this. The real reporters were arriving anyway, with their cameras and floodlights, looking bored and sleepy as they held their mobile phones under the cops' noses to collect a quote or two.

So that was it, she thought, the scene of the crime all gone. She didn't care to know who had set the fire. It didn't matter. Some hired hand, some houseboy. JP would have left Donostia already, would be in Manila, or Bacolod, Hong Kong, possibly even America. She had come to Donostia to perform a simple act of rescue.

What would she send to her boss? She had never written a police report, let alone a crime feature. She had no photographs, except those that Joel might remember to share with her, images of a dead girl with a blackened tongue, a boy pulping his head against the wall. She thought she might document the fire scene, what remained of it, on her mobile phone. When she pulled the phone out of her bag, she saw her daughter had been trying to reach her for the better part of the night. WHERE ARE YOU? Naia had thumbed out. PLEASE CALL THE HOUSE. And then: ARE LOLO AND LOLA WITH YOU? THEY'RE NOT BACK. And: ARE YOU WITH THE LAWYER? ARE YOU COMING HOME?

But replying seemed out of the question; Naia would surely be asleep by now. There was a faint flush of blue on the horizon; within minutes the predawn light would reveal the blackened shell of the house; the avid expressions of the bystanders; her own tired, guilty form huddled in the front seat of the jeep. Joel was out in the road, talking, fairly shouting, to one of the firemen, who gesticulated furiously, as if to rid himself of blame. A police jeep arrived; one of the fire trucks churned past, back to the station, the men in the cab grinning, talking about something that seemed totally unrelated to the scene at hand.

Joel was a mess, shirt wet, the bottom of his trousers smeared with mud. In a short while, as the remains cooled, he would be covered in ash. He was staying, she thought. This was his world; now his life in the next few days would consist of salvaging what he could from the ashes of the case, and she would be superfluous, if not a dismal reminder of the job he had to do. She lifted her mobile phone to call him; amid the noise of engines and the crowd, she heard his own phone ring somewhere on his person, a tiny and contained sound. She saw his mouth work, saw him reach into his pocket and check the name and number as it flashed on his screen. His hand moved and abruptly the call was disengaged, the burring on her own phone silenced. She saw all this but still she stood there some moments more, a disbelieving grin frozen to her face, until he looked her way and their eyes met. He did not react, and she did not call to him. She turned around and began to walk, her eyes smarting from the smoke.

Twenty-five

THE SUN HAD risen by the time she arrived at her parents' house. She had hoped for a bit more darkness, some cover by which she might slip in through the back door, a finger to her lips in case she encountered the maid. A kind of adolescent guilt infused her. Not once, throughout her teenage years, had she slept out without permission. Spending the night in a strange room, with people her parents did not know, had been the ultimate violation of the household rules.

She was yawning and exhausted and desperate for a long, astringent shower, sullied somehow by the night, as though handprints lingered, oily and black, over her skin and clothes. When she saw the car, not in the garage but parked in the road outside the gate, she understood that the night wasn't over yet, and braced herself for the inevitable skewering from her parents.

The living room, facing north, was dim as she entered and at first she did not notice the figure upon the couch, facing the door, as though waiting patiently for the precise moment when she'd appear.

"Mother."

Narita jumped, cast a guilty glance over at the speaker. It was Naia, looking surprisingly composed, her hair freshly washed, her T-shirt spotless.

"There's been a fire," Narita burst out, to forestall any questions. "JP Torres's property is gone. Burnt, razed, kaput — good-bye to all evidence. I was there."

The girl considered this, gave a downturned smile. "Did anyone die?"

She would be waiting for a name, several names perhaps. "No," Narita said. "Not in the fire."

"And the house?"

"It's gone, Naia," she repeated. "No more crime scene. No more evidence. No more case. Do you understand?"

The girl looked at her with a blank, hopeless expression. What do you want? Narita wanted to cry. This is a good thing for you, don't you understand; it means you're free.

"Is it true about the dead girl?" Naia said.

She shuddered at the memory of the blanket-draped form on the stretcher, the young husband pulping his temples against the wall.

"Gemma? How did you know about Gemma?"

Naia shrugged. "How else?" She held up her mobile phone, wagged it in the air. "Was she really murdered?"

Narita was afraid to reply. She went rather self-consciously to the couch and sat down. It was the closest she had ever gotten to her daughter in the week that had elapsed.

"You don't have to worry, Naia. No one will ever do that to you."

The girl took a deep breath, as though debating whether to say more.

"It's not even six, Naia, too early to be about.

"You didn't come home. I figured you knew something about her death. I stayed up waiting for you."

There was disapproval, even dislike, in her tone.

"I ... was part of the investigation. I spent a few hours studying the case ...our case ... afterward."

"Overnight?" Naia said. "With the lawyer?"

"No," she lied.

"Really," Naia jeered.

Narita squirmed beneath the steadiness of her daughter's gaze. She knew that to reveal, even to hint at, details of one's sexuality to one's own child was a dreadful mistake. But Naia was no closer to her than a niece, a cousin who had grown up in a far country. In shame, she tried to smile.

"Your Lolo and Lola …"

"Are asleep. They went to the Hollands' house last night. Came home and locked themselves in and talked for hours."

"The *Hollands*."

The girl regarded her with an expression of wonder. Then she looked away quickly, hiding a smile of contempt: "I thought you spent the whole night studying the case."

I can't do this, Narita thought. This is insane. This person is a stranger.

"You don't know anything at all, do you?" her daughter said. "Tita Antonia told me all about you. How you're all wind. You're hot like fire, but you're all wind. And now you're going to write about me."

For a moment, Narita did not understand. Then she hastened to explain, fighting to speak in slow and clear sentences: "It's not about you. It's about the case — an in-depth report, a long one. It talks about Donostia. About Sweethaven. How something like that could have happened, could have been allowed to happen … it has nothing about you. Nothing personal. I can protect you. I will protect you; your name will not appear…"

She stopped, appalled at the expression on Naia's face.

"Sure you will," the girl said. "Like you have for years. You wrote about me when I was a baby: the diapers and the Kool-Aid vomit and all that crap. You wrote about my pink scissors and my glitter crayons and my pink hearts. You wrote about bad dreams and the best videos for seven-year-olds and what perfumes to buy a kid for Christmas. Go look around in Tita Antonia's room; she's got a whole dossier on you. She clipped all the crap you wrote and kept it, and you know the one great thing about you? You wrote all that and you made it sound so real and *you weren't even here*."

Narita remembered: "The Joys of Breastfeeding," "8 Surefire Cures for Kid Insomnia," a dozen or so hack jobs culled from phone chat with Antonia and secondhand parenting books in exchange for a bit of cash. And Antonia had kept them. Narita visualized her sister clipping her articles out from pulp and glossy alike, and pasting them up in a folder grimly annotated. Overcome with her own frustration — so gifted, too good to sell out, and none of her drawings, none of her wit, ever leaving the four walls of their home.

She realized then how much easier it would be to give up. She would do the article about JP and his friends, the sense of entitlement that money fostered, the tragedy of the murdered girl in the house with the palm frond crucifix on its door. Her usual survival mechanisms would kick in: she would draft everything on the plane out, sit up for a single night putting flesh to the bare bones of her story. She might even call up Joel, swallowing her pride, for a quote or two. She would mention Sweethaven in passing, so skillfully that her readers wouldn't ask for more. She would leave, once again, and this time there would be no false hopes, no real reason to return.

Naia was still looking at her, the disgust on her face dwindling until what was left was something indecipherable — a beautiful blank. They sat, listening as in a trance to each other's breathing. Narita's throat tightened. She knew she would never be more to this person than a distant, sophisticated relation: not even that. But, unfairly, she had so much more to give.

She wanted to explain that not everyone in the world was wicked or cynical, though most people were; she wanted to show the girl the principles, the tricks, by which one held on and, once in a while, flourished.

But what she knew about her daughter, she had invented. She did not know where to start.

Naia rose, to head back to her room. "You want to know about me, Mother? Then stick around. I'll give you plenty to write about."

Twenty-six

THERE IS A spare bedroom in the Holland home where Naia is allowed to lie down. Rigid atop the pink bedspread, she can stay immobile for what seems like hours, eyes turned to the long screened windows, watching the rain streaming silver from the eaves. She is waiting for Brent, for the continuation of what began in the armory. No one suspects.

It is a girl's room; it belongs to Tammy-Shalom. Naia doesn't dare explore. Tammy scares her. Her cryptic rants are all over the Internet, alongside photos of her face, hands, toenails, earlobes, and a parade of fake tattoos. She is a born-again Christian who worships Tori Amos and writes clumsy rhyming verse. Naia dares not cross her. The last thing she wants is to be bludgeoned in a poem.

The room has its own bathroom. On the door is a faded, handlettered sign that reads, DARK ROOM: KEEP OUT. The bathroom stinks of old chemicals; she finds bottles of developer under the sink. This space is the bridge to the next room: Brent's.

Mrs. Holland tells her she may drop by anytime she has a problem, may root around in the fridge if she likes, may help herself to what food takes her fancy. But Brent's room is off-limits. When she uses the bathroom, she must lock up from her side.

Brent receives no such instructions. He doesn't need them. "I trust you," she teases him, giving Naia a conspiratorial wink. The young girl's heart leaps at the promise of warmth and attention and fun, but just as quickly the moment is over, and Mrs. Holland is spewing instructions to her secretary, over her mobile phone.

In the afternoons, the maid lets her in. Mrs. Holland is always late. She keeps a busy schedule of meetings and consultations. They are supposed to talk two days a week, but without warning, she can cancel an appointment, leaving Naia to her own devices, satisfied that the girl is safe in her home. Naia crouches on Tammy's bed, refusing offers of ice cream and cinnamon rolls, listening to the voices from elsewhere in the house. On a couple of Fridays her schedule happens to coincide with her grandfather's. She knows his tread, on the outdoor staircase, the murmur of his voice.

"Is Naia here?" he asks.

"I'll check," Rinky offers, but he does not.

Rinky fears her, or yearns for her, or both. His eyes dart from her face to the round points of her nipples visible beneath her T-shirt. When he passes her a teaspoon or the bowl of sugar, his fingers brush hers; he strives to make contact with her body as he sees her to the door. "It is not acceptable for a woman to receive counseling from a man," he says gruffly, as though warning her against the riptides of desire.

Naia is not interested.

She is not sure what Mrs. Holland wants to hear from her. She is not sure where to begin. All she knows is a choking frustration, a sense that life has passed her by. She is fifteen. She feels useless and untalented, her energies diffused, her time consumed by texting and peacefully watching pirated PG movies with her grandfather. She surfs the Internet for hours. At school, by dint of Daniel's position in the university and a steady supply of pocket money and pretty trifles from Antonia, she moves among the haves, the healthy, attractive kids with their forbidden mobiles and their own computers and their broadband accounts. She feels no particular affection for any one of them. They see too little of each other outside school hours to be true friends.

She yearns for the one defining project that will make her special.

Brent fumbles with the catch on his door. By mutual agreement, she leaves her side of the bathroom unlocked. She stands in silence amid the stench of hobby chemicals, until he comes through. He is a small boy, small and compact, only an inch or so taller than she. Everything about him — from the face with its regular features, the fine nose, and the chin pointed like a hero in a *manga* odyssey, to the gleaming leather shoe tips — bespeaks sharpness and a ruthless perfectionism. He is known to be a terror on the drill field. "Lousy!" he screams at the cadets in his charge. "Squat jump, all of you!" "Morons!" he yells at the band.

They fall into each other's arms, not speaking. As they kiss, the wet, obligatory kiss, she thinks of bubble gum and churning cake batter, vinegar and toads. The clockwise movement of his mouth never varies, not in the three times they have done this, and inevitably she finds herself counting, each second corresponding to one turn, but she enters his greedy embrace without fail, ever hopeful that the next kiss, the next touch will be different, will fulfill the promise of his sidelong and guilty stares, that early tremulous joy at being the clandestine recipient of his attention.

Brent's thin brown fingers are tugging at her underpants.

"No," she tells him. This is not what she bargained for, this clinical distance, this feeling of dismay.

ADAM spends most of his days downstairs, "in his home office," Brent says with a knowing laugh.

One afternoon Naia stands at the foot of the outdoor stairs looking up at the house, not knowing whether to ring the bell or leave. If she misses her appointment, she knows that Emily Holland, despite her cursory cheer, will be displeased. Emily will make inquiries; she is powerful; she is also, Naia suspects, pathologically jealous of the very young girls she praises and teases and plies with questions about their lives.

She has never kept secrets from her grandmother; nor has the task of making decisions ever fallen to her alone. She is only Naia, youngest of the Pastors. She has done everything her elders tell her, and avoided the intrigues that surround pretty adolescent girls. Or at least she has tried. There is a gap, she knows, between herself and the Naia whom others, looking with lust and envy from the outside, perceive.

A low whistle intrudes upon her thoughts. "In here," says a voice.

It is Adam, who is handsomer and kinder than Brent, for at twenty-two, he is a grown man. Those are his chemical preparations in the bathroom. His are the photos of birdmen and clouds that decorate the walls upstairs.

She peers past the whitewashed woven bamboo slats, but sees nothing. The door to the ground level opens a fraction. She enters, stepping out of the hot afternoon light and into that netherworld of furniture shapes and drying laundry, of forgotten bottles of cola parked on chairs and the billiard table.

"What a mess!" she says to provoke him.

"It's not a mess," says Adam's voice. "Your grandfather's house is messier."

"You haven't even been there."

They are already forming the pattern of teasing and complaint that will highlight their relationship.

"But where are you?" Naia says, and then she notices a feeble line of light: a door somewhere has been opened, just a crack. She picks her way, with some irritation, past what seems to be a Formica card table, and an overloaded bookshelf, and chairs heaped with clothes stiff from line-drying. Then she is so close to Adam that his breath is in her nostrils. She stiffens and inhales, her heart pounding in excitement: his mouth has a wet, acidic odor, as of decaying cabbage, in stark contrast to his taut and flawless white skin.

He takes her wrist and, in the darkness, guides her gently over a threshold.

A light comes on.

She giggles. What a room this is, tiny and cluttered, dominated by the computer and the low bed, smelling of paper and dust and clothing in storage. Movie posters, ripped from the backs of video club magazines, decorate the walls: *Top Gun*, *The Right Stuff*. The closet door is half open and she catches a glimpse of a leather flyboy jacket with a ratty sheepskin collar; it looks authentic, a World War II relic, or maybe some cheap rip-off he got on eBay.

Printouts of girls cupping or spreading various parts of themselves cover every surface. This does not surprise her. Nothing surprises her: she is too young to have expectations. Boys and porn, the two go together, a given.

She gives the girls a calculating once-over. She is younger and prettier and wilder and infinitely more delicious than any of them.

In the light of the lamp, she examines his profile, with its fine nose and chin: a *mestizo* profile, the handsomest in the city. A sense of victory, of destiny, sweeps over her.

She weighs her chances while a slow smile, a smile he cannot fail to notice, one that begins at the corner of her mouth.

It would be possible, she supposes, to possess this mysterious individual and keep Brent on the side.

BENDING over her, he crushes the damp white expanse of his face, his soft woman's lips smelling of dead vegetables, against her upturned cheek.

Naia has been anticipating the kiss, but not the click and whirr that accompanies it, nor the series of rapid flashes that blank out the world for a few seconds. Shapes of green flood her vision, and when they clear, she discovers that he has been looking down at her, into her blinded eyes.

"Who were you thinking about just now?" he says. "Who? My brother?"

She shakes her head, unable to speak, her heart racing. She wonders if he will dismiss her now, or kiss her cheek again. Deep within the box of her pelvis, farther up than her own exploring fingers have reached, some uncharted part of her pulses, like a body turning over in sleep.

He turns the camera around — it is a tiny and expensive model — to show her the screen on the other side, which bears a miniature image of her face, white from the flood of light, lips parted and face blank as though in meditation.

"Look at you," he says, as though she has only now come into being.

As she turns her face up at him in joy at her own beauty, he touches her mouth with the tips of his fingers. He presses a button on the digital camera, and with the same series of flashes, blinds her again. She has never been a patient girl, but now she waits for the rules of this game to reveal themselves. He reaches down to arrange her hair, brushing, as if by accident, the lobe of her ear; he tips her chin gently to position her face in a manner that suits him.

Something in his ministrations reminds her of Antonia, their playful hugs, the funny little animals she drew on sneakers, the awful hot stillness of her bedroom after she had gone. Confused, she closes her eyes against the flashes, but they come only when she least anticipates them. He chooses to record her in the interstices, the moment when her shoulders freeze in shock, when she leaps away from the insect's crawl of his fingertips.

She hopes he will stop of his own accord, so she won't have to ask him. She is still promised to his brother; this is not good.

"What's the matter?" he whispers, knowing.

"I'm Brent's girl," she stammers.

"That idiot doesn't know what a treasure he's got."

She begins to weep, in relief at his empathy, but coyly, knowing more of this wonderful attention will be forthcoming.

NOW that these strange events are taking place in her life, she hates to sleep. She can stay awake until 1:00 or 2:00 a.m., listening to the late-night sounds of her grandparents and the maid. She awakens before sunrise, starving, all senses sharpened, reaching at once for the mobile phone by her bedside. There is an unread text message from Adam, his final one for the night. She had not heard it come in, those few hours she had been unconscious. Guilty for the omission, she replies. No answer. Her thumb assaults the keypad once more. She can barely wait for noon, when, awakening, he must find her message and resume their exchange.

Surely today will be the day she collapses in class. The blackboard wavers, the chart on the wall beyond the teacher — "25Mn 26Fe 27Co 28Ni 29Cu 30Zn" — loses all meaning. She stares at the notebook open beneath her nose, reading the same phrases over and over. Her autopilot keeps her aloft. No one notices. The voices of her classmates ricochet about her. She musters the usual smiles, the usual compliments and taunts, for the girls who gather around her, cooing, borrowing her hairbrush, sampling her Gosh cologne, caressing the soft down on her forearms.

She and Brent no longer speak. Sometimes their paths cross, as flocks of boys and girls in their wilting uniforms migrate from home room to science room, from math room to library. Amid a hail of greetings from her former classmates in the honors section, she notes his angry, helpless scrutiny and finds immense pleasure in ignoring it. Once, their eyes meet. He snatches his gaze away, and she is reminded of Mr. Holland, how he studies her clandestinely as he lets her into his house in the early evenings.

Brent must be hurting, she ponders. How strange, that a boy so self-possessed could be dented so easily. She hopes that if he ever finds out about her and Adam it will be years from now, when she is all grown up and on the other side of the world.

Her classmates elbow her and giggle. "Someone's looking at you," they whisper.

"Let him suffer," she hisses back.

If I stopped talking to him, it's as good as saying I don't want him anymore, she reasons with herself. She hasn't double-crossed him. Not technically. Besides, he has never courted her, not in the way her grandmother has outlined: boys in their best sports shirts and khakis, entertained by her grandparents in the living room until she deigns to emerge.

He's never even sent her an SMS worth saving.

How hatefully he behaves on the drill field, how thwarted he looks now. At the thought, she starts to giggle uncontrollably, so that her classmates slap her with their paper fans and sing out, "Naia is in love."

ADAM is restless. He starts at the servant's footsteps directly over their heads. The house cramps his style.

"I wish we could be someplace alone," he says, sighing. "Totally free."

"Well, do you know a place, then?" Naia says. "A room?"

Adam examines her with an expression she has never seen before. What is it? Shock? Revulsion? Triumph?

"I knew you were that kind of girl," he mutters.

What kind of girl? Her mind races in panic. An easy girl, the kind who gets taken to motels? Well, what was so bad about that, after all they had done? What was that look on his face?

"What do you mean? What kind of girl?" she shrieks.

"Oh, shut up," he says, and kisses her. "You're such a kid."

But the Holland car is waiting for her at the high school gate the following afternoon. Adam is at the wheel. "Get in," he snaps.

Her heart thumps. She wants to hide, to lay her head on his lap, but he laughs this off. Relax, he says. She does not ask how he got this car, where he learned to drive, where his parents are at the moment.

He tosses something into her lap. It is a key.

"Hold on to that for me," he says, grinning. They are speeding away from the center of town, through roads she has never seen. "There'll be hell to pay if I lose it."

It is a strange house, nothing more than a room and bath, and so sparsely furnished it gives no clue as to the people who own the place. But she is not afraid. It is only Adam, her secret friend, whose dark and playful nature matches her own. Laying her down on the clammy bedcovers, he decks her body with flattery, murmuring to her breasts, to her belly. She holds her breath in anticipation and fixes her gaze on the light fixture above their heads.

"What are you looking at?" he starts. "There's no one there."

She is completely at home with the camera now. She eases it out of its carrying case herself.

"Touch yourself," he whispers, staying beyond reach of the hot, bright light.

Her fingers pull at her own flesh. The flashes stop: he is taking video. His body becomes immaterial; it has afforded her few pleasures to begin with. The times he has taken her, she has kept her eyes open, staring in fascination at his red, sweat-filmed face, the eyes screwing up into pig slits, the total absorption in his own pleasure.

He puts the camera down to run his hands over her skin, a comforting sensation, different from her grandmother's smacking lipstick kisses, from Antonia's hugs. The words he whispers are the best of all: "My beauty. My angel." She listens close because they are true.

"Put your uniform back on," he tells her. "I want you to model for me."

Twenty-seven

I WILL NEVER understand what it is that draws a woman to the very things that destroy her. There are many things I won't pretend to understand, or know. I don't know whose idea it was to take a digital camera into the room with you; who mounted it on the bedside table while you were undressed; why you took the man in your mouth before that watchful eye; why you, with such gusto, threw yourself into a variety of positions that exhibited your superb athleticism yet surely gave no difference in pleasure except for him. Did you do it for him? Did you do it for the camera? Surely that was your hand that positioned it between your thighs while he homed in for a taste. Whatever your reasons, I won't pretend to understand why your footage was edited, flashing you from one position to the next, changing the music track with each cut. I will never understand what you might have done to warrant such hatred from any man. Up and down you jogged like a puppet on a stick, like a beast scratching fleas: not you, but the pieces of a girl called Naia, pieces that she ceased to own the moment they were taken, pieces she must now disown.

Like your grandmother said to me, you must disappear: change your number, liquidate your social network pages, find something else to call yourself by. Every last photo you ever posted of yourself must vanish from the Internet. The obscene phone calls will peter away; the searches for free footage will lose their appeal. There is little fun in killing someone already dead.

In my fantasy we are looking in the mirror, at our twin faces: you oblivious to my presence, preening, arranging your hair in loose waves to fall over the front of your shirt. Your concentration is so innocent, so full of adoration, that I laugh out loud. You shoot me an offended look that evaporates as soon as you catch sight of yourself again.

This is how I want us to be. We venture into the malls, stop before a pet shop window to gaze mournfully at poodles curled in their cages. We watch movies, surrounded, insensate by the fabulous Dolby sound system. Sink down on benches and gaze bleary-eyed into the fountain. Window shop. Female-bond. The malls are our museum, our leafy park. We walk through the zombie crowd hand in hand.

We tear apart the last Christmas basket that has sat in reserve above the fridge, and investigate the slice of Brie, the roll of pure chocolate tablets from South America, the tub of liver paste — all ensconced like crown jewels on a bed of confetti. You ponder your first taste of red wine. Sit contentedly before the television, watching the endless loop of cable news, forking peach halves into your mouth, tipping the can to your lips to drink.

Our home is a lovely space, on the top floor of the building, small enough to keep clean without hassle, and worth every penny. We fit, like two persons who have grown together over the years, but without the debilitating rivalry of sisters. We are like twins, twenty years apart. This building rears six stories above the asphalt, overlooking a neighborhood of zinc-roofed houses, and nothing blocks the light. In the typhoon season, the wind rattles the glass panes and water streams over the sills, but when the weather is mild, we live in a kind of celestial oyster; we could walk around naked in its whiteness if we dare.

But this is my fantasy, and I am sorry it reads like one of the magazine articles they pay me for. I cannot offer you much more than this. I am sorry that, though your life in Donostia must end, I cannot promise you a viable beginning.

NARITA sat staring at the empty computer screen. The house was silent. She reached for her cup of coffee and drained it.

She had to focus: there was work to be done, an article to hammer out. She had slept — a few sufficient hours; she was a professional. Yet as she began once more to type, using the time-worn phrases of the crime reporter, her mind continued to churn. There was the letter that had to be written, appealing Naia's expulsion. The second air ticket to be bought. There was the serious matter of money — some arms to be twisted, maybe. In a little while, though, her thoughts spiraled down into the text she was writing, and nothing else mattered.

When she stopped after a span of time to stretch, get more coffee, read critically through her work, she was conscious of a new sound, of someone weeping. Cautiously she found her way to Naia's bedroom and opened the door a crack. The girl lay atop the blankets, her chest moving in the slow rhythm of sleep. At her parents' bedroom the door was ajar; she knocked in disquiet, then entered, but there was only her father, sprawled across the bed but snoring peacefully.

The noise, she realized, was coming from the kitchen, a soft and private sound. Luth. Her mother.

She listened in fascination, standing uninvited on the threshold of an alien world. Was it grief or release? This was the person who had blighted her girlhood, for whose approbation she had fought, competing bitterly against Antonia until, in the end, neither sister had flourished, until they were driven apart. But she felt no satisfaction as she stood there listening, just outside the doorway to the kitchen. For a moment she considered going in. The impulse passed: rejection would be certain. Or would it? So much of Luth was a mystery, even more, perhaps, than the cipher that was Naia, and yet both were now implacably in her life — two dark planets, hostile for the most part, and to be reconnoitered with care.

She felt no triumph as her mother wept, only a sense of guilt, as over opportunities tossed away, and the sadness of her own unknowing.

LAKAMBINI SITOY'S published fiction includes the books *Mens Rea* (1998), *Jungle Planet* (2005), and *Sweet Haven* (France, 2011 and North America, 2014). She received the David T.K. Wong fellowship from the University of East Anglia, United Kingdom in 2003, was long-listed for the Man Asian Literary Prize in 2008, and has received a Manila Critics Circle National Book Award and numerous prizes in the annual Don Carlos Palanca Memorial Awards. She holds an MA from Roskilde University in Denmark, where she resides and teaches English.